The
WOMAN
in the
WHITE
KIMONO

The
WOMAN
in the
WHITE
KIMONO

ANA JOHNS

PARK
ROW
BOOKS

PARK
ROW
BOOKS

ISBN-13: 978-0-7783-0814-0
ISBN-13: 978-0-7783-0926-0 (International Trade Paperback Edition)

The Woman in the White Kimono

ParkRowBooks.com
BookClubbish.com

Printed in U.S.A.

For my father, David Gaydos

デヴィッドゲーディス

1936–1988

The
WOMAN
in the
WHITE
KIMONO

Once we meet and talk, we are sisters.

—Japanese proverb

PROLOGUE

My given name is Naoko Nakamura. My married name is Naoko Tanaka. And once, for a short time in between, it was something else—a nontraditional name from an unconventional wedding ceremony held under an ancient tree of flickering lights.

We did not have an ordained priest to perform the ceremony. We were not married in a sacred shrine, and I did not have the three customary costume changes.

But I had love.

That evening, night blanketed the village of little houses and bundled it under a cloak of black, but the orange western sky clung to its horizon, peeking, curious. The humid air kissed my cheeks as I stepped from the porch onto the ground, and when I rounded the corner, I gasped.

Paper lanterns lined the pebbled path and butter-gold orbs illuminated the trees like the yellow *hotaru*, fireflies, swarming after July's heavy rains. So many that when I walked under their branches and looked up, they were like giant umbrellas shielding me from a hundred falling stars.

With a smile, I ran my hand down my gown to feel its lush texture under my fingertips. I had never felt more beautiful or more nervous. My insides crackled in excitement like a sparkler's flare, a charged path that raced through me from toes to fingertips.

Ahead, at the center of the small waiting crowd, was my soon-to-be husband. The lantern's light reflected in his eyes, causing the white wisps at the center to dance like sails across the bluest ocean, and I was lost in them. In him. In that moment.

Each step I took brought me closer to my future and farther away from my family. It was a contrast of extremes in every sense, but I had somehow found my place between them. That was what Buddha called the middle way. The correct balance of life.

I called it happy.

A life with love *is* happy. A life *for* love is foolish. A life of *if only* is unbearable. In my seventy-eight years, I have had all three.

Grandmother would often say, "So it is with sorrow. So it is with happiness. It will pass." But even in my old age, when I close my eyes, I can still see the distant flicker of a thousand tiny lights.

ONE

America, Present Day

Even at night with half the staff, the Taussig Cancer Center ran as shipshape as its namesake. With Dr. Amon at the helm, I prayed my father could somehow weather the storm, but his lapsing health had me perched at his side, watching for signs.

Although I had the lights dimmed and the TV on mute, my father wrestled with sleep. Machines hummed, monitors beeped, conversations rolled like waves from the hall. Someone whistled.

"Whistling up a wind was risky," Pops would say about his days at sea. "It could summon strong gales and rough waters." The hospital wasn't his navy ship from the fifties, but with the improbable coincidence of sharing its name, I wouldn't snub the nautical superstitions. I found my feet and closed the door.

"What..." Pops flailed his arms, causing the plastic IV lines to flap like ropes against a mast. "Tori?"

"I'm here, Pops." I hurried over, placed my hand on his arm. "You're at the hospital, remember?" He'd woken disoriented several times over the last week with shorter periods of rest in between. This had become our new norm.

He strained to sit up and grimaced with pain, so I placed a hand behind his upper back and lifted to work a pillow there. With both arms braced under his, I helped him shift, amazed how light he'd become. He'd joked that he was "half the man" but I didn't laugh. The truth was far from funny and the joke far from true. He was *still* my larger-than-life father.

I handed him the plastic cup of ice. He shook it to rattle the chips loose, then sipped on what had melted. One taste triggered the reflex—a static cough he struggled to clear. I took the cup, gave him tissues and waited for the fit to pass. With a final expulsion, he lolled back and closed his eyes.

"You okay?" Empty words, because of course he wasn't, but he assured me with a nod just the same.

Then he sighed, a deep, raspy breath, his words pushing through it. "Did I ever tell you about the famous blue street? It was the first thing I saw when I stepped off my ship in Japan."

"And the girl who liked your eyes was second, right?" I brightened, happy he was lucid and hoping he'd stay that way long enough to retell it.

"Well, I looked a little better back then."

"You look a little better now." He did. Color warmed his cheeks; his eyes were sharp and focused. His movement had improved. It was wonderful and discomforting at the same time. Dr. Amon said to watch for a "rally of improvement" right before Pops would take his final turn.

For my father, the last hurrah. And for me, a final story.

From the chair beside his bed, I leaned in and propped

my chin under my fist. "So, you took one step, bent low to run your fingers over the reflective stones embedded in the street and...?"

"And I stood up and there she was."

"Staring."

"Yes. And I stared back, saw my future and fell in love." Pops angled his head with a soft smile.

Even though it was the condensed version, I fell in love with that story all over again because it led to all the others.

"Every time I came to port, she would meet me there," Pops said. "But I was always coming and going. That's just how it was. We were two ships passing in the night like in the Longfellow poem." Pops wheezed a labored breath.

I reached for his freckled hand and squeezed.

"After the service, I was landlocked in Detroit and drowning in a bottle. But then I met your mama, and she saved me." His eyes locked to mine. "And here's what you need to know. Are you listening?"

"I am." I hung on every word.

"Mama was the love of my life, but before *that* life, I lived another. That's what I've been trying to tell you." His lips twitched.

When? When did he try to tell me? My mind raced through every moment of the last few weeks, trying to decipher what I'd missed. I didn't even understand what "lived another life" could mean. I wasn't sure I wanted to.

"It'd be easier if you just read my letter. I need you to do that now, okay, Tori? It's time."

It's time?

The swell in my chest was instant. It inflated behind constricted ribs and strangled my heart. I held the emotional bubble in place with shallow breaths, fearing it might burst. I couldn't move.

He reached over, patted my hand. "It's with my stuff. Go and get it."

I found his bag behind the restroom door, placed it on the counter and unzipped the top. With trembling hands, I rummaged through his clothes but froze as my fingers grazed paper. I pinched to pull the envelope free, then stood with it and stared.

The red ink. The kanji script. The creases and folds.

Walking back to face my father, our eyes met.

A dying man. A heartbroken daughter.

"Come here, sit down," he said. "It's okay."

But it wasn't. Because you couldn't take back goodbye. I wasn't ready to say mine, so I didn't want to hear my father's. I couldn't.

The back of my throat ached from the pressure. "I'll, um…" I stepped toward him, then stopped, needing everything to slow down and take a breath, so I could, too. The stress of the last few months, the heartbreak of his slow decline, the unrelenting cancer, and now… A lump rose in my throat as tears formed. I made quick steps to the door.

Pops said something, but I was already in the hall hidden from view. I covered my mouth and took long, deep breaths, trying to fight back the swell of emotion. How did we get to this point? We had researched treatments, applied every home remedy, arranged for a specialist, and it still wasn't enough. Confusion and guilt stacked heavy on my shoulders, and I wilted under its weight. I glanced at the envelope. In hindsight, I should have opened it on the day it arrived.

My father had been watching the game in his living room. "Tori, is that you?"

"Yes, it's me." I tossed my keys and his collected mail on the table, surprised he'd heard me come in with the TV so loud. "There's a letter for you." I leaned into the living room and waved it.

His eyes stayed fixed to the screen. Mine dropped to the empty suitcase still sitting beside his chair. He had yet to pack for the hospital and we were leaving in the morning. Although it was something of a miracle the specialist fit him in, I understood my father's lack of enthusiasm.

I hated cancer.

It ate away at more than just his body. It devoured his spirit, and that consumed mine. I had become desperate, a child at thirty-eight.

I left him to watch his game, one of the few things he still enjoyed, poured myself a cup of coffee, then settled in to sort the excessive amount of mail. It'd been bound with thick rubber bands and stuffed in his PO box as though he'd gone on a monthlong vacation and forgot to place his service on hold. Only he hadn't. It just slipped his mind to have me check it.

I took a sip of coffee and found myself gazing at the letter. Red Asian symbols stamped in every direction. Thick, red lines crossed through the address. Above it, English letters spelled out PARTI. *Parti?* I flipped it over. Flipped it back. It'd been folded more than once, the edge frayed as though it had caught in the automatic sorter; I was surprised it was delivered at all.

The investigative journalist in me itched to rip it open.

I held it to the overhead light. If positioned just so, I could make out the outline of a folded note and a cord of some sort. I shook it, but the envelope carried no weight. Turning it over, I smoothed out the folds, then caught sight of a familiar word smudged in the bend.

Japan.

The ink had bled from the *J*. I traced it with the tip of my finger. Who did my father still know in Japan? Stationed there in the navy, he told all sorts of exaggerated tales about his time overseas, but they were from some fifty years ago. There weren't any emblems or military insignia, so not an official reunion announcement. Maybe an unofficial one? He had played baseball while enlisted—even in Japan.

Once, the Seventh Fleet navy team challenged the Shonan Searex, Yokosuka's farm league, in an exhibition game to a sold-out stadium. Pops would place a cupped hand over his brow as if scanning the crowds whenever he talked about it. "Not one empty seat as far as you could see. Can you picture it, Tori?"

I always could.

The open-air arena, the perfect field of manicured green and my father, so young, so nervous, warming up on the sandy pitcher's mound.

"You can't imagine the noise," Pops would say. Instead of applause, colorful plastic bats thudded the backs of seats—*thump-thump-thump.* Cheer captains ran up and down the aisles, beating drums and shouting victory chants. Organized fan groups in designated sections sang personalized songs and shouted through megaphones. Pops said baseball in 1950s Japan gave a thunderous voice to a quiet culture.

Although the game was a friendly one, the promoted match against the USA carried heavy undertones. Pops said the Land of the Rising Sun wanted nothing more than to beat back the stars and stripes of the red, white and blue.

"I almost wished we'd lost," Pops always said. "My girl's family was up in those stands, and I didn't want to cause insult, especially before I'd met them."

It was always "his girl" when he told those stories. I never got her name. And if Mama was around, I never got those stories. If I asked about his girl, he'd shake his head, blow air from his inflated cheeks and say, "She was special, all right."

So was he. I adored him.

A man who drank fruit brandy like his Slovak father, swaggered like John Wayne and spun colorful yarns like no one else.

Although, with *most* of his stories, it was difficult to discern their truth. "What is truth but a story we tell ourselves?" Then he'd wink, tap my nose and leave me to dissect fact from fantasy. Something I was still doing.

But that letter from Japan—*that* was real.

"Tigers lost," Pops said, startling me as he shuffled toward the fridge. He opened it and stared.

"Do you want some lunch?" He needed to eat something. He was wasting away. At first, his trimmer figure gained compliments, but the admiration ceased when the weight loss didn't. Even his hands—the same ones that had once pitched in a sold-out stadium—had thinned to knobby bone.

He closed the refrigerator empty-handed, cinched the belt of his blue robe, then scratched the stubble on his dimpled chin. "No, I'm okay, thanks." He pointed to the envelope. "What's that?"

"I told you. You got a letter." I held it out. "It's from Japan."

He swiped it lightning quick, squinting at the markings. At once, his expression fell flat. Clasping the letter tight to his chest, he spun on slippered heels and left without a word.

I waited a few minutes before I followed.

He stood frozen, his gaze anchored to the envelope in the middle of his darkened room. Pinch-pleated curtains couldn't keep out the sun's prying eyes. Or mine. I nudged the door an inch or two wider. The breach gave way to long fingers of light that stretched across the room and tapped his shoulder. He turned, clasping a hand over his unshaven face to hide the unfamiliar expression. One as foreign to me as that letter.

One with tears.

TWO

Japan, 1957

G randmother often says, "Worry gives a small thing big shadows." What if it were a big thing? The shadow that looms over me is thick and monstrous, almost alive.

I'm up before the sun to help Okaasan, Mother, with the morning meal of white rice, grilled fish and *miso* soup, but I'm not hungry. My belly's too full of worry.

I'm almost eighteen, and tomorrow starts *omiai*, my arranged marriage meeting.

At least now, with American ideals waging war on this ancient tradition, the introductions are the only part decided. The choice is mine with whom to marry. Of course, having the option and being allowed to make it are two separate matters. This is my challenge. One of many I face.

Taking the plate from Okaasan's hands, I bow to my father

and brother as they enter the room discussing politics. A predictive conversation that flows from the United Nations and the independence of Japan to the dissociation from America.

Father is clean-shaven with short-clipped hair—a preference from his army days—and wears a dark Western-style suit to impress foreign traders. Since Taro is *Oniisan*, eldest brother, and works with Father, he dresses and acts just like him. A perfect imitation, except for his sharp tongue—which isn't held as prudent.

"Soon, Naoko, you will meet with Satoshi, and secure our future earnings," Taro says with a smug tone.

"A fated match," Grandmother adds as she shuffles in behind them. Her thin lips pull into a closemouthed smile, rounding out loose-skinned cheeks.

I met Satoshi years before, so I would know if we were *fated*. A forced match is more like it, and what of my future happiness? Doesn't love count? I place a cup in front of Grandmother and carefully pour her tea. "But first, everyone has agreed to meet *my* intended." I smile closemouthed in return.

A match to Satoshi is my family's strong *suggestion*.

A match to Hajime is my deepest *hope*.

"Chase two hares and you will catch neither," says Grandmother. This is but a single parable in her arsenal of many. She releases them like arrows, but instead of one, which breaks with ease, she slings ten to a bundle.

I'm braced and ready for more when Mother steps between us like a shield. "I think for tomorrow's meeting with your Hajime we'll gather in the garden for tea and proper introductions. That may be best, yes?" To avoid my father's questioning eyes, my mother fixes a wayward strand that has worked loose from her bun.

Everything about Okaasan is neat and pretty. She's dainty with a thin frame and long hair the color of soot used to make *sumi* ink. She keeps it wrapped tight at the base of her neck and skewered with long pins of jade.

I gave a slight bow, grateful for her intervention. Before the war interrupted Father's import and export business, he'd been a king of an empire, and our home had many servants, including gardeners. Now we struggle without help. We struggle in general, as everyone does. So, to utilize the garden means much preparation and work. Mother declaring its use for Hajime's unwelcomed introduction quiets the discussion for now.

Okaasan knows what is at stake. Maybe everything.

Satoshi's father, a powerful buyer for Toshiba, is my father's most important client. This makes me valuable bait. If Satoshi is hooked, my family will reap the rewards in steady monetary gains to ease our burdens. If I refuse and cause disgrace, he could cast my family's business aside, doubling our load.

There is only one way out.

Hajime must be flawless for tomorrow's introduction to be considered a viable choice, and Satoshi must find me ill-suited and choose another. That way, his family will suffer no shame and mine will not suffer the consequence. My family's fortune will continue to rebuild on its own merit and I will have a marriage built on love.

This is my plan.

In the struggle of stone and water, water eventually wins. Since my family's mind is set like stone, I must persist like water to change it.

"I'll be late, Okaasan," I say, ignoring the tightening in my chest. "Since I'm missing traditional dance club for the next few days, I'll need to stay after school with Kiko to practice." It's only half a lie since it is a rehearsal. But instead of dance with Kiko, it's preparation with Hajime.

Kenji, my little brother, races in and lands with a thump on the floor cushion, rattling dishes and startling Grandmother.

He is nine and too cute for his own good. Bright eyes and long dark lashes allow him to get away with everything, even bad manners.

I cast a stern look. Kenji sticks out his tongue.

With everyone present, we say, *"Itadakimasu"*—"I gratefully receive"—but my head remains low as I ask for additional blessings. *Please let tomorrow's meeting be perfect so Hajime's lack of significant family name won't shame ours or add weight to Satoshi's prominent one.*

Yes, a belly of nerves, but a heart filled with hope.

The school day inched forward like a snail, slow and labored. Even now, waiting for Hajime at Taura Station, it drags. As I step from the train platform, the afternoon sun bounces off steel rooftops, blinding me. I squint from the glare, seeking Hajime's face among so many. *Where is he?* I'm eager to practice.

American men in uniform eat while walking past. Hajime will not make such rudimentary mistakes. We have been working on etiquette to impress my family. Never walk and eat. Sit to show respect for the time and sacrifice it took to plant, harvest and prepare. The Americans don't seem to notice or care that everyone shields their eyes from their lack of courtesy. Everyone except for Hajime. He cuts right between them.

He's dressed in a white T-shirt and tan trousers. With his fine hair—the shade of cast-iron—slicked back and worn high, and the deep dimple in his chin, he looks like Elvis or a movie star. Maybe James Dean. We're both crazy for all things modern. I wish I could have changed from my uniform. At least my ponytail sits high on my head in the popular Western style.

I wave as he draws near.

My smile already hurts my cheeks. Love and a cough cannot be hidden for it takes everything not to run or shout.

We meet in an awkward moment of wanting to leap into each other's arms, but settle with small bows, then laugh as we almost clunk heads. Hajime takes my hand—a social taboo—and, with quick steps, pulls me between storefronts into a narrow alley.

I duck my head, worried we'll attract the judging eyes of hardened hearts. "They circle like moths. We should go, Hajime."

"Well, like moths, they're just drawn to your light. So I say, let them look." He grins, revealing the sliver-thin gap between his front teeth. He leans out, yells, "Hi! I love this girl!"

"*Shhh!*" I dart to his other side, press flat to the wall, laughing, but then ask, "What light?" I smile but keep an eye on the street.

He turns and retakes my hand. "The one behind your eyes." He squeezes my hand, then reaches for the other. "The one that shines from your heart." He gives each palm a quick, soft kiss.

My cheeks burn hot. Now I only look at Hajime. He's such a tease, a boy but also a man, and the mixture of the two is delicious.

He leans closer, presses his forehead to mine. "Hi, Cricket."

"Hi, Hajime." I smile wider, amazed at how brave I am with him. To contradict a lifetime of lessons—show humility, stay quiet, place others first. All good things and yet... I look down, breaking his stare. His eyes will swallow me up if I'm not careful, but he cups my cheeks, tips my chin.

"I'm going to kiss you right here, on the lips, okay?"

I lean up on tiptoes and kiss him first.

My heart bounces between panic and bliss. *Who is this girl I've become?* Like morning's bloom welcoming the early sun,

I open to him. Yes, he is delicious, sweet like *kompeito* on my tongue. And just as with the sweet candy, I am greedy and tempted for more. To take what my heart desires? It is liberating. But we promised. Not again until we're married.

So, we break apart.

I smile. Hajime grins. I smack his chest and laugh. Yes, *who* is this girl? He hugs me, and I know. I am his. Still me, but bolder, brighter, *free.* If I shine a light from inside, it's from the happiness he creates.

"I have a surprise," he says with a kiss to my head before my release. "Come on." With long steps he skips out of the alleyway, then turns, waving for me to follow.

"Where are we going?" I double-step to keep up as he veers from the street into a field of tall untended grass.

Hajime turns and walks backward with a playful smirk. He reaches down to pluck a seeded blade of grass, breaks it short and chews the end.

"*Where*, Hajime?"

His eyes, blue like a just-rained sky, narrow, then close as he turns. "Nope. Can't tell you." He peers over his shoulder. "It's a surprise."

My eyes grow wide. He runs.

"Wait!" I laugh, chasing his long, scissor-legged stride. The tall grass whips my exposed calves, but I will myself faster when he's too far ahead, then slow when I no longer see him. "Hajime?" I look toward the nearby trees, glance back the way we came, then turn.

"Ah!"

I squeal from his scare, then cover my face, locking elbows in tight. Laughing, he wraps his arms around me, rocks me back and forth, whispers he loves me.

And like that, I'm happy.

I slide my hands down just a little, lean out and peek up

over my fingertips. Hajime bends down and plants a kiss upon my forehead. Yes, I am his. He is mine. This is fate.

"Come on, it's just ahead," he says, and tugs my hand.

We stroll, fingers intertwined. Hajime with a new seed head to chew and me grinding worries. "We still must practice, remember? You understand the importance?"

"Of course." He regards me with a sideways glance. "That's why we've practiced at least a hundred times."

"A hundred times is nothing." My heart thrums discontent. "To fully master the art of tea, it takes *years* of practice, maybe a lifetime. To fully master the rules of etiquette, we now have only this moment." I stop, so he does, and plead with my eyes. "Tomorrow's meeting is everything. Please, we must practice."

"Okay..." He looks up to find the answers. "First, I admire the bowl, then rotate it two times, apologize for drinking before others to show humility and bow before taking a sip." He lowers his chin. "See? We're ready, now come on." He tugs my hand.

I'm not convinced, so I continue to drill him as we work our way up a steep hill far from the crowded street below. I'm not sure where we're going, but I don't let it distract me from our goal. "What do you do before you *pass* the bowl?"

He hesitates.

I burst. "You must wipe the rim with the napkin, or risk causing embarrassment, remember?" My stomach turns. Such a mistake will not be forgotten or *forgiven*. "Which direction do you pass the tea bowl after you clean its edge?"

Hajime's expression remains blank.

Mine fills with alarm. "Left. *Left!*" My heart races and I walk faster, now taking the lead. "How are we going to convince them we're a suitable match if you can't remember?"

"Cricket."

"We must be *perfect*." I keep on. Marching, lecturing, pan-icking. "No mistakes. Not even one small error or they could refuse our request and force me to marry Satoshi." My arms swing as my words run wild. "*You* are my happiness. *You* are where I belong. Do you understand? *We* are fated, so we must be perfect and make them see!"

"Naoko!"

I turn from the sharp use of my real name.

"Do you see that?" He tries to hide a smile, then motions ahead. "Look. How could they refuse us when we already have a home?"

Turning into the sun, I blink away spots and find scat-tered rows of tiny houses clustered along the hillside to form a hamlet. They are small, thatched-roof structures in need of repair. I pivot back to face him. *We already have a home?* Then my heart stops. *"Here?"*

Spinning me back around, he rests his chin on my shoulder and points. "There. That one on top of the little hill is ours." He smiles near my cheek and waits for mine.

I only bite my lip.

"I know it's not much. It's small and old, and not at all what you're used to or deserve." He speaks excited and rushed. "And I have nothing really to offer except a promise to love you and…"

He loves me.

What boy uses these words? None I've ever known. Not even Father to Mother. While he talks of planned repairs, I lean against him for comfort and breathe him in—fresh tanned leather and citrus. The uncommon aftershave has an exotic smell. I like everything about him because nothing is expected.

"…and there, beside the deck, I could clear a patch for a

garden. Can you see it? I know you'd live with Satoshi and his family in some big, modern estate, but—"

"Who needs a big, modern estate?" I face him, surprising myself with the quick rebuttal. "Who wants a hard-to-please mother-in-law, or to dance around another family's hierarchy and rules? Not me, so a small one-storied home, if it's with you, is perfect." With Hajime, my heart and mind are more than tolerated, they're celebrated, but... My heart falters, and I look away.

Why must this prove so difficult?

"What's wrong?" Questioning eyes search my guilty ones. "You don't like it?"

Dread climbs my spine.

"Cricket, you know with me you can say anything. You never have to hide your thoughts, okay?"

I nod, grateful. With Hajime, I am free to express opinions or act silly because he likes my thoughts as well as my smile. *But how to explain this?* It's not the run-down little house that causes my alarm, but the community. It's in a region that houses *Eta*, outcasts. The *Burakumin* are at the bottom of the social order. They are poor, some of mixed blood, and work necessary trades of death: butchers, leather tanners, undertakers. Therefore, they're deemed tainted, unclean and *unlucky*.

I am the unlucky one.

My family will forbid it. To live here would damage Father's reputation and Taro's prospects to earn one. Hajime doesn't know my family already favors Satoshi and to heap this on him, too? Another strike to an empty drum. I rub my nose and look at my feet.

Such big shadows have been cast, for these are no small worries.

THREE

America, Present Day

The morning of my father's doctor's appointment, we packed up his Cadillac convertible and headed east. The two-lane highway would take us all the way to the Taussig Cancer Center in Ohio, passing fields of soy, stalks of corn and miles of whirling metal. The massive turbine pinwheels filled the horizon with wind farms as far as you could see. Pops lifted the bill of his newsboy cap, dabbed his brow with a handkerchief and watched them through the rolled-up window.

With sidelong glances, I watched him.

We hadn't spoken about his letter from Japan—what it meant, who it was from, how he reacted—but it didn't mean I hadn't thought about it. How could I not? He'd brought it. I caught the familiar flash of red on the dash before we left.

Pops tracked where I looked, picked it up and folded it in his pocket. He didn't say a word and I knew better than to ask, but besides worrying about his running fever, I thought of little else.

Who had sent it? An old shipmate perhaps, but then the letter would have originated in the States, not traveled from overseas. A charity thank-you or newsletter crossed my mind. Pops did sponsor kids and causes all over the world, but it wouldn't have garnered that kind of reaction. I'd only seen him with tears like that once—at Mama's funeral.

Pops barked a chesty cough, trying to clear his throat in vain, then glanced in my direction. "You're quiet."

"I'm concentrating," I said, and I was. While the 1958 convertible was a showstopper—red-button-tufted interior, pearl-white body and deep red pinstripes that ran from finned headlight to exaggerated tail—the extended size made it difficult to drive. It was also the first time I had driven it.

Although, when I was younger, before my mother could object, he'd have me slide in between them and I'd help steer. She'd scream when he'd release the wheel, keeping it steady with only a raised knee, and scold him to "slow down" when he pushed past the posted recommended speed. Riding in my father's Caddy was always a fun adventure.

Driving the classic convertible was a different experience. It was hard to manage, and as cars flew past, we were wind-whipped from all directions. Even with the windows up and my sunglasses on, I couldn't keep the hair from my eyes. Having the top down wasn't quite the thrill I'd remembered. I told my father as much.

Like magic, he conjured a streamer of red from the glove box. It colored the wind and billowed like a majestic sail.

My eyes grew wide with recognition. *Mama's scarf!* I hadn't seen it in years. I could still picture her wearing it—her ash-blond hair, pin-curled the night before, tucked in and under the pretty floral design.

As I tried to position it over my hair, Pops reached for the wheel—the irony wasn't lost even though the lane was. We drifted, causing another car to swerve and honk. I hurried to tie the tails under my chin, then grinned at my father.

He smiled in return. "It suits you. You should keep it."

I glanced in the rearview mirror, saw my face instead of my mother's. "I couldn't. It was hers."

"No, I mean it." He shrugged a shoulder. "Truth is, I always intended for you to have it, but your mother found it, and then what could I do?"

My heart rose high in my chest. "Are you sure?"

"Yes. I want you to have it. It's important."

I straightened it in my hair and smiled. I did love that scarf. When worn, the red-and-white motif converged to paint the most beautiful color story, but when opened and smoothed flat, according to my father, the scarf's design told one.

"A secret one," he'd say, running his fingers along the hand-rolled hem. Then he'd tell me how China kept the secret for almost two thousand years. He'd point to the floral in the scarf's design, say they were the same flowers found in the palace garden, where the young empress first discovered something valued more than gold—silkworms.

"She'd been enjoying tea when a cocoon fell from the sky, and to her surprise, it landed square in her cup." His eyes grew wide to demonstrate, and I'd giggle when he made the face. Then he'd pretend to fish it out, just as the empress had, claiming it unraveled into a single shimmering thread almost a mile long.

The royal family, so impressed by the pearlescent sheen, used the delicate filament to weave exotic fabrics to trade throughout the world. And because the rare silk grew to that of legend, the emperor issued an imperial decree to keep the source—the silkworms living within their garden mulberry trees—a secret. "And it stayed that way, until..." Pops would hold up a finger.

I'd move closer, knowing from there the story would change.

Sometimes it was a spoiled princess, betrothed to a prince from a faraway land. She couldn't bear to live without the luxurious garments, so she hid cocoons in her wedding headdress.

Other times, my father claimed two Nestorian monks used their tall bamboo canes to smuggle out the worms. But my favorite was always the Japanese spies who traveled the long Silk Road of China—which my father said was woven into the scarf's design. I'd spend hours imaging their 4,000-mile journey while tracing the design's varied lines.

If the Caddy was my father's prized possession, the memories of my mother's silk scarf with its intricate pattern and hidden stories were mine.

"You're quiet again," Pops said, tugging me from memory.

I looked over. "I was just thinking about the empress, and how the silkworm cocoon fell into her tea."

"You remember that?"

"Of course. I remember all your stories. There was the one about the ships battling far out at sea, the fight for the Japanese princess..." Sometimes in that one, he'd claim the boy was a Samurai whose clever words were swifter than his sword. Other times, a wealthy prince who could afford to give her everything except the one thing her heart desired. When I'd ask him what that was, he'd smile lopsided and say, "Me."

"Oh." I tapped the steering wheel. "And there was Tea with an Emperor."

"Empire." My father laughed through his nose. "He was

a merchant king with a vast trading *empire*. How could you forget that one?"

"You have a lot of stories with tea." *And Japan.* I glanced at my father. "You could remind me."

He favored me with a smile. And in that exact moment, time slid back. To when a larger-than-life man told epic stories to a little girl who loved them. It was a welcomed reunion.

"Well, I can tell you this much, aside from silk..." He cleared his throat. "Nothing good *ever* came from tea."

FOUR

Japan, 1957

I wipe the sleep from my eyes, fighting for consciousness. A glimmer of light steals my attention. Then a fluttering outside the window. A white butterfly fans its shadow wings. They stretch tall and fade into nothing only to flatten wide again.

My eyelids grow heavy, captivated by the dance. With a deep yawn, I consider the primitive stories of living souls wandering the world in the form of insects. I imagine I am that butterfly, carried on the morning's breeze. Free, content and happy. I visit Hajime and whisper reassuring dream words about today's match meeting. *We have practiced. We are ready. They will love you.*

"Naoko!"

I blink against the intrusive light to replace the paper wings of my mind's eye. My mother again calls from the kitchen. Sitting up, my head spins, so I lie down until it passes. Then I shift and roll my bed and make my way to her.

"You should've woken me, Okaasan!" I scramble to her side, almost knocking into Grandmother in my haste. The salty smell of fresh *miso* soup pervades my senses. Everyone has eaten and little brother's putting on shoes to leave for school.

"Good luck with your boyfriend, Naoko," Kenji says, followed by puckered lips and kissy noises.

He howls when I seize him for a punishing pinch.

"Kenji, go!" Mother scolds, shoving an empty bowl into my hands and pointing me to sit at the table next to Father. "Eat whatever's left, then we prepare. We have a significant day ahead."

Father scowls, blowing out a breath before sipping his tea. The vein at his temple throbs under newly grayed hair. I'm sure I am responsible.

Grandmother likes to say, "That which is too obvious can make for a quick regret." What is clear to me is Father allows this first meeting with Hajime for the sake of appearance. What will become evident to him is that I'm allowing the second meeting with Satoshi only to guarantee the first.

My nerves prickle as afternoon preparations for Hajime's introduction get underway. I'm almost ready, but Okaasan's not happy with my placement of the traditional white-and-pink ornamental hair comb, so she is redoing it. I hold it in my lap while she rakes a brush through my hair.

My thumb rubs back and forth across the comb's smooth enamel, knowing it doesn't matter if it's positioned correctly in my hair. Hajime will not know if it's correct any more than if the garden maintains symmetry in rules of three, or if the tea bowl is for the summer season, but Okaasan does not know this.

Or does she? Did she somehow learn what I've been hiding? Does she fear Father's reaction?

I do.

Grandmother only adds to our nervousness. "That's no good, see? The hair comb still slants," Obaachan says with a grunt as she lumbers by. She pretends to have no interest in the preparation but finds reason to pass through and offer opinions.

They all do. The perfect presentation of the meeting reflects my family's honor and importance. This is true even if its guest of honor carries none.

My mind jumps through hoops of rules and protocol. Did I explain to Hajime where he should sit? When he should speak? How much to eat? My pulse quickens. *Did I tell him to only take small portions?* Hajime has a big appetite; I should have told him. I don't think I told him. I feel hot. Dizzy. Nauseous. The *obi*'s too tight around my ribs. Tradition threatens to choke my every breath.

"There. Yes." Okaasan pats the sides of my head, then steps back to eye her handiwork. The hair comb's plum blossoms hang with delicate precision to one side. "This is good. Yes, I think this is good."

Father and Taro walk by without even a curious glance. For Satoshi's meeting, I'm sure they will act differently. Today, I'm invisible. A ghost.

Okaasan makes last-minute adjustments to my kimono. It's attractive, but ordinary, unlike the *furisode* I'll wear during Satoshi's visit. That one has sleeves that hang low and wide like colossal, colorful wings.

"Hmm…still crooked," Grandmother says from behind

us. She tilts her head to the side, eyeing my hair ornaments. "Crooked top on a crooked kettle."

My stomach drops. *Does she know about Hajime, too?*

Little brother believes Grandmother has foxes under her employ and that they tell her everything they hear. I always make fun, but now I'm not so sure.

Mother regards the headpiece once more and puffs a breath to dismiss Grandmother's opinion. She motions for me to follow her into the garden, where the stage is set for the upcoming exhibition. The soft reed mat covers moss-laden patio stones beneath the table. The flower arrangement on top comprises a single bloom of white. And the ritual prep for making tea waits at the ready.

Only Father and Taro are out of position.

They sit in the garden, backs to the entrance in silent opposition. The smoke from their pipes climbs the air above them, two snakes intertwined along an invisible vine. My insides strum in discord.

It is almost time.

Hajime knows the importance of showing up at the precise moment, not a minute early or a second late. He knows to walk along the dewy garden path sprinkled with water to rid himself of worldly dust and to approach the middle gate for official introductions before tea. So, I stand at attention, the sticky heat building against my skin, nervous for that moment when Father and Taro turn, their eyes falling on him, and judgment passes.

Since the house sits at an angle from where I stand, I can see where Hajime will approach. I keep watch, but there is not enough air for my lungs. My chest aches for trying.

What was I thinking?

I should have told *them.*

I should have told *him.*

"Ah, see? A sign of luck, Naoko." Mother motions to my sleeve, where a white butterfly takes rest on the pink floral design. Its paper wings ebb and flow with the breeze, and at once I remember the morning's vision and breathe.

"I dreamed of you, little butterfly," I say with a smile, my nerves quieting as I regard my returning friend. "We rode the wind, you and I. Do you bring me promising news?"

"Maybe you are still asleep like in Chuang Tzu's butterfly dream," says Grandmother as Taro helps her into a sitting position on the mat.

I stay focused on my tiny visitor, holding my arm so it can explore more of the silk fabric. The great Taoist master dreamed he was a butterfly with no thought to his former human self. When he woke, there he was. A man once again. So, was he a man who dreamed of being a butterfly? Or a butterfly, who now dreams of being a man. What is real?

"Maybe Chuang Tzu fixated on the wrong thing, Obaachan," I say to Grandmother. "Instead of which is real, maybe it is both. True happiness existing in the in-between."

Her lips cinch to retain her words.

I quieted Grandmother?

Okaasan reaches up and adjusts my hair comb, deciding that, after all, maybe it is crooked. Grandmother smirks.

It is a short-lived victory.

The butterfly spreads wings of white and takes its leave. I follow its graceful looping path until my eyes fill with a new vision. My future.

Hajime is *here.*

The butterfly swoops low to greet him, hovering momentarily as if to whisper a blessing before fluttering past. The butterflies in my stomach are not nearly as graceful. They bump and flit in a wild frenzy.

Our eyes meet as he nears. He takes in my traditional kimono, swept-up hair and powdered makeup, but his smile drops flat since mine is lacking.

I am frozen in panic.

My heart, lodged high in my throat, beats at an impossible speed. Hajime's clean-shaven with trimmed hair and looks like a movie star, but *why* did he wear his service uniform? Why didn't he wear a suit? I didn't think of this. My oversight will ruin everything!

His eyebrows draw close, confused by my reaction. He mouths, *What's wrong?* But it's too late to explain. They've spotted him.

Okaasan's eyes snap from him to me to ask in silence what she dare not speak out loud.

"Whaaaa…" Grandmother dares for both. "I *knew* it!"

Taro shifts at her outburst, darting eyes in our direction. They widen in surprise to draw Father's curiosity. He turns.

"What is this?" Father bolts upright, disturbing the nearby tea bowl so it lands with a loud *thud-smash* and breaks into pieces.

Okaasan gasps.

Father points accusatory eyes at her, then shifts them to me.

My stomach jumps. I drop my chin, knowing I must work fast. "Father, I wish to present—"

"You will do no such thing." Father's outrage is a barb, sharp and piercing.

My eyes fall to Hajime. His lips form a tight line. He's puzzled by their reaction but lowers his head and bows. "It's an honor—"

"Honor?" Father huffs. "No. *No.* There is no honor in *this.*" He pushes past us.

Taro follows, his shoulder clipping Hajime's hard as he does.

I turn to Mother, confused. "Okaasan?"

"Please, Naoko, say goodbye to your friend and come inside." She bows in apology and trails after them.

"Look what you have done." Grandmother points to the broken tea bowl. Her glare is sharp and cutting. "A jagged split through the center cuts it in half. You can't put it back on the shelf. It belongs nowhere." She juts her chin. "See, Naoko? There is no happiness in between. Not with a *gaijin*." She spits the word, then mumbles as she leaves. "Foolish, stupid girl."

I stare at the broken pieces, then turn to Hajime on the cusp of tears.

He rocks on a foot as though unsure if he'll step forward or back. "After weeks of practice you didn't even tell them?" He removes his cap to run a hand through neatly combed hair. "Why?"

"I *couldn't*." My voice cracks, as jagged as the split bowl. Tears fall. I move closer, desperate for him to understand. "My silence is what allowed this meeting, Hajime. I wanted them to meet you, to see the face of the man I love and want to marry. This was the *only* way."

"You should've told them, though." He steps back, a hand scrubbing the back of his neck. "Because *this* way, all they see is the face of the enemy." His eyes shift to the window where Taro and Grandmother stand watching, waiting, judging. "An American *gaijin*."

The vile word hangs between us.

Today was meant for happiness. I knew it would be difficult. That Father and Brother would be challenging. Even Grandmother, but I thought, I hoped... I was wrong.

With open palms, I collapse into my hands. "I'm sorry." I bite back emotion, not able to bear the shame.

"Naoko." There is a pleading in the way my name rolls from his tongue. He peels my fingers from my face, then

frees strands of hair from my tearstained cheeks. "No, I'm sorry. This isn't how I wanted things for you. For us. Not even for them, I—"

Knock-knock-knock. We jump oceans apart as Grandmother bangs the glass. She shoos him away with angry, frantic waves. Hajime bows, then walks backward, but stops at the corner of the garden, out of her view. He pockets his hands.

I am lost in the liquid blue of his eyes. The disappointment they hold. He wanted nothing more than my family's acceptance. I want nothing more than his. My lip quivers. "Have you changed your mind?"

The air is still. Birds do not sing. Everything holds its breath.

He shakes his head. "No, *no,* but you have to change theirs."

"How? They won't listen to me."

"You're smart and clever, Cricket. Use your voice." He moves closer. "Make them listen."

Grandmother again scolds with her banging, yelling for me to come in.

We look at each other.

A silent conversation of wants and wishes.

Hajime walks backward, mouths, *I love you.*

I love you, too, I mouth back.

He smiles. Nods. Then turns to leave.

"Hajime!" I plead.

Grandmother pounds, but I step forward. "I will convince them."

"If anyone can, it's you," he says, then again turns.

With a sigh, I watch until he disappears around the corner. A ghost. A shadow. It stretches tall and fades. And then no more.

Grandmother's right.

I am a foolish, stupid girl.

But I am also a girl Hajime believes is smart and clever and who has a voice. And I have every intention to use it.

For I am also a girl in love.

FIVE

America, Present Day

When my father and I first arrived at the hospital, we'd gotten lost. Not hard to imagine, considering the sheer size of the expansive medical campus. It formed an intimidating maze of tall glass buildings that were situated one right after the next, and as the afternoon sun bounced between them, it created a distorted hall of mirrors.

Once we located our entrance, we walked side by side toward the door, our exaggerated reflections bounding forward to greet us with youthful energy in long graceful steps. But then they shrank in size, slowed in gait, and all at once, eye to eye, we faced our current selves.

A sick old man. A worried daughter. What we saw. What we were. The constructs of a fun house.

"The *Taussig*." My father stopped short and examined the

hospital name on the door. His mirrored image gaped from the other side. "That was the name of my ship. She was a Sumner-class destroyer, did you know that?" He removed his cap and finger combed his hair. It curled from the perspiration dotting along his fevered brow. "Yes, sir, seventeen years old, and that was where my life began. Who would have guessed it'd end there, too?"

End? I cast a sideways glance as I opened the door, then considered the odd coincidence in name.

As an investigative journalist, I wasn't one who believed in signs or fate. I subscribed to the rationality of reason and its either-or language of hard-edged truth. But for the hospital and his ship to have the same name? Maybe the universe *was* trying to tell me something. And maybe that truth, where my father was concerned, spoke not in absolutes, but in the subtle shades of nuanced whispers, and I only had to listen.

"It was 1955… That was when I joined the navy."

As we walked through the lobby, my father strolled down memory lane.

"It was a year of rock and roll, civil rights and complete unrest." He dabbed at his brow with his handkerchief. "*Rebel without a Cause* was the voice of my generation. We didn't want to conform. We wanted change. I certainly did. And I had to fight for it."

"I know, Pops." It wasn't the first time I'd heard the story. "This way." I motioned toward the elevators.

"Two things transformed everything for me that year." He held up his hand, counted them off with knobby fingers. "One, James Dean died in a car crash. And two, Rosa Parks refused to give up her seat." He explained that while one had nothing to do with the other, for him, a young man coming of age in the '50s, they formed a small epiphany.

"How much time we had wasn't in our control, but what

we *did* with it was." My father placed a hand to his chest. "And if I wanted a different life than my father, I had to stand up to him. So, I faced him square and told him I was joining the navy."

"But you were only seventeen and needed his permission," I said, imagining him going toe-to-toe with my grandfather—a formidable man.

"Yes, but I had a speech. A good one." Pops threw his shoulders back, raised his chin, then told me how he used his grandparents' immigration as an example. How, because they escaped an oppressive Slovakia before the outbreak of World War I to chase a better life, we all had one. And while following in his grandfather's and father's footsteps to work at the factory—like every other immigrant in their neighborhood—was a *good* life, for Pops it wasn't enough.

"Then I drove it home. I said, 'Don't I owe it to Grandpops, who made that sacrifice, and to *you*, who benefited from it, to stand on your shoulders and reach for more?'" Pops gave a wide self-satisfied smile. "And that was it. The winning line. My father found a pen and signed permission for me to enlist then and there."

"It's a good story, Pops," I said, signing him in at reception.

"I set sail on the *Taussig* not long after, and here I am again." He looked at the logo sign mounted on the wall, coughed into his handkerchief and nodded. "Yes, sir, 1955…"

Not six months before he enlisted, the Detroit Master Plan zoned my grandparents' struggling neighborhood as heavy industrial. With the grossly polluted river and air, people had begun to abandon their homes or burn them for insurance money. As families moved out, trouble moved in. For the poor Hungarian village in Detroit, these were telltale signs of hard times ahead.

And while I appreciated my father's fight-for-independence

story, I'd bet my grandfather's reasoning had less to do with Pops's speech and more to do with easing their family's foreseeable burdens.

I only hoped my father hadn't agreed to see the specialist just to ease mine.

Dr. Amon's bright smile and yellow bow tie put me right at ease. He made small talk as he reviewed my father's health history and joked during the initial exam. So, when he sent my father to radiology for a CAT scan, I didn't think twice about it.

When we met with the doctor the second time, some three and a half hours later, his bright smile had dimmed to match a new, serious disposition. It hovered over the conversation, and I thought of nothing else.

He apologized for our wait, explaining he'd wanted to consult their extended team, then he smacked his hands together and delivered the news.

"...the cancer has metastasized..."

"...enlarged lymph nodes and pleural effusions in both lungs..."

"...pneumonia."

My mouth went dry.

Coughing, shortness of breath, fever, perspiration, the bluish tint to his nails, low levels of white blood cells, and with his compromised immune system... Other things were said, doctor things that drifted in and around my altered state.

But my chin snapped up with his final assertion.

They were checking my father in.

The private room, even with the comforts of a nice hotel, couldn't conceal the medicinal smell and noisy medical equipment of a hospital. It was astounding how fast the tide had turned. I sighed and rubbed the tension above my eyes. "This has been a long day. You must be exhausted."

"I'm okay." Pops set his magazine aside, then threaded bulbous knuckles across his middle. "You know what I was thinking? In a way, it's good I got cancer."

"Pops…"

"No, listen. What I mean is, with cancer, we have more time. Time we didn't have with Mama."

My chest tightened. Sure, cancer gave us time, but it stole its quality. Whittled away patience with pain, spitting out tainted last memories not worthy of remembrance. I wanted *him*. Not what cancer couldn't swallow. "I miss her." I wasn't ready to miss him, too.

"With the heart attack, she went quick, and I thought of that, too. At least, that way we still remember her the same. She was still Mama right to the end." His sky blue eyes clouded with memories, then drooped heavy under baggy lids. "Not like me."

"What are you talking about, not like you?"

"Like this." He swept his hand up and down in the air to indicate himself. "I'm grateful for the time, but I don't want to be remembered as some grouchy old man."

It was true. My father was grouchy one minute from his aches and pains and fuzzy the next from the pills that dulled them. But what fell between were flashes of the spirit within. The determined boy who didn't let circumstance define him, the restless dreamer who sailed across the world and the stable family man with a flair for fun.

I sat tall, determined that he knew that. "That grouchy old man is *not* my father. I know who my father is. He's a kind and thoughtful man who loved his wife and lived for his family. I know who you are. I see you, Pops. And *that*…" I copied his sweeping gesture. "That is the disease. It's only the disease."

"But that's what people will see at my funeral."

My heart dropped to the floor. Cancer was killing him, but he was killing me. "I wish I could just wave a wand, say some magic words and poof." I wiggled my fingers. "It all disappears."

Pops chuckled, leaning back into the stacked pillows. "Abracadabra."

"My magic tree." I smiled, thinking of the story, then pulled the thin blanket up over my father's too-thin frame.

He tutted. "The tree wasn't magic. It was the words." His yawn overtook the smile.

"They were good words, Pops."

It was a good story.

We'd been planting a sapling he had sprouted from seed in our backyard when he first told it to me.

"Not too deep, not too wide, just enough room to breathe." He packed it in nice and tight. When I stepped back, I expected the branches to wave or sparkle—something. After all, he'd said the tree was magic. I told him it was broken.

But Pops said the magic was in the *words*. A written message given to him while standing under a tree just like the one we had planted. "Only this one was fully grown and almost thirty feet tall. And that night, Tori, paper lanterns filled every branch with shimmering light. So many, that if you held on to the trunk and looked up, it was like a giant umbrella shielding you from a hundred falling stars."

"But what are the magic words?" I asked, my own lisping through the gap of missing front teeth. "Abracadabra and hocus-pocus?"

Pops laughed. The quiet kind that shook his shoulders. He placed a hand on top of my young head and tousled my hair, so my braids swung back and forth like a handheld bead drum.

"To understand your direction, you must know both your

roots and your reach." My father said the saying was magic because of where he stood in life—leaving the roots of home and reaching for a new one. "It just spoke to me."

For the longest time, I thought he meant the tree spoke to him. I regarded my droopy sapling with new eyes, tried to remember the magic saying to make it talk. But then I wrinkled my nose, asked if I could maybe just say abracadabra instead.

Pops laughed, pulled me close and tickled me until I squealed. We spent the next hour making whistles from thick blades of grass. That tree still stands on our old property. It never reached thirty feet tall, but it talked.

With Pops's story, it would talk for years to come.

"Hand me that, will you?" Pops pointed to his cup of ice. I sprang to my feet to retrieve it. Then, without thinking, I readjusted his blanket and cinched him in along his sides.

Droopy eyes flickered to mine. He laughed through his nose.

"What?" I mocked him with my smile because I knew. He used to do the same for me. "You want a story, too?" I asked, angling my chair to keep a better vigil. "I've got some good ones from work. How's this? Falsified reports of illegal logging? I could make it a fairy tale with profiteers and furry woodland creatures."

Pops's chest shook. A silent laugh. For me, a triumphant win.

He wet his lips. "My magic tree story. Did I ever tell you *why* I was there?"

I thought back. No. He hadn't. "But you can't just add more to my story."

"I'm old. I get to do what I want." His eyes locked to mine. "Are you listening?"

"I'm listening." I scooted closer.

"Okay, so this ancient tree, as you know, was forty feet high, truly majestic."

"And magic." I laughed. "It gets bigger every time you tell it."

He shushed me with a faint smile. "And because it was in bloom—thousands of pink flowers—it was the perfect place for a wedding."

My father said instead of an ordained priest to perform the ceremony, it was a spiritual leader in a robe of white. Instead of family, perfect strangers and brand-new friends attended. Instead of a ring, it was an ornate silk pouch. Inside, a single seed from the majestic tree with a small scrolled message written in English on one side, and Japanese on the other. "That was the magic saying I told you."

"It's a beautiful addition to the story, Pops."

He blinked sleepy eyes and closed them. "You should've seen the bride's gown."

I brightened. It was always about the dress. My mother's was a classic '50s fit and flare—sleeveless, high neck and cinched tight to the waist. Then it exploded in a plethora of tulle to float above her knees. "Was it like Mama's?" I asked.

"No, no." He sighed. "It was a kimono."

SIX

Japan, 1957

My mother is off to retrieve her treasured *shiromuku*, wedding kimono, while Kenji and I admire her wedding photos. She worries about my sullen mood since the failed meeting with Hajime yesterday and hopes to lift my spirit.

I hope yet to change her mind.

A photo catches my interest, so I pull it close to study. Okaasan had three costume changes: a reception gown of pink, another in bold red for their departure and, the most elaborate in design, her layered *shiromuku* gown of white for the ceremony. She wears it in this portrait. The faded image hides its glory, but not Okaasan's beaming happiness.

"So beautiful." I hold the picture out to show Kenji. "And Father looks so handsome." He seldom smiles, but when he does, his expression changes from one of regal dominance to that of a contented cat with his underbelly exposed. He saves that face for Okaasan. Here, it's captured for all to see.

Kenji scoots closer and pulls down the snapshot. "Like me." He flashes a grin. "And you're like Haha," he says, using the child's term for *mother*. His eyes dart from me to the photo.

Squinting to regard Mother's features, I smile. It is my face that stares back. We have the same defined cheekbones, narrow jaw and high nose bridge. "They're so young, only babies."

"You'll make babies soon." Kenji wrinkles his face in disgust.

I mock him, then feign interest in another picture. I have no plans to discuss such intimacies with my little brother, but now I think of nothing else. The stolen kiss that led to more. And how that led to Hajime's proposal of marriage. I smile to myself, remembering my surprise.

"You want to marry me?" I asked, eyes wide.

"More than anything." Hajime pulled me so close our racing hearts beat as one.

"Where would we live?" I asked, contented in his arms. While America's youthful energy colored my dreams, Japan's cultural traditions rooted me home. I nuzzled under his chin, my previous happiness stifled by truth. "Hajime, I could *never* leave."

"Well..." He kissed my temple, then leaned back to rake fingers through my hair. "What if I stayed here?"

"Stayed?" My chin shot up. "What about your family?"

He shrugged. "I'll miss them something awful. I mean, I already do, and my *mom*? Yeah, it'll kill her..." He angled his head and shook it. "And I'll miss the weekend ball games with the guys and Sunday brunch with my folks. I'd miss that life for sure, because it's a good life. And yeah, I could just go and live it. But then one day, before I know it, I'm an old man and I'd always wonder, what if? Because I'd know..." He brushed knuckles across my cheek. "Don't you see, Cricket? I'd give up all the comforts of home because you're my home. And if my life doesn't have you, it's no life at all."

I kissed him. He asked for my hand. Instead, I gave him my whole heart.

"Look!" Kenji waves a picture in front of my face to startle me from memory. "I want to join the army, too. That way I can kill evil *gaijins*." His sweet face contorts.

"What? *Don't say that...*" I glance to the image. My stomach twists. It's Father wearing his military uniform. Kenji isn't aware that Hajime is American. He knows nothing of what happened at the meeting because he wasn't here. I push the photo away. "War is what's evil, Kenji."

"A necessary one." Father's deep voice startles us both. His narrowed eyes scan the memories scattered about on the floor.

How long has he been standing there?

With two fingers he motions for Kenji to give him the military photo. Regarding it, he grunts with a bunched expression. He has experienced war more than once. "One too many," Okaasan says any time it's brought up.

I borrow Hajime's courage, swallow hard and dare to speak. "Necessary but over, Father. Otherwise we are forever in a monkey–crab battle."

His eyes glare daggers, then dart toward Grandmother shuffling by with tea.

"Monkey and crab...such a foolish battle, tsk, tsk, tsk." As she turns into the garden, her lightweight summer *yukata* blends into the deep indigo of the evening sky.

For once I agree with Obaachan. A silly story to illustrate a horrid truth. The crab has a rice ball, and the monkey convinces him to trade it for a persimmon seed. The crab agrees and plants the seed for the fruit. But then the monkey climbs the tree and steals the fruit. The crab's children are so angry they seek revenge, and so on, and so on.

When I look up, Father still stares, so I lower my chin and my voice. "Revenge only creates more revenge," I say, hoping to soften his resolve.

"Tut, tut, tut. Enough of all this." Mother waves off the unpleasantness as she enters the room. "Naoko's match meeting with Satoshi is only days away. Let's speak only happy words, yes?"

We silence our conversation as we know not to upset her. Okaasan's enlarged left heart chamber sometimes beats to its own rhythm when stressed. A small abnormality seldom discussed, but always considered.

Satisfied, she holds out her traditional ceremony kimono and smiles. "Here, Naoko, try it on and let us see."

"Try it on?" My eyes drink in its lush fabric. It is a visual feast of tripled white fine silk and detailed workmanship. The intricate pattern is revealed or masked, depending on how it flirts with the light. It is stunning, and I dare not touch it. To wear this on my wedding day is to honor my family and signifies I am unblemished and presented pure for my husband. I shake my head, full of guilt for failing both. "It's too beautiful, Okaasan, too much for me."

Father turns toward her. She drapes the cherished kimono over his forearms, and I catch a shared glance of warmth that lingers between them.

Facing me, Father nods. "Try it on. It's not too much for a daughter who will marry into such a prominent family. Not everything must be a battle, Naoko."

There it is. A conditional offering of peace to a battle that has only just begun.

After our evening meal, with a clear view of Father and

Taro on the patio, I take over washing the dishes while Mother dries and Grandmother returns them to their display.

"Do you not want to take your tea in the garden, Obaachan?" I motion outside. "You could rest your feet, and I could bring you a fresh cup."

Mother casts a curious glance in my direction. *Maybe I'm too obvious?*

Grandmother hobbles closer, smelling of custard and jasmine, eyeing us both with suspicion, but moves to join Father and Taro on the patio.

I place the kettle over the flame and, when I'm sure Grandmother's in the garden, begin. "You look so pretty today, even more than usual, Okaasan." It's not a lie. Her hair is pulled tight in two sections and fastens with combs of gold and dark sapphire. "Your summer kimono flatters you."

"As you flatter me, Naoko." Mother glances sideways, only this time with eyes that glint and smile.

Giving a small head bow, I stay focused on my rehearsed words.

They are a trap of poetic truth.

Okaasan takes the overwashed bowl from my hands. "You have my ear, Naoko."

My heart's beating wild, like a tiny bird trapped in my chest. I take a breath for courage, and release, hoping her fragile heart holds its rhythm as I cast my plea. "Do you think it is possible that Satoshi can change his mind about me?"

"Is this what troubles you?" Her shoulders drop as though braced to carry a heavier load.

"Please, Okaasan, is it possible?"

"Of course it's possible, but I don't think—"

"So, you agree that minds can change?"

Her eyebrows draw together. She knows I pull water to my own rice paddy, so she says nothing.

I lean close. "What if we learn Satoshi doesn't wish to marry me, either? Then there's no risk of losing his father's business."

Okaasan's drying hands stop.

With a deep breath, I start the petition I have practiced to perfection. "I only ask you to consider this. If you agree that minds *can* change, and if Satoshi's mind is changed—without offense—can you not change Father's? Can you not open his heart to see what is in mine? I wish for a marriage of *love*, Okaasan."

"Naoko..." Okaasan tilts her head.

"I love Hajime." I dare his name in a whisper. "And he loves me. So much, he would give up his home in America. Leave his family to make a life here with ours." I don't yet say where. "He's a good, honorable man who embraces our customs and ways, and also respects me." I smile, emotion bubbling up and misting my eyes. "He encourages me, Okaasan. To speak up and act freely because he loves *all* that I am. And I love who I am with him. It's as though I can do anything. Do you know what he said to me?" His beautiful words have decorated my thoughts since he spoke them. My smile widens.

"He said I'm smart and clever, and if anyone could convince you and Father why we should be together, it's me." I take her hand, squeeze. "So, I say this to you... *You* are smart and clever, and if anyone can sway Father to reconsider, it's you. Please, I beg you to find the courage and persuade him."

Okaasan turns her gaze forward, placing both hands on the counter. She stares out the window where everyone sits. The nervous twitch of her little finger gives movement to her consideration. *Tap-tap-tap.* Then again. *Tap-tap-tap.* We stand next to one another at the sink, each holding our ground by holding our tongue, until—the kettle trumpets steam.

She motions to the boiling water and resumes drying

dishes, a signal my answer must wait. Hurt is often the hole that truth whistles through, and even in silence, it squeals in my ears. *What if Okaasan doesn't answer at all?*

I prepare the after-dinner tea and present it to Grandmother outside. Father and Taro's discussion on foreign trade stalls with my arrival. Taro regards me with a pointed look, but Father doesn't consider me at all. Instead, he observes Kenji, who studies a bug beside his book.

"Kenji-kun..." Father calling his name is correction enough.

Grandmother accepts the tea with a nod and I am dismissed, but never acknowledged.

As I turn to leave, Taro resumes their conversation, the word *gaijin* emphasized in spite for my ears. He's more of a threat to Hajime than Father because his zealous nationalistic views feed Father's old ingrained prejudices.

He's gasoline to a slow-burning fire.

The best insurance against fire is to own two homes, so I wait on Okaasan's answer. If I've persuaded her oversize heart, maybe she can coax Father's narrow mind to open, and our house will no longer stand divided.

SEVEN

Japan, 1957

The train's vibration aggravates my sour stomach, making me queasy. I should have gone home right after traditional dance practice, but I went to the pier. Hajime's ship is out at sea—they travel every other week between Yokosuka and neighboring ports, but I left him a note with the guard. In it, I wrote,

The Red String of Fate is an old East-Asian belief. It is said the heavens tie a red cord around the little fingers of those ordained to be together. It is an invisible thread that connects those who are destined to meet, regardless of time, place or circumstance. The thread may stretch or tangle, but it will never break. Follow ours to find me waiting at our little thatched house.

I snipped two small pieces of red yarn—one for us each—
and enclosed his in the envelope. He needs to know that my
feelings and intentions haven't changed. I left out how Father's feelings haven't changed, either. Although I believe my
mother supports me, I understand her submission and her silence. She's of a different generation and has never had someone like Hajime to inspire her words and actions. I'm hoping
mine will encourage hers.

With a sigh, I lean back in the train seat and watch the
woman and child sitting across from me. While I'm crammed
in with others, they sit alone. Passengers pretend indifference,
but the overgenerous space demonstrates disgust. It doesn't
matter that their clothes are clean, hair is neat or that they
wear no surgical mask to indicate illness, no one risks con-
tamination from the child's obvious mixed blood.

The little girl catches me looking, so I smile. Reaching in
my pocket, I retrieve two pieces of cubed *dagashi* candy and
offer her one. She only stares.

"Please," I say, holding it out farther. "I have plenty."

With enthusiasm, she reaches out and claims it.

Now no one pretends indifference.

The man seated to my left bolts upright to stand. The
woman beside him shifts farther away. The sleeping woman
is awake and glares with disapproving eyes. I've become in-
fected, so I pretend indifference.

In truth, it hurts my heart. If Hajime and I have children,
it will be the same.

With her light skin and almond eyes, the little girl is a living
reminder that we lost the war, that America's radical Western
beliefs intrude upon our traditions, that they have tainted our
blood. She's a mixed-race child, and although innocent, her
existence shames and scares them.

My country's opposition and my family's fear are what shame and scare me.

Tears well up. For them, for me. For not knowing what to do. I dig in my pocket and pull out what remains of my candy cubes. She gets them all.

The train squeals as the brakes squeeze. Impatient passengers stand and make their way toward the door, itching to be rid of us both.

I focus on the horizon as I step from the platform to walk the long road home. I should hurry, but I'm already late, and as Grandmother says, "If you are going to eat poison, you may as well clean your plate." I kick the gravel, causing angry puffs of loose dirt to rise in protest.

"Naoko!" The deep voice travels from the top of the hill.

I squint to make out the figure. A charged thunderbolt shocks my insides. Heat soars up my neck and prickles my skin.

Satoshi!

Oh, no. *Did I forget?* I thought our meeting was tomorrow! I quicken my pace but then slow. Hajime said if anyone could change my family's mind, I could. Now is my chance to change Satoshi's, as well. I shuffle-step, pretending a leisure stroll even though he approaches in haste. I want him to find me discourteous.

"Your father sent Taro and me out to search for you." His voice softens as he nears. "He's gone to your friend Kiko's house, so I headed for the train and here you are."

"Here I am." Leaves rustle as I stand a captive audience. Maybe just a captive. I'm still confused. "Isn't our match meeting *tomorrow?*"

"Yes, but your father invited us to visit informally *today.*"

Which I might have known if Father had told me.

For the moment, we study one another. Me, plotting a plan.

Him, cursing his luck? I'm a mess. *Good.* I hope he storms off to declare me unacceptable. I slouch to inspire the idea. Hajime would laugh and beam with pride. I slump more.

I pretend not to notice how he's changed. I remember him as cute, but now, I must admit, he's attractive, although not like Hajime. His hair is longer on top and slicked back, but I would presume on a normal day it is not as neat and worn more fashionable. His face is angular, with a high nose bridge and wide-set eyes that fix on mine.

I drop my head and toe the dirt, aggravated from my misfortune. He should be hideous, so I can complain to my family. *How could you ask me to marry such a beast? Think of your future grandchildren! Did you not see how striking Hajime was?* Instead, my arguments would fail.

From midwaist, I bow an apology to test him. "Forgive me, Satoshi-san, I must have forgotten today's arrangement. It slipped my mind. Such carelessness. Weak character makes for a weak wife." Flippant remarks, but now I can study his reaction. The strong, square jaw, is it tense with irritation? Is his chin held high and smug like Taro's? Do his eyes hold contempt like Father's?

"And I am sorry for the confusion." He returns the bow gracefully. Smiles. "Shall we walk?"

I cast a sideways glance, not trusting the performance, but stroll beside him.

Birds give pause to consider the steam whistle. One long signal indicates the train's withdrawal. Japan runs on a strict schedule of arrival and departure, everything at its own proper time.

Except for me.

Grandmother says, "Truth has a proper time, too. If it comes too early or too late, it is both a lie." The push for Satoshi as a match is not fair to him or me. I don't wish to lie, so the proper time to tell Satoshi my truth is now. My teeth grind hard as I decide how to present it without igniting outrage. I want him disinterested, not offended. He is still the son of my father's client.

Hajime says I'm smart and clever. But convincing? I stop and throw the words to the wind. "I'm sure someone of your quality has another match. Somebody obedient and mindful. Someone that's perfect for you. In fact, I find myself in this same challenging situation." I face him but focus on his impeccable brown shoes.

"I see." His polished foot taps once, then again. "Do I know him?"

"No, I'm sure you don't, just as I haven't met your intended. But I'm certain she's always considerate to your busy schedule, unlike me—an unlikely match. What were our parents thinking?" I almost laugh. Hajime would say I should go into acting.

"Does he attend your school?"

"No. He's completed his education."

Satoshi shifts his weight. "Does he work with your father, then? I may have met—"

"He doesn't, and you haven't." I grind my jaw in agitation. *Did he not hear anything I said?*

"But how do you know? I may—"

"I know because he's *American*." My head jolts up, surprised by my own audacity. Then, at once, lowers. My stomach plummets. *What have I done?* "I'm very sorry and wish not to offend you or your family. Please don't tell your father or… I can't…" I can't breathe or think. Now I want someone to tell me what to do.

This emotional storm is too close. I would like to seek shelter in the forest with the now-laughing foxes. They may tell Grandmother everything, but they tell me nothing.

From flash to boom, I mentally count the seconds between them.

One one-thousand.

Two one-thousand.

Three—

"I must admit, Americans are hard to resist."

What? I peek up through lashes. Satoshi is not angry or cross that I choose another match—an *American*—and he is... *smiling*? Does he, in fact, have another match and therefore an understanding heart?

He resumes our walk, so I follow, not taking my eyes from him.

"You know baseball, Naoko?"

I nod, still surprised by his casual demeanor, but also cautious. Hajime plays baseball. Does he know this? Is it a trick because the American team won the highly promoted match? Will his words yet rain down in ire and disgust?

"The American baseball player Joe DiMaggio married the famous blonde movie star. I saw them in Tokyo when they were here for their honeymoon." He turns, casting a fixed gaze to me. "I swear she hypnotized me with her big blue eyes."

He laughs, which makes me smile despite myself.

This blue-eyed spell I understand well. When I first met Hajime in Yokosuka, his eyes charmed me. They captured light and sparkled like water absorbing the sun.

"So, yes, Naoko, I, too, understand the appeal. But..." Satoshi stops, his wide smile replaced by a softer one. "I also like midnight eyes that glint like rare black diamonds." He winks. "Maybe you do, too, hmm?"

My face warms, so I stare into the trees, confused. So, he is charming; it's still for show. In Japan there are two types of love. Family love for wife and children and relationship love, which the husband continues outside the home with others. I want both within the marriage and I want my *own* home. Not one governed by a spiteful mother-in-law.

We walk in silence.

Why isn't he angry? He should have declared our match unacceptable, forcing my family to at least consider Hajime. Satoshi's not following the rules.

"You're lost in thought. Where are you?" Satoshi asks.

"Oh..." I glance in his direction but look away with haste. If this were our official match meeting and I were trying to impress him, I'd talk about the garden's various plants to show my knowledge and attention to detail. Or I'd ask about his studies in electronics and exclaim how impressive his ambitions are. Instead, my tongue betrays me. "I am thinking of the ritual cat story and its silly rule."

He laughs and regards me with an amused expression.

"Much like these match meetings, wouldn't you agree?" I ask, glancing at him sidelong to see if that, too, makes him smile.

It does. He clasps his hands behind his back and looks up to the trees. "There was once a great spiritual leader whose meditation was disturbed by the constant noise and whine of the displeased monastery cat."

"Yes." I nod because he knows the story. "And to solve this problem, they tie up the cat during service, so the great leader will be able to concentrate."

"And when the cat eventually dies..." Satoshi holds up his index finger and speaks in a dramatic fashion. "They get another and tie that one up, as well. This becomes a *required* rule for perfect and proper meditation for centuries to come."

This time we both laugh.

"Naoko..." He stops as we near my house. "Please know I admire your honesty and would not betray it to my father or hold it against you or your family. You can trust me." The corners of his lips turn up. "And while I understand your heart is full, can you understand when I ask if there's room for consideration?" His mouth opens to say something else but closes as Okaasan and Satoshi's mother approach from the front door.

Dread crawls up my spine. I'm already exhausted by this day, but to have caused embarrassment to Okaasan? I am white bones and weary. A daughter who cannot be found signals a mother who is also lost.

Father must be furious.

Polite conversation finishes up the visit I all but missed. I bow an apology again for my tardiness to Satoshi's mother, and Satoshi quickly interjects that it's not needed, as the visit, although short, was thoroughly appreciated and enjoyed. This stops his mother from responding and saves my continued embarrassment. We exchange smiles, and with a slight nod, he escorts her from our home.

From the doorway, I watch them walk away. Satoshi's one arm motions as he talks; the other extends for her to hold for balance. She leans into him and says something, causing his head to throw back in a robust laugh.

"You're smiling," Grandmother says from beside me.

I turn, my cheeks dropping fast. "He just surprised me."

"Like having a rice dumpling fly into your mouth, it's unexpected and sweet." Her lips pucker smugly.

Just as unexpected is Taro's tight grip on my arm as he tugs me aside. "First you insult us by bringing home a filthy *gaijin* and then when Father attempts to discredit any rumors it may have caused, you show up late? Had you not been found, all would be lost. Do you not understand this, sister?" His eyes bulge.

"I understand no one cares what I want." I yank my arm from his grasp but maintain my piercing glare.

"What *you* want?" Taro's thin lips twitch into a sneer. He steps close and growls. "Do you want us to lose everything? Do you know how hard Father works since the war?"

"The war ended twelve years ago, Taro." I fire the words back.

"The war ended *millions* of lives, Naoko. It almost destroyed our country and the American Occupation has barely dissolved and you...you whore around with them, wearing their clothes, listening to their music, wanting to *marry* one." Taro begins to pace. "How do you think this reflects on our family? Our chance to rebuild?"

"Do you not do business with them?" My eyebrows rise with my point.

He stops. "Buying and selling wares in a mutually beneficial agreement is *not* selling your family's name."

"No, instead you wish to sell *me* out for the sake of business." I cross my arms to hold my pounding heart in.

"Look around, Naoko." Taro motions wildly. "Do you not see our shrinking station? Do you wish to see Obaachan and Okaasan reduced further if you cause offense with these games? For Father to lose face? Me, my birthright? Trade you off..." He huffs. "Father trades you *up*. He secures a prominent home for *your* future when ours is still uncertain because of them. Are you so selfish?"

My stomach drops in confusion. *Am I?* I flip my hand to reject his words and spin to leave.

Father stands right behind me.

Kenji roars past to taunt. "Naoko, you're in so much troub—"

"*Enough!*" Father's tone halts Kenji. With a sweeping motion, he dismisses both him and Taro.

Kenji bows, the teasing eyes replaced with worry. Quietly, he back-steps to where Grandmother and Okaasan stand near the kitchen. Taro stabs me with one last cutting glare, bows to Father and leaves in a huff.

My breath shortens; a sharp ill-ease brews in my belly.

Father widens his stance. Fire burns behind his eyes to redden his face and scorch his words. "*Where*, Naoko?"

Grandmother's adage floods my mind. "Truth told too early or too late is both a lie." It's too late. "Otousan, please forgive me. Time slipped away an—"

He smacks me.

I wobble in shock. Okaasan gasps and runs toward me, but Father pushes her away.

"Don't touch her!" I move between them.

"It is not my place to interfere. Forgive me, husband." Okaasan lowers her chin.

"No, it *is*. I'm your daughter," I say, facing her. Tears itch behind my eyes. "You have a voice, Okaasan, and every right to use it. This is 1957..." I turn to Father, my heart enraged and beating fast. "Women make their own decisions and I—"

Another strike across my cheek jolts me back. This one hurts. My hand covers my prickling skin as tears fall over my fingertips, but I hold my head up. Next time he won't catch me off guard.

"You reflect our family's honor, Naoko. That does not change. And tonight, you shamed us by your unexcused absence. And now you disrespect me with your insolence." He barks the words, nostrils flaring with each breath. "I blame the *gaijin* filling your head with nonsense. *Women* make their own decisions." He scoffs. "I decide in this house."

I study the rise and fall of his Adam's apple as he swallows his anger. I clamp my jaw to hold back mine.

"And I have decided to give my blessing for you to marry

Satoshi at once." A snarl through clenched teeth. *"If* he will still have you."

"But, Fathe—"

"Silence!" His mighty arm cocks but holds position. "It's done."

I drop to my knees, distraught. Bury my face with tears.

His words strike harder than any hand.

Satisfied, Father leaves me there alone. In his mind, a match with Satoshi guarantees I'm well cared for by a family he respects, a family that ensures the continued success of ours. This pleases him, gives him comfort for everyone's future. I understand, but what happiness is there in a future that isn't mine?

Unable to rise, I whisper a small prayer and send my request into the storm. I ask for the glue that mends jagged edges. If not possible, I ask to be stronger than the bowl I broke. If still not possible, I ask for help from someone regarded with even more importance than the ritual cat.

For in Japan there are many fearful things under the sun: the great earthquakes that bring down entire cities, deadly thunderbolts from an angry sky, raging winds of lethal fires and the father.

The last is not the least.

EIGHT

America, Present Day

I'd checked in at a nearby hotel, but I spent little time there. Instead, I'd brought most of my things to the hospital and made do with the oversize chair. It had been over a week, and with the intravenous fluids and antibiotics, I had expected my father to start getting better. He'd gotten worse.

The teal blue gown hung two sizes too big and washed out his already pale complexion. My heart twisted at how gaunt he'd become. He wasn't eating and only took water through a straw, and even then, only in sips. And while medicine settled his chesty cough, it made him drowsy and increased his wheeze. My father was slipping away, and no one was doing anything.

A quick knock, then Pops's door opened, releasing a ribbon of fluorescent light. A nurse my father liked walked through.

Natalie? It was hard to keep track of names when I could hardly keep track of the day.

"Hello," she whispered, trying not to disturb my father. "I'm here to check on our guy." Her ponytail bobbed as she set to work.

It was always *our* guy, *our* friend and *we* think this or that. As if the hospital staff were one collective consciousness instead of a mass of individual souls. Perhaps a necessity. *Our guy* allowed an emotional distance. But our guy was *my* father, and he had a name. I wished they'd use it.

"Do you think you could get my father some oxygen?" I asked before she could slip away. Pops's congested breathing had shallowed, sometimes with long pauses between. "I don't think he'd want tubes, but you have the mask kind, right?"

"Dr. Amon is on his rounds, so he should be here any minute." She shut the door, taking the answers and the light with her.

When the doctor finally appeared, I leaped up from the chair and herded him back into the hall.

"What is happening?" He craned his neck toward the room, alarmed.

"No, sorry, he's fine. I just wanted to discuss other treatment options. The antibiotics don't seem to be working— he's getting worse." Once I started, it was full steam ahead. I clenched my fist and pounded through my concerns and suggestions one after the next: the antibiotics, the resistance to them, his lack of appetite.

"Please." The doctor held up his hands. "I understand—"

"No. You *don't* understand." I pointed inside. "That is my father, and no one is doing anything."

"Please..." he said again, and guided me from the hall back inside the room. "Let us include your father in this discussion." He flipped the dimmer up. Harsh light shocked the room. "Mr. Kovač?" Dr. Amon leaned over him. "Hello, Mr. Kovač. I am sorry to disturb you."

Pops blinked, squinted and inventoried his surroundings.

"Yes. Hello, Mr. Kovač, hello." Dr. Amon took a small step back, motioned to me. "I'm afraid your daughter is most upset. It appears you haven't talked with her about your medical decisions, and I recommend we do before the others arrive."

"What others?"

"Mr. Kovač?" Pops rubbed at his eyes, confused, so Dr. Amon repeated himself. My father shifted his head on the pillow in my direction, then gave a nod to Dr. Amon.

"Yes? Okay." Dr. Amon spun to me and pushed back his shoulders. "Against my wishes, your father requested we not share his recent medical decision with you."

"Wait, back up, what decision? And when did *that* conversation even take place?" I'd only left once or twice for the hotel. I got coffee a few times. Ice.

"After the CAT scan results." Pops's words crackled as he tried to prop himself up.

I wanted to help, but my feet rooted in disbelief. "Okay, so you want to make your own medical decisions, which is fine, but you didn't want them to share anything with me?" I scrutinized Dr. Amon. "It's not like his cancer is a secret." I eyed my father, spoke louder. "Pops, that's why we came here, remember? To discuss treatment options for your *cancer.*"

"Doc…" My father furrowed his brows. "Please."

"Yes, all right." Dr. Amon drew his palms together in thought, rested them under his nose, then flipped them free with his words. "Your father and I discussed palliative care after he received the test results, and as of this morning, your father informed me that was his decision. Do you understand this?"

I didn't. My silence said as much.

Dr. Amon dipped his chin. "Your father has chosen not to continue treatment and opted for end-of-life hospice instead."

"What?" The punch of his words was so quick and sharp it drew tears from the shock alone. I stepped back in disbelief.

Dr. Amon clarified that aggressive therapies would prolong suffering. He explained the interventions to provide symptom relief for a patient without curative options. He said other things, indistinguishable doctor things of what to expect, but my mind fixed back to my father's words upon our arrival. *My ship. That's where my life began… Who'd have guessed it'd end there, too?*

My father didn't guess, he *knew*. And maybe underneath the tea, the vitamins and even the last desperate appointment with a specialist, I did, too.

That night I didn't sleep. Instead, I peered out the hospital window and watched the sun break through the haze. *Red sky in morning, sailors take warning.*

The storm was just ahead.

NINE

Japan, 1957

There is no after-school tutoring session, so my friend Kiko and I ride home from the train station unhurried. Twisting my bicycle's handlebars back and forth, I make serpentine tracks in the gravel as I think of Hajime, hoping he's read my words. I stare at the red string I've dared to tie around my finger, then stand on my bicycle's pedals to build speed for the hill ahead.

Kiko lags behind. I'm lost in thought, while she's loud in silence. She's upset with me for even considering going against my family. But how could I not?

At the top, I skid to a stop and turn. The skirt of my cotton school uniform clings to the backs of my thighs. I shake it loose and wait. Kiko takes her time pedaling and pretends not to notice my impatience. Her feet touch down to walk in the gravel. She does not stop, just passes by with tight lips and high-arched brows, like an insolent child holding her breath.

"I am aware you're angry with me." Sitting on the seat, I push the bike with oversize steps to catch up. "But you don't understand."

"What is there to understand?" She puffs a breath to free her eyes from blunt-cut bangs that settle in the same spot. "First, you date a foreigner, and I think, okay, he's handsome, we both love everything American, so it's fun, but now?" Kiko's round cheeks dot red with anger as she stops to make her point.

I brake, too, braced to fight it.

"I can't believe you want to *marry* Hajime despite your father's wishes. And to tell Satoshi he is American was foolish. What if they close their account with your father's business? Your family fortune will dry up and they won't be able to secure another match." She tucks her short hair behind her ears to better frame her scowl. "And you *know* what everyone will think." She sniffs.

"I'm not *trapping* him," I snap, and cross my arms, embarrassed.

"But that's what people will say. That you sold out for a ticket to America like the *pan-pan* prostitute girls who hang out at the base." She leans over the bicycle's handlebars. "They may even say you're pregnant."

I hide my face into folded arms on the handlebars.

"Naoko?"

When I don't say anything, she shakes my shoulder. "Tell me you're not?"

"I'm late," I mumble.

"What?" Her voice rings shrill. "Oh, *no*..." Kiko's shock shifts to sympathy. "How far do you think? There still may be time to get rid of it and fix everything."

I gasp. "Get rid of it? *No...*" I shake my head to dislodge the thought.

Kiko pedal-walks closer and almost whispers. "We could lie on the permission forms. And I have some money—I'm not sure if it's enough. And we'd have to find a doctor who would bend the rules a little."

"Stop, Kiko!" I push off from the ground to move the bike forward and leave her horrible words behind.

"How many cycles missed? Tell me."

I drop my head, disappointed with my situation. The one I wouldn't admit but can no longer deny. "If I miss this week, it'll be three moons. Too many weeks."

"You should have told me sooner." Her words stipple in hurt. "I would have helped you. You would have had time. But now?"

"But nothing. I *want* this baby." Twirling around to face her, I plead my truth. "I love Hajime. Does that not mean anything? And Hajime wants *me*." I kick the gravel road, scattering sand and pebbles in various directions, then start pushing my bike again for home.

Kiko glides beside me on hers, buzzing like an irritated bee set to sting. "People will talk."

"We planned to marry, anyway," I say without glancing over. "So, that leaves the gossiping hens nothing to cluck about." Another kick, this one raises dust along with Kiko's ire.

"That gives them *more!*" She pedals faster, making sharp circles, ensnaring me in the middle. "Rumors will follow your family at every turn."

I pivot as she circles to keep her judgmental eyes in view. Mine burn hot with tears.

"They will call you a *whore*, Naoko, say your family has no honor, and no one will associate with you. My family will force *me* to stay away. Is that what you want?"

I balk. "You know that's not what I want."

"No one wants half-bloods." Kiko snorts a fast breath, coasting closer. "And no one will want *you*. Where will you live? Foreigners cannot own land and your family will cast you aside, so where? On the American base?"

"No." I plant my feet because I'm losing ground. "Hajime has rented a house in Taura." I jut my chin, determined. "We will be fine."

She skids to a stop. "You mean in the old *Eta* community, don't you?" Her eyes go wild. "Oh, Naoko, you *can't* live there."

"I know…" My heart plummets and sours in my stomach. "But maybe I won't have to."

I tell her the plan I put into place, how I petitioned for Okaasan to sway Father. And if that doesn't work, how I'll share where we would live—and because the *Eta* stigma would impact them, perhaps they will help us secure better housing. Even if only to save themselves.

"*That* is your plan?" Kiko taunts. "Hajime was *intended* for memory, Naoko. A secret, wonderful memory to return to one day. But if you do this, that's what you'll become. A memory, to all of us. Exiled. Have you worked *that* into your plan?" She shakes her head. "I'm not going to let you do this."

"There is nothing to be done. I love him."

We stare at one another.

"Then you're a fool." She glares tearful eyes, then pushes off.

Why must this be so difficult? If it were Satoshi's child, everyone would claim an early blessing and rush the marriage. Touching the red yarn looped around my finger, I watch Kiko pedal away through my steady tears. Her words slice through my heart, but not my resolve. We've been friends since we were children, so our threads have run together side by side. We've never once crossed to move in different directions.

Until now.

"Naoko."

My name is whispered from somewhere far. Who is calling? I run with outstretched fingers to sweep the wind and chase the sound. Looking around, everything fades and blurs until I focus. I am awake within my dream.

My arms rise to command the air. I am the composer, coaxing Nature's elements to perform. At first, gentle, the indecipherable rustle of swaying branches and leaves. Then, with force, and in one gust, the foliage rips from limbs to swirl around me. Faster and faster in a mad whirlwind dance.

"Naoko, wake up."

The voice stills the gale, and the leaves drop in unison. My eyes flutter open. Mother leans close. Her hand jostles my shoulder to shake the fog of in-between.

"Okaasan?"

"Shh, follow me now," she whispers, then rises and pads out.

I stand and blink away my dream, while moving on tiptoes after her toward the back door.

My eyes widen to adjust as I step outside. The sleepy orange sun peeks from a thick blanket of dark, not committing to push it away, maybe irritated by our early disturbance.

"Come." Okaasan tugs my arm, walking us along the garden's path, away from the house.

"What is it?" My skin bumps like a plucked chicken from the cool air.

Mother stops at the wooden bench that sits to the west. I sit beside her, sensing the moment's importance. Does she have my answer?

Her shadowed eyes lock on to mine. "Naoko, it's good that Satoshi knows of your American and shows a compassionate heart. And now confirmed, it releases our family of future burdens. It also allows you a choice. You have two paths, but only one opportunity to select which one you will walk." She pulls my hand between hers. "But there's no going back. Is this clear?"

I nod, wanting to comprehend, but struggle in confusion.

She forms a soft smile. "Daughter, since you present an American military man as your intended and deny consideration of Satoshi—a good match—your father suspects a pregnancy."

"What? Why would you think...?" My heart falls. *Kiko.* "She told you?"

She waves to silence the words that dangle from my lips. "Because I know my daughter and watch her appetite wane and see her sick with morning worry, I already suspected." Her hand squeezes mine. "So then, has the bloom remained on the branch? Or is the pregnancy Kiko spoke of *possible*? Now, I am asking for your courage to answer with truth."

Not wanting to admit the shared intimacies of marriage, my chin drops, and I look away humiliated. My silence is answer enough.

Again, her slender fingers, wrapped around mine, squeeze. "Your father won't accept Hajime, with or without a baby, daughter. And Satoshi cannot accept you as a match if your womb grows another man's seed. There's a midwife Grandmother can contact who can confirm either way and, if you are, can deal with such a thing in discretion."

I glance up to absorb the meaning of her words. "Okaasan, *no...*"

Her eyes soften. "Satoshi still wants this match if you do,

Naoko, as does your father. It's still possible. Do you understand?"

"I understand both sides of the coin contain sorrow." My shoulders fall and I lean onto Mother. Her hand runs through my hair from crown to tip in slow, comforting strokes. The sun no longer fights its slumber. With a deliberate stretch, it drags fingers of light dipped in orange across the gray-blue sky.

Okaasan sighs. "When I was a young girl, no older than Kenji, I tried to trick my mother. She was not so different than Obaachan—stubborn and opinionated. Determined to show her up with a clever riddle, I pretended to hold an imaginary bird behind my back. I asked her, 'Is the bird I have hidden alive or dead? What is your answer?' I grinned, so proud, knowing I couldn't lose. If she replied, 'Dead,' I would act as though I set it free, so it would fly away before her eyes. If she said, 'Alive,' I would feign a small squeeze to snap its little neck.

"I watched my mother consider my puzzle, and I repeated my question, ready to bask in my moment. 'What is the answer? Is the bird alive or dead?' My mother's chin lifted. She smiled and said, 'The answer is in your hands.'"

There's a pause while the meaning sinks in.

"So, this is what I say to you. The answer, daughter, is in your hands. You choose baby bird's destiny, and your own, by what you do now. Right now."

Okaasan places a hand on both of my shoulders and speaks in a somber tone. "Have the morning meal and prepare for school just as always. Then, as you leave, understand this. At the bottom of the hill, within the trees, I have hidden a small suitcase for you behind the old stump. You know where?"

I nod, straining to listen over the thumping of my heart.

"If you choose Hajime and the possibility of his baby, then

take the bag. Go to him. Do not ever come back or we will all suffer for it." Her eyes glisten with moisture. "If you choose Satoshi, then go to school, come home and prepare for the wedding. Grandmother and I will make arrangements with the midwife to confirm the womb is clean…and clean it if it is not." She leans closer. "But you must never breathe Hajime's name again. Not even as a whisper."

Salty tears fall one after the other and rest near my lips. Panic bubbles up to burn my throat and nose. "How do I know which path? How do I know, Okaasan?"

"To pick the correct one is fate. To pick the wrong one is also fate. So, you must choose your love, and be prepared to love your choice." With her thumbs, she wipes under my eyes, then holds my cheeks. "At day's end, if you return to me, I'll embrace you with all my love. But, if at day's end, should you not return…" A sharp intake of breath swallows her words.

I feel my own stagger in my lungs.

"If you should not return, my love is as your shadow, unshakable and always behind you."

My lips purse. Okaasan pulls me to her; one arm wraps me tight, while her other hand frantically strokes my hair. She kisses my forehead, the top of my head, then one cheek, then the other and then…no more.

No more.

My mother loosens her hold and sits back. She doesn't look at me again. Only stares ahead with glossy eyes that have gone blank. Standing, she forces a long breath. "This day has begun, Naoko. The bird is in your hands."

TEN

America, Present Day

Standing outside my father's hospital room, I stared at my father's letter—the kanji script, the smudged *J* of *Japan* and the envelope's tattered edge. I considered opening it, but first pondered his words.

Mama was the love of my life, but before that life, I lived another. That's what I've been trying to tell you...

What "other life" and when did he try to tell me? During our road trip to the hospital? When we'd first arrived? I'd traced every step of our journey here and every word and story since they checked my father in.

It'd be easier if you just read my letter. I need you to do that now, okay, Tori? It's time.

It's time. He was dying. Tears slid down my cheeks with that truth. I could no longer ignore it or wish it away. I couldn't fix things. There was nothing else to be done. I blinked and forced a full, slow breath, then brought the envelope close to lift the flap, but it was still sealed. *He never opened it?* Pops said he wanted me to read it, but why hadn't he?

I studied the circled marks, the stylized symbols blurred within them, the strange assortment of English letters stamped at the top, the return address beside it.

There, the most noticeable clue stared me right in the eye. My father's PO box. It'd been there all along. At once, I understood why the letter hadn't been opened.

The letter wasn't *to* my father. It was *from* him and had been returned. But who was Hajime?

"Pops?" I wiped at my cheeks and walked back into his room.

He blinked sleepy eyes.

"Pops, you wrote this letter?" I held it up, so the address faced him as I approached. "That's your PO box but that's not you." I tapped the odd name above it with my index finger. "I don't understand."

Pops regarded the envelope, me, then his eyes drifted. "Did you...?" His breath caught under thick, stubborn phlegm. His exhale rattled, determined to break it free. "I wanted—" He attempted to clear it, held up a one-minute finger, then folded with the succession of coughs that followed. It didn't let up.

"Should I call someone?" I placed my hand on his back as though it would calm the fit, make the cancer stop and leave my father alone. I scanned the bed and table for a towel or tissues, swiped the box from where it fell on the floor, then held out several. He convulsed into them.

They soaked in blood.

"Oh!" My heart lurched. I searched for the corded help button within the tangled sheet, found it and clicked. "Hang in there, Pops. They're coming."

More coughs. More blood. I panicked and ran to the door. *"Somebody!"*

★ ★ ★

My father was dying. And like everything else in his life, he chose to do it on his own terms.

Sedated, Pops drifted in and out of sleep. I sat beside him, listening to him breathe. A beautiful sound, even though it wasn't. A beautiful man but with such an ugly disease.

My father had said that was what people would see at the funeral. At the time, I'd argued, told him what I saw. A man who had loved his wife and had lived for his family, but right then, I saw the disease just the same.

A monstrous serpent with morphine-filled fangs that pierced his arm. And like the snake who eats its own tail, it had begun the fatal cycle to devour him whole.

Pops twitched awake, studied the room into recognition.

I moved closer and leaned my head near his.

He blinked heavy-lidded eyes.

I blinked teary ones. "You okay?"

A nod. An eyebrow raised to ask the same.

"I'm okay, Pops." I smiled through tears. "I'll be okay."

We looked at one another.

It was the conversation of our life.

It was our last conversation.

With sleep, my father slipped into a coma and from there struggled to breathe. As he requested, there would be no life support. And soon…no life.

I didn't leave his side again.

I told him that I loved him.

I held his hand.

Hours later, he let go.

The night became a blur of doctors, staff, paperwork and condolences. One minute I'd been sitting with my father and the next he was gone. I didn't remember the car ride back to the hotel, but there I was, alone in the dark. Alone in the world.

Before, the thought of my father's letter frightened me. I couldn't understand what it could mean, but hours after my father's death, I was desperate for any meaning at all, because it was all I had left.

"Okay, Pops..." The words brought instant tears. "Okay, here goes..." I opened my eyes and, with trembling hands, opened the flap. There was a single folded sheet tucked inside and, inside that, a red piece of yarn. *Yarn?*

I looked to the paper, to my father's familiar cramped handwriting, ran my hand over the ink, then read his words.

My Dearest Cricket,

I hope this letter somehow finds its way to you, and that it finds you in health and surrounded by loved ones and family. I pray that family also includes one of my own.

Please, without any expectations, I wish only to know our daughter is well and, if it's within your heart, for our Little Bird to know she's always been in mine. Even now.

I'm an old man, Cricket, at the end of my life when pain comes due. I need you to know, in loving you, I've never had a single regret. But in losing you? In the how and the why? So many.

Your Hajime

Daughter. It said *daughter.* My heart lodged high in my throat. *I wish only to know our daughter is well...* My vision blurred from flowing tears. I blinked and wiped them away, bringing the letter close as if I'd misread.

I hadn't. I placed a hand to my forehead and left it there

while I read it again in its entirety. I didn't understand. That was what he wanted to tell me? How? Where is she? I stared at his words, then managed my own. "How do you have another...?" A hitched breath snagged the word. My heart hammered constricted ribs as I rocked forward to force it out. *"Daughter?"* I didn't understand.

"Pops?" My voice cracked. The words mixed with tears, salting a freshly sliced wound. I looked around, searching for answers.

But my father was no longer there to give them.

ELEVEN

Japan, 1957

I sit with my family for the morning meal, a day like any other, and yet, after the conversation with Okaasan in the garden, it is a day like none before. Grandmother's words haunt me: "Worry gives a small thing big shadows." But a possible pregnancy is a big thing and the shadow it casts isn't only monstrous, it's life-changing.

Chewing each mouthful of rice, I stare and marvel at my mother. I may have encouraged her to speak up, just as Hajime encourages me, but it is she who inspires. When she attempted to persuade Father, and he silenced her voice, she used her savvy to outsmart him. She's more than clever, she's brave.

I study them over my bowl's rim, committing every detail to memory. Father: the silver-white hair near his temples, his thick eyebrows and the deep-set lines that permanently rest between them. Taro: determined eyes, shoulders wide and high. Grandmother: knowing smile and meddlesome spirit. Kenji: Buddha cheeks and boundless energy. Okaasan...

"What are you saying, Naoko?" Grandmother asks. "Hmm?" She holds her cup out, so I pour.

"I didn't speak, Obaachan."

Taking a sip, she smacks her lips and harrumphs. "A silent man is the best one to listen to."

I remain silent.

Grandmother wipes her mouth. "I remember when Okaasan prepared for her wedding, she became quiet, too. It's a mixture of happy and sad to start a new life, but meeting is always the beginning of separation. You become a new daughter for Satoshi's family, and we in turn will receive a new daughter once Taro marries." Grandmother's eyes cast to Taro. She's insistent that he settle down.

"First secure a fortune, Obaachan, then a wife." Taro turns from Grandmother to Father, who nods his agreement.

"Ah..." Grandmother raises a knobby finger and shakes it toward him. "Fortune and misfortune are two buckets in the same well."

Taro swallows his bite. "He who has the fortune brings home the bride."

"You do not wait until you are thirsty to dig the well," Grandmother says, undeterred.

Kenji laughs. They all do. There is no beating Grandmother.

My throat constricts to hold back my sadness. My vision blurs through unshed tears. This is what I would miss most of all. I smile.

Mother's expression drops. "Yes, and you both will miss school if you do not hurry." She gathers the bowls and moves toward the sink, turning to hide her face. "Go on, or you'll be late."

Kenji leaps up to change from slippers to shoes, bumps the table and rattles the dishes. Taro and Father discuss plans for the day. Grandmother watches me. I hesitate. Am I saying goodbye? My eyes fix on Father. He looks up. But I have no air, so I have no words.

He raises his chin, but before he speaks, I bow—low and deep with respect.

As apology. Just in case.

"Naoko, hurry! *Itte kimasu*," Kenji yells to announce he is leaving, but before anyone answers he is already gone.

As I change my shoes, Grandmother shuffles in my direction and stops.

I rise but cannot meet her stare. Instead, I focus on her plump middle and weathered hands, the liver spots that decorate them.

"Naoko, look at me." She lifts my chin and stares. But she offers no wise words. She only nods, blinks and then hobbles away. The foxes tell her everything.

I stand alone. Not ready to move. I glance to my mother. "Okaasan…" My voice cracks, unable to form the word.

"Oh, so late, Naoko. Go. Go!" Her hand waves in the air behind her, but she does not turn.

So, with a deep breath, I do.

Outside, the sun blazes bright. Squinting, I spy Kiko coasting impatient circles at the bottom of our small hill. I know she betrayed me, so why does she wait? I march toward her, fists clenched.

"Naoko!" Mother runs from the front door, waving a bento box above her head. "You might be hungry later." Her chest rises and falls from the short sprint. Her eyebrows crease as though to fight back emotion.

My lips tremble, but what to say? She pulls me to her and, just as quick, lets me go. With swift steps she returns the way she came.

Like that, I am released. Set free. Left to test my wings and choose my fate.

My feet ache to chase after her but Kiko yells for me to hurry. She has one foot propped on the pedal, the other positioned on the road, ready to push off and glide away.

I wish she would.

My nostrils flare from a fast inhale. I stomp in her direction with a weighted heart and loaded tongue. *She had no right to tell Okaasan my secret!* Instead of spewing accusations and questions, I clench my jaw and march right past, leaving her and my bicycle behind.

She pedals after me, but I move from the road to the tall, damp grass. They snap beads of dew.

"Naoko..."

I peer back over my shoulder, but don't stop.

"Where are you going?" She abandons the bike, so it topples on its side and the suspended front wheel spins, traveling nowhere. *"Wait!"*

"Go away, Kiko!" I pick up my pace, making tracks for the trees. Yesterday, her teakettle disposition—soon hot and soon cold—confused me. Today, it hurts. Does she really believe I don't know what she's done? I veer from the easy path and cut through dense foliage. The woodland undergrowth nips at my ankles, jutting shoots, scratching at bare knees.

Still she follows.

I stop and turn. "How could you tell Okaasan?"

Her lips open but offer no explanation, so I continue forward without one. Ahead, trees part to open sky, and under a canopy of blue sits the remnant of a once-giant camphor tree.

My suitcase beside it.

I run, swipe up my bag and perch on the stump.

Kiko's eyes go wide at the sight. Blunt bangs hide high arched brows. She storms toward me and shrills, "You are *leaving*?" Birds flap their wings, some take flight. "How can you even consider such a thing?"

"How can I not?" I remind her of our many trips to the temple's Wishing Tree. How the temple priests offer a daily prayer for the granted wishes the winds set free. "Did I not tie white-ribbon requests from every limb, Kiko? So many, in fact, that the branches bent from their weight? Every week I asked for the same three things—my true love, a family of my own and a home to protect us all. Did mine not catch the breeze? Are they not granted?"

Kiko gathers her face into a frown, then using her words like an ax, chops down my wishes, one after the other.

"You're blinded by love and cannot see what is true, Naoko."

Chop.

"Your baby will be of mixed blood and therefore a mixed blessing."

Chop. Chop.

"And your house is with *Eta*, in the old *Burakumin* community, so instead of protecting your family, it adds to your shame."

Chop. Chop. Chop.

The last takes down the whole tree.

Then she turns and leaves me on its stump with only my decision.

Okaasan said to return home after school if I choose Satoshi. So why go to school at all? I should use this time to weigh my wish. Instead of staying in the woods, I find myself at the little house Hajime has rented. The one with splintering rails and sun-dried lumber in need of repair. I sit on its step, kicking against the brittle wood, listening to the *furin* bells bicker with the breeze.

Restless clouds play in the early-afternoon sky. They float high in dark rows that are in constant transformation. One a swift-moving mackerel, another a tall-footed crab. Now the animal clouds melt together, forming a giant sheet to billow as a sail. The prevailing wind guides its direction.

The prospect of a new life governs mine.

I *could* be pregnant. I have been ill, and I am late, but I believed it due to a belly full of nerves. Not anymore. Whether to go east or west depends on one's heart or feet. My feet would take me home. But my heart? To leave Hajime and to clean the womb? That thought is unbearable.

Elbows to knees, I rest my chin in my hands and look around. The little village is alive with activity. There is a rhythm to its noise. The intermittent beat of hammers from a group of men who restore a battered building in the next row, chatter between women as they gather laundry from the lines and the young ones' song as they play *Kagome Kagome*.

I watch them, weighing Taro's and Kiko's words of warning and Okaasan's words of choice. Kiko said I would add to my family's shame by living here, but Okaasan said by choosing Hajime and his child, I could never return to my family, so what indignity would they face? Quiet gossip over my disappearance? Okaasan forced to lie about my whereabouts? But they'd suffer no public scorn as I'd never return.

Never return.

It would be easier for everyone if I could go to America, but Hajime has yet to get the marriage paperwork approved, so it isn't an option.

My heart drops lower than the knotweeds clustered near my ankles. And if I'm pregnant as I suspect… Will my future children pay for my selfish indulgence? Everyone suffers from the stigma and ugly history of this village.

Rumors say the *Eta* or *Burakumin* are pariah deviants not worthy of marriage or trusted to hire. The worst say they are *hinin*, nonhumans that lack one rib' and have deficient sweat glands, and that's why dirt never sticks to the bottom of their feet.

A muddy boy waves from next door. His mother ventures out to collect clothes from the line. She is thin with short hair in pin-curled waves and moves in quick, fluid motions.

The boy is at most four and dressed in clothes too big. He smiles and waves again, venturing closer.

"Hello, little *boku-chan*," I say more to myself, and return the smile.

His curious eyes beam. He points to me, then wipes the back of his hand across his cheek, adding more mud there.

"Tatsu, Tatsu!" his mother calls, a basket of clothes balanced on her hip. "Tatsu, do not bother the woman. Come." She holds out a hand to gather him near.

When he turns to run, I strain to glimpse his bare feet. They are filthy. *See? Rumors.*

I jump from a distant thunderclap. With the threat of rain, I hoist my travel bag up and drag it to the door, but warped wood sticks. With a lift and steady pressure, it slides. Stale dust dances with the disturbed air. I cough, then stare.

The main room, furnished with an old futon, is the size of one partitioned space at home. The small bathroom attaches near the back. I peek in and blanch. It's a porcelain squat toilet. It sits in the floor without a seat. My stomach rolls queasy from the rancid stench.

A translucent screen of handmade rice paper sections off the kitchen. The back wall consists of a counter with a bowl-sink to hold water. It's small, dirty and in need of much repair.

I stand in the middle with my suitcase. What will happen at home if I remain here? What will Father say to Okaasan when he discovers I'm missing? And what of Kenji? My mind jumps from one thing to another, a grasshopper avoiding puddles.

A burn builds in my belly and coils high in my throat. My eyes prickle from the pressure. *No crying, Naoko.* I push it down. Spilled water cannot go back to the tray. I consider the dimming sky to calculate the time left before my decision is due. A few hours at most.

I *must* choose.

With a sigh, I set my unopened case on the futon's edge. The latches release with a simple *click-click*, and with exaggerated care, I lift the lid to see what Okaasan has packed.

Sorting through the clothes, I find casual skirts and tops, basic kimonos, sleeping wear and even my slippers. I slip them on and wiggle my toes, happy to have their comfort. I run my hand in the lid's pocket to feel for *tabi* socks and...*wait*. Paper?

I pull the fabric pocket out, peer inside and spy silk-bordered paper, *sumi* ink and stone, and two of my calligraphy brushes! Another luxury from home. Okaasan thinks of everything. I contemplate how I'll use them to pass the time. I place my hands across my middle and consider the probable life I carry. A gift? *Yes*, a scroll for Hajime that announces his child.

Boy or girl?

An old method to predict the sex—that midwives claim with ninety-eight percent accuracy—is to add the mother's and father's lunar birth month with the date of conception, then divide by three. If there's no remainder or if it's two, then you will have a girl. If it is one, a boy. I do the mental math with the date, then recalculate to be sure, and smile.

If I am pregnant—a girl.

To wait out the rain, I set to work on my announcement.

If I stay, it will serve as a wedding present. If I leave, it will serve my conscience, forever marking the possibility of this baby's presence in the world.

Fat round drops splatter on the deck. First dotting, then building, till nothing remains dry. The sky strobes bright, then darkens again. I concentrate on the clean lines of *Shodou*, the art of calligraphy, trying to ignore the jagged flashes that rip through the sky. I plan the message—the time frame, his blessing, a girl—and with each stroke of my brush attempt to transfer my spirit so the words contain life.

The heavens crack and I jump, dragging ink in the wrong direction. This changes the intended meaning. One slip and the straight line of moon has become the prolonged tail of a dragon in the wind.

I stare as though it stares back. Grandmother's dragon story whispers from memory.

There once lived a man who loved dragons. He kept paintings and statues of them everywhere and could talk on and on about the majestic beasts to anyone who cared to listen.

One day, a dragon heard of this man and his appreciation for his kind. He thought it would surely make him happy to meet an authentic dragon. So, he caught a strong wind and changed his course to visit him in his cave dwelling.

When he arrived, the dragon found him sleeping. The man woke to see the giant beast coiled by his side with glistening teeth and green scales reflecting in the moonlight, and he was terrified. Before the dragon could make his introduction, the man reached for his sword and lunged, causing the dragon to jump back and slither away.

Sometimes, when Grandmother told this story, she said the dragon represented liking the idea of something more than the thing itself. Other times, she said the true dragon is our real selves, a truth we must sit with and face.

I sit with mine. He curls at my feet. We share a silent conversation and I know. It's him, casting my big and monstrous shadow. The one I feared. The one I sought. The one I stare at even now. Tears build and the back of my throat aches from trying to hold in what I've known all along. Hajime holds my heart and I may hold his child, so there was never any choice.

Only an acceptance.

For I am granted every wish: my true love, a family of my own and a home to protect us all.

But just like the man in Grandmother's story, when faced with it, I am terrified.

TWELVE

America, Present Day

The cottage-style condos in my father's retirement community were quaint, with the rust-colored stonework and arched entries, and I'd miss the neighborhood, even the neighbors, but I'd miss my father more. The afternoon of his funeral, neighbors and friends linked hands on his lawn as Mama's old pastor recited Longfellow for Pops's final send-off prayer.

"Ships that pass in the night, and speak each other in passing,
"Only a signal shown and a distant voice in the darkness;
"So, on the ocean of life we pass and speak one another,
"Only a look and a voice, then darkness again and a silence."

A shared amen, then we released each other and my father's memory. Pops used the "two ships" saying back at the hospital to reference his significant, although fleeting, first love. But I pictured Mama—the love of his longer life—as the one waiting at heaven's port to welcome him home.

"Fair wind and a following sea, Pops." I whispered the sailor's farewell, eyes wet with tears. And just then, the breeze kicked up and stirred around me. I stood there a moment, then wiped the moisture from my cheeks and headed inside, where food, drinks and comfort waited.

A simple service like he had wanted. No fuss, no fanfare, just a few kind words at the church and more than a few toasts at his place after. I drank till my glass was empty, some guests stayed until the bottle was, and then that was that. I sat by myself on his patio and, for the first time in my life, stood alone in the world.

Except, according to his letter, he had another daughter, so maybe I wasn't.

I blew out a breath, took a sip of my brandy—I'd found a hidden bottle stashed in Pops's pantry—then stared up at the evening sky. Pops's yard wasn't elaborate by any means, but it was the kind of place you could prop your feet up and, on a clear night, stargaze.

The Big Dipper was always the easiest to find. And to its left, the North Star. As the northern sky moved, it held, anchored in position.

If heaven was an ocean of stars, then I imagined Pops sailed across it, vying for passage through the Great Divide. I smiled at the thought, remembering the story of his first Pacific voyage in the navy where I pulled the image from.

He said they followed the North Star on the crest of a giant wave. That the groundswell traveled so fast it slammed them into the massive gates that separated the west and east. "They rose from the heart of the sea and extended to the heights of heaven," he'd say. "And with our ship pinned against them, the court of King Neptune himself tested our valor for days."

He had so many stories. While I questioned the facts behind most of his tall tales, that one, I learned, held truth. The Great Divide separating east and west was the International Date Line. The tests of valor were the navy's fraternity-like rituals of initiation. And the official court of Neptune were sailors who had crossed before. It was a ship of boys being boys and my father the youngest at seventeen.

Seventeen. To have enlisted so young, and then to have fathered a daughter? And to have never told anyone? It didn't line up. Pops was as fixed and steadfast as the Northern Star. There were no variables. And yet his letter challenged everything I knew about him. The thought squeezed my rib cage, building pressure, which released with frustrated tears.

Maybe that was why I'd scheduled an estate company to clear out my father's things. I didn't want to find out more. I didn't want anything to change.

In theory, the recommended service was the perfect solution to manage a stressful and difficult task. They'd auction what held monetary value, donate what didn't, and I'd pack only what I wanted to keep.

I leaned elbow to table, eyes fixed on his stainless-steel twenty-five-year commemorative ashtray. That was something to keep. It had puddled from the late-afternoon rain, leaving floating butts in muddied water. Emptying it into the outside bin, I wiped it with a napkin until the bottom engraving shined, then held it up and marveled. Twenty-five years was a long time to stay at the factory, and while the token of appreciation wasn't worth much, the lifetime of hard work and service it symbolized was.

Unless my father thought his years of service were wasted.

The memory of him retelling his "fight for independence" story when we entered the hospital came to mind.

And while following in my grandfather's and father's footsteps to work at the factory was a good life, for me it wasn't enough.

It wasn't enough, and yet he ended up there, after all. He was happy, though, wasn't he? My throat constricted. Maybe that was what he'd been trying to tell me. That he resented the course his life had taken and regretted what he'd given up.

At once, the ashtray took on a different meaning—a symbol of what he'd lost. Another daughter and a different life. What was wrong with this one? Anger dipped its toes in the waters of grief and stirred. I caught my pained reflection in the metal surface, then set it down and looked away, but the ripples carried everywhere. What else did I have wrong, and what was I supposed to do with all of this?

It was me, not my father, who was trapped and tested at the great divide.

I glanced to my father's empty metal chair with its red peeling paint, then tipped my glass, swallowed the last bit of burn and stood.

Another daughter. I was fooling myself if I thought I could leave it alone. I couldn't unlearn what I'd discovered, so the only way forward was through my father's past.

In the morning, I'd call and cancel the estate company, and I would pack my father's belongings and, by doing so, attempt to unpack his other life.

THIRTEEN

Japan, 1957

I didn't sleep well, tossing all night on the musty futon while my thoughts battled *Baku* demons that devour dreams. Did Kiko tell Taro what she had learned? Will Father show up and drag me home? What if Hajime ignores the note I left with the guard and never returns? My eyes snap open with the absurd thought.

Early light stings them. Blinking to sharpen my focus, I reacquaint myself with new surroundings. Water stains the rice-paper kitchen partition and pools on the uneven plank floor. An invasive knotweed grows up and through the boards. I cringe. I had half convinced myself the house's dilapidated state was only a figment of my imagination. Instead, it's worse because it's worse than I remembered. Everything needs repair.

The skewed door of the little house rattles. It moves an

inch, then hitches. Quick fingers jut through the small opening for grip.

I jump up startled, ready to run. But where? There's only one way in or out. It could be anyone. An outraged landlord, a half-crazed neighbor or, worse, my father.

The door slides open. Tan trousers. Green duffel. Slicked hair.

"Hajime!" My soul leaps. My feet follow.

My hug knocks the air from his chest.

"Whoa." He laughs, takes a step for balance and drops his bag with a small *thud*. He kisses the top of my head and returns the squeeze. "Hi."

I crumble within his strong embrace. "Hi." Nothing else spills out. Only happiness. Only relief. Only tears. The night was a long journey with a heavy load; now Hajime is here to help carry its weight.

He smiles crooked, then pulls me up on tiptoes for a kiss. He hasn't shaved and his stubble scratches under my fingertips. Relaxing into him, I slide down to stand on solid ground for the first time since yesterday's arrival.

"The place is pretty bad, right?" He steps back and looks around. "I planned to have it cleaned up before you..." His eyes lock to my suitcase, then cloud in confusion. "Cricket, what's going on?"

"I asked Okaasan to help persuade Father, and she tried, but he—"

"He kicked you out?" He stares with wide eyes.

"Oh, no, no, but..." I wring one hand into the other, tell him how I pleaded with Okaasan to help. "And while she listened to *me*, he did not listen to her." I explain how Father declared my match to Satoshi without consulting me. "But guess what Okaasan did?" I smile, beaming with pride.

"Without consulting him, Okaasan put the choice back in my hands. So here I am."

"But your father doesn't know?"

I shake my head.

He rocks back on his heels. "We should go talk with him." He picks up my suitcase and takes wide steps to the door. "If he finds you missing it'll make things worse. He'll never accept me."

"Hajime, if I return, I must marry Satoshi." Stepping forward, I ease the suitcase from his white-knuckle grip. "I chose you. So, there is no going back."

His lips part. He scoffs. "What kind of choice is that? You can't give up your family."

"Are you not giving up yours to stay here for me?" I place my bag near my feet and cross my arms.

"It's not the same. I'll miss them, sure, but—"

"You said it would break your mother's heart if you stayed. And what about weekend baseball and Sunday meals at your parents'? I know what you will give up, Hajime. And yet you choose to stay with me, so…" I shrug one shoulder, smile hopeful. "I choose you, too, okay?"

"But it's not, Cricket. It's not *okay*." A small step back creates distance. He slants his brows. "You can't lose your whole family over me. You'll never get to go home? See them again? What about Kenji? That's crazy." His hand scrubs his jaw, then he shakes his head. "No way. I can't let you do it. I won't. That's too much. No."

"No?" Anger rips free from a tongue too often silenced. "It's my choice! It's not Father's. Not Satoshi's. And no, Hajime, it's not even *yours*." The declaration rings loud and hangs in the air between us.

He opens his mouth as though to speak but says nothing. Instead, he looks away and drops his shoulders.

Mine push back, braced to support what I must say. "Do you not understand?" Hot tears burn behind my eyes. "The choice is made. Okaasan risked everything so I could make it. And I have. So, now you must decide..." My heart pounds in my ears. "If you still wish to marry me. *That* is your choice. Your only one."

"But, Cricket, it's not that simple..."

"It is. It *is* that simple. Unless..." He has changed his mind. Maybe he sees his own dragon, and faced with what he asked for, it is too much. My heart drops. *A baby.* I haven't even shared that possibility. My knees wobble so I sit on the edge of the futon and focus on my opened hands. On the decision they hold. The one I've already made.

The one he could refuse.

Hajime crams his hands into his pockets and paces. One step, then another. "It wasn't supposed to be like this. We should have their blessing. I wanted them to be a part of things. Plan a wedding, maybe have them talk to my folks on the phone..." He sighs, rakes his hair. It splays in different directions between his fingers. He leaves his hand there, looks around at the dust-covered room. The water-stained wall. The puddled floor. He sighs, winces. "I thought I'd have time to fix this place up. You'd plan the wedding while I'd get our house ready, but..." A curse floats under his breath.

"Okay." My breath hitches in my throat. "I understand. You no longer wish to marry me. It is all too much." A dying has begun. I feel my spirit dim and flicker with the bad connection.

"No. No, that's not what I meant." He sits beside me, angled so we are eye to eye. "Of course I still want to marry you." With both hands he cups my cheeks, then leans his forehead to mine. "More than anything."

"Then what is it? What's wrong?" I whisper.

He lifts his gaze to mine. "Remember I told you about the community day on the ship? They have us leaving right after to patrol the Straits. They changed the schedule." His eyes soften. "I can't stay."

The shock straightens my spine. I expected him here for the week. "How long will you be gone?"

"Just for two weeks, but... You're *here*. I can't leave you here unmarried in this place alone." His chin drops.

His body relaxes forward into my arms, and I wrap my arms around him.

"Your lieutenant still won't sign the marriage document? I signed it." I run fingers through his hair.

Hajime lifts his head, fixes his eyes on me. "I know, and I got it notarized. I went twice to get it translated, but he keeps avoiding me because the navy frowns on, well, you know." His blue eyes look away. "None of it matters, anyway, because we need your parents' approval unless you're eighteen."

"I'm almost eighteen." My voice is high-pitched. This is a disaster.

"I'm so tired of asking everyone for permission and hearing no. First my lieutenant and now your family." Hajime stands but then his eyes brighten. "What if we did it, anyhow? We could do it tonight."

"Do what?"

"Get married." He hoists me up, then pulls my hands tight to his chest. "We could have the ceremony tonight and straighten out the paperwork later. Why not? Then everyone in this village will know who you are, that we're married and that you're with me."

I drop my gaze to our hands.

"I love you, Cricket. I want to spend my life with you. Forget everyone else. This is you and me. Your mom supports us, so we work on your father until we win him over. I don't care if it takes a lifetime, I'll keep at him, okay? Say you will."

My mind spins around details. The idea that Hajime would still try to change my father's heart warms mine. "But I don't have a dress."

"Wear what you have on."

"This is a sleeping kimono!" I laugh, which makes him laugh.

"Then wear whatever else you've got in that suitcase. Just say you will." His thoughts rush out in excitement. "We can do it here. I'll get some of the guys to help. Everyone can bring a dish, and I don't know, I'll find a pastor, or a Buddhist priest, or whatever you want." Hajime lifts my palms to his lips and kisses them. "Cricket, I can't leave you here unmarried and alone. I want to marry you. That is *my* choice, right? That's what you said." He smiles. "Well, I choose you, so marry me tonight."

Tears blur my vision to create a hurricane of happy. "Okay, yes." I burst.

"Yes?" His smile widens.

His kiss steals my answer.

It's late morning and Hajime is off to prepare for the evening ceremony. He has left me with Maiko, the neighbor woman I watched hanging clothes yesterday. She apologized for not coming over, admitting I'd spooked her. She thought I was a spy there to collect land taxes. We sit on her step and laugh about it while making decorations with two others. Grandmother Fumiko, an elder woman who lives two houses over, and Ishuri, a young mother from the next row.

Ishuri has a new baby boy with chubby cheeks and dimpled fingers. Maiko's daughter, Yoshiko, watches him and keeps an eye on her little brother, the dirt-covered Tatsu. He runs wild, trailing fistfuls of ribbon from each hand while Yoshiko chases after him, scolding.

Even cursed, people here are happy.

"So, babies soon?" Ishuri asks with thin eyebrows arched high. Her skin is tan and pocked, but her bright smile more than makes up for it.

Since I'm not sure what to say, I only nod and continue to weave the light green ribbon strip through the paper lantern's handle. We plan to hang the lights from the trees.

"No. She should wait to have babies." Grandmother Fumiko nudges my shoulder and gives me a wink. "She should enjoy practicing first." She's frail with long silver hair pushed under a threadbare headscarf and is as lively as I imagine its colors once were. "Youth fades soon enough. Look at me." She laughs, thin cheeks lifting upward.

Maiko adds, "Grandmother Fumiko was once a spring festival's Plum Princess."

"Now just a prune!" More laughter shakes from her belly.

"And what of your dress?" Maiko asks, a different lantern held in her lap.

"Oh." My mind scrambles for the right way to answer. "My mother's *shiromuku* is so beautiful, but…" My shoulders drop. The story is too much to share with new friends.

"Then wear my *uchikake*," Ishuri says, placing a hand on my arm. "Although it is a reception kimono, it would still look pretty on you."

"Yes, pretty, but so bright," Grandmother Fumiko says.

The three women prattle on about the bold colors and how best to minimize them. I'm touched by their kindness but saddened by its truth. I won't wear Okaasan's gown and my family won't attend. Instead, I'll dress in a stranger's garment and celebrate without them. I sit under the plum tree, graced with its beauty and shade, but I am unable to reach its fruit.

★ ★ ★

Crouched on a tiny stool in Maiko's bathing room, I scrub, lather and rinse so I can soak in the tub of scented water she has prepared. In Japan, we wash first, then bathe. Hajime still does not understand one is to cleanse the body while the other to purify the mind.

Maiko and Ishuri will fix my hair and help me with Ishuri's kimono. It is pretty, though its edges fray and the color has faded.

Wedding kimonos, with the high quality of fabrics and elaborate patterns, are costly, and most families must rent them. Okaasan's is *owned*. Heavy in sentiment and expense.

With grateful humility, I accept Ishuri's offer, of course. It would be insulting to wear my own everyday kimono, even if its condition is far superior. Besides, unless I'm wearing Okaasan's, what does it matter? I will pledge myself to Hajime with open arms and accept this new and different life as they've accepted me.

Today is about heart rather than appearance.

Maiko discusses what flowers they should add to my hair, but then pauses. "Are you okay, Naoko?"

"Yes," I say from the small tub infused with vanilla and spiced plum. The rich, sweet scents fill me with gratitude. They have so little, and yet give it all. I'm undeserving. I cup handfuls of warm water and release, attempting to calm nerves with the sound.

It is my wedding day.

A ritual of light and cheer, and although pleased, I am weighed down with want. I *want* to hear the nonstop opinions of Grandmother as Mother helps me get ready. To have Okaasan's reassurance and laughter. Kenji's teasing, Taro's watchful eye. Even Father's…

I sigh and descend farther, so the water rests under my nose.

I want too much.

Taro is right, I am selfish. But why does Father have to be so difficult? Deep down, I know it's his pride, not his nature, which demands so much of me. But does he understand it is my nature, not my pride, which dreams for so much more?

"Naoko?"

Hajime's voice excites my spirit and the women.

They yell at him in Japanese, "Out! She's not ready!"

"Wait, Maiko," Hajime says. *"Wazuka sū fun."* He's laughing because they won't listen. "Cricket?"

I find my feet at once, creating a small tidal wave, and wrap in the bathing towel. Careful with my steps, I move toward their shadows. "Hajime?"

"Tell them I need to talk to you for a minute. From here, okay?"

I laugh, then reassure Maiko it is only for a moment. The voices quiet to a grumble and the shadows move away. Except for his—it stands tall and narrow.

I inch closer and whisper, "Hajime." My smile drops, and I'm struck with worry. "Is everything okay? Did something happen?"

"Everything's perfect. In fact, I have a surprise for you. An early gift."

A gift? I bounce on my toes. His shadow drifts away until it is so small it disappears.

Inside the wash room, I hold my breath to listen. There are footsteps, more, then whispers and the door slides again. Now, silence.

Did they leave?

Should I go out?

A new shadow appears. Not as tall, not as narrow. The door opens. "Oh!"

Okaasan!

Tears begin with an agitation of hands.

Her hands pull me to her, not caring if I'm wet. She rocks me, her chin over my shoulder, desperate fingertips clutching at my back. My heart beats high in my chest. My words render useless and separate like earth and clouds. How can I hope to express the relief, gratitude, pure comfort I find in her embrace?

I cannot.

After a moment, maybe two or three, Okaasan lessens her grip and leans away. Her lips pull in tight. Her eyes, glossy and bright, seem to ask, *Are you okay? Are you happy?* My answer reflects in mine. *I am now.* Satisfied, she nods, then wipes under my eyes with her thumbs.

She pushes out an airy breath and laughs. "Good thing they didn't do your makeup yet."

My heart, high in my throat, blocks all speech. I swallow hard to push it down, still not quite believing she is here.

"I cannot stay, Naoko. Father is not aware I have come. But I hear your wish on the wind. It calls to me like a dream, and then your Hajime appears, and..." With a long inhale through her nose, she gathers her resolve. "I recognize in my soul it is your destiny to be married—" The explanation is consumed by another quick breath of air. She points instead, to the low table near the kitchen.

Draped over the silk casing is her *shiromuku*.

Now I am a river. I am not deserving of such love. There are no words. Only tears. My throat tightens to control the rising sobs.

My mother smiles to push back her emotion, then steps to the door. *Is she leaving?* She opens it only a nudge and motions with her hand. Maiko and Ishuri rush inside, closing it back behind them. Hajime, having delivered his most perfect gift, has disappeared. I love him all the more.

The women's eyes shift to the *shiromuku*, and my stomach drops. *Ishuri's dress.* After they've been so welcoming, I'd cause insult.

My neck warms from panic as I try to find the right phrasing. "Ishuri, I—I am..."

"Do not consider such a thing, Naoko." Ishuri's voice is warm, understanding. Her eyes are wide. "Of course you will wear your mother's *shiromuku*. Of course."

I lower my head in a deep bow, humbled, relieved, overwhelmed by so much kindness. "Thank you, Ishuri," I say with fruitless dabs at my eyes.

"The moon is terribly impatient," Maiko says, her smile beaming bright. "Soon it will drag out the night, so we must hurry. First makeup and hair, then let us get this bride dressed."

I look to Okaasan and take her hand in mine. Without asking, she seems to recognize my question.

"How can I go before I see you dressed? That is too much to ask of a mother, too cruel." She lifts my hand to her chest and leans into it, so I feel her heart. The steadfast rhythm. "Yes? It beats full and strong. I am here. We have this moment. Heaven does not deny me this, daughter."

I take nothing for granted. Although I am not entitled to such happiness, it is given. Heaven's blessing is capricious at best. I recognize this. So I smile at my mother, at my new friends and fate. Even with the dragon's breath hot on my neck—a possible child, Hajime leaving for weeks, me here alone—I understand that when heaven drops a plum, you open your hands.

FOURTEEN

America, Present Day

O ver the course of several days, I'd made significant progress in clearing out my father's condo but discovered little that unraveled his past. The emotional roller coaster of grief and confusion proved exhausting, as did my father's well-meaning neighbors and friends. They kept stopping over with covered dishes and condolences. The fridge was stocked with casseroles, but I had no appetite, and nothing new to add to the same old conversation. At least, nothing I'd say out loud.

"…he was a good man…"

A good man with a big secret.

"…now he's with your mama…"

Did my mother know about his daughter?

The thought grabbed my heart and wouldn't let go. Either they both kept it from me, or it was my father's secret alone. I didn't like either possibility, so instead of focusing on what-ifs and imagined scenarios, I took breaks from packing, shoved the emotion down and did something useful—research.

My father's letter stated he fathered a baby girl, which meant there had to be a record of birth somewhere. On my laptop, I typed "Birth records in Japan 1950s," then scrolled through results.

The US Embassy in Tokyo kept no records, birth or otherwise. And according to the Tokyo Legal Affairs Bureau, all birth records of non-Japanese citizens were maintained by the city of birth but were not kept permanently. Would the baby have been considered a citizen in the 1950s?

When I looked up from the screen, an hour had passed, and the only thing I discovered was that Japan didn't have a records system back then. Not in the traditional sense. Families kept track of birth and death in something called a *koseki*, but without a full name, you couldn't make an official request.

My heart sank. I didn't even have the mother's name, just the nickname my father used for her in the letter—Cricket. What kind of name was that? I scoffed. What kind of name was *Hajime*? And why had Pops signed the letter with it?

I squeezed my eyes shut and rubbed my temples. *What was I missing?* I knew the location of the base, the years of his service—the military. What about those records?

I tapped away at the keyboard. If my father had a child while enlisted, there might be a record of birth on file. I clicked link after link until I found the correct site, the right department, then did a search through their FAQ.

As his next of kin, I could request his records, but not online since his discharge date missed the archival cutoff by two years. There was a wait time of six to eight weeks and several documents were required: his social security number, the branch of service, dates of service and a copy of the death certificate—all of which I had. I got to work.

I gathered the items from my records box, made copies to mail in the morning and was in the process of filing the online fee when Pops's alarm clock kicked on from his bedroom. He'd set it to remind himself to take his nighttime medication and every day I clicked it off but didn't remove the reoccurrence. With the alarm set, I'd been forced to enter his room every day to turn it off. It was a way to gird myself to the overwhelming task ahead—sorting my father's most personal things.

Following the incessant beep, I worked my way through the maze of boxes and bins I'd packed to my father's room—the only place still untouched—followed the cord, then pulled. The clock's digital readout blanked.

I stared.

It was time to sort his room, and I knew it.

My gaze shifted from the alarm clock to our family photo album beside it on the nightstand. I picked it up and sat on the edge of my father's bed. The inexpensive book was falling apart. It was the kind with defective adhesive cardstock covered by clear protective sheets. There we were, our little family of three, faded, yellowed and gummed to the page. And me, the only one left.

Or so I had believed.

The thought kept digging at me. As though my father having another daughter took something away from me. It didn't, because I had *him*. There was a life of love documented in every photo. I ran the tip of my finger over a snapshot from Little League. Pops was my coach, both on the field and off, and he used the lessons of the game as schooling in life.

Tired? You push through.

Winning does matter, but how you win matters more.

You're an exceptional pitcher, solid at second base, but not as quick around the bases. Know your strengths.

Know my strengths... I didn't even know him.

My mind kept reorganizing what I believed—a good father, a good man—with what I feared—a man who abandoned a pregnant woman and left his child. I didn't want to believe that. Pops wouldn't do that. I stared at his photo, close to tears. The truth was, I didn't know anymore.

I slapped the album shut, knowing it didn't hold the answers, moving toward his dresser in search of something that did.

Birthday and anniversary cards filled the top drawer of his dresser. A few were from me, but most from Mama—none from Japan. T-shirts filled the next drawer, socks and undergarments in another, but in the last, a manila envelope sat along the bottom. I stared at it, then with a racing heart and careful fingers lifted it out and unwound the circle clasp.

Inside were the Caddy's title and insurance documents, things I'd need, but nothing more. I refastened the top, placed them in the box marked Records and pushed out a sigh of disappointed relief.

In front of my father's closet, I put hands on my hips and shook my head, amazed at the amount of stuff he had packed inside. I spied his Tigers baseball jersey, then slid it off the hanger and pulled the shirt on over mine. It hung shapeless, but I was relieved to have found something untainted.

I sorted through the rest of his clothes, checking pockets of each item before I moved on to the next. Most hadn't been worn in ages and some still had tags. Seasonal sweaters and miscellaneous boxes filled the shelf above. On tiptoes, I reached for a shoebox, knocking over several. Black-and-white images spilled across the floor.

Photos from my father's time in the navy.

There were pictures of his ship in the harbor and photos of the crew on the deck. Boys, really. Someone's son away from home for the first time. Someone's high school sweetheart who promised to write. Someone who looked at the course of their small-town life and wanted more. I flipped the images over to find my father had scribbled their last names: Valentine, Elliott, West, Spain.

What if I posted a search for the names on the navy's reunion sites? If these guys were still alive, remembered or were reachable online, they could maybe shed some light on what happened. A long shot, but worth exploring if they confirmed what I hoped was true—that my father learned of his daughter long after he'd shipped out and couldn't get back. Maybe he wasn't certain the baby was even his?

There were several articles I'd found online that touched on the subject with titles like "Occupation Babies," "Babies of the Enemy," "Postwar Pan-pan Prostitutes," and each raised a different question.

Was the baby a possible ploy to trap my father into marriage? Was the woman he wrote the girlfriend from his stories or someone else? Surely one of his navy buddies would know, but how many of them were left?

And, of course, there were photos of my father. *Hi, Pops.*

He was the quintessential poster child for the '50s with his mass of dark, slicked-back hair. His wide grin carried the overconfidence of youth. All he needed was the leather jacket and a motorcycle instead of the uniform. I stifled a laugh through tears. No wonder Mama swooned.

There were sightseeing pictures titled "Hong Kong," one marked "China's coast" and several tagged "Japan"—the colorful Goodwill Gate in Yokohama, street vendors peddling wares in Kyoto and a beautiful woman dressed all in white. A kimono. The flesh on my arms prickled.

Did I ever tell you why I was there? A wedding.
You should have seen the bride's gown.
It was a kimono.

I brought the photo close. The woman's chin canted down, so I couldn't make out her face, but her stained lips, the elaborate folds of the layered material and the half-moon headpiece sang of ceremony.

My father really did attend a Japanese wedding?

My arm dropped to my lap, but I didn't let go of the picture. While I always knew my father's Great Divide story held grains of truth, I never considered the other stories.

I would now.

FIFTEEN

Japan, 1957

The humid air kisses my cheeks as Maiko helps me step from her porch onto the ground. Night blankets the village of little houses and bundles it under a cloak of black, but the orange western sky clings to its horizon, peeking, curious.

For a normal ceremony, the bride and groom are led by a Shinto maiden and form a processional caravan. But without my family's involvement, we forgo these traditions.

Maiko has my arm, but the distant lights have my eye. As we round the last house, I gasp. The paper lanterns we made line the entire path and butter-gold orbs illuminate the trees like the yellow *hotaru*, fireflies, swarming after July's heavy rains.

My thoughts also swarm. *I'm getting married.* I wish Okaasan could have stayed. With a smile, I run my hand down her *shiromuku* to feel its lush texture under my fingertips and to hold on to her connection.

The built-up motif of layered white organdy feathers gives the garment fullness and life. Silk floss, in long and short stitches, embroiders the fabric to create its opulence. The brocaded *obi* sash has a thin ribbon cord in blush and silver to coordinate with the array of flowers woven throughout my hair.

I have never felt more beautiful or been more nervous.

Each step I take brings me closer to Hajime and farther away from my family. It is a contrast of extremes in every sense, but with Okaasan's visit, and now wearing her *shiromuku*, I have somehow found my place between them. This is what Buddha calls the middle way. The correct balance of life.

I call it happy.

Ahead, at the center of the small waiting crowd, is Hajime.

He stands tall, broad shouldered, his crisp white uniform pressed and polished. The cap is low on his brow, and his hair trimmed neat underneath. His dimpled jaw, clean-shaven, looks chiseled in sharp angles.

He becomes a blur of white as I scan new faces on either side: Maiko's husband stands with their children. Grandmother Fumiko with Ishuri's family, and Hajime's shipmates Valentine and Spain, to Hajime's right, dressed in uniform. Everyone smiles. Tatsu, Maiko's son, shouts my name, provoking giggles.

Almost there. I glide in Okaasan's *shiromuku* to close the distance. My insides crackle in excitement like a sparkler's flare. Its charged path races through me from toes to fingertips. I look down with a nervous smile as we move forward. *This is it.*

I take deep, slow breaths to calm my racing pulse. I sense Hajime's stare, but only when I stand before him do I dare to lift my gaze. Bowing, I peek up through long tinted lashes, no longer as a young girl, but a woman and, soon, his wife.

My heart thuds in my ears. I can't breathe. *Is he pleased?*

He bows in return but never lowers his gaze. In it, I know my answer. The lantern light is reflected in his eyes, causing the white wisps at the center to dance like sails across a blue ocean, and I am lost in them. In him. In this moment.

The Shinto priest, dressed in *Jōe,* a pure white kimono robe with a tall peaked cap, clears his throat and asks all to stand. The ceremony begins.

We bow to our ancestors, to our guests and to each other. Then we partake in the three-by-three exchange with three different-size bowls of sake. Each one represents the inseparability of the newly formed bond with an earthy taste like moss kissed from dew. Just as in marriage, not all things endured are pleasant.

Only with the third bowl, on the third tip, do we allow the pungent mix to spill over our tongue. This is the ninth, so we drink. Nine means triple happiness. I catch the twinge of surprise on Hajime's face. *Did I warn him of its bitterness?*

Everyone claps twice at its completion to gain the attention of the deities, for they must bear witness to the spoken words of commitment.

Turning to Hajime, the priest begins his inquiry. He asks if he will love me, respect me, console and help me until death. He asks Hajime for his promise. This is what I have been waiting for. Will he understand? *Should I interpret?* Just as my lips part to speak, he turns.

"Yes, I promise."

His fingers squeeze mine and he leans closer, speaking in low rounded tones. "I promise to love you *now*… I promise to love you *always*."

My chest is tight trying to hold back emotion, the words. They burst. "I will love you forever, Hajime."

The crowd laughs because it wasn't my turn.

My cheeks flush and I smile, then look to the priest. "I promise, too." I do not need him to ask.

More quiet laughter.

The Shinto priest then hands us each a small silk pouch that holds a special wedding blessing to close the ceremony. "Let the words serve as a guidepost as you now travel life in a new, singular direction."

But before the priest can announce the official proclamation of man and wife, Hajime draws from his own tradition to announce it with a kiss. Even with the remnants of the bitter drink on his lips, it is the sweetest taste I have ever known.

When Hajime pulls away, well-wishes and cheers bless us, but I hear nothing; I am transfixed by his gaze in the middle of a suspended moment of happiness. We stare at one another, a shared acknowledgment between husband and wife that despite the world's preconceived notion of propriety and order...we love.

We love.

After the ceremony, we share a meal under the trees and listen to stories. How Maiko and Eiji met, of Ishuri's want of sleep since her baby's arrival and all about Grandmother Fumiko's many suitors. We laugh and celebrate our new beginning.

Now it's late and even the fireflies are sleepy. Their show of light lulls in intermittent sparks. We listen to the steady rise and fall of the crickets' song, the whisper of wind through the trees, and say good-night to the few remaining guests.

Maiko stands with her husband, Eiji. Tatsu is slung on his

shoulder, his head draped in sleep. Their daughter, Yoshiko, stretches and yawns. It has been a long night for all.

"Maiko, wait." With quick steps I move toward her.

Hanging lanterns dapple light across her rounded cheeks and soften even the finest of lines. "What is it, Naoko?"

"I just wanted..." I adjust my sleeves, trying to find the words to express how much her kindness has meant. A fresh surge of emotion builds. My throat tightens. "Without my family here or Okaasan..." Tears well and hold on the lower lid, ready to spill. "I wish to say you honor me." My lips stretch tight and I bow.

She smiles and returns the gesture. Peering over to Hajime, she grins. "You'll be fine."

Are my nerves so obvious? I glance to Hajime, who talks with his shipmates, then back to Maiko and smile. I laugh with a breath. Yes, I am sure it's noticeable. She pats my arm and turns to rejoin her family.

Although Hajime and I have shared the intimacies of marriage, they were stolen moments rushed for fear of exposure. Now that we're married, we'll have a full night to discover each other. We will be alone as husband and wife. No hiding. No concern of time. Nothing between us.

Except for the secret that I may carry his child. That, I'll share in the morning.

For now, I promenade toward my new husband with slow, deliberate steps. He stands alone and captures my gaze. *What is this look?* My heartbeat quickens. It's now just us. Everyone has gone. Yes, I know this look. Head slightly cocked. Serious eyes. My stomach flutters.

He tucks his cap under his arm and holds his hand out for me. "Wife."

Wife. I like my new name on his lips. Placing my hand in his, a charge ignites from the contact—just fingertips and I am consumed by heat. We walk toward our little house holding hands, stretching our arms apart to separate around an uneven patch of earth, and coming back together on the other side. From the corner of my eye, I catch him watching me.

"You're quiet," Hajime says, and squeezes my hand. "What're you thinking?"

"Oh…" My eyes dart to his, then away, blinking back through my contemplations. I am not willing to share these thoughts. With a shrug, I give a sheepish half smile.

Hajime lifts my hand and presses a kiss there. "Well, I'm thinking I'm the luckiest man in the world. I'm thinking… what could I possibly have done to deserve you?" He gives another kiss to my fingers and stops. He moves close. "I'm thinking…damn, she's beautiful." His gaze drops to my lips, he leans down—

I kiss him, not able to help myself. Warm lips mold to mine. And now I think of nothing, I only feel.

I'm scooped up in his arms without warning and laugh. "What are you doing?"

He moves as though I weigh nothing, taking quick short steps to reach our deck. He shifts so he can slide open the stubborn door. "The groom always carries the bride over the threshold."

"I don't know this custom," I say as he turns so we can both fit through the doorway.

"Welcome home, my wife."

I bite my lip and smile, his odd tradition forgotten.

My stomach clenches, and I wrap my hands tighter around his neck. With ease, he sets me down, but we do not break apart. We pull close and his lips again find mine. There is a slow building hunger to his kiss. His hand waves through air until it strikes the door to slide it closed. He glides hands over my sides to rest on the *obi*. His fingers fumble.

Pulling back, he motions to my mother's dress. "I'm afraid I'll damage it. I don't want—"

I quiet his lips with my fingers. "It took three women to dress me, Hajime. Please, if you're patient, to remove, it will take only one."

I take off my shoes and *tabi* socks, nodding for him to follow suit. Then, taking his hands, I guide him to the futon. I motion for him to take a seat. He undoes the top buttons of his dress shirt as he sits on the edge, and pulling the collar loose for comfort, he rests back on elbows.

I watch him watch me, curious. My heart skips, and I swallow hard.

With shaky hands, I retrieve the silk cloth the *shiromuku* wraps in and place it at my feet. Then, with eyes on Hajime and with great care, I reach behind my back to free the decorative cord.

In soft tones, I speak in Japanese, knowing he will not understand all of what I say. It is not everyday conversation. But they are words I have selected only for him and just for tonight. "You are now my husband. So, without shame, I make myself ready."

I wet my lips and take a long breath to steady my nerves, then loosen the sash. It threads through my fingers as it falls. Every movement is measured for a pleasing aesthetic, every touch imagined as though my hand is against his skin.

I have his complete attention.

Reaching behind, I unfasten the *makura* pillow to release the folds along the back. My hands tremble as I pleat one end over the other. Bending only at the knees, I place it near my feet on the open silk.

"I have no need of cover." My voice is a throaty whisper.

I untie the *obi* knot next. It falls loose in my hands. I set it aside, then undo the *himo* that holds the excess folded fabric underneath in place. My heart thumps against my chest, causing short breaths.

Hajime stares, his eyes hooded, stormy. Black pupils crowd out the color, leaving only the thinnest ring of blue.

As I stand, the unbound *shiromuku* hangs loose over my body, losing all shape. Now it can be removed.

"This night…" I continue while gliding my hand under the robe at my shoulder and removing to reveal the under-garment. "My lips, my skin…" I release the other shoulder and hold the loose fabric with my hands. "My all…"

Hajime tilts his head in recognition of my simple words. My cheeks burn hot. Again, I bend my knees and place the gown on the opened silk. Chin down to show humility, I crouch and look up at him.

Hajime no longer sits back. He edges closer, leans in.

Inches from his face, his lips, I whisper, "I welcome your touch. I am for your pleasure."

The flutters inside build into a frenzied swarm, know-ing what I am about to do. A thousand years of wives lov-ing husbands has awakened in me. It is an ancient knowledge ingrained in my very essence, nature's own primitive design of courtship and invitation. And like a blueprint, I use it to guide and enchant. I want nothing more than to please him. To show him my love. To feel his.

With a sharp intake of breath I stand. The undergarment drops, and I am presented to my husband.

I hold my breath as his falls from parted lips.

He scans my bare body. My heart beats erratic. Everything is exposed. I am his to admire. My chest rises and falls in short breaths. Heat builds low as I wait, searching his eyes as they search every inch of me.

I dare not move until he does.

My husband takes his wife.

SIXTEEN

Japan, 1957

Hajime and I stayed up talking, laughing and loving as husband and wife well after the moon surrendered the horizon. This morning, we lie entangled, two wisteria vines reaching for the same light.

As sparrows squabble, worry returns to remind me of what's ahead. After a night of showing him my love, I want to share how it may have already bloomed.

I breathe the ocean off his bare tanned skin and feel the rise and fall of lean muscle beneath my flattened hand. I am contented. Sated. Nervous.

I study him while he slumbers. Will our baby have the slight indent of his chin? Eyes like the sea? The subtle wave of his hair? At least his locks hold rich, inky shades. I'd love our child regardless, but this way, one less burden on such tiny shoulders.

Hajime pulls a lazy breath in through his nose and forms a languid smile. "Morning." There is a deep scratch to his early waking voice. Another new aspect to cherish.

As I prop myself up, my hair falls forward. He tucks it behind my ear, combs through the length just to do it again. The repeated movement is soothing, and like a cat, I stretch my neck and lean into him.

I smile at my husband. *Husband.* My emotions swim circles. He leaves to patrol the Taiwan Straits today. Should I wait the two weeks to tell him? I stir the water with my words to gauge its temperature. "Ishuri's baby is beautiful."

Liquid blue eyes stare into mine. "You're beautiful."

His fingers trace my smile, but I stay focused. "I consider him perfect. He hardly cried, did you notice?"

"Ishuri's tired. She said she never sleeps." He sucks in a breath that stalls from a sluggish yawn. It swallows his words. "I like sleep." He stretches, pulls me tighter to him.

"You don't like babies?" My voice almost squeaks.

Hajime guides me to his waiting lips. With a grin, he croons, "I like *making* babies."

A full kiss and my insides hum. For the moment, my attention is diverted. Fingertips follow the length of my spine, leaving a trail of heated shivers. The kiss is hungry and delicious, but this cannot wait.

"Hajime." I push away and sit up. Shifting my weight, I reach for the scroll tucked near the cushion's side. The one I made alongside my dragon upon my arrival. I nudge the material closer, grab its edge and place it between us.

His eyebrows arch. "For me?" He props himself on an elbow, smooths disheveled hair and rubs his eye. Sliding back, he reaches for me. "Come here."

I roll onto my side into the crook of his arm and place my head near his chin. I press a finger over the raised letters of the metal dog tag on his chest as he unrolls my wedding gift. I'm frozen with fear. *What if this is unwelcome news?*

He holds the silk-bordered paper close and reads the elaborate grass-style kanji. I close my eyes to wait, listening to his heart, and pray it's open to a child. Three seconds, five, ten? *How long will he stare at my words without reaction?* My toes squeeze with impatience. To give birth may be easier than announcing its possible arrival.

"This is amazing." He kisses the top of my head.

My eyes pop wide. *That's it?* I scrunch my face, confused. His reveals no happiness. Although pleasant, it's blank.

He shrugs. "What does it say?"

"Oh…" I sink into him, relieved. "Grass style is hard to read even for Japanese. It is more for aesthetics than readability." I point to the vertical symbols along the left side. "This here says six. The next, moon…" I debate if I should explain the dragon's tail but decide against it. "The last reads as blessings." My stomach flutters. "In six moons we are blessed." Pregnancy in Japan measures in lunar months at four-week intervals. So instead of the Western nine, we are pregnant for ten. It's still forty weeks. And if I am pregnant, I am four moons along. I would deliver in February.

I wait on his reaction without glancing up.

"What about this one?" He taps the larger kanji to the right.

"That says…" My heart beats wild, a frantic bird caged inside my ribs. There is no misunderstanding that symbol. "Girl."

"Girl?" He readjusts the scroll for closer study. "Six moons we are blessed, *girl*?" His forehead bunches.

I open my mouth to speak, but let the silence linger and reach for his hand and place it over my middle.

He takes a sharp breath.

"You're saying you're *pregnant* with a girl?" His gaze drops to where our hands rest over the tiniest swell.

"Maybe. It's not confirmed."

His gaze finds mine. "But you think so?"

I nod.

He stares. I knew my news would be water to a sleeping ear, unexpected and shocking, but I don't think he's happy.

My chest constricts. I sit up. "You're not happy."

"No, it's not that." He leans up and cups my checks. With his thumbs, he wipes at their moisture. "Why didn't you tell me?"

"You remember the story I shared when you found me here? How Okaasan told me of the baby bird? And that the choice of what to do was in my hands?"

He nods.

"This little bird…" I motion to my abdomen. "And you, that was my choice. I didn't want to force yours. I wasn't trying to trap a husband. So, I waited until we married, but…" I consider his eyes through the tears of my own.

"Come here." Hajime wraps me into his embrace, strokes my hair and whispers, "I chose you, too. And I am happy. I'm stunned, is all. I wasn't exactly thinking about a baby yet."

"You're lucky," I say. "I have thought of nothing else."

Tokyo Bay was once rich in the fishing industry and known for shipbuilding. Now industry makes the coast rich by poisoning the fish and polluting its shores. The smell is a mix of salty air and fumes and makes my already queasy belly roll.

Fanning my face, I try my best to smile and be of good company. Community Day invites everyone, so we agreed to bring Maiko's daughter, Yoshiko, and her friend Kimi. This is to thank Maiko, but also as company for my ride home.

The congested ship hosts crew, family and grade school children. They are everywhere, and navy photographers capture it all. Hajime waves one over and kneels between the girls, then goads me to stand beside him. The girls join in with his pleading, but I don't like the attention, so I only take a small step closer. With plans to persuade Hajime's commander to sign the US marriage documents, I'm nervous enough.

"Did they forget to wear their school uniforms?" the photographer asks, noting how the other children wear theirs and wave regional flags to show their school spirit.

Maiko's daughter and friend have plenty of spirit, but no school. To avoid discrimination, the mothers take turns to teach within the village. Today, I'm the teacher, and Hajime is our guide. To avoid the repeated question, it will be our only photograph.

After the camera flash, Yoshiko and Kimi spring up still smiling, unaware of my irritation. Hajime rests his hand at the hollow of my back, all too aware. I reach for Yoshiko's hand and she takes Kimi's as we return to our stroll around the deck.

"Why is a ship called a she?" Kimi asks.

I translate their nonstop questions as we walk in unhurried steps along the rail.

"A ship," Hajime says, looking among us all, "is like a beautiful woman. She's admired for her slim waist, heavy stern and cute fantail." He eyes me mischievously.

I smile. The girls give him their absolute attention, eating up his foreign words.

Yoshiko tugs at my dress. "What does he say? Why is a ship called a she?"

Oh. I smile, not sure how to translate. "He says because they're pretty."

They stop and give incredulous looks to Hajime. Adolescent fingers perch high on too-skinny hips.

He laughs. "And if you take care of her, really good care…" Leaning close, he bumps my arm and smiles. "Then she takes you on a journey you never thought possible." His eyes drop to my middle, where my hand rests, then glances back to the girls. "I might be a father. Baby, *akachan*."

Their eyes grow wide, darting from me to him. I laugh and nod, happy for my news, but happier for his reaction. If a ship is a woman, then a man is the sea. He is respected for his depth, his wide reach and immense power. He is one thing on the surface and a million other things beneath. I enjoy what is underneath. A happiness. He tries on the word *father* like a new coat and is proud of its fit.

Yoshiko and Kimi imitate Hajime's salute to a passing officer. This has become their game. He pretends to catch them, and they laugh, feigning innocence. Even though they can't understand him, they gobble up his constant attention until someone steals it away.

"I'll be right back," Hajime says, and takes off through the crowd.

He approaches a stout man with white-gray hair peeking from under his cap. He's a bullfrog, with an overlapping neck and jaw, and lips that stretch wide into a thin frown. After a minute, Hajime motions in our direction.

Is that his commander? His narrowed eyes slice through me, leaving me cold. I give a respectful bow, anyway, hopeful he respects our marriage per Shinto tradition and agrees to sign. He doesn't acknowledge or return my greeting.

I watch their faces for clues and try to guess their conversation. Does Hajime explain how we will live *here*? That I'm not wanting a ticket to America? The girls laugh, so I turn.

A group of children taunt lazy seagulls with bits of sesame bread the sailors give them.

"May we?" Yoshiko and Kimi ask together.

I nod and spin again to Hajime.

He is busy talking. His commander is busy looking elsewhere, weight forward as though ready to jump away. Did Hajime confess how I may carry his baby? Will it matter if I do? Why must this be so difficult?

The girls squeal, again grabbing my attention. Brave gulls dive to snatch treats from their exposed fingers. Wings flapping, they caw and screech and stir up laughter. When I look back, Hajime is walking toward me, and the commander has sprung away.

"What did he say?" I ask as he leans on the rail beside me. "Will he sign now?" My brows arch high with hope.

"No, but I'll keep working on him." Hajime lifts his cap and rakes his hair only to reset it. "When exactly do you think you're due?" His brows have creased. It's as though, now, the news of a baby has settled and allowed worries to surface.

I shrug. "Our Little Bird is a February baby, but I have yet to see a doctor."

"There's a navy hospital near the base. I'll get you set up when I return." Adjusting his cap again, he begins to walk.

"Girls." I wave for them to follow, then fall in line beside him.

He talks more to himself than to me. "But what about when I'm gone for weeks at a time? What if something happens? Or if..." He jerks his head toward me. "I need to make sure getting back isn't a problem."

"What do you mean?" I furrow my brows. "Why would getting back be a problem?"

"Cricket, I'm out of the navy in a couple of months. My service is up in October, and I have to travel to the US for discharge, remember? And we knew if the commander didn't sign the marriage paperwork, I couldn't apply for a spousal visa."

"Yes, but you can get a work one."

"Right. But that takes time, and I'd need to find a company to sponsor me. Before, we had lots of time, but now?" His worried gaze drops to my midsection.

I stop walking. "But now we are *married*. Your commander must sign."

The girls run ahead, now waving for us to follow.

"I'll keep trying." Hajime squeezes my hand with a quick tug and walks. "And if he won't, I'll figure something out, okay?"

My heart sinks. We talked about the difficulties of his return, I knew of the delay, but I didn't think of how a baby changed their importance.

We circle to where we boarded the ship. The girls continue to ask questions as I translate, but it's not fun anymore.

It's also time to leave.

The girls bow goodbye, then wait for me near the pier just off the gangway. Hajime and I stand at the ship's handrail. Since outward shows of affection are taboo, only our shoulders touch. Me, hands clenched around the metal banister. Hajime leaned forward on forearms, one hand wringing the other.

Gulls swoop in, curious if we have treats to share. Gentle waves lap the ship's side. Schoolchildren laugh and dart around us, but we remain silent. We are fish seeing three sides of a raised net. Even as we focus on the open sea, we're trapped and sense the woven fibers cinch.

"Two weeks is too long," I say at last.

"I know." He shifts to face me. "I left money in your suitcase, but if you need anything else, ask Maiko and Eiji. I asked them to look out for you. And when I'm home, we'll set up all the needed doctor appointments, okay?" His words weigh with worry.

I reassure him, telling him how I'll spend his time away—getting better acquainted with our neighbors, making our little house a home and counting days until he is in my arms once more.

We perform like the wooden dolls of the *bunraku* puppet theater, on display for all to see, while our true selves stand, shrouded in black, hooded robes, just within the shadows. I want to say so much more—*I love you, I'll miss you, I'm scared*—but a personal gift and its story will have to do.

I reach up and unfasten the silk scarf knotted around my neck. "When my father traveled for business, he'd bring us small trinkets from faraway lands." I run the red-and-white fabric through my fingers. "When he handed me this scarf of hand-painted silk, I knew he'd made a mistake. It was too grown-up, too exquisite, for a such a little girl. He must have intended it for Okaasan. 'No,' he said. 'It is for you. For the honored woman you'll become.' I wear it always, hoping to reach this expectation." I hold it out and offer it to him. "In loving you, as your wife, I believe I can."

Hajime straightens and shakes his head. "No, I can't, that's too important. That's from your dad."

I place it in his hand and close his fingers, allowing mine to remain on top. "By sharing its importance, I guarantee its safe return." Through lashes, I find his eyes. "And yours."

Hajime's eyes lock on to mine and glint. A translucent flash that rivals the shimmer of stone chips embedded in Yokosuka's famous Blue Street, where we met. And like that, it's as if we are alone. No bustling passengers, no swooping gulls, no lapping sea.

Without regard for rules or protocol, he pulls me close. A

kiss to my head. Another near my temple. A whispered promise at my ear. "I love you now and always, Cricket."

I hold on tight, both to him and his words, hoping he heeds the familiar tug home from the gravitational pull of Little Bird's moon.

SEVENTEEN

America, Present Day

I parked the Caddy in my father's driveway, gathered my shopping bags and opened the door to his condo. "I'm back."

The words echoed in the near-emptied space. I stood in the doorway, stunned the habitual greeting had slipped out.

I released an exhausted breath and stepped inside. In place of my father watching the baseball game with the volume too loud, there were boxes and booming silence. Pops's things were, for the most part, packed and sorted. And as for his life, aside from his military records, I had nothing more to search except for his stories, which was why I'd stopped on my way and spent a small fortune on supplies. I had tacks, sticky tabs, dry-erase markers and three maps. One of the world and two of Japan: the first showed roads, rail and cities in detail, and the other was an oversize educator's edition used in class-rooms. It spanned six feet with gorgeous illustrative eleva-tions and featured a write-on laminated finish.

Using a kitchen chair as a stepstool, I hung the large map of Japan on Pops's emptied living room wall first. Beside it, I tacked up the detailed street guide and, above it, the world. I pinned my father's letter, snapshots of his shipmates and the woman in the white kimono underneath, then I stepped back to take it in. An investigative wall was something I used as a journalist. By flagging locations and tacking up my research—in this case, my father's past—it helped to see the bigger pic-ture and zero in on possible connections.

I'd start with what I knew for certain.

Pops was active military from 1954 to 1957. He'd served primarily aboard the USS *Taussig* and, on it, crossed the Great Divide. I flagged the international dateline within the Pacific Ocean on the map, then found the US Navy base on the pen-insula in Yokosuka and tagged that, too.

But what did I know from my father's stories? I glanced at the naval base pin. Pops said a giant anchor weighing sixty thousand pounds sat at the entrance gate where he would sometimes meet his girl. I slid my father's kitchen table into the middle of the living room as a makeshift desk, then searched the navy website on my laptop.

As a young girl, I had tried to understand. "If the anchor was so big and heavy, how did it end up on land?"

"An earthquake," my father had said. "One so big it stirred a massive sea monster from a thousand-year sleep. When it woke, it swallowed the harbor of ships in its yawn."

He said the anchor was all that was left behind. Maybe my father should have been the writer. I laughed to myself as I clicked through the navy's photo gallery on my laptop: an aircraft carrier recently deployed, the navy exchange shop, a sign for family housing and—I froze—a massive black anchor. There it was. And while it wasn't skyscraper tall as I'd envisioned as a girl, even tipped on the T-bar it reached higher than the gate.

Only it wasn't at the front gate anymore. According to the caption it'd been relocated to the Womble Gate entrance in 1972. I added a pin to the map. Pops would have had a great story on how they moved it.

My gaze dropped to the photo of the woman in the white kimono. I needed to confirm the kimono was, in fact, a wedding dress or it didn't tie in to my father's "wedding under an ancient tree" story. Back at my laptop, I searched "Japanese traditional wedding kimono" and within seconds, I had several matches.

The same layered white fabrics and half-moon headpiece filled my screen. Unlike Pops's photo, these images were crystal clear, showing intricate patterns woven into the outer robe with delicate stitch work along the padded hems. Captions called the dress a *shiromuku* and said they were often seen in traditional Shinto-style ceremonies held in the famous shrines near Tokyo.

Is that where my father had seen one? There were photos marked Tokyo.

Excited, I searched "shrines in Tokyo" and discovered dozens—some featured elaborate gardens, others war memorials and museums, and almost all claimed an ancient tree.

Tokyo earned a pin even if I couldn't narrow down a shrine. What else?

What about the "street of blue" where Pops took one step, found her staring and fell in love? My fingers danced across the keyboard to type the query, and in one simple search for "Yokosuka's blue street," my father's story came to life.

I smiled, because there it was, just as he'd described. A

dark asphalt street with imbedded blue and white stones that sparkled like a river of light. No wonder he stooped down to touch them, even in the photos it gave the illusion of movement.

In my father's full "Blue Street" story, he'd said it started at the gangway and spiraled through the city like the path from *The Wizard of Oz*, but the street I found was straight and narrow and didn't connect to the pier. A slight exaggeration, but it *did* exist. Just like the Great Divide, the gigantic anchor and the bride.

I pinned the location on the map, then stepped back and stared in awe, because, like Dorothy, I'd been swept away to another world. A familiar one. One where my father belonged. For the first time since I'd read that letter, a sense of harmony returned. Through my father's stories, the man I knew had returned, and in looking at that map, I saw him everywhere.

If only I could forget the letter and everything it implied. I wanted to. I was desperate to talk to him. To understand. I kept spinning over the same two questions. Was my father's letter an attempt to clear a guilty conscience or a life's regret of unfortunate circumstance?

I was desperate to believe it was the latter, that everything I knew of my father held true, but his secret shook me to my foundation, and to rebuild it, I needed proof. But I wasn't finding anything, and while my father's stories held truth, they weren't giving me answers.

What if I never got them?

My gaze dropped to the envelope tacked below the map. I'd already checked the address several times only to find the house as numbered didn't exist, but it was a safe assumption the city on the mailing address was correct.

I located Zushi on the opposite coast from the base and

placed a pin on the map. It was a mere ten-minute trip by train. But in the 1950s? Minutes later I had my answer. Zushi Station opened in 1889, and while the travel time was extended, the lines did connect. I flagged it and, with a thick red dry-erase marker, traced a route between the two.

The seaside town was small, which surprised me. According to my father's "Tea with a Merchant King of Empire" story, it was a traditional house that time forgot. Within such a small area, how many traditional homes could there still be? Back on my laptop, I searched "traditional houses in Zushi, Japan," and while I scrolled the results, I remembered his words.

Her home sat at the top of a small hill, and she'd said I'd know it by the curved, clay roof tiles.

When I asked him why they were curved, he'd said to ward off evil spirits because demons only traveled in straight lines. For days after that story I'd spun in circles, taking the meaning as literal. I laughed under my breath, because here I was, a grown woman, searching for the home's literal description.

But it paid off. Photos showed buildings in Zushi with curved roof tiles, but none were homes, and not all were old. Two were converted into *ryokans* or hotel-like inns, and three were refurbished as restaurants. Since all had curved roofs, all five locations were printed and pinned underneath the map, but there had to be an easier way. I needed someone who knew the area, someone in Japan whom I could call and ask questions, but who?

Yoshio Itō at Tokyo Times.

I straightened at once. I'd worked with him on a piece about the safety of Japan's nuclear reactors and then again when their Democratic Party leader fell under suspicion of taking bribes. Although Yoshio didn't live near Zushi, he spoke the language, and as a Japanese citizen and local journalist he might have access to records that I didn't.

I scanned the envelope after blocking off my father's PO box with tape, then emailed Yoshio, requesting "off the record" help in locating the property. That was all I told him. Aside from past online chats, shared resources and work-related email correspondence, Yoshio and I were strangers, and this was personal.

Thunder rumbled.

I'd lost track of time and the afternoon had lost its light. I peered out the window. One thick drop of rain followed another to splatter on the walk. *The Caddy!* I had left it out and the top down. I scrambled to find Pops's key chain, then raced out the door.

Just as I pulled into the garage, the sky cracked open. Heavy drops pummeled the cement and pounded at the gutters like a hundred angry fists. Filled with nostalgia, I stepped from the car and stood with hands slung in my pockets to watch the downpour.

One summer my father and I had been out in the yard when a storm came on just as quick. Pops set up lawn chairs in the garage to wait it out and made up stories about my chalk drawings running pastel rivers down the drive.

Lightning lit the sky. I unfolded one of Pops's lawn chairs and took a front row seat. He was missing a heck of a show, and I was missing him.

After a while, I stood, pushed the button that closed the garage and stepped inside, tossing his keys on the counter. Something I'd done at least a dozen times in the last week or so, and yet, I froze, eyes fixed to them. There were four. A typical house key for the condo, the original set for the Caddy and one for a padlock.

The self-storage unit.

My father had agreed to downsize and move into the retirement community a year or so after my mother had passed.

We got rid of most of the furniture, yard equipment and everyday items he'd no longer need, but moved what had been in the home's attic to a self-storage facility.

That was years ago, and I'd forgotten.

Within minutes, I had my bag, and was back out the door.

EIGHTEEN

Japan, 1957

The sun sails high and proud above ridge clouds, a white fluffy ocean with small cascading waves. A perfect after-noon in the little village, and yet, I sense the coming storm. I twist my hands, one inside the other, and squint at the sky. It's been a long week, and I face another one without Hajime.

Everywhere I turn today, I see Grandmother's omens. It's only old-folk wisdom and nonsense, but last night a spider inside the house escaped my capture, so I couldn't release the bad luck it carried. And this morning my *zōri* sandal's band snapped, which signals pending misfortune.

I try to ignore the ominous signs and concentrate on the children who gather around my rotting stoop. Every day more and more arrive for impromptu English lessons. Including Maiko's children, Tatsu and Yoshiko.

It's taught in school, but no one in this village attends, just as Kiko warned. My heart breaks, but it builds on my resolve to change things. Because Hajime teaches me conversational English instead of the memorized lines we learned in class, the children will gain the advantage of both.

When I first met Hajime, we both spoke English, but couldn't communicate. It was Saturday, day of the Earth, and Kiko and I had traveled to Yokosuka. I spotted him crouched as though trying to pry up stones from the road. Such a silly American boy! Kiko and I inched closer, amused. But when he looked up, I gazed into eyes as blue as the stones the street was named for.

"*Arigatōgo,*" he said.

Thank you? Kiko nudged my arm, laughed.

"You are welcome?" I said in Japanese.

"Ah..." A slow smile with wide, deep lines crept across his tanned and angled cheeks. "English?" He rubbed at his dimpled jaw. "*Watashi wa hanasenai...*English?"

He can't speak English? *What?* Kiko and I again exchanged looks. In Japanese I told him, "You cannot speak Japanese, either."

That time, he laughed, but it was obvious he didn't know why. "Man, if you're not a living doll."

"No," I said in English, showing him my hair. "I am a girl. Naoko."

Tatsu, Maiko's son, tugs at my leg and drags me from memory.

We've been at it for over an hour. "Really...re-lee," I say, articulating how to form the word with my mouth. Japanese language does not have an *L*. It doesn't exist, and this is the source of much confusion. "Rea-la-la-lee."

"Ri-lee," Tatsu says, and beams.

I pat his head. "Yes, good."

Although much younger, he reminds me of Kenji. He has the same bright eyes and long lashes. His hair sticks up from a cowlick and he is always moving. The comparison makes me ache for home. And I know my little brother also aches for me.

I asked Hajime how he snuck Okaasan here without Grandmother or her fox spies knowing.

His grin split his face. "I found a fox spy of my own," he had said. "One who likes baseball cards and misses his big sister."

Now I miss them both.

Maybe I could visit home in secret again? Watch as Kenji returns from school? I had done it once before. If I leave now... I stand.

"Arigatō, gozaimasu, Sensei." One after the other the children bow.

I return the gesture, overwhelmed by how grateful they are for my time. But I'm the appreciative one. Time is a stubborn creature that delights in goading you. When happy, it sprouts wings and flies. When waiting, it drags through thick mud with heavy feet. The children help me to trek through the terrain.

"You're a good teacher, Naoko!" Maiko calls as she gathers dry clothes from the line.

Tatsu races to her, chanting, "Ri-lee-Ri-lee-Ri-lee!"

I dip my chin with a head bow. *Am I a teacher?* The thought is a seed, planted for later. Right now I'm desperate for the familiarity of home, even if only from a distance.

The train rumbles under my seat as I watch the landscape rush by in splotches of green. Between my finger and thumb I roll lavender sprigs plucked on my way to the station. It's the leaves that hold the fragrance, and I crush their scent to my skin before holding it under my nose to inhale its comfort.

Such a day. A sigh escapes, my hands drop to my lap and I consider my sandal. I had to fix the strap again before I left. An additional unlucky sign. You're not supposed to mend your clothes before you leave the house. All this good luck–bad luck is silly.

Standing, I wait until it's safe to exit the train, almost tripping for want of my family and home.

The familiar trees along the road welcome me with high waving branches. The sun flirts between them, still warm. Still happy. The caw of a black crow catches my ear, and when I look up, I catch his eye. I turn away. It's another forecast of misfortune.

These omens stalk me.

I stare at my feet as I walk, trying to concentrate hard on pleasant thoughts. I think of our wedding and the night of love that followed. Of this baby, the one I now hope to carry. Of Hajime's ship and how it is only seven days from carrying him home.

Gravel kicks up on the road ahead of me under the weight of a car. *A car?* Although Japan's economy grows, vehicles, even among the prosperous, are rare. Father has yet to consider a purchase. I move to the side, allowing its passage, then stop.

It's a funeral coach.

Not the elaborate *miya* hearse with the gilded gold-and-red shrine on the rear, but the modest van used to transport a body to the funeral home. My thumbs tuck in each fist as a precaution. Thumb in Japanese translates to parent-finger, and hiding it serves as their protection. A superstition, but this one, even I do not challenge. The menacing sensation that has soaked my skin all day now drowns me.

I watch it pass in the direction I just traveled from the train. Then turn back with dread. Where had it been? Over the small hill there are just three homes.

One of them mine.

My stomach drops.

Maybe it doesn't mean anything. Maybe it's our dear neighbor's widowed mother-in law. But maybe it's...

Blood rushes my ears, creating panic in its pulse. My feet begin to move. One step, then another and another. Faster and faster they push off to propel me forward until I'm running. The sandal with the homemade fix frees itself. I scoop it up and continue running.

At the top of the hill, I stop, breathless, with one foot bare. My heart slams against my ribs. There's my house, undisturbed. My eyes dissect every detail. The landscape... tended. The door...inched open to catch a cooling breeze. The quiet... I'm sure Grandmother enjoys her tea in the garden.

Yes, maybe everything is okay, after all. There are tire indents near my feet. I bend to the earth and scoop the loose gravel in my fingers. There is no maybe in their direction. I trace the tread marks and follow them home.

The steps I took between the top of the hill and my front door do not exist in my memory. I see only flickers in my mind's eye, images that will haunt me for the remainder of my life. I blink and float through time. I'm on my porch. A white lantern hangs to signal death. I'm at its door. There's a wailing. Sobs. *Who?*

I want to hold my ears, make it stop, make this go away. Two shadows move inside. Grandmother and Okaasan would be the only ones home. *Taro? Father? Oh, not Kenji. Please not...* Shaky fingers fumble the door the remaining way open.

My father turns.

His eyes are red under heavy, downcast brows. They're swollen with emotion. When they fall on me, his lips twitch with surprise, then press tight to suppress it. The crying comes from Grandmother. She's hunched into her hands and shakes with grief.

I bend and step from my remaining shoe, then run around them both. More flashes to burn into memory. The empty kitchen. The empty bedroom. The other bedroom. *The garden?*

My bare footsteps pound the floor. Grandmother calls my name, but I'm gone, running the outside path in slow motion. Rocks and dirt dig into my unprotected feet. I turn my head in every direction.

"Okaasan?" Her name spills from my lips and catches against my throat. I scream the childhood nickname: *"Haha!"* It's sharp. Piercing. Desperate. *Where is she?* Is she alone grieving? Did Taro have an accident? *Please not Kenji.*

I sprint the grounds, blinded by tears, searching. The empty tea garden where I presented Hajime. The Zen garden to the east where Okaasan and I shared secrets. The small shrine to the west. *Oh!* My hand slaps my gaping mouth. It's already covered in white paper to keep out the impure spirits of death.

Taro. I spot him walking with Kenji from the hill. I am paralyzed by the sight of them. They are together. Grandmother and Father are inside.

Blood rushes my head. I may faint. There's not enough air. *"Haha!"* Her name rips from my lungs.

I don't remember entering the house again. But here I am. Empty kitchen. Obaachan's tea sits untouched and dishes are out. Empty bedroom. My parents' sleeping room smells of patchouli and sandalwood. It's earthy and damp, like the garden after a rain. A small table filled with flowers. *Did I see these before?* Father's outside, walking to the boys. It's all in slow motion, underwater.

Hands to face, Grandmother stands in the middle of the main room. Her shoulders shake. Her hair's in disarray. The bun at the nape of her neck slants to the side, and strands have worked free to rest in peculiar directions.

As I inch toward her, her fingers drop and hover near her chin. Her eyes sag with grief. My lips quiver, trying to form the question my ears can't bear the answer to. Grandmother nods before I can ask.

This isn't true. I shake my head. *No. No. No.*

"Her heart—"

"No!" My arms fly up to wave away her words.

Stepping away, I scream at her. "No! She's *not* dead!" *She can't be dead.* My hands claw through my hair and pull. I tug hard, ripping from the roots to transfer the pain, needing to feel something else. Anything else. *This isn't happening.*

Grandmother speaks, but I'm too far inside myself to hear. I rock on my heels…back and forth, my head buried in my arms, my heart bleeding out. *How could she be dead?* A sharp gasp of air sucks in. I release violent sobs out. I am shackled with them and fall to my knees, distraught.

My tongue pushes to the roof of my mouth as my throat constricts to keep screams from escaping bloated lungs. Grandmother steps closer. I clutch her legs and weep into them with loud cries and rivers of tears. She strokes my hair, but I am inconsolable.

My mother is dead.

NINETEEN

Japan, 1957

Time does not discriminate. It does not care if we are happy or sad. It does not slow or hurry. It's a linear creature, traveling in one direction, constant even through pain.

Today is Okaasan's funeral.

I have only been to one, and I was a child. I remember Okaasan saying, "Death is only a doorway. We are here both to honor their life and help them pass through to the next." This is what I told Kenji last night when he snuck in my room. His pained expression mirrored my thoughts. *I do not want her to pass through. I want her here.*

White summer chrysanthemums blanket the main temple area and frame the altar, their light scent dusting the air. It blends with the agarwood incense and grows stronger with each passing minute. Normally, the resinous heartwood is pleasing. But here behind closed doors, it is a cloying odor that clings to my skin, my clothing, my memory.

Grandmother sits beside me dressed in an all-black formal mourning kimono. Her hair sweeps up neat into a round and perfect bun, and her eyes are hollow. Like the famous Chinese painted dragons of Andong, they are without her spirit. I listen as she rolls prayer beads back and forth. Her lips tremble with silent words.

Father and Taro sit tall, resigned. I'm allowed to attend Okaasan's ceremonies because I'm expected to stay on at home. Father and Taro are preoccupied with business, Grandmother's growing age. And because my family does not recognize my marriage, Kenji now resides in my care. He tucks under my arm and stares at nothing. In his dark suit, he looks more like a young man than a nine-year-old boy. My guilt is infinite. I'm not fit to take Okaasan's place.

Soft footsteps pad up the middle aisle. One after another, mourners file in, bow to us and offer incense at the altar. This goes on forever. Kiko's family offers their respect, but in refusing to look at me, Kiko grants me none.

I clamp my teeth. Guilt eats my insides raw. Sleep is the brother of death, and I am in need of his company. I wish to be anywhere else. Since my tears will find no comfort, they are best not shed.

When I look up, I spy the Tanaka family returning from the altar.

Satoshi.

His hair is slicked back to reveal angular features and warm eyes, and the suit fits him well. He looks like a modern man of business. I stare at his feet as he passes to sit behind us.

His family must know I have chosen an American and the divide it's caused. To feel something other than shame, I dig my thumbnail under the other so deep it almost draws blood.

The back of my neck burns hot from Satoshi's judgment. A mind conscious of guilt is its own accuser, and Hajime's absence only makes this worse. *Do they wonder where he is?*

Kenji wipes his face when the Buddhist priest begins to chant a section from the sutra. Everything runs together. The hollow *click-click-click* of Grandmother's beads, the hum of quiet prayers and the priest's explanation of utmost bliss and those that dwell there. It all fades in and out.

I sit rigid in my emptiness.

Because I was not home for the last-moment preparations, I didn't dare ask Father or Obaachan what personal items resided inside the coffin. Did they add the six coins for easy passage of the Sanzu River?

The Sanzu is the river the dead must pass on their way to the afterlife. Your life's virtues determine the place of crossing, and there are only three.

A bridge, a shallow ford and rapid waters infested with snakes.

Okaasan will cross over the bridge because of her good life and blameless heart.

Kenji's tears dampen my shoulder. I hold him tighter and whisper comfort as they announce Okaasan's new name to close the ceremony. The length determines the price, and Father paid a small fortune to honor her. We're required to call her the short form version of this name to ensure we do not rouse her spirit from beyond.

I want to call her back right now.

Kenji and I stand to the side while guests file out. It is a sea of black. Black suits, black kimonos and blackened spirits. Mr. Tanaka speaks with Father and Taro. Mrs. Tanaka bows to Grandmother and pats her hand. No one looks past them to me, except for Satoshi.

I drop my chin, stare at his suit coat, concentrating on the fibers.

He leans to Kenji, who hangs on my arm. "If you need anything, you just come over, okay? And next week, we'll still play ball. Don't forget."

Kenji only nods and lifts his chin, a brave face in front of his newest friend.

"An inch of time cannot be bought with an inch of gold, Naoko. You can't go back or speed it up, it must be endured..." Satoshi sighs. "I am so sorry for this."

Silent tears continue to fall. *How can I have so many?* I wipe at them, trying to keep them away.

Satoshi whispers in English, "I wish to speak with you in private."

I lift my chin, surprised.

Without my having to say a word, he understands.

He nods. "When appropriate, Naoko."

It's been two days since I stumbled home to discover Okaasan had died. A day since her funeral, evening feast and the ceremonial separation of her bones and ashes. Only hours since her burial.

Kenji cries as he runs off for a second time, his little feet trying to outrun the truth that follows. This, I would give anything to forget. It shreds me straight through. Taro and Father wait on the porch for his return, blank eyes fixed on the tree line. I pick up in the kitchen while Grandmother drinks tea for comfort and eyes me from the table. She wants to talk. Or rather, for me to listen.

I'm listening to the water as it runs instead. The dishes are clean enough, but I rinse them again to stall, thinking of Obaachan. There's an intimacy with water. It molds to its surroundings and yet changes everything's shape over time. I twist my fingers through the stream and glance over.

Grandmother's brows rise on her pale face. The black silk kimono washes out her complexion, leaving a pasty, sickly cast. "There are people who fish, and those that just disturb the water," Grandmother says, then coughs to clear her throat.

She disturbs me with her fishing. "More tea, Obaachan?"

"No. My tea is fine." She tips the cup to thin lips, staring from behind the rim. Her pupils, small and fixed, resemble a stalking fox.

I know she has much to say. I respect and love her, but my patience is thin. With a frustrated sigh, I tilt my head as a signal for her to begin.

"Satoshi still favors you, Naoko." Her voice is croaky, from tears and wailing. "Yes, we saw him give you comfort, acting like a husband should toward a wife."

My heart pounds heavy in my chest. She won't stop here.

She sets the cup down, one finger tapping at the rim. "Where is your *gaijin* when you need him?"

My stomach constricts. "Satoshi was being a friend because my *husband*, who loves me, and who will be heartbroken to learn what's happened, can't be reached. That's all."

"Does he even know about the *baby*...hmm?" Her eyes narrow as if concerned, but she speaks with a flinty tone.

So they all are aware? Of course. Okaasan said Father suspected and I would guess Grandmother is partially why. Her foxes have outsmarted me again. "Yes. He learned of the possibility after we married." I take a step toward her, a bowl in one hand, and the cloth in the other. "You should have seen him, he was so happy!" I spin with a huff back to the dishes, turn off the water and focus on drying. My hands rub so hard I see myself in the shine.

"So, he thinks it's acceptable to leave you in that *place*, in this condition? Gaah…" She waves a hand in the air, dismissing the thought.

"That *place* is my new home. Love lives in thatched cottages as well as palaces, Obaachan."

"Humph, that love poisoned your mother. It tore her apart."

"No!" Anger rips through me and pulls my spine straight. I point the bowl at her, no longer able to hold everything in. "You don't know as much as you think, Obaachan."

"And what do you know, child?" Grandmother grimaces, mocking me.

"I know Okaasan stood behind me and my choice to marry Hajime. She came to see me on my wedding day. She even brought me her *shiromuku* to wear!" I step closer. "Did you know that?"

Grandmother lifts her chin and stares. A vexed breath puffs through her nostrils, causing them to flare. "Foolish girl. We all know." She snaps her words like a cutting whip. "Only when your father learned of this did his anger stop her weak heart."

"What?" My insides tighten, my stomach cramps.

"Yes, because of you." Grandmother confirms as if she knows my thoughts.

"Because of your selfishness, Naoko." Father startles us both from the doorway.

My eyes snap to his.

"You will now listen." Father growls, low and gritty. The warning constrained only by an inch. He steps closer. "You're like the mindless cook. Taking whatever suits you from the garden of life and hastily chopping it up to serve as soup for others. Just as the cook, in your haste, you snare a snake and include it. You force everyone to drink of your poisonous mixture. The snake's severed head floats in your mother's bowl, Naoko. It was too much for her to swallow."

He means this baby and Hajime. He means my wedding. He means me. I am responsible for so much discord it caused my mother's death. I am a tsunami of emotion. The sand beneath my feet draws back. The next big wave is coming. I want to crumple onto the floor and brace myself.

"Naoko?" Kenji's voice is so small. "Naoko!" He rushes past Father to me, and I am hit with emotion. The groundswell overtakes me.

My eyes lock with Father's. Kenji's face buries in my chest and my arms wrap him to me, but I do not cry. I swallow my sorrow to comfort his.

Another tightening stretches across my middle. I fold over and palm my belly. "Oh!" *Oh, no...* Another sharp cramp. There's a warmth between my legs.

"Obaachan?"

Grandmother had me lie down and insisted I not move until a midwife could tend to me. I heard her tell my father she would fetch a woman who owes her a favor. Many owe Obaachan.

It's been hours, and I take deep, controlled breaths to keep from crying, but after everything, this is impossible. Although the tears are endless, the bleeding has stopped. I tried to tell Grandmother this before she left, but she worries if I'm pregnant and miscarry I could hemorrhage. Her concern is for me, not for my child. After Father's accusing words, I'm lucky for any concern at all. From anyone.

For Kenji, I've been strong. For my father and Taro, I've shown remorse and respect. For Grandmother, I've been nurturing. For myself, I've been cruel. I soak myself in blame and deny forgiveness. When it's my turn to cross the Sanzu River, I'll not be as fortunate as Okaasan. Her death now stains red on my hands and soaks the weight of my clothes. I already battle an unforgiving current of vengeful serpents.

Grief releases in spurts.

This is heaven's design. If it didn't offer moments of repose, we would die beside those we mourn. Like a switch, it flips agony on and off. On, we are strangled by death until we are near it ourselves. It clicks off before we suffocate. This is the void, the vacuum of nothing.

This is where I am, in my old room, numb from the inside out, waiting for the next wave to hit. *Please let my baby be okay.* To lose Okaasan and then my baby? It would be too much.

My ears catch muffled voices, footsteps, and then the door slides, allowing in light. I wipe at my wet cheeks and turn to Grandmother and her guest.

"This is Eyako. She'll take care of you." Before leaving, Grandmother whispers something else to the midwife.

Eyako closes the screen. The lantern she carries casts sharp shadows across her face. She's not as old as Grandmother but wears a considerable age. Deep creases form between her brows. She smiles but the lines stay. She sets the lamp to her side on the floor and folds her hands. "So, you are how far along?"

I clear my throat. "I've missed three…"

She peels back my thin blanket with care and undoes my shirt. To remove the chill from her fingers, she rubs them together, then places a hand over my somewhat swollen middle. The push is gentle and with purpose, first high, then low, and then again. She lifts my skirt and looks within.

I look to the heavens and squeeze my lids shut.

"All signs point to a fourth-moon-month pregnancy." She covers me back up.

My fingers clutch the blanket as I study her face for answers. Our eyes meet, and she pats my arm.

"Signs also indicate everything is okay. There was only a small amount of blood and cramping. There's no pain?"

"No." Relief surges through me, and I exhale a long breath. *This baby fights.*

"But I prefer for another midwife to make certain with proper testing. We'll move you to the maternity home first thing in the morning, and there you can rest, okay?"

My eyes widen with tears.

She pats my arm in reassurance. "Sleep. Stay calm." She leaves as she came, taking the light with her. More hushed voices, footsteps, and then silence.

My mind runs through all the scenarios, every option available to my life. The life that is no longer my own. It now belongs to this baby, to the man I swore my heart to and to Kenji, the little brother I must take as son. *As son.*

"How can I even hope to take your place, Haha?" I whisper through tears. New expectations and old traditions eternally bind me. Father will never accept Hajime in our family home, and I can't remove Kenji from the only one he has ever known. And what of this child I carry?

Please let her be okay.

TWENTY

America, Present Day

In the Midwest, the rapid swings in temperature can quickly explode into a storm. I knew better than to drive through one, but once I remembered my father's storage unit, a category five twister couldn't have kept me away.

The Cadillac's wipers fought a losing battle with the torrential downpour. To make matters worse, the wheels hydroplaned on the standing water and the flashes of lightning created afterimages. I should have pulled over, but I was determined to press forward.

By the time I reached the self-storage facility, the storm had abated to a steady drizzle. I leaned out the window to punch in the gate code, then flipped on my brights, trying to find row H and unit 101, but the markers were hard to see.

I crawled down one aisle after the next until I found it, then parked alongside it.

I sussed out the key from the others and stepped through a river of rainwater to reach the lock. Threading it in and with a turn it clicked. I reached down and hoisted up the roller door, beads of collected water sprinkling over my head. As the light flickered on, I moved inside, pushed wet hair from my face and looked around.

Where to begin?

Pops had a specific system for how he wanted things stacked. It didn't seem so long ago that we had moved the attic boxes here, and yet the drop cloths were coated with a thin layer of dust. I yanked one off, and in an instant, the stagnant air took on the texture of forgotten years.

As I moved through the aisle between boxes, my shoes left prints across the dusty concrete floor. At least the unit hadn't leaked.

The first box held my great-grandmother's handmade quilts—heirloom quality, painstakingly crafted and heavily used. I pulled out the one that had sat on the foot of my bed. It was a simple patchwork of pink and white squares, but every eight-by-eight block displayed the colors in a different pattern. The blanket hid me from monsters as a child and comforted heartaches as a teenager. Now it would keep out the chill. I draped it over my shoulders and peeked in another box.

My mother's silver-edged china. An eight-piece collection that had been her mother's, and then became mine—although I'd never used it. I closed up the box, knowing I most likely never would.

Several plastic bins held Christmas decorations. I popped the latch and riffled through the one that held the tree ornaments in muted grays, pinks and whites. Mama was obsessed with French decor and preferred the softer hues to the garish greens and reds. I admit, the nontraditional shades were lovely. Before Mama died they'd colored every Christmas, a part of our family's tradition, but Pops hadn't decorated since she'd passed. I moved the bin near the storage door, deciding to take them and use them myself.

I worked through more Christmas decor, stored magazines, another set of dishware and an old luggage set. I popped the gold metal clasps of each suitcase but found them all empty.

Behind the luggage sat a box wrapped with shipping tape in both directions. It was heavy, but I tugged it to the center to sit under the light. I picked at the tape corners to peel it back, then ripped them free.

I opened the flaps to find a newspaper lined the top of the box, but it wasn't crumpled to add padding or protection. Rather, it was folded and saved with intention.

The facing article, titled "The Girl with Red Shoes," featured a photo of a bronze statue of a little girl with braids. She held a single stemmed flower and looked over the ocean as though waiting for someone. I skimmed through the text.

San Diego and Yokohama, sister cities located on opposite sides of the Pacific Ocean, now have another link, thanks to Yokohama's gift of friendship. The Girl with Red Shoes sits on the tip of Shelter Island, near the US naval base in San Diego, and portrays a Japanese orphan who was adopted by a loving American couple. Her touching story became first a poem, and then a well-known song in Japan.

The rest of the article talked mostly of how the statue was a symbol of alliance between countries, but when I took out my phone and searched "The Girl with Red Shoes," I found a different story. The real one.

The famous poem and song, "Red Shoes," was inspired by the girl's life but took creative liberties. The lyrics placed the mother on the Yokohama pier, hidden and watching as her little girl—clad in red shoes—left to board the ship with blue-eyed foreigners. In the song, the mother cries out how she will think of her daughter every time she sees red shoes and she wonders if one day her daughter will look back across the sea and yearn for home.

The real-life child was born in a small village at the foot-hills of the old Shizuoka Prefecture. The unmarried mother, finding life difficult with an illegitimate child, moved, and when the opportunity presented itself, she married.

To ensure a better life for the child, the woman's new father-in-law arranged for mercenaries to adopt the little girl and take her to America. However, the child contracted tuberculosis—then incurable—before setting sail, and was turned over to a nearby orphanage instead, where she remained until she died at the age of nine.

The child's mother and husband never knew.

Theories suggest the father-in-law had fabricated the mer-cenary story for the mother and delivered the little girl di-rectly to the orphanage himself.

I pocketed my phone, confused, eyeing the photo of the statue in the paper. Why would she give her up? I under-stood that an unmarried woman with a child would find life difficult back then, but after she married, the child wouldn't have been considered illegitimate anymore. They could have moved, and no one would have known.

But then I understood. Maybe the child was mixed-race just like Pops's daughter would be. Was that why he saved the article, because it resonated with him? Carefully, I refolded the newspaper, set it aside and looked in the box.

A folded garment bag took up the remaining space. I pulled

it out and placed it flat over the other boxes. In white letters it said US NAVY. I dug under the zipper panel and pulled it open. His navy dress whites. Separating the hangers, I removed just the dinner jacket. Was Pops ever that small? I smiled to myself, trying to imagine him so young. *Seventeen.*

My father wasn't an officer, but the style of the uniform was close in style. Silver navy-eagle buttons, with a narrow, pointed lapel, and three white stripes over black on the upper sleeve. It looked good despite being stored incorrectly. I smoothed out the deep creases across the front, but something bumped inside.

I ran my hand along the lining, then hooked a finger into the interior pocket and poked around. A balled-up handkerchief? I tugged it out. Not a handkerchief. A white silk pouch beaded with metallic, silver thread. The kind with a ribbon drawstring hidden within the hem. My father's words floated from memory.

And inside, a single seed from the majestic tree with a small scrolled message.

Heart pounding, I held my breath and pushed at the fabric. The contents crinkled.

It couldn't be. With trembling fingers, I pried at the bunched part, then tipped the bag. A small scroll shook free. I carefully worked it open. Dumbfounded, I stared at the words. At *my* magic words.

TO KNOW YOUR DIRECTION, YOU MUST KNOW BOTH YOUR ROOTS AND YOUR REACH.

It, too, was real. Which meant the photo of the woman in the white kimono was possibly the bride in his story. She had to be. But Pops said the silk pouch was given *instead* of rings. That's what he said, right? Why would *he* have the pouch?

I looked at it, turning it over in my hands. Were they passed out like wedding favors? The magic tree story I knew by heart. Pops added the wedding part at the hospital. Now I questioned what I'd heard. It didn't make sense.

I checked the pockets of the slacks that hung within the garment bag. Nothing. But I caught sight of something at the bottom of the box.

There was an envelope. It wasn't as tattered as my father's letter, nor was it as creased, but with the familiar red-inked Asian symbols, I sensed it was just as important.

I took a deep breath, opened the flap and wiggled the contents free. It was a form written entirely in Japanese except for my father's signature and the title.

AFFIDAVIT TO MARRY

I looked at the silk pouch, the one he said was exchanged instead of rings, then gazed at my father's name on the marriage document. His name listed on a *marriage* document.

I shook my head, refusing to believe. Tears welled up. He said he *attended* a wedding under a giant tree. He attended one. That's where he'd received the magic words.

He didn't say it was *his* wedding.

He was married before Mama? Did she know that, too? The tears slid down my cheeks. To learn there was a child left behind, combined with a wife and coupled with grief was…a lot. I kept replaying my father's words.

Before that life, I lived another.

It'd be easier if you just read my letter.

It wasn't easier. Because the letter didn't tell me he'd been married or where his daughter was or what happened. It didn't explain anything. There was nothing easy about any of this.

I thought of the photo of the woman in the white kimono,

how I'd found elements of truth in all his stories, then I stared again at his signature on the marriage document and the one underneath. The last name was smudged, so only a handful of symbols to make up the first remained.

Wait. Didn't Japanese write their last name first? Yoshio did. I wiped at my eyes and looked again at the symbols. There were three and then a defined space before the illegible others. *Oh, my God.* Was that her last name? Did I just find her name? I reached for my phone, snapped a photo and attached it to an email to Yoshio, asking for translation. I held the document and stared at the marks.

"Abracadabra," I whispered, because, like magic, I'd finally found the key that could unlock my father's "other life."

Her name.

中村

TWENTY-ONE

Japan, 1957

A fog has settled low and blankets the ground. Father has business matters and I am to travel for tests, so we walk toward the train station together. There, we will part since Father's work in Yokohama and the maternity home in Hiratsuka are in opposite directions. The haze paints the landscape in inky, muted pigments that only heighten the stark silence between us.

This road is endless.

Because I carry this child, Father carries the small suitcase Grandmother insisted I bring. She said, "Better to have the sweater and suffer its load than have gooseflesh and suffer the chill." I suffer either way.

If Father was the rock, then Okaasan was the appeasing water that over time softened and shaped it. Now he sits in an empty riverbed taking on the full scorch of the sun. The shadow under each eye tinges dark. Behind his eyes he carries pain.

We are both responsible.

He clears his throat but says nothing. Only Grandmother's meddlesome foxes entertain conversation. I swear they whisper as we pass, "Who will tell Hajime where you are? What will he think when he learns you must care for Kenji? What if you lose his baby?"

I agree to go to ensure my baby's well-being, but I'm wrecked with worry. *Calm thoughts, Naoko.* My baby is fine. Hajime loves me. He will show Kenji compassion. Together, we can discuss with Father what to do.

"Naoko." Father's pace slows. He draws out his steps with an arduous sigh as we near the station, then stops. "Do what they say in all matters of your health. Do not be stubborn. Do you understand?"

Our eyes meet, mine guilty, his compassionate. He has concern for me, but what of my baby? To ask is a temporary shame. Not to ask, an eternal one.

"Father, I..." Where to begin? There is much to say.

My hesitation robs the chance. His gaze moves past me and sets rigid again. I turn to what has captured his attention. My heart skitters.

Satoshi?

My head snaps back. "What is this?"

Father's hand rises to settle my protest. "He believes you have taken ill and a family doctor cannot travel to see you. Satoshi will serve as chaperon to where it is convenient."

"But, Father, I—"

"Enough." His hand chops the air. "This is *not* negotiable." Father's tone reclaims its stern edge as he gives the crane's word, the final say from someone in authority to settle a difficult debate.

I glare my displeasure in silence. Anything I voice will only splash water on the sweltering rock—a wasted effort.

"Think of your brother, this family, and accept." Father sets my bag down and speaks under his breath, exasperated. "*Accept*, Naoko."

Accept.

When will he accept Hajime and our baby? Me?

The train follows the scenic coast of the Sagami Bay to the rebuilt Kanagawa Prefecture of Hiratsuka—a small city nearly destroyed twelve years ago by air raids at the end of the war. Its strategic location and vast beaches were a planned ground invasion site, but it ended and spared the surviving residents this added humiliation.

After thirty minutes Satoshi and I exit with the small crowd. I've not spoken to him until now. "Why did you agree to escort me?" I plant my feet on the platform.

"You should not travel alone." Satoshi switches my suitcase from one hand to the other, then nods for me to follow him outside.

The air still holds a light layer of fog as we begin the straight walk to the *Take Josan-shō*, Bamboo Maternity Home. It clings to the simple structures that line the town's main road and paints them mottled gray.

"But how is my travel your concern?" I ask, matching his stride. I have no idea what I hope to accomplish. Maybe to make him furious so he turns, gets back on the train and leaves. Maybe just because I'm mad at Father for forcing me to leave in the first place. "You know I am now married?"

"Yes, I know this." Satoshi pauses, waiting for a barefoot man on a bicycle to pass before crossing the uneven road.

"And still you oblige my father's request?"

"I did not think it necessary to cause him embarrassment." He shrugs.

I am the one embarrassed. Heat warms my neck, then boils to anger. I lift my chin to challenge. "Do you also know I am *pregnant*?"

Satoshi stops. His eyes remain forward.

I circle in front of him. "I am not meeting a family physician like Father told you. I am to meet a midwife." With the matter settled, I turn smug and start walking. Now he can leave. I spin to reclaim my suitcase, but startle. He is right at my heel.

"All the more reason for an escort, wouldn't you agree?" His brows arch over his direct gaze. "Especially with an absent husband." Suitcase in hand, he moves past me.

Who does he think he is? "He is on his ship in Formosa but will return any day." Satoshi is no better than Obaachan or Father. I scramble between a woman with a young child and an older man in a tattered coat to walk beside him.

Satoshi glances sideways. "So, you do not know?" He blows out a breath and places his free hand within his pocket. He slows his pace. "I wondered if your father informed you. This is what I wanted to discuss with you. Remember, at your mother's service?"

The day is a blur and my father told me nothing. My blank stare is answer enough.

"I don't have all the specifics, but tensions over Taiwan have again escalated and a US Navy ship on patrol was caught in accidental cross fire."

"What ship?" The question is out before I have thought to ask it. "What ship, Satoshi?" I grip his forearm, heart pounding, imagining the worst.

He shakes his head. "I am not sure. But do not worry, it

may just mean a possible delay." He places a hand over mine and squeezes.

I yank away as if burned, embarrassed to have placed it there in the first place.

"Please." Satoshi glances to my middle and sighs. "For the baby's sake, accept my friendship and let me escort you the rest of the way." He motions ahead. "See? The clinic's bamboo fence is just there."

Tall golden slats woven together go on as far as I can see. My eyes skitter sideways to Satoshi and narrow at my father's word. *Accept.*

"For the baby's sake," I say, and begin a worried stroll, twisting a strand of hair between finger and thumb. Of course Father did not mention any news of conflict in the Straits. Why would he? He would prefer Hajime never to return. My skin bumps. What if he doesn't?

A large entry with a crossbeam support and rusted brackets mark the entrance. There is a small *Bonshō*-temple-styled bell with embossed bamboo design for visitors to ring, but the gate is open. Satoshi swings it wide, then steps aside for me to lead. Out of respect, I grasp the suspended wooden beam and ring it once before we enter. Like the larger temple bells, the low, clear tone resonates to carry over a great distance to announce our arrival.

The uneven pebbled path winds like a serpent through dense woodland. The trail is well-tended with the encroaching forest pruned back, but the profuse groundcover tells me it is not well-traveled. I am careful with each step, almost stumbling over a raised stone. Satoshi reaches for my arm to steady me, but I've already found my footing and make a show of not needing his assistance.

Through the trees, I can make out bronze tiles of a roof.

Squinting, I try to pinpoint more details. "I thought this was a clinic. It looks more like a house."

Satoshi shrugs. He would not know of these things any more than I do. The path drops down an incline to swallow both the structure ahead and the street behind. Under the heavy canopy, we enter a hidden world between. Quiet, except for trilling birds and katydids. And something else—a continuous whisper. I tilt to listen. *Water.*

A small river of green appears around the corner. We climb the red wooden footbridge and pause to look over its high rails. Light dapples from above to illuminate the shallow water's gentle flow and its many inhabitants. Butterfly koi, plump and established, meander with winged fins of gold, white and black. It is peaceful here. I watch them but cast a quick glance to Satoshi.

Not only did he understand about Hajime, he kept his word and kept it quiet from his father to save our families' business relationship and spare my humiliation. Then he learns I've married and already carry a child. And still he escorts me. My cheeks warm. Guilt pokes holes in my insolence. "I'm sorry."

Even if I don't want to admit it, I'm grateful for his company and his friendship. I face him. "I am thankful for everything, Satoshi. Even that you are here. And I apologize."

Satoshi's gaze stays fixed to the water, leaving my words to dangle between us. I focus on the painted fish, not sure what else to say.

He leans his forearms on the splintered rail and clasps his hands. "There is no need for an apology, Naoko."

He does not want my apology? Flustered, I place my hands on my hips. "You confuse me with your opinions. I am grateful, but still..."

"Still you wonder *why* I am here?" Satoshi turns to look me in the eyes. "Yes, I understand your confusion. But understand, by you, I have never been confused." He masks a smile. "Even when you were a little girl, I understood your true nature."

My true nature is selfish. I look down, not wanting to face his criticism.

"From time to time, I would see you at company gatherings with your family. You were as beautiful as your mother."

Without raising my chin, I glance up at Okaasan's mention, a fever of curiosity.

"And once, I caught you sneaking *mochi*." He laughs. "Do you remember?"

I straighten and face him; his smile is infectious. "I was sneaking rice cakes?"

"You had one in each fist." He pats his mouth. "And sticky sweet all around from many more. When I scolded, you shoved a cake in my hand and ran away, turning with a smile."

I laugh, but I do not remember.

"The next time I saw you, you were not so little. And now…" Satoshi's gaze lingers.

I look away again. I am sure my cheeks burn red.

Leaning low over the rail, he points. "You see him?"

A fat yellow koi, bigger than the rest, with black markings on his head, swims around in the middle. I nod.

"See how he ignores the others? He jumps and keeps himself in the center even though we drop no food. He reminds me of Rosetsu's painted fish." Satoshi walks again.

"He was persistent," I say, following him to the winding path that now climbs up. I think of the story. Rosetsu found himself near a pond of koi. He watched one fat fish jumping up on the ice to retrieve a fallen treat. He bumped his head, cut his fins and lost many scales trying to nab it but never quit. "Rosetsu marveled at its determination."

Satoshi peers sideways, nodding. "Yes, I'm like Rosetsu and you are—"

"Like the *fish*?" My lip pulls up with my displeasure.

Satoshi laughs and then lowers his chin. "Persistent. I mean to say you are persistent. And like Rosetsu, I admire your efforts. You still have your own mind just like when you stole rice cakes as a child."

My cheeks warm again but my discomfort is short-lived and replaced by curiosity. Ahead, the trees open to a clearing and at the far end sits the one-storied clinic. A planked wood deck wraps the entire face, and the surrounding grounds, while clipped and manicured, lack ornamentation.

Before we reach the entrance, a middle-aged woman approaches with quick steps as though she's been waiting. Her hair is pulled in a tight twist and her shoulders hunch to swallow her neck. The woman's eyes flick from Satoshi to me behind round-rimmed glasses. "I am Housemother Sato. You are Nakamura Naoko?"

I bow. "*Ohayou*, yes, I am Naoko." I open my mouth to say something about Eyako, the midwife who sent me here, or Grandmother, but nothing else comes out. Why is she staring at Satoshi?

"Registration papers? You have them?" The woman waves her empty hand for me to fill, eyes still darting between us.

"Oh, yes. Yes, I do." I retrieve the envelope from my pocket and hold it out.

She snatches it and opens it to count the payment. "Ah... okay, then you may come inside. But not him." She gives another look of confusion to Satoshi, then in haste returns to the clinic, leaving us to bid farewell.

"I can wait at the gate to escort you home, if you like?" Satoshi hands me my small suitcase.

I am tempted but tell him no. "You have done too much

already, and it could be hours," I say, putting on a brave face, then offering a small bow. "Thank you for your kindness, Satoshi. I will not forget it."

He returns the gesture. "Just remember you are the persistent fish, Naoko. And know that I admire your fight."

My fight.

Pregnant and alone, and now with news of a possible delay for Hajime's ship, I fear I may need it.

TWENTY-TWO

America, Present Day

Travel the world to search but return home to find it.

The quote came to mind because I'd been searching the world online for kanji meanings from the comfort of home. If you could call my apartment home. In caring for my father, I had spent most of my time at his place instead of my own. With his passing, I wasn't sure I'd remain in the area. One benefit of journalism is you could write from anywhere.

As though on cue, the crooning of an Italian melody drifted up from the waterway below. Although I lived in the Midwest, the downtown featured a man-made canal with an intended Venetian charm. The city even hired an Old World gondolier to serenade passengers on the weekends. I waved as he passed under my balcony. He tipped his hat without missing a note. It was always the same song, "O Sole Mio." A story of love and sun and beautiful days. For that, there was no translation needed.

Unlike the Japanese symbols I'd been trying to decrypt. Kanji didn't form sounds, so were they word pictures? One had a line with an overlapped rectangle that looked like a square-rigged sail, and the other two marks resembled swords.

I had to restrain myself from contacting Yoshio over the weekend for an update but couldn't stop checking my email for his reply. I'd become obsessed, frustrated at having to wait. Had the kanji been digital in the first place, I could've pasted them into my browser and translated it right away.

I tried various applications to get a translation, but they didn't recognize the symbols. I then searched for online kanji charts only to learn there were eighty thousand in the Japanese vocabulary. Even the shortcut graphic showing just the most common contained over two thousand. I had three kanji and not one probable match.

I rubbed at my eyes, tired from staring at the laptop screen, then checked for Yoshio's email again. Nothing.

With a sip of coffee, I gazed at the crowd walking along the canal below. People crossed the concrete footbridge in droves, like shoals of colorful fish all moving in the same direction.

I never could follow the masses. Instead, I pushed against the current and forged my own lane. Stubborn independence that often got me into trouble. I took another sip of coffee and stifled a laugh. *Like father, like daughter.* By choosing to marry a Japanese girl in the 1950s, Pops exemplified taking "the road less traveled."

An irony, since many misinterpreted Frost's poem. One understanding of the last stanza claims the traveler was reflecting on how, in life, we create fictions, assigning meaning to what was nothing more than a string of random selections. My father crafted stories, but his choices were anything but arbitrary. He elected to marry the Japanese girl, and he chose not to share that part of his life until near the end. They were conscious decisions. And I had to start accepting it.

According to my research, the Affidavit to Marry served as legal proof of eligibility, one step short of a license. It required both parties', a witness's and a notary's signatures, and the family's signed consent if either participant was under the age of eighteen.

The form carried my father's signature, the bride's, an embossed seal and another set of marks next to that. It was either a witness or a parent. But why would the girl's parents grant permission when they hadn't even allowed Pops to stay for tea? Pops signed the letter *Hajime*. Maybe her parents didn't know he was American. What a mess that must have been.

I typed "translate Hajime to English" in my browser. It meant *begin*. Then I selected the sound icon to hear the pronunciation. *"Ha-je-mit."* I typed "James" and repeated the steps. *"Jam-a-se."* I then did the same with "Jimmy," what Pops went by in his youth. *"Ji-me."*

Ji-me. Hajime. It contained his name, but I needed hers. I opened my email and checked again for Yoshio's response. Finding nothing, I reopened the shortcut kanji graphic and got back to work.

Light edged the drawn drapes of Pops's living room window, telling me to hurry before the donation truck arrived. I'd been at his place for hours, loading my car with belongings I wanted to keep and moving the remaining boxes into the garage for easy pickup. I still needed to remove my investigative wall. Then that was it. I'd turn off the lights and close the door of my father's condo for the absolute last time. But I wasn't ready to close out his life.

My father died, but I had become the ghost. It was my restless spirit that lingered and couldn't leave well enough alone. How could I? Like a house, we build foundations from family, and from experience, we construct our walls. But when the ground shifts under your feet as mine had? The father I thought I knew was now someone else. The family I grew up in had expanded to include another. Regardless of your age, that changes you.

It changed me.

Knowing what I did about my father, it must have changed him, too.

I gazed at the oversize map of Japan. Then, with care, I detached the articles of historical interest I'd printed, the snapshots of my father in the navy and the crew, including the picture of his Japanese bride, and placed them all in a large envelope for safekeeping.

I removed the location pins next. And as I did, I retraced my father's life. From the crest of a giant wave to where he slammed into the Great Divide, to the massive anchor at the gate of the base, to a street of blue where he first saw her, his future, and fell in love.

One thumbtack remained. The coastal town of Zushi, where just beyond the bustling marinas and up a small hill sat the traditional house that time forgot.

Had Yoshio forgotten about my request? I'd been patient through the weekend, and though it was early Monday morning here, it was well into the evening in Japan. I dug out my phone, selected email, placed my finger on "compose," but caught sight of his reply. *Finally.*

Dear Tori Kovač,
Wishing you sunshine as the rainy season comes to an end.
I regret my delayed response, but I am happy to provide the following information.

First, regarding the translation you requested. 中村 is the family name Nakamura, which means "middle village" and one of the most common surnames in Japan, much like your Jones or Smith in America.

Concerning the property, please know that, in Japan, addresses are distributed in the order homes are built, and due to Zushi's rapid and continual growth, the postal codes have shifted many times. As you have discovered, the address you provided no longer exists, but according to my source within the Land Ministries department, the home does. I expect to have a copy of the official record with updated address soon.

Please understand, this document of the house will not reveal the family's name if ownership has not changed hands, as full disclosure on existing land and property is not a legal requirement in Japan. However, paying property tax is, and I have made several inquiries. The name might also be obtained through direct contact with the current owners, and I would be happy to inquire on your behalf should you desire an interview and tour of the home.

I look forward to your response.
Wishing you continued health,

Sincerely,
Itō Yoshio
伊藤良夫

I paced the room, my mind three steps ahead. The woman's last name was Nakamura and Yoshio found her house. They might still own it. Or maybe not, but if he approached whoever did, they could offer key information. I smiled to myself, giddy from the idea, but then I was stopped by a thought—an interview. I raked my hand through my hair, leaving it there.

I'd have to present myself under the guise of being interested in the property and its history and use the pseudonym I wrote under. No need to unload my father's past unless it was required. If it were the same family living in that house, would they even talk to me? What would I say to the woman? How would I even begin to explain? Had she told her daughter about Pops?

I dropped my hand and straightened.

While I'd been digging for truths within my father's life, I never expected to confront them, nor had I considered what it meant to mine.

I might find my sister.

Would she look like Pops? I had his thick dark hair that curled in the humidity, and although my eyes weren't as translucent, they were also light blue. Were hers? Unlikely, but she might have his dimpled chin and angular jaw. She might even resemble me.

I paced again. A mindless walk through imagined scenarios and possibilities. While I was playing catch with Pops in the backyard, or running through a sprinkler to dive onto a slip-'n-slide, what was she doing? Did she have birthday parties and go on family road trips? Did she have a good life?

I never went without, because my father as a child often had. As an adult, he'd insisted Mama spend a small fortune every week on groceries. I remembered our pantry, fridge and an extra freezer in the basement always stocked and overflowing because "his" child would never go hungry. She was also Pops's child, so had she? They might be angry at him and resent me. My jaw clenched. They might have good reason to.

Let them. I unpinned the last item from the wall—my father's letter. Unlike my father, who looked up from Blue Street and saw his future in the girl's eyes, I'd stare into hers and hand her the envelope that held my father's past. Then she'd know the regret in his heart by reading his words. Maybe that was what Pops wanted from me.

I turned the letter over in my hands. Had I known what secrets it contained, how they would reshape and color my view of the world, of my *father*, would I have opened it? I opened it now and reread his words. *In loving you, I've never had a single regret. But in losing you? In the how and the why? So many.*

I was still waiting for my father's military records, but those might only offer a confirmation of marriage. I already had the marriage document, the letter, a name and, soon, the address, so what else did I need?

The how and the why.

And that required a ticket. I'd need to go in person, talking over the phone would never work. And if her family no longer owned the house, the new residents might have information that could lead me to them. I had to know. I had to do this for my father and for me, but how? In caring for Pops, I'd lived off my savings and only worked in spurts. A lump formed in my throat as I considered my finances, how bills were stacking up and my savings had dwindled. I couldn't afford to go.

I gazed at my father's letter, reread his words, then fixed on the only word that mattered—*daughter.*

I couldn't afford not to.

TWENTY-THREE

Japan, 1957

The maternity home is large, clean and filled with a pleasant scent. Sandalwood and maybe clove. The incense wafts in a steady stream from a white ceramic burner. Although agreeable, I do not like it. I do not like anything about this place. I am half tempted to turn around and chase after Satoshi. Why did I dismiss his offer to wait?

A young girl not old enough for marriage, but ripe in pregnancy, appears. She is unadorned and with a child's haircut—short with a blunt, heavy fringe. Her plain everyday kimono folds askew under her belly's swell and hangs awkward. Does no one help her dress? She does not say a word, just stares with big, curious eyes.

A high-pitched shriek curdles the air from the rear of the house. I spin to face its direction and find Housemother Sato instead. She walks with hurried steps, wiping hands with fervor on an unhemmed *tenugui* cloth.

"A baby arrives today," she says matter-of-factly. "Jin, take Naoko to the empty room." She snaps to me. "You are to stay there, understand?" She turns without my answer, but barks over her shoulder, "And the baby's father cannot return to visit. Only girls are allowed here."

She thinks Satoshi is the father?

The girl named Jin waves me to follow as shrieks tear through the walls. Another girl, also pregnant, runs through the hall with her arms bursting with towels. We pass two more. They gape in my direction. One, about my age, is just starting to show. The other, like Jin, is ripe and ready, but older.

The cries vibrate my bones. I have never been present during labor. Because Okaasan had a difficult pregnancy, she delivered Kenji in a hospital. My stomach drops. I wish she were here now. I wish they would perform the tests and send me home.

Jin slides the farthest door open and steps aside to allow me through. She closes it and disappears without a word.

The space is small. It is partitioned by a *shoji* rice-paper divider wall. There is a futon. A table. A *sumi-e* painting— a simple stalk with split leaves with seamless shading. The light transitions to dark, evoking a subtle dialogue between the two.

The not-so-silent shouts continue from the next room over.

Moving to the thin cushion, I sit and rub away the tension above my eyes. Since Housemother Sato is busy with the delivery, there is nothing for me to do but wait.

The shrieks grow louder. Lying back, I listen wide-eyed and stare at the exposed ceiling. The bamboo beams weave high above me. I count them two dozen times, thinking of my baby, Okaasan, Hajime. Is he okay? What has become of his ship? Will they encounter additional delays? The screams come faster, even before I get to the last row.

Eyes squeezed shut, I plug my ears with my fingers to mute out the cries. They echo from my hollow insides. My hands cover my face to hide the tears. I just want to know my baby is healthy and go home. I am tired by it all.

The door slides. "Girl. *Girl.*"

Looking over, I see Jin with a food tray. Behind her, peering over her shoulder, is another. She is the one who speaks. Not as young or cute but far from plain. With midlength hair set in big waves and lips painted bright red, she is hard to miss.

Self-conscious, I right myself and wipe at my eyes. Only here for a few hours, and I am crying like the baby they try to deliver.

"Please…" I wave them in, then smooth my shirt to tidy myself.

Jin carries the platter over her protruding belly. Without a word, she bows, then places it in front of me.

"Thank you," I say, but Jin fails to acknowledge me and instead turns on her heel and leaves.

"Do not mind her. She hardly talks," the new girl says. "She is next to deliver and will leave soon, so what does it matter?" Without waiting for an invitation, she plops down beside me and points to the food. "Lemon *Ban-cha* tea to make you feel better, and Housemother Sato had me prepare a special late lunch. See?"

Cold udon noodles and simmered dipping broth make up the meal. "*Arigatō gozaimasu.* I am actually a little hungry." I manage a smile and nod.

"Pretty soon you will always want something. So, eat up before Housemother begins watching every bite." She inspects her nails as she talks, picking at the chipped red polish. "You cannot gain too much, or you will cost too much."

I look up surprised, because I am not staying.

"Do not worry, I always sneak extras and can share. Oh, I am Chiyo. Chiyoko, but I am not a child anymore, am I?" She smiles wide with crowded teeth and pats her small rounded belly.

It is a decent little bump, and if I were to guess I would say she is in her fifth or sixth month, but I am not sure.

"Naoko, right? Yeah, I read your papers. You come from Zushi, well-off family, and..." The smile slides from her face. It's replaced by a nose wrinkle and disdain. "There is talk you have a handsome husband." She huffs.

It does not surprise me that Grandmother informed the midwife of my marriage. It is to protect my reputation as much as our family name. And I am certain she sent Satoshi as an escort to give the impression my husband is Japanese. I paste on a smile and change the subject. "So, who is everyone?"

"Oh..." Chiyo looks up and tallies the home's occupants. "Jin—the simple girl you already met. Aiko—who is like me, into fashion and everything modern. There is Yoko, the one shouting, so she should not count, and Hatsu." She rolls her eyes. "Hatsu is a bore and thinks she is smarter than everyone, so we ignore her."

The mouth is the front gate of all misfortune, so I nod, then raise my bowl and fill mine before I speak and add more.

Chiyo leans close. "You and I will be the last to leave since we are not as far along. So, we will be great friends, yes?"

"Oh..." I swallow fast. *Last to leave?* "No, I am here only for the day, maybe overnight if she can't see me right away. The midwife, Eyako, sent me for tests to make sure my baby is okay. Is she here?"

Chiyo's red lips grimace. "Who's Eyako? Housemother Sato is the only midwife. Maybe you misunderstood."

"Oh, yes, maybe." I sip on my tea, trying not to appear unsettled. It does not matter, as long as the tests confirm my baby is healthy, then I can leave. *Soon.*

Another yell fills the house.

Chiyo keeps talking. She tells me how her family is old-fashioned and boring (everyone is boring to Chiyo), and she does not care if she had to abandon school because she plans to go to Paris or maybe America. I smile, grateful for the company, but confused by her words.

She never mentions her baby.

No midwife comes to check on me. Not Eyako, who Chiyo does not know, or Housemother Sato, who is still busy. The screaming girl, Yoko, has yet to deliver. She has been in labor since my arrival, and we are now into the early night, poor thing. The girls have been my only visitors. One by one they file in to talk and hold vigil.

We sit on the *tatami* mat, all five of us huddled together, all five of us pregnant. I imagine it is quite a sight. I am the new student, popular for the moment while everyone sizes me up. I try to figure them out, too. Who is friendly? Who is most like me? Who should I be careful of? Although, soon, I will leave, so what does it matter?

The cries from the other room go on and on. They cut through the air with a guttural force strong enough to make me cringe.

Housemother Sato's impatience carries through the walls, as well. "Push!" she yells over the cries. "You must push harder!"

I cover my ears. "I do not think I want to give birth."

The girls laugh. Chiyo is the loudest. She thinks everything I say is clever. But they are not all friends who laugh with you, so I keep one eye open just in case.

Chiyo motions to Jin, who sits across from me. "That is you next, Jin. Will we finally hear your muted voice? Will you make even one tiny sound?"

Jin does not respond. Her cheeks are pink from constant embarrassment. Is she even fourteen? Maybe younger. I dare not ask how she came into this condition.

"Oh, yes, she will yell. Maybe louder than us all." Aiko sits between us. She's twenty-three, the oldest, and six and a half months along. She's put together head to toe with gelled and pinned hair like the girls I see hanging around the American base, modern and Western in style. No wonder Chiyo idolizes her. I understand the appeal. Aiko is glamorous, even while pregnant. Although the look accentuates Aiko's delicate features, it highlights Chiyo's lack of them. She tries too hard.

Hatsu, the one Chiyo says is a bore, is eighteen and begins her seventh month. With high cheekbones and long lashes, she is pretty without makeup, which might make Chiyo jealous and explains the contempt. There is also a sadness about her.

Hatsu pats Jin's leg. "Do not worry. I bet your birth is the easiest." She nods, then tucks her thin straight hair behind each ear.

"So, Naoko." Aiko looks to the other girls, then stabs me with her made-up eyes.

I stiffen for an instant, wary of her tone and already aware her beauty resides only on the surface.

She smirks. "We are told you are married and according to Jin he is very *handsome*." She drags the word so Jin feels the impact.

"I did not say that!" Jin takes a big breath, her cheeks flushed.

"What? What, Jin?" Aiko leans in, invading Jin's space,

her hand cupped to her ear. Her playful manner has a biting edge. "Are you saying I am *lying*? I am a liar? I bet you lied that she is married, too."

Jin looks down, frustrated. Lips puckered tight, she shakes her head.

"Thank you, Jin," I say with a smile, trying to lessen Aiko's hold on her and divert their attention. "I think he is handsome, too. And yes, Jin spoke the truth. I am married."

It works, all eyes point in my direction. Jin glances up but looks away.

"I do not believe her, either." Aiko talks to Chiyo as if they deliberated it. Discussed me. "She is no different than the rest of us."

"I *am* married." I shake my head, confused by this turn.

Screaming pulsates through the walls followed by the housemother's yells to push.

"Then why are you here?" Aiko rallies to the others. "Am I right?"

I want to yell. My cheeks burn. I am sure they rival Jin's. "I am here for tests. I had some bleeding, spotting, really, but Eyako, the midwife, thought—"

"No." Chiyo huffs, eyes darting from Aiko to me. "She means, why are you *here*?"

"Ah, maybe she tricked him. Maybe it is not his." Aiko's lips curl.

Before I can protest, another shriek stabs the night, louder and longer. We all look at one another with wide eyes. There is a long pause.

Then we hear the cries of a baby.

I laugh. It is like a bell. If given a soft tap, you will only get a tiny ping. Strike hard and you will receive a strong resounding peal. This baby rings loud. *I am here.* It demands everyone's attention.

My hands cover my smile. For the moment, I have forgotten the accusations and want to run in there to welcome this new little life. Will we all get to hold him? This will be a nice diversion and good practice. I imagine the day my baby arrives and how excited Hajime will be. I picture him with a wide, beaming smile.

"Lungs like the mother," I say, but no one laughs this time, not even Chiyo. My smile drops as my eyes take in the girls' somber expressions. No one looks at me but Hatsu. Her sadness is no longer hidden. She has tears. The skin on my arms bump.

"What is it?" I ask Hatsu, leaning forward. I am answered by silence.

There is a stillness all around.

My head slants to listen.

Why isn't the baby crying?

Everyone is frozen, holding their breath. Hatsu sighs. Is the baby feeding? Little ones enter the world hungry. A sharp tremor climbs my spine. The floor squeaks. Quick footsteps grow loud, then fade. Another creak and then soft cries. These are not from the baby.

They come from the mother.

"Why is Yoko crying?" I ask in a whisper, but my insides scream. *What happened to the baby? What happened to the baby?*

Muffled voices bounce off the walls, then heavy walking. I search each of the girls' faces for answers. Jin studies the floor. Hatsu stares into nothing. Aiko and Chiyo look to one another and then without a word they all stand and move toward the door.

"*Wait.* Chiyo?"

She looks back as the others file out. Her red lips pull up in a sneer. "What do you think, Naoko? We all have handsome husbands we can trick into marriage?" She huffs a breath and slides the door shut behind her.

My heart pounds heavy in my chest. My hands shake. The prickling of tears burns the corners of my eyes. She cannot mean... I must have misunderstood. *Yes, of course I did.* But everything inside me fears the worst.

On all fours, I crawl to the partitioned wall, place my ear close and listen. I listen for the baby. I need to hear this baby.

I listen for its cries over the mother's.

Over my own.

TWENTY-FOUR

Japan, Present Day

Less than a week after Yoshio contacted me about the property and family name, I had boarded a Boeing 777 and headed east. The plane taxied, pushed off and within minutes cut through morning clouds. I settled in for the sixteen-hour flight, but never settled down.

Instead, I watched movies, charted the plane's route with the on-board app and leaned against the window to peer into heaven. Was my father out there watching? Would my trip to Japan make him happy? I knew the way I paid for it wouldn't.

When my father first drove the Caddy home, my mother wasn't convinced of the flashy extravagance, claiming it was too big and expensive. "We already own a reliable car," she'd said, but Pops cited the $7,500 purchase—promoted as GM's crown jewel—as a winning investment. Turned out, he was right.

A 1958 Cadillac Eldorado Biarritz convertible in pristine condition could fetch between seventy and two hundred thousand dollars from serious collectors. I landed somewhere in between. It was more than enough for the trip and expenses, but the guilt was almost more than I could bear.

When they loaded my father's prized Caddy onto the flatbed truck and drove it away, I stood in the drive and cried. I'd sold the one thing of value passed down to me.

But in the end, the chance to restore my father's character, my memories of him, my trust in everything I'd known, and to understand what happened, was worth more.

I just wished I knew what to expect.

Yoshio still waited on property tax records to reveal the homeowner's name, but he'd acquired the home's reassigned address and promised to travel to Zushi and try to arrange a tour and interview. While I was grateful for his help, he didn't share the house numbers, and that small oversight had the journalist in me on high alert. Yoshio—an accredited reporter in his own right—understood the moment I had the information he was out of the mix. And since I didn't write human interest or lifestyle pieces—my best guess was he smelled a story.

It wouldn't be the first time he and I chased after the same one. We'd both been pursuing an interview with the then director general of the IAEA, but I'd landed it. When it was picked up internationally, Yoshio switched sides and wrote an opposing piece to discredit mine that garnered just as much traction.

Not that I blamed Yoshio then or now. Journalism was a game of information, one we both played to make our living. Plus, I only informed him this research was off the record, and I hadn't stated why. I planned to explain more when we met for lunch in Tokyo. I'd just need to be judicious in how I approached him and with what I shared.

Somewhere behind me a baby cried, and with the captain's announcement, the fasten seat belts light came on. My ears popped with the gradual descent. I folded my seat tray, packed up my things, then lifted my window shade.

Narita International Airport was an hour outside of Tokyo, so there were no stunning views of the megacity and, with the hazy sky, no glimpse of Mount Fuji in the horizon. Only snaking water channels, clustered buildings and the characteristic patchwork quilt of land. But instead of the agriculture grid of the Midwest, it resembled a sprawling golf course of sand traps and water hazards. I leaned closer to the double-walled glass, narrowing my eyes to focus. The fields were submerged. I'd thought the rainy season had ended? As we neared, the shallow pools with muddy bottoms came into focus—they were rice paddies. I jostled from turbulence, then gripped the chair handle, braced to land.

After the long flight and with the fourteen-hour time difference, I arrived in Japan exhausted. I turned in my landing card, health form and customs declaration, then stood in long lines to process through immigration where they snapped my photo, collected two fingerprints and an eye scan and recorded my temperature. I was grateful my phone's network was supported, but frustrated by the navigation app—it pointed me toward the trains when my hotel, located on airport grounds for convenience, required a shuttle.

An hour later, finally checked in, I swallowed a sedative and, as soon as my head hit the pillow, prayed for the sweetest of mercies…sleep.

The following morning, I found myself aboard the crowded Narita Express train, but with the spacious seats, spotless interior and beautiful views, the frustrations of extended travel were long forgotten. From my window seat, I took in the rich rural landscape of Chiba Prefecture while traveling to the most populated metropolis in the world—Tokyo.

The high-speed rail cut through marshy fields of rice and expansive rows of green, skirting the edges of sleepy village towns that, according to my travel app, were saturated in history. In one, a Dutch windmill surrounded by acres of seasonal flowers—a goodwill gift from the Netherlands to celebrate four hundred years of trade. Another was the hidden city of Samurai. Had my father stopped to see the castle ruins? Did he walk the secret paths and tour the few remaining homes of those sworn to protect it?

Once we crossed the water, the scenery changed from rural green to city gray with tall, thin buildings all fighting for the same space. Through the distortion of the train's curved glass, they welcomed me with a midwaist bow. I considered myself well-traveled, but nothing I had seen compared to Tokyo— not Chicago in size, nor New York in congestion.

The skyline was spectacular.

I verified my stop on the four-language screen, eyed my luggage, then readied myself for release. Outside, the humidity hit me first, then the realization—*my father had been here.* I was stepping into his stories and onto a literal map. Instead of pinned locations to trace his other life, I'd follow in his footsteps. The skin on my arms bumped.

The restaurant Yoshio selected wasn't more than a few minutes' walk from the station, but I arrived early to take in the sights. In true tourist fashion, I snapped several photos of the station's redbrick exterior and gilded, peaked crown. Then I stepped back and took several more. The architecture, albeit beautiful with the stone facing and decorative reliefs, looked European. It belonged in Italy or Britain, not in the capital of Japan.

Buildings covered every inch of land and people crowded every space between. There were more vending machines than trees, and while the city itself gleamed spotless and trash free, the sky was littered with billboards. I leaned back, trying to imagine their neon at night.

There was intrigue everywhere. An electronic bird chirped as I crossed the street. I stopped, trying to locate the source. A group of rainbow-dressed teens gestured to the device above the crosswalk screen and smiled. I smiled in return. No translation needed.

Electronic menus offered everything from fish cakes to tofu, and when passing street vendors, I learned not to look too long and risk the obligation to taste.

I expected the old to somehow stand with the new, like in Europe, where the Colosseum and the Trevi Fountain rested among boutique hotels and kitschy shops. There, everywhere you turned, the modern world rubbed elbows with its past. You sensed history. Felt it on your skin. Breathed it in the air.

But not in Tokyo.

Tokyo shined brand-new as though it had just stepped out of a traditional bathhouse, its history scrubbed clean.

I just hoped my visit could do the same for my father.

"Hello, Tori? Tori Kovač?"

I spun around to find Yoshio waving just outside the restaurant door. Of course he recognized me. I wasn't hard to miss. First, I had my luggage; also Tokyo, like all of Japan, was almost singularly Japanese. While not uncomfortable in my skin, for the first time I was acutely aware of it. I smoothed out my gray trousers and straightened my short-sleeved button-up. It was hot enough for a sleeveless shell, but shoulders were covered in Japan. "Hello. Yoshio?"

He looked just like his bio pic. Midforties, with a square jaw and a wide, confident grin. I extended my hand, uncertain, but he shook it, then clasped his other hand on top, and shook it again.

"Please... I have a table reserved." He opened the restaurant door, then followed me inside. "Did you enjoy the train ride through the countryside?"

"It was beautiful." I widened my eyes, trying to adjust to the dimmed lighting. "And not as packed as I imagined," I added, slowing so he could lead the way.

"Oh, yes, but you rode on the express. Had you ridden the commuter and traveled during rush hour, it would be a different story. There are so many people, the white-gloved *Oshiya* are hired to push passengers onto the train." He motioned to a short-legged wooden table with red circle floor cushions situated along the far wall. "Away from the sun and noisy street, so we may have comfortable conversation."

I was already uncomfortable. There was a lot riding on this conversation. I tucked my carry-on beside me next to the wall while Yoshio and the hostess spoke in Japanese.

"Please allow me to order for you?" Yoshio turned toward me to ask. "I promise you will not be disappointed. It is a world-famous cuisine."

The street vendor's sample came to mind, the odd texture I'd barely managed to swallow down, but I gave a nod and smiled, anyway, refusing to fall into the stereotypical caricature of the difficult American. I knew better from other travels abroad. In Italy, when I attempted to convey my food preferences, I was told in no uncertain terms by the short Italian cook, "You eat what Mama makes." And that was that.

With tea served and orders taken, we made polite small talk. He inquired if the hotel met my expectations. And I, in turn, asked questions about his remarkable city.

"Did you see Shibuya Crossing's traffic lights?" Yoshio asked. "They all switch red at once. In an instant, people pour onto the road from every direction like glass marbles spilling from a bag."

Discussions of the house in Zushi and its owners, I knew, would have to wait. I'd read that polite conversation was the currency for information in Japan, so I bided my time and played along.

"Renowned Kobe beef with seasoned vegetables," the hostess announced as our food arrived. "Please, try a taste."

Both Yoshio and the server waited for my reaction. One bite and I understood the accolades. My eyes went wide as the meat melted on my tongue and I nodded, giving the server the assurance needed before she turned to go.

Yoshio laughed, then whispered as though divulging a secret, "The delicate flavor is due to the pampering. The cattle are given beer to drink and receive a daily massage."

I laughed, too, but I was also becoming impatient. "Yoshio, I can't thank you enough for your hospitality. I'm so excited to be here and anxious to dig into my research. You said you had news?"

"I do, yes. Although municipalities maintain separate property registries for taxation purposes, I was able to confirm the home's ownership."

I leaned in. "Is it them? The Nakamura family?"

His smile widened. "It is. Records show the Nakamura family has paid taxes on both the home and the property for many generations."

"This is amazing, thank you." It had to be the woman's family. *I found them, Pops.*

"I have a photo, if you would like to see?" He opened his messenger bag and produced an image.

I drank it in. The large, multisquared one-story traditional home was both simple and sophisticated with exposed bamboo frames, white paneled walls and a tile gable roof. It was situated high on a hill of green but blended into the surrounding elements as if they were one. That was what I'd expected of Japan—exquisite Old World charm and timeless elegance. "Wow." It was the best I could do.

Yoshio gave a satisfied nod at my oversimplified reaction, eyed my almost-empty tea and refilled it while he spoke. "It's built in the traditional *Sukiya* style, known for the natural and unpretentious aesthetic. The lack of superficial decoration stresses internal self-improvement while the wide eaves create peaceful shadows in which one can reflect. Teahouses were first built in this design. See how the roof and tiles curve?" He motioned to the photograph. "It's to confuse evil spirits."

"Because they never travel in straight lines." I laughed even as tears welled up. "It's beautiful." And matched every description of the house in my father's tea story.

"Can you tell me of this article you plan to write? You mentioned it was on the history of the home, but have you found something interesting on the Nakamura family?" He gave a tight-lipped smile and held it too long.

The small hairs on my arms rose. "Have they agreed to the tour and interview?"

"Will you not share your intent?"

"Will you not reveal if the interview is arranged?" I jutted my chin.

The thin smile all but vanished from Yoshio's face. "Although you have traveled all this way, I'm sorry, Tori, but I do not think an interview will be possible."

My heart dropped, then quickened. "I don't understand. Are they worried I'm going to write some exposé about them? Because I won't."

"That is what you write."

"I write fact-based reports on large companies."

"That expose people of power and their controversial activities."

"That enlighten the public, who have a right to know. As do you, Yoshio." I threw my shoulders back, incensed. "So, forgive me, but now I really don't understand. Here I thought you were trying to scoop me and you're actually protecting them?"

He gave a blasé shrug. "I am simply curious of your intent."

"I knew it." I huffed an exasperated breath. "You're *screening* me because you're curious if there's a story."

"Of course." He set his chopsticks on their rest, dabbed his mouth with the warm towel and leaned back. "And is there one?" He arched a brow.

I shifted my legs and gave the photo of the house another glance. I wanted the address, so I'd have to tell him some of my father's story, but there was no way to guess his reaction to such a contentious subject. "What if I told you I wasn't planning on writing an article about the house or the family at all?"

"I would find myself very curious indeed."

"May I ask a somewhat delicate question first?" With his nod, I took a deep breath, and debated where to begin. I had his full attention. I didn't want to squander it. "The American Occupation ended when?"

"In 1952."

"Yes, 1952." Pops served from 1954 to 1957. Only two years after. "From what I've read, there were many children born between US servicemen and Japanese women, as well as many marriages. Is this a correct assessment?"

"There were some marriages, yes, but they were not common and many of the babies did not survive."

"Didn't survive?" My shoulders fell. "Because of…?"

"Sickness, for one, and lack of adequate care." Yoshio lowered his voice, leaned into the table. "Tori, the women who were in this situation found themselves alone in the world and unable to properly care for their children. Society shunned both the mother and child. Remember, Japan is rooted in ancient tradition and it was so soon after the war."

"War or not, it was deplorable to shun them, don't you agree?"

"Quite. But you must also agree that America didn't welcome the Japanese brides their young men brought home so soon after the disbandment of Japanese internment camps and the war."

My mind spun back to American history: to articles and photos of Japanese war brides accused of trapping soldiers, and the Japanese Americans forced to give up their homes and businesses and imprisoned like criminals. I gave up my seat of judgment, realizing my country, just like his, had no right to sit there.

Yoshio nodded. "So, you see? It isn't one country or culture that holds responsibility, but one race. The human one. And such deep wounds of war take more than a single lifetime to heal. It takes many. Even now, in such modern times, it would be a difficult situation in Japan."

"And yet, so many babies." I gave a small smile, attempting levity.

"Yes, yes, because as I said, we are human, aren't we? Even with war, there's always *that*." He gave a soft laugh.

We smiled at each other, again on common ground.

"So." Yoshio leaned closer. "Have I passed *your* screening? Will you now share with me the story's intent? What did you learn about this family?"

His words stretched between us and hung there a moment.

"Yoshio, there isn't a story. At least, not one I plan to pub-

lish." I turned my teacup. Turned it back. "I want the interview for personal reasons. Matters that pertain to *my* family."
I gambled with the vague comment. "Do you understand?"

Yoshio's brows twitched, then his eyes dropped as though in
thought. After a moment, he lifted them to mine and gave a
nod. "Yes. I think I do. Thank you for sharing this with me."

I smiled, grateful I wouldn't need to clarify. "And who
knows, seeing the house, meeting a family member, it might
be enough to answer my questions without asking any that
could cause embarrassment. That's why the interview is so
important."

His face wilted. "While I am happy to provide you with
this photo and the address, as I said before, an interview might
not be possible."

My heart stilled. "They declined?"

"No. There is no one living in the home to ask."

I sat back, stunned. "It's empty?"

"Yes, according to the neighbors, the home has sat empty
for some time, but as you can see in the photo, the property
is well maintained."

I gazed at the beautiful landscape in the picture. "So, who's
taking care of it?"

"I wondered that, as well. Forgive my curiosity, but I did
some research of my own. I found several Nakamura families in Kanagawa Prefecture, but only one with such deep
generational roots in Zushi. A family with a large, privately
owned business located in nearby Yokohama called NTC.
Although they have added other industries, they made their
fortune dealing sundries and tea."

I took a sip of my own, then asked, "What does NTC
stand for?"

"The Nakamura Trading Company."

My eyes widened, and I stifled a laugh. *A merchant king of empire.*

I smiled at Yoshio through the sudden swell of emotion because it was more than fitting, it was perfect. It was where my father's story started. Pops said, "Nothing good ever came from tea," but just then, something had.

TWENTY-FIVE

Japan, 1957

I sit up with a sharp gasp, choked by morning's persistent light. I push hair from my sweaty forehead, taking in my surroundings. A small table, a *sumi-e* ink painting hung beside the window and my suitcase below it. I blink in recognition. I am at the Bamboo Maternity Home, where a baby was born last night.

Where a baby may have died.

Everything floods back to awaken my sleepy mind. The girls. Young Jin, the silent one. Aiko, snide but fashionable. Hatsu, the girl with the sad eyes. And Chiyo, so loud and bold. Her words wash over me. *What do you think? We all have husbands we can trick into marriage?* My hands cover my belly, the miniswell that has begun to take shape.

I glance at the wall, wishing I could see through it. Is Yoko

still here? Does she rest? So far, my stay here has been anything but restful. I listen for her but only the bustling of the
house makes noise from the other direction.

No one woke me.

Dressing in a simple skirt and blouse, I hurry to get ready. I
do not plan on staying, so I return everything to my bag and
place it by the bed. I have yet to see Housemother Sato about
my tests. My stomach twists because I am not sure I want to.

I slide my door open and stick my head out. Voices carry
from the front of the house. Each step I take is quiet but with
purpose. I am here for assurance. That is all. Then I will go
home and return to Hajime.

Hatsu washes dishes in the kitchen, while Aiko argues with
the woman who runs the clinic. Only Jin still eats. She looks
over, so I offer a soft smile.

"Ohayou," I say to everyone.

Housemother Sato spins from Aiko, her wire-rimmed
glasses low on her wide, flat nose. "Ah, you missed the morning meal. There is no fish but grab a bowl and fill up with
miso. You are lucky anything is left."

"So, I do not eat, but she does?" Aiko spits the words, in-
dignant. "If we do not prepare, we do not partake. That is
the rule." She presses a manicured hand to the counter and
leans in to challenge the housemother. Her belly hangs low,
giving her back a slight sway.

Housemother Sato waves a stubby finger in the air. "She
eats because she is new and is just learning the rules. Go on,
Naoko. Take the bowl."

I pick one up, darting eyes to Aiko. She folds her arms and
watches me pour the soybean soup. It is watered down and
runny, but the fermented smell excites starved taste buds. I sit
across from Jin, trying to ignore Aiko's pretty scowl.

"And when's payment coming, Aiko?" Housemother rests

her hands on pronounced hips and shifts her weight to her back leg. "You're lucky you are not on the street. Eh?" She twists back to Hatsu, who is putting the dried dishes away. "Find Chiyo, then come help me clean Yoko's room."

My back straightens. Yoko is gone?

"Chiyo!" Hatsu hurries off in search of her.

"Housemother Sato?" My voice shakes. I want to ask about the girl, her baby, but instead focus on why I am here, so I can leave. "The tests?"

Housemother turns, wiping hands on her apron, and regards me with indifference. "What tests?"

I stare at her, incredulous. "We are to do tests today before I go home, remember?"

Her nostrils twitch. "Tomorrow."

"Tomorrow? But my husband is expecting me tonight." My pulse quickens, knowing if he is delayed he will not be expecting me at all. But I can't stay until tomorrow.

She shakes her head and shoos my words with waving hands. "I must discuss this husband with your grandmother, and you need to rest." Her chin lowers. "Tomorrow. Now eat." She turns from me and leaves the room.

She's meeting with Grandmother? And what does she mean "this husband"? What is there to deliberate? Aiko slides my bowl of *miso* away. I glance up. Her lined eyes narrow to slits.

"The rule is, if you do not help prepare the meal, you do not eat the meal." Aiko lifts the bowl and slurps.

"You did not prepare it, either." Jin's words are whispered as light as a feather.

Both Aiko and I gape in surprise. Jin stares at her rice, braced for Aiko's response.

"See? I knew you had a voice. Too bad you don't know when to use it." She gulps more into her mouth and leans close to Jin's ear. "What? You have nothing more to say? Did you forget your words again?"

Aiko grins at me and dumps the rest in the sink. I keep quiet, but do not glance away. She flashes her eyebrows, then leaves us alone at the table. Jin looks up and slides her bowl over.

I wave my hand to protest. "No, Jin, it's okay. I can wait."

She shakes her head and pushes it farther. "No, I have had enough."

"I have had enough of Aiko," I say, making Jin laugh.

"She is jealous because you have a husband and her boyfriend is married." She motions to the bowl. "Please..."

I nod, grateful for the offer, and accept. My stomach rumbles as it is filled. I deliberate on Jin's words and debate my own. I must know about the baby. To hear what I fear spoken out loud. "Is Yoko in another room?"

"She has left."

I stop eating and lean in. I lower my voice to a mere whisper. A soft tap to a quiet bell will still produce an answer. "What about the baby?"

She wets her lips and sinks her chin low. "Gone."

"Gone?" The word rings hollow. I tap again. "Do you mean...?"

"I want this baby gone, too."

Okaasan's words flood my mind: *There is a midwife Grandmother knows, who deals with such things.* My insides seize. This is *not* a maternity clinic. It is a dwelling to hide the mothers and deal with unwanted babies.

What has Grandmother done? What did she tell my father? Does he know? Is he in agreement? And what of Satoshi? No, he didn't understand any more than me.

A long, shuddering sigh escapes. Everyone here is unwed and young. Based on Aiko's and Chiyo's stories, does that mean they also all carry babies of mixed blood? These children are regarded as less because they don't have pure Japanese blood racing through their veins. This makes mine race faster and boil.

Poor Yoko. That poor baby.

My attention falls to Jin's ballooning belly. If ignorance is the mother of suspicion, what is truth when it confirms it? "How old are you, Jin?"

Her timid eyes flick to mine. "I turned thirteen last month."

My heart drops. She is not much older than Kenji. I am almost eighteen, just five years older, but five years is the difference between adolescence and womanhood. Five years is a lifetime.

With a breath, I force the question. "What of the father?"

Her lips move but no words come out. She chews them instead and shakes her head. Her eyes drift to seeing nothing.

I slide closer and lean in. "You can trust me, Jin."

"I said no," she says, barely audible. Her fingers open and close into a fist. "My parents blame me even after I told them." She shrugs. "That is why I choose silence. What is the point of speaking if no one will listen?"

"I'm listening." I despise the pity in my voice. It festers inside, threatening to surge.

Jin stares at her belly as if she reads my thoughts. Her mouth twitches to a grimace. "My mother says this baby is my punishment. It won't let go. It will be born so I am forced to look upon its mocking pale face and devil eyes at least once."

I straighten and speak with authority. "He was a devil for what he did to you, Jin, not because he was a foreigner. And your baby is innocent."

Her eyes grow moist, but not one tear falls. "You are lucky, Naoko. You have a suitable husband, so you will have a proper baby." She wrinkles her forehead. "So, why *are* you here?"

I don't answer because I will not be for long.

★ ★ ★

Housemother Sato has left, and everyone takes advantage of her absence. Aiko fixes Chiyo's hair in their room, and they cackle on about music and movies while Jin sits alone and reads. Hatsu is the only one who attends to her chores.

I plot my escape.

Walking past Hatsu, I nod, and slide the main door open, saying I need some fresh air. I slip my shoes on, peek back at Hatsu and wander out to the front deck. The sun's bright smile causes me to squint and grimace. A beautiful day after such a dismal night and morning.

To not raise suspicion, I pluck a sprig from an evergreen shrub, then walk around as if I am curious about the grounds.

Kicking at the grass, I edge toward the path that led me here. The air tickles my nose, but I hold back the sneeze. One glance over my shoulder tells me my performance is without an audience, so I make my exit.

I am going home.

Together, Hajime and I can figure out how to approach Father and what to do about Kenji. Grandmother is a different story. I have some wise words of my own to share.

My small bag sits packed in my room, but I do not need it. It is all replaceable. This baby is not. I quicken my pace as my mind churns over recent events. Jin's question stabs at its center. "Why are you here?" This explains Housemother Sato's confusion when meeting Satoshi. Why she needs to discuss things with Grandmother. But what does it change?

I do not plan on staying to find out.

My ankle rocks from stepping wrong on the narrow path, so I slow to be more careful. Stretched tree limbs hold hands high above to form a canopy. Concealed in its shade and away from that house, I breathe easier for the first time. The footbridge should be ahead, then just a little farther to the gate.

Easing myself down the shallow embankment, my foot slides, and I skid a step before grabbing hold of a branch to keep steady. The sound of trickling water fills the air, and I spot the bridge.

In crossing, I peer over at the butterfly koi to catch my breath. My mind spins. I am not a girl kept in a box. The real world is all around me—I see how it works, I know there is injustice. Even with my family. There is Father, a retired military man with strong views; Obaachan, opinionated and set in her ways; and Taro, who is blinded by nationalism.

But me? I fall in love, marry and carry a child of an American despite it all.

I may be of my own mind like Father, but my heart comes from Okaasan. Otherwise, how could I have given it to Hajime? My chest heaves a slow pained breath.

I need to get out of here.

Ahead, I see the tall bamboo fence with black ties. I lift the wooden latch and, with an open palm, push on the gate, but it doesn't budge. I shove it again. Nothing. It only sways to absorb my weight.

My pulse quickens. *Why won't it open?* Using my side, I press my hip onto it, but it is stuck and only bends more. Panic creeps over me. I scan the height of the fence, then the length. Should I follow it? Climb over? With both hands, I grip the crossbeams in the gate's construction and rattle it hard, willing it to open and let me free.

"That will not work."

I spin. It is Hatsu. "You followed me?"

She steps into clear view. "Housemother Sato secures the latch from the other side when she leaves." She ambles toward me. "Normally the lock is on the inside."

I step back, my lips parted in shock.

"She says it is to keep squatters out, but everyone knows it is to hold us until full payments are made."

Without thinking, I move past her and edge along the bamboo fence, pushing branches to clear a path.

"Wait. Naoko, where are you going?"

I am not staying here. "The fence cannot encircle the entire property, can it?" The ground crunches under my sandals with barbed brush biting my calves.

Hatsu follows. The nicks itch, so I scratch as she catches up. With her behind, I push forward. She holds a hand high to block her cheeks from the branches' snapback. The tangled brush grows thicker with every step.

Voices carry from over the fence. People are walking down the street. My heart jumps. We both stop and stare at the bamboo fence. I close an eye and press the other to the bound stalks, trying to see in between. Two monks. Older. And one in a long white robe.

"Hello?" I try to sound calm. "Hello? Excuse me?"

The talking stops. Something is mumbled and then, "Yes, hello?"

"Hello?" Hatsu steps closer, pressing her face beside mine. "Can you tell us if the fence goes on much farther? We are trying to follow it out."

"Out where?" the monk asks.

"Out there," I say, hoping we are closer than we thought. "We are trying to get to the other side."

A pause precedes the serious tone. "My children, you *are* on the other side."

Hatsu and I look at each other. What does that mean? They are leaving?

I smack my hand on the fence. "Wait! Please! Excuse me?"

"Forget it, Naoko. Unless it is Brother Daigan, those monks will not help us. Not even the nuns, who work and live in the adjoining community. They know what this place is, and as long as we are *inside*, they cannot interfere. Those are the rules."

I straighten and brave the words. "What *is* this place, Hatsu? Say it. I want to hear it said out loud."

She studies me. "Housemother provides a service for those who waited too long to get an abortion." She shrugs. "It is a business. That's all." With that, she pushes through the brush again back the way we came.

This time I follow her. "I want my baby, Hatsu."

She whirls around with a huff. "Yoko wanted her baby, too. She planned on sneaking away to that home before she delivered, then leaving it on the steps. But she went into labor early."

"What home?"

Hatsu flips stray hair from her forehead and rolls her eyes. She turns, seemingly tired of my questions.

I pull her shoulder. "Hatsu, what home?"

"The one for mixed-blood children." Again, she walks, pushing branches to the side. "It is over in Oiso. Some lady takes them in, I do not know. I hear they are overcrowded and overrun with sickness, so how is that better?"

I step high to avoid the bramble canes at my feet, my mind spinning her words into something I can understand. Branches bite my cheek. I shove them aside undeterred. "Yoko's baby was mixed?"

"Yes. I found out he was a boy. He did have some lungs, didn't he?" she says. "He cried so loud."

And then he was silent. I stop. "Hatsu."

She faces me, and I can see the pain in her pinched expression. She knows I am going to ask. What I must know. What I must hear.

My heart beats louder than my words. "What did the housemother *do* to Yoko's baby?"

Her mouth draws into a tight line.

I step closer, eyes locked on to hers. "Tell me."

She looks away, forcing a hard breath. "She holds their noses."

I stare at her, stricken, gripped by the enormity of this truth.

"Housemother Sato does it as soon as they are born. It's usually before they sneak in a breath, but that one had fight."

My hand covers my mouth. Fresh tears build along my lashes. The spirit only enters the body with the first cry of life. Her baby cried. *I heard him.* He announced his arrival to the universe. An image plays in my mind of the little boy's body squirming in vain while his mother watches him suffocate.

She is a monster. *A monster.* And what does that make Obaachan? My father? I heave, leaning on the fence, unable to catch my breath. Every thought screams with sadness and anger. No one will touch my baby! From this moment on, my family is no more. Only Hajime. Only Kenji. Only this child who will cry out with mighty lungs.

Hatsu steps closer, her voice is steady, but detached. "She is a woman of business, Naoko. She profits from those like us by providing a hidden place to avoid shame and family dishonor. And for those who cannot afford her fees, she charges only once. For delivery and disposal."

Disposal.

The word is a knife, puncturing my resolve. My tears fall of their own will. I wipe under my nose and sniff. "Why doesn't she take the babies to this home you mention? That must have occurred to her as a better option."

Her brows furrow. "How many sick babies do you think that home can keep? And why?" Again, she resumes her walk.

"No one wants them. Where will they live when they grow up? *If* they grow up. With so many unwanted babies who will only starve or die in the streets, Housemother Sato feels this is more humane for mother and child." She steps from the woods back onto the main path and turns to me. "And maybe it is."

Stepping out, I shake my head. "It is not more humane." I don't say more. My instinct is to push through the thick forest in the other direction, regardless of the burrs. This fence ends somewhere.

"I am married, Hatsu." My voice shakes. I smooth the fabric over my miniswell, picking off twigs that snare it. "And my husband supports me. We have our own house, and we want this child."

"So, you do not live with his family?" Her eyebrows knit together, and her mouth drops open from my obvious slip of information.

My breath falters at her words. When married, the wife moves into the husband's family home. Of course, with Hajime, that is not possible.

Her lips curl to a semismile. "That was not your husband, was it?"

I only stare.

"Come on." She waves me forward, turning with a step. "I need to show you something."

TWENTY-SIX

Japan, 1957

I trudge behind Hatsu in silence toward the maternity home, but she leads me around it. We walk a narrow, overgrown foot trail that winds through the woods in the other direction. This property is endless.

In life, the wise make their own heaven while the fool complains of hell, but I think both are inevitable, and both are temporary. Heaven is not some place for your future spirit to rest. It is finding happiness in your current state. And likewise, there are no locks on the gates of hell; it is only suffering and only for a time.

But there is a lock on the gate that keeps me here.

With every step, the woods darken. The tree limbs no longer playfully hold hands. One binds the other to choke out the light. Sweat forms in tiny beads and collects in my hair even without the sun's direct touch. I am tired and want to go home. Or rather, I want to go to my home with Hajime.

"Hatsu…" I stop, using the back of my wrist to wipe my brow. "Hatsu, wait."

She pivots, her seventh-month belly cradled in one hand, her other holding a found walking stick. A branch snaps behind me. We both spin to glance along the trail.

Nothing.

Another rustling stirs a brown-eared bulbul bird, and it scolds us with a screech.

Hatsu rolls her eyes and sighs. "Jin, I know you are following us. I saw you leave the house. Just come on, Housemother will not be gone long." She continues forward.

I wait. Sure enough, Jin appears from the brush. Our eyes meet, and she shrugs.

"Come on!" Hatsu yells from farther up.

We begin again. A prickle travels the length of my spine. At the base of a large tree sits a small *Jizō* statue. He is the Buddhist monk known in life for helping babies, and now, in spirit, helps their souls. It is said that *mizuko*, water children—the stillborn, miscarried and aborted—cannot cross over alone. A *Jizō* wears baby's clothing, a bright red bib and cap, to show their connection. This one has none.

Ahead, up a slight embankment, Hatsu stops. It is bright before her and the long, narrow shadows cascade off her back as though the light repels them. Jin and I climb and stand beside her. A soft breeze cools the skin, and far below in an open field, large wild red blooms decorate unkempt grasses as far as I can see. It is beautiful, but misleading.

My heart stutters.

I shield my eyes and squint to focus.

The red blooms are not flowers, after all. They are markers like the one at the tree. They are *Jizō* statues in babies' clothing.

And there are *hundreds*.

The concrete statues with fabric bibs and caps of red position every which way, with no set order. Some sit in neat rows, some climb the embankment, others face one another in silent judgment. From the clearing's mouth, the earth bleeds red, and I peer into death's pregnant, bloated belly.

Hatsu's mournful eyes glance at Jin, then find mine. "This is their resting place. Their bodies come here."

So many.

The three of us stand in silence, staring at the tiny markers, all three of us carrying babies of our own. Hatsu with a seventh-month belly. Jin rounding nine. And me, around four.

Tears fall hot with anger. My nostrils flare with a resolute breath. "My baby will not end up here alone and waiting to cross."

"No. Mixed-blood babies won't. At least not *here*." Hatsu points to a vast orchard of small strange trees. She steps down the embankment and walks in its direction, careful to maneuver around the tiny *Jizō* figures.

We follow. I cannot help but stare at their stone faces as we pass. All different. This monk has chubby cheeks and closed eyes in meditation. That one scowls angry. Another sad with furrowed brows. Its bib has blown sideways from a distant wind. Some have only faces carved in ordinary boulders. No bonnets to keep them warm, and the bibs tie near the narrowed tops.

The grove of trees holds its own secrets. We walk between them. They are not like any I have seen before. Dark gray peeling bark and leaves like spindled fingers reach to us as we pass. Some climb the sky and tower above. Most skim the top of my head.

"They are nonnative trees from the West like the nonnative babies that rest among them. This is where those babies lie. This is their paradise." Hatsu stops and points to a fresh pile of dirt just ahead. "Yoko's baby…"

My eyes widen with understanding. I spin to take in the landscape. Small mounds are scattered everywhere. So many. There are no *Jizō* statues to help them cross. They are not even respected in death.

They are left unmarked and alone, forgotten.

I clutch my belly as if to reassure the little soul within. She will not spend a single minute bound alone in darkness. Housemother Sato will not condemn my baby's spirit to an eternity of hellish unrest.

The cry of Yoko's little baby fills my mind. The sound of his sudden silence breaks my heart. His tiny trapped spirit calls out. Warm tears fall one after the other from eyes that have seen too much.

I have had all I can take. I storm to the high grass and start picking through for wildflowers, ripping them up near the roots. I will make markers for their graves.

"Where are you going?" Hatsu calls to me.

"I have not forgotten," I yell to the trees, to the lost souls that cry within them. "You will cross. You all will find peace!" Disturbed bees buzz in my ears, but I wave them away, and keep reaching down, pulling and risking their sting.

"Naoko." Jin, or maybe Hatsu, calls my name.

I drop to my knees, my fingers clutching bundles of grass, flowers and weeds. Everything comes out, everything rips up and everything spills. Why did Okaasan have to die? Why? *"Why?"* My cries fall from trembling lips. *This is all too much.*

Squatting with feet flat, I lean back and tug harder on a stubborn root. Both hands wrap its thick stalk, and I rock back, pulling and screaming half sentences. "I have had it. It is all too much." I refasten my grip and jerk harder. "I just want Hajime. Why, Haha?" Another yank. "Why?" The root snaps, and I fall over with the jolt. My back hits the ground first, then my head, and I stay there and sob.

My fist slams the earth over and over, then I dig nails into the dirt. All I can do is cry. Haha, Yoko's baby, all these babies. How could Grandmother send me here? How could Father let her? Why hasn't Hajime come?

Someone sits beside me and strokes my hair. I lift my head, and Hatsu gathers me in her arms. I press my head to her belly; her hands continue to stroke my hair, and I weep.

I weep for these babies. For mine. For me.

But this will be the last time.

I will weep no more.

Hatsu and Jin help me gather bouquets of wildflowers for Yoko's baby. We find a stone and create a colorful wreath to place at its base. Before, I heard her baby cry, and now, I hear his spirit. With our makeshift *Jizō* statue, he crosses over. He finds peace.

"I hope you never get angry at me." Jin swishes a long-stemmed knotweed cane. A hidden smile colors her tone.

I look up from my mindless grass-plucking and stifle a laugh. Hatsu smiles and shakes her head. The three of us sit together under a giant unfamiliar tree. The largest one in the field.

I share with Hatsu and Jin the loss of my mother and how she brought me her treasured *shiromuku* to wear on my wedding day. Although Hatsu suspects Satoshi is not my husband, I am not ready to confirm this, but I do not deny it, either. Let them still believe my husband is Japanese. Sudden trust brings sudden regret, so I am careful, even among new and cherished friends.

"Where do all the *Jizō* statues come from?" I ask Hatsu.

She sets the small garland she weaves on her protruding belly and thinks. "The families either send them over or Housemother Sato charges them for their purchase."

"But not for these babies. They are forgotten even in death." I look over to the unmarked mounds.

"No, not these babies." Hatsu continues her flower wreath. "Even if the families send money, Housemother Sato does not use it for them, so their spirits stay trapped."

"She is a demon midwife." Anger drives my words. "Jin, I know you say you want your baby gone, but that…" I point to her midsection. "That is a living baby. And regardless of the pain that surrounds its conception, the baby is innocent. Maybe we can find the orphan home?" I shift my position, so I am sitting up on my knees, and take a deep breath to gain momentum and draw courage. "I say we make a pact."

"A pact?" Hatsu's eyes narrow. "What kind of pact?"

With another breath, I look to each of them. "First, I say we band together as guardians of these forgotten mixed-race babies. Each mound needs a *Jizō* statue—even if only homemade—so every little spirit may cross. Not one is trapped or forgotten. And second…"

I grab a hand from each and hold them. "Let us pledge a guardianship to our unborn babies. We are charged with their care in life and in death. Let us swear here and now that Housemother Sato's bony fingers of death will *never* stop their breaths and leave their spirits waiting. That if we cannot keep our babies or keep them safe, we must seek Brother Daigan, the guardian monk of babies, and allow him to take them with honor and respect to a better home."

Hatsu and Jin exchange dubious glances but then link their hands together, so the three of us form a circle.

Hatsu squeezes my hand. "I promise."

"Me, too," says Jin.

"Good, then we have a solemn pact. Now we just need an escape plan."

For the first time since losing Okaasan, I have strength and a renewed sense of direction. I cannot change the world that we live in, but through the example of Okaasan's courageous heart, I can change the lives of a few.

TWENTY-SEVEN

Japan, Present Day

Before Yoshio and I parted ways at the restaurant, he gave me the photo of the traditional house in Zushi along with its new address. I tried to pay for lunch to thank him, but he wouldn't let me.

I found myself rather optimistic as I waited to board the Yokosuka line. Finally, there was progress. The home was registered under the name of Nakamura, the same name translated from my father's marriage affidavit, and although the house stood empty, we'd found it, and there was a strong possibility the Nakamura Trading Company in Yokohama, with founding members from Zushi, were the owners.

It had to be them. A trading company fit Pops's story.

I checked my JR rail pass, then looked around for signs to verify if I stood in the right queue. The day's excitement and lingering jet lag made navigating the congested stations that much more confusing.

As was the white-gloved employee pointing at trains as they pulled in and out from the platform. He wasn't one of the white-gloved people-pushers Yoshio described earlier, and although Pops once mentioned employees leading calisthenics on the platforms, the man wasn't exercising. No one even watched him except for me.

I studied the odd LED blue lights attached to the overhang above him. Were those cameras that broadcast to a traffic control center?

"Suicide lights."

I spun around to find a young man, blond, freckled and maybe all of twenty. He had the telltale buzz haircut of the military. He gestured to where I'd been looking. "Those lights, ma'am. They're supposed to calm the crowds and keep people from leaping in front of the trains."

"Really?" I stepped back from the painted line, the only barrier before the open tracks below. I'd just read an exposé on LED streetlights and how they doubled skin cancer risks. Why did Japan believe they were calming? I gave a half smile of disbelief. "Are you sure?"

"To be honest, I don't rightly know." He shrugged with a sheepish smile. "I only arrived from North Carolina this week and my designated buddy over there..." He motioned to his friend flirting with a group of Japanese girls. "Well, he could be pulling my leg." They waved him over. "Welcome to Japan, I guess, right?" He laughed, then trotted off to join them.

He was no different than I imagined my father had been. Young, perhaps away from home for the first time, and craving adventure. Watching them laugh and posture, I pictured the young man, older and married, telling his children tales of Japan and the girls he met there. I smiled. I hoped his story had a happy ending.

I hoped mine did, too.

I glanced again at my rail pass, then back to the pointing train employee. "Excuse me." I stepped toward him while motioning to my queue. "Is that the line for Yokosuka line?"

"Yo-kas-ka?" he asked without stopping his pointing gestures.

I'd been mispronouncing the city name. The *o* was short, and the *u* was silent. "Yes, is that the line for the Yo-kas-ka train?"

"*Hai*, Yokosuka." He smiled, then gave a nod toward my line.

I found most Japanese could understand basic English, but few attempted to speak it. Instead, I was met with smiles, nods and gestures. I returned to my line with confidence and searched the Nakamura Trading Company website while I waited.

On a page designated "Company Heritage," it explained how the family had a long history of importing manufactured goods and exporting raw materials but had recently expanded into industry. The distribution center was located near the harbor and the company was headquartered in the Minato Mirai 21 business district, a short hike from the Yokohama station. I considered calling them to set up an appointment, but my train arrived.

The doors opened, and as a mass of people poured out, we wove between them and crowded in. Unlike the nonstop express train from Narita Airport with roomy, upholstered seats, the Yokosuka line was a standard commuter. I unfolded one of the plastic outer wall chairs but offered it to an older man who came in after me. Signs posted the rules in pictures. No smoking, eating or talking on your phone, and the elderly, injured and pregnant had priority.

Clutching the strap above my head, I leaned into my arm, and caught the curious stare of the woman beside me, the man crammed behind her and the eyes of several others. I looked around to find everyone but me faced the outer walls, so I turned. There weren't any signs about that.

The Yokosuka line, built over a century ago, traveled along the southwestern flank of the Miura Peninsula alongside Tokyo Bay. Not that I could see any of it. From the inside aisle, all I saw were people, and since I looked down, all I saw were shoes. I found mine were the only sandals.

I planned to check into my hotel in Zushi, get a good night's rest and formulate a plan, but as we approached Yokohama, where the Nakamura Trading Company was located, I gripped the handle of my carry-on luggage and found myself edging toward the door.

Yokohama was the second largest city by population in Japan, and its train station was a city unto itself. Both the east and west entrances connected to an underground shopping district that spanned up several levels and linked to surrounding skyscrapers.

Once outside, I typed the Nakamura Trading Company address into my navigation app, and was on my way. I still didn't have a plan. Had I landed an interview I would've prepared questions, but this was nothing short of an impromptu visit to gather information. I had one goal. Learn if the Nakamura family who founded the Nakamura Trading Company was the same family that owned the traditional home. And if they were, ask if they were available for a meeting. If Yoshio had already contacted them, I'd explain we were working together.

The wheels of my carry-on luggage rumbled along the pavement as I walked toward Tokyo Bay. It was the largest industrialized area in Japan, and as I neared the water, the scent of development—sulfur and smog—saturated the air. And yet, everywhere you looked, there were signs for tourist fishing excursions.

I had covered this in my article on the Fukushima nuclear incident. How, after the quake and subsequent tsunami in 2011, damaged reactors had continued to seep radioactive cesium into the ocean, collapsing the area's fishing industry. And because of that, Tokyo Bay—once considered too polluted for the seafood trade—celebrated a resurgence.

I crossed another busy street and dabbed at my forehead. The short walk to the central business district turned into a thirty-minute hike under an unforgiving sun, but as I turned the final corner, it eclipsed behind the Yokohama Landmark Tower. The fourth tallest structure in all of Japan housed a five-star hotel, restaurants and shops, and various corporations, including the Nakamura Trading Company.

I picked up my pace.

As I cut across the garden plaza toward the mirrored door, I remembered the walk alongside my father to the hospital entrance in Ohio. How we strolled side by side, and our exaggerated reflections bounded forward to greet us. And as I neared, just as before, my reflection shrank in size, slowed in gait, and I faced my current self.

Only this time, I stood alone.

The vaulted lobby opened into an expansive five-story shopping mall with roman columns and two grand staircases on either side. People bustled along, but quietly, and the wheels of my carry-on warbling across the tile floor were anything but. I retracted the handle and opted to carry it to the elevators. According to the Landmark Tower directory, the Nakamura Trading Company was on the thirty-seventh floor.

I stepped inside, punched 3 and 7 on the digital screen and tried to calm my nerves with each passing floor. The family might be there, and I wasn't really prepared.

I knew from research that Western culture had seeped into Eastern traditions and muddied the waters after the war. And how Americans were a curiosity for the young and an abomination for the old after the Occupation. And how babies born between Japanese women and American military were often abandoned just as Yoshio had said.

But *my* father abandoning a child?

Pops?

It was a horrid thought. A sickening idea. I could *not* believe it was true, but what if the Nakamura family did? What would I say? I'm sorry? I had my father's letter of regret, money from the sale of his Caddy, and while I needed answers, I had none to give.

My stomach dropped as the elevator slowed, then opened.

Straight across the hall was a frosted glass wall with the etched logo of the Nakamura Trading Company. My heart pounded my chest as I walked across the small lobby. I'm here, I'm going. *Wish me luck, Pops.* I opened the door.

Stark white walls, red upholstered chairs and a curved desk with a vase of oversize white flowers.

The receptionist, smartly dressed in an ivory blouse and thick-rimmed glasses, smiled as I approached. "Hello. May I help you?"

English. I gave a smile of relief. "Hello, I don't have an appointment, but I was hoping to speak with someone within the Nakamura family?"

She glanced at my luggage. "Are you wishing to establish an account with us? We have several salespeople available."

She placed a finger on her headset as though to call for one of them.

"No, thank you. I'm actually wanting to speak with a member of the family regarding a traditional home they own. Well, I believe they own it. It's registered under the Nakamura name, and I was hoping to get some information."

"Are you in real estate?"

My heart jumped; she didn't even blink. "I'm actually a journalist. Is someone in the Nakamura family here I could speak to? Or set up an appointment with?" I found myself glancing over her shoulder for someone in the back offices.

"I am afraid Mr. Nakamura is away on extended business, and he is the only founding family member." She pushed up her glasses.

The only? "Do you know when he might be back? I would only take a few minutes of his time." I held my smile.

"I would be happy to give Mr. Nakamura your information when he returns."

"Of course." She wasn't going to tell me. I reached into my pocket for a business card and handed it to her. "Do you mind if I take a company brochure?"

"Please..." She motioned to the stand that held them.

I took one and looked it over as I made my way to the door. It repeated some of the information I found on the website, but this included several photos of family members who held the title of CEO over the years, including the original founder, a man named Nakamura Kenji, who currently held the position. He was maybe sixty with a slight tinge of gray bordering his widow's peak. It listed Nakamura Taro as his brother and former CEO. Just as I was about to ask if he was available, I noticed the dates below his name. He had passed several years ago.

I turned back and held the brochure up. "Thank you again."

★ ★ ★

After I checked into my hotel, I hiked to Zushi Beach, needing a moment to wander and think. The Miura Peninsula, known for its broad and rugged coastline, was beautiful and Zushi was no exception. Since it was early evening, the swimming crowds had thinned, leaving only a rash of red umbrellas to speckle the still-fevered sand. I chatted with Yoshio on the phone as I walked barefoot through the wide, rolling swells that lapped the shore.

I'd amused him by my impromptu visit to the Nakamura Trading Company. "That is why I love Americans, always so inventive."

"You mean impatient." I smiled, knowing he was just being polite.

"*Hai.*" Another laugh.

"What do you think about actually writing a feature on NTC in *Tokyo Times*?" I stopped and toed the wet, gray sand. Although technically a volcanic beach, Zushi's wasn't the characteristic black. "You think you could arrange that?"

"I thought this wasn't a real article, that it was of a personal matter?"

"Well, yes, that's true." I switched the phone to my other ear and continued walking—a slow, hand-in-the-pocket type of stride. "That part is personal, but I was reading through the company's brochure, and the history is interesting. They survived the Great Kanto Earthquake and somehow managed through the postwar depression. And the eldest son, Taro, took over after the father died, but he died prematurely, leaving everything in the hands of the youngest son."

"The current Mr. Nakamura?"

"Yes, and although he's in his sixties now, when he took control, he was the youngest CEO in NTC's history and has by far proven to be the most innovative. So what do you think? Worth a story in the paper?"

"I think you are feeling guilty for your American cowboy antics."

"*Grateful.* I'm feeling grateful that my cowboy antics confirmed they are in fact the same family. Plus, it gives them a real reason to call us back. So how about you use your Japanese charm to wrangle them a real story?"

"I knew you thought I was charming."

I stopped and laughed, letting the cool water surge over my feet. I blinked toward the setting sun, low and sleepy, decided that I was sleepy, too, and turned to head back the way I'd come. "Oh, wow."

"What is it?"

High hills hugged the peninsula coast, untouched islands dotted the horizon and, in the gray-pink haze of an early-evening sky, Mount Fuji floated majestically between them. "Mount Fuji."

"Ah, yes, Mount Fuji," Yoshio said. "You are wise to climb it, but a fool to do it twice."

"And that is why I love the Japanese, always so insightful," I said, teasing him with his earlier words.

He laughed. "Actually, it was on my tea bag."

"Of course it was." I smiled. I planned to head back to my hotel, but after we hung up, I found myself sitting on the beach, watching the sun feather the sky in pinks and reds across a restless ocean. I was just as restless. Had my father been here? Did he see this, too? I didn't find a photo of Mount Fuji among the pictures, but I had to assume he had.

I dug out a small piece of driftwood and drew the kanji lines that meant Nakamura in the sand. They owned the house. And although a tour of the property hadn't been arranged, I wasn't leaving Japan without seeing it.

I had the address, so I would find it in the morning.

TWENTY-EIGHT

Japan, 1957

Hatsu, Jin and I sit on the steps of the maternity home's wraparound deck to enjoy the cool evening breeze. Summer packs its flowered bags in hues of mossy green in preparation for its upcoming departure.

We do, too.

Safe from prying ears, we talk of nothing else. But I grow impatient.

It has been two days since we made our pact to help the lost spirits cross over by making *Jizō* statues. Two days since we pledged to seek out Brother Daigan if we cannot keep our babies or keep them safe. Two days of checking the gate's lock and searching the grounds for ways to escape.

It has been two days too long.

So far, we search in circles. I sigh with a substantial breath. It can't be helped. I have a heavy heart.

"What's wrong?" Hatsu asks with a nudge.

I glance over my shoulder to ensure Aiko and Chiyo are not in earshot, then lean in. "It's just we search these grounds several times a day and every time we find only more of the same. We know there is a front path between the locked gate and the maternity home and a back path to where the spirit babies wait. But the rest is an infinite wood surrounded by an endless fence."

"That's why we keep looking." Hatsu lowers her chin.

"But there's too much ground to cover and too little time to search. Housemother's only gone for quick errands, so we mostly cover the same ground." I sit tall to gather my thoughts. "We're like the three blind monks who are asked to describe an elephant. Their perception is only a fraction of the whole."

Jin and Hatsu glance at one another.

Hatsu crosses her arms. "But what else can we do? We cannot just walk out a locked gate."

My eyes pop wide. My heart thrums. *Why not?*

It is as if I climbed on the elephant's back and can see what is obvious. "What if we could?" I ask, looking between them. "The surest way out is the way we came in, right?" I take a deep breath, excited by this revelation. "We do not need to find another exit, we just need to find the key! We know she keeps it in her room, right?"

Hatsu's eyes round, then cloud with worry. "But how? If the key is here, Housemother is, too, and she is always nearby. When would we have the opportunity?"

"We *create* one." I am giddy with possibility. "When they are inside, we draw them out to the clearing. You and Jin create a commotion of some sort."

"Like what?" Jin asks with nervous eyes darting from me to Hatsu.

I shrug. "I don't know, pretend you are hurt or fighting, something. Anything. Who cares? Just create a big distraction. Then I will go in screaming like crazy for help." I almost laugh. This could work. "When they come out. I will stay in and find the key. It is simple."

"It is risky." Hatsu shakes her head.

"It is a bigger risk not to try." I sit tall, resolute, hoping my spine is strong enough to support their doubts. "I *know* I can find it. Then we can leave. I cannot stay here."

"Stay here? What is this whispering, hmm?"

We startle and turn. Housemother stands at the door with suspicious eyes behind wire-rimmed glasses. Her unlit cigarette dangles from her starburst mouth.

I paste on a smile. "Oh, we were just discussing friends and family, right?" I face Hatsu and Jin and speak as if continuing a previous conversation. "And like I said, Kiko may not even know I am *staying here.*" I raise my brows to encourage their participation.

Hatsu plays along. "Kiko is your sister?"

"Like a sister. She is my childhood friend."

Satisfied, Housemother pushes the brass lighter's thumb button and inhales deeply.

"Or at least she was." My chin drops, no longer pretending. "At my mother's funeral, she still held her grudge and refused to look at me. My grandmother would say, prosperity grows friends, adversity proves them."

Hatsu, sitting between us, bumps my shoulder, then Jin's. "Then we are the *best* of friends. The three monkeys."

We smile at one another. This is what we call ourselves. Hatsu is the one who covers her sad eyes—she's seen too much. I am the one who covers her ears—haunted by the cries of spirit babies. And Jin is the silent one, who speaks quiet and with few words.

Housemother harrumphs from the doorway. "You are three *foolish* monkeys grasping at the moon's reflection to believe such nonsense. You arrived alone, and you will leave alone." She stifles a smoke-filled laugh.

I cover my ears. "Did you say something? Sorry, I cannot hear you."

Hatsu covers her eyes. "Who said that?"

Jin covers her mouth and giggles.

Housemother rolls her eyes and blows out another smoke-filled breath.

We wait out her presence with everyday conversation. "Do you miss school?" I ask.

"Not math club," Hatsu says with a laugh. "Why do our parents get to choose our club? Then we are stuck our entire school career." She says under her breath, "If my baby wants to switch, I will fight the teachers to allow the change."

"What would you have chosen?" Jin asks.

"Mmm…" Hatsu crinkles her nose. "Calligraphy—no, dance. What about you?"

Jin does not say; she just shrugs, staring at the blade of grass she rolls between her stained thumb and finger. She isn't feeling well. I am sure Housemother's toxic smoke cloud isn't helping.

"I am in dance," I say, fanning the air, then quietly add, "Maybe my little bird will be a dancer, too."

Hatsu straightens. "Did you study *Nihon Buyō*?"

"We studied many traditional styles, but my favorite was *Nō Mai*. Do you know it? The *Mai* masks are magical. The carved *hinoki* wood allows light and shadow to alter the expression."

From inside, Aiko and Chiyo yell in disagreement.

"Quiet down!" Housemother yells, then clucks her tongue with a long exhale of smoke.

I keep talking. "*Mai* means to dance, but only after one's studied do you move."

"I am going to move everyone into locked quarters," Housemother gripes when something inside crashes. "Maybe three days' punishment for all, eh?" She spins on her heels to scold the girls inside.

My heart jumps. "We need to begin our own performance before she makes good on her threat. *Please*. We are the three wise monkeys, right? Let us not act like the three blind monks."

My pulse races wild. I nod. They nod.

"Good, go! Before we lose the chance," I say, pushing at Hatsu's shoulder. She grabs Jin by the arm and they run to the middle of the clearing.

We stare at one another.

"Did you say Jin fell?" I yell out, hoping to spur them on.

"Yes, Jin fell. She hurt herself!" Hatsu shouts back with cupped hands. Hatsu gently shoves her arm. Jin just stares. When Jin still doesn't respond, she prods her again.

We both motion for her to fall. When she finally does Hatsu almost laughs until Jin shrills an ear-piercing screech. Hatsu and I both look at her, surprised.

Jin smiles.

"I will get help!" I yell, not wanting to lose momentum, but trying not to laugh. I wave for them to keep going. Hatsu shouts of blood and broken bones while Jin sits folded over, pretending an injury with fake cries. Together they create quite a commotion.

"Housemother, come quick!" I howl, running inside. I find them in the kitchen. "Jin is hurt!"

"Now what?" Housemother lifts her arms in exasperation.

Aiko smirks, drying the dish she was forced to wash. Chiyo laughs and hands her another.

I point to the door. "She's hurt and—"

Another piercing scream from Jin. This one even louder. She is quite an impressive actress! Maybe her club was theater?

"You must hurry, Hatsu said blood and bones! She is in so much pain, her mouth spits fire!" I say, not to be outdone in performance.

Another cry, but this one's from Hatsu. It inspires fast movement from all three. Aiko, Chiyo and Housemother dash for the door.

I stay behind.

My heart thuds so loud it almost drowns the commotion. As soon as they are out of sight, I dash into Housemother's room to search for the key. Two futons positioned side by side rest center against the back wall. Low tables on either side give balance. A single *sumi-e* painting hangs on the facing wall.

I slide the storage door and peer inside. Linens, clothes, boxes for personal items. Everything is neat and orderly. Pushing my hand between them produces no key.

Heart racing, I peek out and listen. Jin's screams curdle in my ears. Housemother's voice matches in volume, but not in pitch.

Their voices draw closer!

I look left and right, then fix my eyes on the decorative box on the side table. I open it and stir the contents. No key.

There is another scream and Housemother's voice barking for Chiyo to help propels faster movement. Kneeling, I feel between the futon and *tatami* mat. Nothing. Their voices gain in volume. My heart slams my ribs. Where, where, *where*?

I turn, eyeing the room.

Something glints from under the box I had just looked in.

The space underneath created by its feet. I lift the entire box and there it is. A single key.

"Naoko!" Jin cries out.

I spring to my feet, stepping from Housemother's room just as they step through the door.

My brows push down. Jin has one arm slung over Chiyo's shoulder, the other over Hatsu's. Aiko and Housemother prod them forward from the back. "What's wrong?"

Did she hurt herself for real?

Jin's hunched, crying and...

Wet.

"What has happened?" My voice shakes as I step close to help. Did she learn of our plan? Did she strike out at poor Jin?

Housemother barks, "Chiyo, help Jin to the back. Aiko, help me with these two so they do not interfere." She grabs Hatsu by the arm and yanks, throwing her off balance.

Aiko snatches my arm, but I push back and scream for an answer. "What has happened? Tell me!"

Aiko clamps her fingers around my wrist and pulls at me to follow. I lash out, but stumble into Hatsu as they shove us together in my room. The door is shut and locked as we pull and push against it.

"Housemother!" I continue to shout and smack the door, yanking at the handle. Then cast my eyes to Hatsu.

She folds to the floor, hands wrapped around her pregnant belly.

"Hatsu?"

Footsteps pound the hall and scurry about the house. Housemother dictates orders. It's like my first night here. My chest constricts. Jin weeps from the other room. Another scream.

"*Hatsu*, please, what happened?" I say, crouching.

She lifts her chin. Tears fall one after the other. "We were

performing just like we had discussed, but Jin stopped acting." Hatsu's sad eyes meet mine. "Her water broke, Naoko."

So has my heart.

"We waited too long." Hatsu's face crumbles. She covers
it with her hands.

I slide down beside her, lean onto her shoulder as she shakes
with frustrated sobs and cover my mouth to silence my own.
What do we do? What can we do?

Scrambling to the wall, I yell to Jin. "We are here with
you! You are so brave, everything will be okay."

Hatsu joins me. "You are doing great, Jin!"

"Please let us help!" We beg through tears. "Please let us—"

"Shut up in there!" Housemother shouts, then screams for
Aiko to find more towels.

Jin's screams pulsate through the wall followed by Housemother's yells *not* to push. Something is wrong. We listen to
Jin cry with Housemother's explanation of breech. We hold
our breath in silence. We wait.

The screams grow louder. I listen wide-eyed and find myself staring at the exposed ceiling again. The bamboo beams
weave back and forth high above and I count them two dozen
times. Twenty-two, twenty-three... The screams come faster,
even before I get to the last row.

As night falls, we sit in the dark and watch their frantic
shadows through the *shoji* rice-paper divider wall. An unnerv-
ing performance scarier than the demons of *Nō* plays. Even
with closed eyes, their silhouettes remain.

With Housemother's words to push, we thank the heavens
and add our own to encourage her.

"You can do it, Jin!" we yell. "Everything is okay!"

And after a short time, near the final push, our reassurance returns to begging. "*Please*, Housemother! Let her baby

live! Please have mercy—we can take the baby to the orphan home!"

Jin screams. A final push.

The floor creaks. Quick footsteps grow loud, then fade. Another floor creak and then soft cries. These are not from the baby or the mother.

They are ours.

We cry because Jin's baby never did.

As the moon tiptoes across the sky, silence swallows our tears. The busy footsteps cease, and night's symphony of singing insects resumes.

The house settles for sleep.

This nightmare will haunt me.

"Jin," I whisper, still sitting beside the *shoji* dividing wall, "can you hear me?"

She does not answer. *"Jin!" Will she ever speak again?* I press my open hand against the wall. "Jin, your baby will cross over warm and loved. Hatsu and I will use our best clothing to dress your baby's *Jizō* statue."

"We promise. We will not forget," Hatsu says beside me.

Tears stream down my cheeks. "And we will never forget you. Friends forever. We are the three monkeys, remember?"

Jin's small hand matches mine from the other side. We sit connected, a million things unsaid. Then, after a beat, her fingers and their long shadows trail away into the light. Another image burned into memory.

Tears fall, but like Jin, I refuse their voice. Instead, I hold a blank expression, like the enchanted wooden *Mai Nō* masks. Our play did not have a happy ending, only an end. I look around the room, choked by unbearable emotion. Small table. *Sumi-e* ink painting. My luggage in the corner. I am *still* at the Bamboo Maternity Home. Where another baby was born.

Where another baby has died.

I have come full circle and it spins to make me dizzy. With a deep breath and new determination, I face Hatsu, then dig in my pocket to produce the key.

Our eyes lock.

We are leaving.

TWENTY-NINE

Japan, 1957

The sun is slow to make its way across the late-afternoon sky, and the impatient moon encroaches the same space. As I teeter on the uneven path below, they wink at me through the trees' thick canopy of green.

While Hatsu finishes her chores, I wander to collect my thoughts, calm my nerves and piece together what happened with Jin. Like Yoko, Jin wasn't there in the morning. Did her parents come and get her? Did Aiko and Chiyo help House-mother move her to another place? We don't know, and they won't say. I wish I had remained awake. Instead, I slipped into the abyss, then woke to find Hatsu beside me on the floor and our door opened.

Since we have the key, we planned to leave first thing. But Housemother's watchful eye has been on us every time we are together. And when we are not, she uses spies. Even now, Chiyo follows me.

I step up onto the weather-worn footbridge with one hand outstretched for balance. "Hello, *Ganko*, stubborn fish, remember me?" I drop a sliver of sweet roll filled with red bean paste. A blur of yellow and black disrupts the water. He fights the others to guarantee his share and doesn't quit until he wins. I like him. Satoshi was right. The fattened carp and I are both the same. *Persistent.*

Has Satoshi wondered why I haven't returned? Did he inquire of my whereabouts and did Grandmother again mislead him? Has Hajime come back from the Taiwan Straits to meet a similar fate? Or does destiny keep him there still delayed?

My hand rubs reassurance to the emerging bump at my middle. Housemother says it should be bigger, but without proper health care and such meager meals, I am lucky she grows at all. My baby fights. So, I do.

Usually when a woman is ready to give birth, she leaves her husband's home and travels back to her kin. My family sent me here. I imagine Grandmother has told Father I am better off in a maternity home. My guess is she left out what kind. He would trust Grandmother, as a woman, to know best. She has created a lie with more than feet; it has sprouted scandalous wings and flown beyond my forgiving reach. To imagine my father knows otherwise is the foot of a lighthouse. *Dark.*

Hatsu cannot go home, and it is risky to return to my house in the outcast village. With Hajime detained, my family, knowing I have run off, may look for me there and drag us back. I cradle my belly and think words of comfort: *It is okay, Little Bird, I'll keep you safe. The monastery will not turn us away.*

I sigh, knowing all my worries are sparrow's tears. A small thing compared to the larger picture. This baby. Hatsu's baby. The pact we made. The one we will keep.

We named Jin's baby Minori, which means Truth. One of many I contend with. Because we leave tonight, Hatsu and I cannot keep our promise to Jin. At least, not right away. I swear to the heavens I will return to honor my word and her baby's spirit. She won't wait long.

"Oh? More?" I crumble the last bits of sweet roll and toss them in the stream's eddy, then continue my walk, listening for Chiyo's noisy feet. She follows me everywhere.

In many ways, I must become like these koi, able to accommodate myself to the water. I should not force my direction. Instead, I should enter the current's swirl and flow out the current's spin. This is how we will manage our escape.

Ahead, the tall gate looms, the same one we check every day. Housemother Sato's rusty lock hangs crooked. With a tug, I confirm its hold. Still locked. I smile. It won't be for long.

Hatsu holds the key. One of us must. As a safeguard we keep exchanging it.

If I had it with me now, the temptation to free myself would not prompt me to take it. Not at Hatsu and her baby's expense. How could I? We get one shot to leave, and we are taking it together.

I listen as monks and nuns walk by for their daily outing. The same monks and nuns who will not intervene while we are on this side of the fence but are obligated to help once we cross over.

I close one eye and widen the other to see them through the high bamboo stalks. Blurs of brown and rust. I imagine Brother Daigan is among them in a robe of white, his pleasant face and rounded cheeks pushed high from a smile, causing eyes to curve like two crescent moons. I pretend he can hear my secret thoughts. *Not yet, Brother Daigan. I'm not ready*

to hand over my baby. I still have a chance to keep her. We will es-
cape tonight!

We only have one additional obstacle to overcome. Housemother's rat spies. Still, they are not as bad as Grandmother's
foxes. At least we know who and where they are.

With new girls arriving at the maternity home next week,
Housemother Sato allows Hatsu to share my room. She need
not worry about space, because after we escape tonight, there
will be plenty. Night pulls down its shade, but we lie side by
side awake, listening to the bush crickets' three-pulse song.

"I know everyone's stories," I say just above a whisper.
"How Aiko learned her boyfriend already had a family and
left her, how Chiyo got pregnant on purpose only to have him
deny the baby was his and how Jin suffered such an ordeal."
I angle my head to face Hatsu. "But I do not know yours."

She stares at the bamboo beams in the ceiling with the thin
blanket tucked under her pointed chin. Her hair fans out in
different directions. She blinks in silence.

Restless, I shift to cover my exposed feet. "Satoshi, the boy
that escorted me here, is not my husband. You were right to
suspect as much." I curl my toes, uncomfortable with the subject, but share my story in hopes she will tell me hers. "But
I did not intentionally mislead anyone. It was just easier to
allow the confusion."

"So, you are not actually married?" She angles her head
to meet my eyes, then sighs. "I almost hoped it were true."

"No, I am." I roll to my side and prop myself up with an
elbow. "Satoshi, the boy everyone saw, was my family's choice
as match. He's honorable, but I had already given my heart to
another." A soft smile fills my face. "I call him Hajime, but his
real name is Jimmy. Jimmy Kovač—he's an American sailor.
Right now his ship sits in the Taiwan Straits. He does not

know where I am or what has happened. We married before he left." I share how my mother gave me the choice, how my choice split my family and how I ended up here.

Hatsu moves to her side so we face one another, and our whispers have less distance to travel. "But your mother, she came to your wedding? She actually was there?"

"It was such a magical ceremony, Hatsu." I share the details and relive them with every spoken word. How the lanterns twinkled from the trees like a thousand glowing fireflies. How handsome Hajime looked in his crisp white uniform. How his promise of love expressed so many times sustains me even now. I also tell her of the morning after. How I shared the possibility of our baby.

"And he was happy?" Her chin dips almost unbelieving.

My smile beams. "Yes, yes. Although..." I rock my head from side to side. "At first, surprised."

We laugh.

Hatsu swivels again onto her back and pushes out a long, dreamy breath. "Your baby will have such a good story of how she came into this world. One of want and love and a beautiful wedding." She sighs again. "I wish my baby could have the same."

I wet my lips, debating if I should dare the question again, then brave it. "What *is* your baby's story, Hatsu?"

She bites her lips, then loosens them. "You know how Chiyo and Aiko share similar tales? Even Yoko. Almost everyone's stories are the same."

"Except for Jin's," I say.

"Yes, except for Jin's." Her expression falls flat and shadows. "And except for mine."

My hand covers my mouth.

"Jin is somewhat lucky. At least she only battled one demon."

My heart drops. Tears follow. Their moisture floods my fingertips and seeps through. That is why she took Jin under her wing. Stood up for her. Mothered her. I didn't know. I didn't guess. *I didn't ask.*

"So, you see?" Her lips pull high and her shaky words fight to work through them. "When my child asks his or her new parents, 'Why was I given away? Where did I come from?' they won't have a wedding story of magical lights and forbidden love to share. They will have nothing to offer, because with a story as horrible as mine, I have nothing to leave."

"You leave *life*, Hatsu." I slide close, wrapping her in my arms and whisper through tears. "You leave life."

Hatsu managed to drift off to sleep. Small snores rattle with each inhale. I have been listening to her for hours and thinking of her words. What was said. What was not.

Such ugly truth.

The word *rape* in English is ugly. It is a pucker of lips, then a hard pop. But the word, ugly or not, almost always connects to a bigger story.

Hatsu is right. I am blessed to have a good one. That is why Hatsu will now share mine. She can leave her baby a story of love and a magical wedding, too.

I shift to my other side and stare at the wall, thinking of my husband. *Husband.* My fingers drum my belly, causing featherlike flutters inside. So light, if I was not statue still, I would miss them. Hajime is missing them. I am missing him. He consumes my thoughts. *Is he safe? Does he think of me? Is he working hard to return?*

I stretch with a lazy yawn, trying to keep tired eyes open, and roll over to find Hatsu awake and staring back. Her expression asks if it is time. I blink, look up and listen for the answer.

My erratic heart.

The heaters buzz, and there are soft irregular taps like tiny pebbles on the rust tiled roof. *It's raining?* I breathe in deep to taste the air. It is chilled and damp. Kerosene taints the flavor, which means Housemother Sato has left the wick too high again. My eyes wheel back to Hatsu, and I nod. The house sleeps.

It is time we did not.

We are dressed in layers to steer off the evening chill and to keep our bags light and manageable. Hatsu has the key.

"Let's go," I whisper.

Hatsu lifts her bag and takes careful steps. The floorboards groan from the disturbance. We pause to allow night's normal rhythm to reestablish before trying again. Then, moving as one, we both lift a foot and set them down together. This is tedious but assures we are not detected. *Has the distance to the door always been so great?* The floor creaks under our weight near the entrance, threatening to snitch to Housemother and her spies.

We freeze with wide eyes and listen.

No one stirs.

Maybe it is lucky that it rains. The light patter helps hide our maneuvers. I pry open the front door. My heart thuds in my chest. *We are so close.* On the deck, I wait for Hatsu to move through, then close it with measured care. I resist the urge to run.

Dark clouds hide the moon and most of its available light. I didn't plan for the weather and we're without a lantern. A man surprised is half-beaten. I'm vigilant with each step, knowing our babies' lives are at stake.

"Come on," I whisper, taking her hand. The ground is slick, and with her protruding belly out front, she is already unbalanced. Steady rain falls from low clouds to accumulate on the grass. Our hems soak from their moisture as we dart through the clearing toward the narrow path.

The overhead canopy of branches acts as an umbrella and offers some sanctuary from the downpour. I stretch a drenched foot in front to test its placement before committing, but puddles collect where the ground dips. I can't see them and only know they are there after I have stepped through. "Be careful," I warn Hatsu. The air bites, leaving me to shiver regardless of my many layers.

With the rain, it is taking us twice as long to make the trip.

The slight embankment in front of us worries me most. The rain makes it slippery. I drop our bags to take Hatsu's hand. "You go first. Hold on to me for support."

She rotates, positions backward and steps down. Then she swings her leg to find stable footing. The rain pelts my back. Trickles run down my neck to add stinging cold. I lean all my weight back to assure my hold. She takes another step, digs that foot in and moves farther still, almost beyond my reach.

"Oh!" My head jerks back.

Hatsu cries from the sudden release and fall.

Housemother Sato screams. "You both try and sneak away, eh?" She yanks my hair again, so I stumble into her. "I knew you were up to no good!"

I flail with wild hands, trying to remove hers.

"Without payment? I don't think so." She shakes me, so I shriek.

"Run, Hatsu! *Run!*"

"Naoko!"

"Run!" I yell again, and swat at Housemother. She pulls back, causing imbalance as I claw for release.

She drags me. With every labored step, the distance between me and the gate increases. I thrash and fight even as hair rips from root, grateful Hatsu has the key, and pray she makes the gate.

I kick. I scream. I *bite*.

"Ahhh!" Housemother releases me, reeling back in pain, cursing.

I whirl around and run, the taste of blood in my mouth. The taste of freedom slipping away. She's right at my heel, screaming threats in rage.

My heart beats like a rabbit so I move like one. Fast steps with only one desire. Out. I'm not fast, but I can maybe out-maneuver her and hide. I veer from the familiar path into the dense, overgrown woods.

Fallen twigs snap from my weight. Wet, tall grass whips at my calves. I push through barbed brush and keep going. Farther and farther I go to create distance until her shouts fall away, and I'm exhausted to the bone.

Out of breath, I stop, hunched over to listen.

Inconsistent drips filter through branches to land on the forest floor. It's almost musical as they strike one leaf to the next, a hollow chord progression of *tap-tap-tap* followed by a pause before changing tempo and key.

But that is all I hear.

No distant shouts. No nearby footsteps. No one follows me here.

But where is *here*? Where is Hatsu? I pray she is far away and safe.

I blink in the darkness and look back the way I came. I ran erratic, a hare stalked as prey, going left, right, maybe in circles.

Sliding to the ground, I clutch my knees, having lost all sense of direction and losing hope. Snares have scratched my legs. Raised thin lines wind up my calves and swell in ser-pentine welts. They itch. I don't care.

I dig at the earth, squeezing mud and twigs between my fingers, and gently rock. I will stay put, wait out their search—if they still search—then move at first light.

We left so late, morning can't be long off, but with this rain, it's hard to tell. Rain drips from drenched hair and beads along my cheeks. It collects on my lashes, blurs tear-filled eyes. Open, shut…open, shut. I squint, trying to keep focus.

When I am with others, it is almost bearable, but here in the blackest of nights alone? Grief and worry are intolerable. My head spins in the past, remembering my choices, choices made for me… *If I had chosen different would Okaasan be here? Would I? But then what of my baby?*

My head pounds from memories. The muscles around my chest pinch so I cannot take a full breath. Instead, I focus on my hands. The twig I hold and strip of bark. When it is bone-bare, I drop it and claim another to begin peeling off its many layers. I imagine Hatsu at the monastery, warm, fed and looked after. This thought warms my heart and sustains me as I wait…

Minutes. Hours. And then…morning clouds drip red with the long-awaited yawn of light.

My mind scrambles to reacclimate my surroundings. What did I say to Jin and Hatsu? "We know there's a front path between the locked gate and the maternity home and a back path to where the spirit babies wait. But the rest is an infinite wood surrounded by an endless fence."

I lift my chin. *That is it.*

I just need to climb back up on the elephant and march him in a straight line. Eventually, I will either find myself back on a path or blocked by the fence. Either way, one of them will lead me to the gate.

Pressing muddy hands to soaked thighs, I rock myself up. I pivot left, then right, then spin back the way I'd come. A thousand-*ri* journey begins with one step, and so what does it matter? This way will do. A stiff step forward. Then another. Then one more.

With outstretched arms, I push through. I catch on an exposed root, stumble over mud and moss, but don't quite fall. It goes on and on this way. Under the rain-soaked canopy and in drenched clothes, I am in another world. Damp earth fills my nose. A dank chill rattles my teeth. And it is quiet. Except for squabbling birds and something more—*something familiar*. I cock my head.

Water.

The stream! Am I so close? My heart propels stiff legs to up their pace. To move faster. To get out! Stepping high over brush, I snap back branches with still-wet leaves, dart to where the woodland clears and find the small river. I accommodate myself to the water, remembering its direction. I chase the current's swirl to flow out the current's spin. And there it is.

The red footbridge. The path. And what it leads to...the gate.

I run.

I run along the uneven stone path as it winds through dense woodland. I run until I spy golden slats of tall bamboo. I run and slam open palms into its crossbeam gate.

It sways from impact but jolts me back.

I push again.

Again.

Leaning close, I peer through. My stomach drops. A new lock hangs crooked on the other side. Housemother's not here. Has she gone to look for Hatsu? Me? Maybe she believes I've gone.

My emotions run feral. First, calm in a suspended disbelief. How did this happen? How did Housemother know? Then anger rips through me with a quiet scream. I strike the gate again and again, then spin on my heels to find Chiyo's smug smile.

"Hello, Naoko."

I now understand how Housemother knew. How she found us so quick. We were foolish to underestimate her.

Spies and foxes are no match for such a rat.

THIRTY

Japan, 1957–58

In the course of a month, the forest changed its seasonal wardrobe, shedding late summer for fall. The *momiji*, maple trees, are now blush red and wear a coat of haughty yellow and burnt orange. I settle for a hand-me-down sweater in gray for warmth. Without the sun's face, the breeze blows cool through too-thin walls. My six-moon belly, although small, makes the worn cover-up awkward to close. That and it is missing two silver buttons.

Sitting up, I knead between my brows. The room seems to rock, so I lie back and close my eyes. Things have not been right with me since Hatsu's escape and my capture. The rain's damp fingers had soaked through my skin and gripped my spirit. My teeth rattled as it shook me. The ordeal cost me my good health. I am wasting away skin to bones.

A labored sigh blows through my weary lungs.

Without Jin or Hatsu, I am all alone here.

Maybe everywhere.

On my side, I lay in a ball, cradling my belly. I have not gained enough weight, and my limbs ache from lack of use. Housemother Sato keeps me bedridden and warmed with special tea to encourage my good health's return. Her concern is I might miscarry and then she will lose months of fees.

Mine is for my baby.

There has been no word from Hajime. No word from my family. No word on Hatsu's well-being. She is in my constant prayers. I dream of Okaasan and cry out to her. *"Haha,"* I scream. But she never answers, and I wake drenched, cold in sweat and burning up in fever.

Chiyo's chatter and big laugh enter my room. "That girl is Naoko, but don't mind her." She spits the words in a pretend whisper to a girl I have never seen. "She thinks she's *married* and that her husband will rescue her." Something else is said but hidden by her cackle.

The new girl glances my way, curious. She's all angles, high cheeks and a tiny chin. Her long hair is tucked behind her jutted ears, and the side part highlights wide-set, questioning eyes of the deepest acorn brown. Her belly rounds but isn't ripe. With closed lips, she smiles.

I do not. It is as though I have blinked, and all the familiar faces have changed except for Chiyo.

"Come on." Chiyo tugs her arm and she is gone, as well.

Months have passed, and the disagreeable climate and autumn foliage now slumber under January's cool watch. The temperature drops enough to chill my thinned blood with its dry, crisp breath, and freeze mine in a solitary puff. Here, in Kanagawa Prefecture, it seldom snows, but winter is sleepy. I am *still* sleepy. I lie in bed, waking from an afternoon nap only wanting to rest more. It has been this way an entire season.

My hand rubs at my face, then into my hair. I stroke it back, comforting myself. Tears well up and I bury my face in my hands. Okaasan. Hajime. *Someone.*

Death would be easy. The difficulty is in the living.

The new girl often visits. Her name is Sora. I sometimes wake to find her sitting beside me, and although I am now like Jin, quiet and not up for conversation, she talks, anyway. I listen through my fog, grateful for the company and saddened by her now-familiar story. Her American soldier denied the baby as his and accused her of sleeping around. Only later did she learn he already had a baby and a wife. Another foolish girl.

Cruel-hearted Aiko delivered and left. Although I mourn for her baby, I'm not sad to see her go. Two others came and went. Sora shares their stories and their stories are the same. This one was reckless in hopes to snag a husband and that one was careful but not careful enough. Neither wanted their child. And with me so weak, I could offer no other option. This weighs heavy on my soul.

And what of my baby? I remember our pact, the one Jin, Hatsu and I swore to one another. I think of Hatsu, her baby somewhere safe, and Jin, her baby's spirit still waiting to travel safely home.

"Naoko? Naoko, wake up." It's Housemother Sato.

My eyes stay shut in hopes she might leave. Bony fingers of death rock my shoulder, the same fingers that pinch tiny noses and dig shallow graves.

The same fingers that will reach for my baby.

That took Jin's.

"Naoko, up, I have made more tea. You can take it at the *kotatsu.*"

Her voice grates on my ears. Sharp like glass but transparent. She pretends concern. I pretend to sleep.

She shakes me again. This time hard. It rattles my senses. "Come on. It's warm and toasty and all ready for you. Does that not sound nice?"

Having my legs warmed under the large blanket that drapes the heated table does sound nice. I roll over, giving in.

"Ah, there we go." Her eyes are soulless orbs behind wire rims. They narrow with her contrived smile.

I watch her leave, her wool kimono dragging across the floor with each step. Sitting up, I wait for the room to steady and then gather the strength needed to rock to my feet. My brain is mottled and fuzzy, my limbs sore and feeble.

With slow movements, I slog myself to the *kotatsu* in the main room. Sora, with her high cheeks flushed and pink, sits on the other side. I scoot up close, so my baby bumps the table's edge, and pull the blanket around my lap to warm us both. It is cozy and comforting underneath from the burner. I stretch stick legs and wiggle numbed toes to aid in circulation.

"You are so pale, Naoko," Sora whispers. "You are like the *yūrei*, ghost."

I am, it is true, except I am still here floating between worlds, finding comfort nowhere. It is a disconcerted state between feeling too much and too little.

Housemother Sato sets down the tea and pours. With one hand, she holds the lid secure, and with the other she tips the pot to fill my cup. Steam swirls, filling my nose with its sweet and grassy scent. I bring it to my lips and blow a cooling breath.

"Drink every drop, yes?" Housemother waits for my nod, then disappears to check on Chiyo. Her labor has begun.

"Wait." Sora holds a hand up as I start to drink. "I need to ask you something." She scoots around the table to sit beside me, our legs now fighting for the same limited space.

I set the cup down but keep my hands wrapped around it to soak up its heat.

Sora glances over her shoulder toward the back room where Housemother Sato attends to Chiyo. She tilts her head to listen, then leans even closer. "Is it true you helped a girl escape? That you want to keep your baby?"

This grabs my attention. Did I hear her right? Did I answer?

"Naoko…" With beseeching eyes, she starts again, only slower. "Do you still want to save your baby?"

My lethargic heart pumps a beat faster. I rub a hand through tangled hair. Hair that has not been combed in weeks or longer. I blink.

Her fingers wrap my emaciated wrist. "Naoko, do you trust me? Have I not been a good and faithful friend?"

I nod. She has. Who else has visited my bedside? Brought extra blankets or a cooling rag for my fevered brow?

"Good." Sora's eyes brighten and dance like liquid ink. "Then we leave tonight."

Her words jolt me. *"What?"* My breath catches in my throat, as though I have not spoken in some time. Have I? I cannot remember.

Sora leans closer still. "Yes. It is perfect. Chiyo only starts labor, by dark she will steal Housemother Sato's full attention, and we will steal away into the night."

The gate. I stare at my knobby fingers and paper-thin nails, trying to focus. "Hatsu took the key."

"And I have taken the new one." She smiles.

I frown, remembering. "It was wet and dark, and I was lost. I am too weak."

"Naoko, you are like the blind man who traveled at night carrying a lamp. He did not need it to see, it was lit so others could see him. You still carry the lantern for us all. You never needed it to know *your* direction."

My head shakes. *Stories, always stories.* "His lamp blew out, Sora." Just like mine. Just like me.

"Yes, you're right." She reaches out and places her other hand over mine. "And are we not lucky it did? How else would I have bumped into you?"

Almost a smile. This is all I can manage. Sora and I are indeed friends.

"Please," Sora says. "I am scared to try alone. Say we leave tonight, and you will fight to save your baby from that demon midwife."

Demon midwife. My promise to Little Bird. The pact with Hatsu and Jin. My baby's spirit stirs inside to wake my own. My eyes lift to meet Sora's.

"Yes?" Sora prods.

I nod.

Her eyebrows drop low and knit together. "Then...do *not* drink that tea."

THIRTY-ONE

Japan, Present Day

My earlier research for traditional homes in Zushi had led me to several that were converted into *ryokans*, traditional Japanese inns. They each sounded lovely. One included a *hinkoyi* bath, a wooden tub of white cedar where you soaked in steaming water mixed with soothing essential oils. Two had elaborate gardens with reflection pools for peaceful prayer and meditation, and all had the simple futons over *tatami* mats and personal *yutaka* kimono robes. That was where I wanted to stay, but I couldn't. Guilt wouldn't let me.

I sold my father's Cadillac to cover the expense of travel, not to indulge in luxuries as though this were a personal holiday. So instead of a beautiful traditional inn, I opted for the budget-priced Seijaku Capsule Hotel. Seijaku translated

THE WOMAN IN THE WHITE KIMONO

to "silent." It was anything but. There were constant door clicks as guests ventured back and forth between the community living space, the shared bathroom and the luggage locker room.

The minipods were built around an elongated twin-size bed. They were narrow and long and, at most, four feet high and stacked one on top of another in double rows. Those in the top row were required to climb a small ladder to gain entrance. Inside, there was a ceiling-mounted TV with headphones, a mirror, a single coat hanger, an electrical outlet and a light over the bed. That was it.

It wasn't for the claustrophobic, for anyone of significant height or size, or for those expecting privacy. The pods were for single occupants and separated into gender-specific rooms of twenty. But, to me, it was still better than a bunkbed at a hostel. I did have my own space and could close the bamboo blind over the see-through door.

It was late, but I couldn't sleep, so I rested on my back, and skimmed hundreds of neglected emails while my thoughts ran rampant. I was thrilled Yoshio found the traditional house and that records of ownership matched the last name on the marriage affidavit, but what if they didn't connect to the family? What then?

I adjusted my pillow and propped myself up, then selected several emails to delete, but opened one from the records department instead. Although my father's military records would arrive by mail, I'd gotten impatient and requested a status update.

Thank you for submitting a request to the National Personnel Records Center. We service approximately 20,000 requests each week, and while the average response time is six to eight weeks, you may experience a longer response time due to a fire in 1973 at the National Personnel Records Center that destroyed some sixteen million military files, and unfortunately, no duplicate copies exist.

While we cannot confirm your requested records were among them, this correspondence is to alert you of a possible delay for our search.

Thank you.

I pinched the bridge of my nose and closed my eyes. If the company in Yokohama wasn't a match to the family, and Pops's records were lost, what else did I have to go on? Worry burrowed like a worm, tunneling right to my core. What if I'd sold Pops's Caddy and traveled all the way to Japan just to see a vacant house?

Working through the rest of my emails, I stopped on one with "USS *Taussig*" in the subject line, then glanced below to find several more responses from the military forums. Blood rushed to my head and I sat up taller. I'd forgotten I'd left contact information on the navy reunion site.

The first was from a crewmate that served as an interior electrician but didn't remember my father. He shared reunion information but cited how most of the crew had passed or were too old to travel.

The next was from a woman whose husband worked within the engine room aboard the USS *Taussig* during the same time frame as Pops. He had passed, but her brother-in-law also served, and she would reach out to him.

Another shared how their father had served aboard the *Taussig*, but now suffered from Alzheimer's. He'd showed his father the photos I'd shared, but he didn't have any reaction.

There were a few others, but they all had similar stories. And then…

Dear Tori Kovač,
I found your post requesting information on the Taussig and some of the crew, including your father. I was aboard the Taussig from 1954 until 1957, making three Far East cruises. I don't remember seeing your father and don't recognize the other names listed, but with over three hundred souls aboard, and over fifty years gone by, I'm afraid my memory fails me. I did pull out my copies of the cruise books, however, and found a picture of your father in the roster. I've attached it in hopes it helps you in your search.

Respectfully,
Sal Dia

I opened the attachment. The swell in the back of my throat was instant.

There was Pops, standing in uniform, front and center with a semismile. He had his chest pushed out and his shoulders back. A brave young sailor ready to take on the world. Tears welled.

It was just a simple group photograph of the first division from their yearbook, but it was a photo I'd never seen before. It was as though, somehow, I got a piece of my father back. A piece I didn't know was lost. It hit me in that moment just how much I missed him.

With the overhead light on full, I sat up in my miniature room and sent thank-you emails, overwhelmed that perfect strangers, who didn't even remember my father, took the time to reach out. And for someone to dig through personal keepsakes and attach a photo from the ship's cruise book? Such a simple thing and yet it made an enormous impact.

It was just the hopeful nudge I'd needed to carry on with my search. I gazed at the photo of my father. I wasn't going to let him down, or myself. I wanted answers. Tomorrow, I'd visit the traditional house, question neighbors, and if need be, I'd extend my trip and wait for the person who cared for the grounds.

The house might stand empty, but I wasn't leaving Japan empty-handed.

I'd risen with the sun and enjoyed the free "well-balanced, body-friendly" breakfast of *no omoi*, which translated to "heavy." There were pickles, tofu and even fried cheese and chicken bites. I sampled a little of everything but filled up on rice. Then I secured my belongings in the locker and packed a few things for the day, including my father's letter. I'd hoped the home's old address on the envelope might bridge the language barrier should I run into neighbors. At least they'd have a general idea of why I was there.

The walk to Zushi Station took about fifteen minutes, but only because I'd hurried. I'd rushed past teenagers touting surfboards on their way to the beach, wove around locals shopping the outside market and waved away merchants who beckoned obvious tourists like me inside. The Yokosuka line ran every thirty minutes and I wanted to catch the next train. I jogged the last hundred yards and arrived just as it approached the gate.

Once aboard, I found an empty seat and clicked through my travel app's destination highlights. In Zushi, there was the Enmeiji Temple with a giant ancient red maple tree. I raised my eyebrows. The tree was over a thousand years old. Before, I thought Pops had snapped the photo of a traditional bride at a shrine near Tokyo, but now suspecting the photo was *his* bride, I needed to consider shrines closer to the base and the girl's home.

Taura was directly between them, and it, too, listed one.

The Yokosuka-shi Taura, also called the forgotten shrine since the woods had reclaimed the bright red gates that adorned the walking path. A giant stone fox waited at the end to reward those that braved the hike. The app cited hundreds of fox statues also adorned the woods, but it didn't say why.

I marked both locations, then glanced up as the train curved around a corner. Tall, elegant yachts lined up along the pier and small colorful sailboats bobbed in front of the marina. To my right, lofty trees swayed in the breeze, and as we continued the broad arc, rooftops appeared between their branches. Within minutes, we glided into the Higashi-Zushi Station in the Numama district.

While the ride through Zushi was quick, the walk from the train depot to where the traditional home stood would take longer. I didn't mind, as the surrounding woods were peaceful and, the breeze flapping their leaves like paper, warm.

Pops had once made this trip, and in spirit, I believed he was with me now. As I traveled to the traditional house that time forgot, I remembered...

"I almost turned back twice," Pops had said. He'd dressed in uniform and fidgeted with his cap, nervous to meet her father—a merchant king. I was nervous just to see the house.

As I neared the top of the small hill, I stopped as I'd imagined Pops had, looked up and squinted against the late-morning sun. *She told me I'd know it by the roof tiles.*

And like my father, I knew it, too.

A white mist rose from the curved clay tiles as the sun warmed the morning dew and rolled over the edge like the dangling petals of a cherry blossom in an ornamental hair comb. Backlit by the sun, the large, white-walled structure almost glowed. There was a quiet, understated elegance to how it perched atop the hillside. And while the photo Yoshio took was stunning, to approach it in person was surreal. Time had indeed stopped. It was right out of my father's story.

After Yoshio talked about the architecture, I researched the teahouse style and found the construction fascinating. I couldn't understand how the interior paper walls could endure everyday use. Wouldn't they tear? But the rough textured paper was crafted from the mulberry tree, the same trees the silkworms were found in, and were surprisingly strong. And what made it durable was the latticework that held the paper taut. If only I could peek inside. Movement from the side yard caught my eye.

My lips parted.

An elderly woman clipped white flowers from the low, dense foliage. They overflowed from the bamboo basket hanging from her arm. I squinted against the sun, then shielded my eyes but couldn't get a good look due to her sun hat. I thought the house was empty?

Was that *her*?

There was only one way to find out. I smoothed out my hair, adjusted my blazer and, with a deep, calming breath, walked toward the house.

THIRTY-TWO

Japan, 1958

Back in bed, I rest with a full belly. I forced down the *udon* noodles that Sora snuck in. I need the strength if we are to escape tonight. Curled on my side, I shift to find a comfortable position, but there is none. Leaving sparks too much excitement, even my baby stirs.

My thoughts jump from Hajime, my baby and Sora, like a monkey swinging from one tree to the next. *Three Monkeys.* Hatsu, Jin and me. My heart squeezes. Sora could be the fourth. There are four in the old stories. He's called *Shizaru* and crosses his arms to refuse evil. It fits. Sora surprises me with her help and want of her child. She pushes the action, and heaven pushes the intent. There must be a greater purpose to all of this.

Unless I'm blind? *Did Grandmother not say that?* No, no…

it was Kiko. She yelled it when I told her my choice, of what I was considering. "You are blinded by love and cannot see what is true," she had shouted.

My heavy lids open and close. Open and close. The wall is there and then it's not. I curl up tighter and think of Hajime's translucent-blue eyes and his parting words. "I promise," he said. "Now and forever."

"Always." *Were those true?* Before long, I am lost in memory. Lost in love. Lost in dreamless sleep.

Better blind than hopeless.

"Ayieeeee!" Chiyo's cries shake the house and disturb my slumber.

I blink, not yet awake, but no longer sleeping. She screams again. Then heavy footsteps and another shout.

Only this one is from Housemother. "Do not push, Chiyo! Wait. You must wait."

Sora's at my door. "Naoko, we must leave *now.*" She grabs my bag and throws random clothes inside. She looks frantic. Her eyes are wide, and her breathing is fast.

"Now?" I sit up, startled. I had only closed my eyes.

"Ahhieeee!" Another cry cuts through the night and jerks me to my feet. Okay, yes, we must leave now. *Poor Chiyo.* No, *poor Chiyo's baby.* I move to stand but wobble. Adrenaline pumps through sleepy veins, willing my lethargic muscles to act. I push back my sweaty, matted hair and try to balance. Sharp needles prick my left foot, numb from sleeping wrong.

Sora steps to the door, leans out and listens. "Get dressed. I'll be right back."

I shake my foot to revive some feeling, then rub at my eyes to better focus. *Is this really happening?* I need to think. *Socks...* I pull on a second pair, remembering how wet my feet were last time with Hatsu. I grab a third pair to keep in my pocket just in case. *What else?*

I spin, turning this way and that. I pull on an additional cotton slip to layer under a long Western skirt, a sweater that no longer fits my belly and rides up, then my gray hand-me-down sweater to keep my arms warm. I won't need my bag if I keep adding clothes on my back. I even cover my head, taking no chances. There's no telling what will happen, and this time, it's bitter cold.

Chiyo's screams have turned to sobs. She begs Housemother Sato, "Do something, please, do something."

There's another shriek, then more back-and-forth from Housemother Sato and the other girls. I stand frazzled in the middle of my room, eyes darting every which way. *Oh, the lamp.* I swipe matches from the table and cram them in my pocket.

Sora runs back in. "I told Housemother you were ill, that I'd fix your tea and stay with you all night." Her brows bunch when she sees my outfit. "What are you wearing?"

"Everything," I say.

"Okay, good. Let's go."

Sora ducks her head out the door again, then waves me to follow. I thread my arm through my coat's sleeve, grab the lamp's handle and teeter after her, lopsided. Heavy footsteps pound the floor, and we freeze. One second, two…but no one appears. Chiyo's cries mask our remaining steps to the door.

"Go," Sora whispers, opening it.

I don't look back.

With my bag in hand, Sora falls beside me, then takes the lead. The moon sits high and casts long silver shadows. We hug them, scurrying through the clearing as fast as my underused legs will allow. A frost has set, and the brittle ground crunches with every step.

"Come on, hurry," Sora says over her shoulder as we near the small footpath. Like a smoke-breathing dragon, a white puff of frigid air blooms with her words. "Be careful."

I push weary legs faster. My scarf falls, exposing my face, and I puff my own dragon's breath with the exertion. The thick, overhead canopy of bare-boned branches grabs the moon's light and squeezes, releasing only glimmers to filter below.

I hold up the lantern while she digs in my pocket for the matches. I position the lamp.

There is a flash of sparks, then a steady flicker appears. The flame takes to the wick with ease, and with a quick shake of her hand, the stick is extinguished.

Sora takes the lantern in one hand, holds my almost-empty bag in the other and leads the way. Light bounces over the trail to illuminate the path. I'm careful over the rough surface, taking slow, even steps. The crisp night air bites with fierce teeth, but I'm bundled and temporarily warmed with hope.

I am leaving.

Without the rain, the steep embankment is easier to manage. My bag is tossed to the bottom, and I hold the lamp while Sora steps down. It sways from the handle, the yellow beam rocking with uneven coverage.

"Okay, ready?" She holds her arms up as if to catch me and my mind flashes in memory to Housemother's yank. To Hatsu. To how she fell.

Positioned backward, I step down, and swing my leg to find lower footing. I hand her the lamp, then brace myself. *I can do this.* My body's tired, but my spirit is alive and fueled by the taste of freedom. It's right in front of me. Another step down, one more, and I practically fall into her outstretched arms.

"Come on." She lifts my bag, holds the lantern high and starts toward the footbridge.

My heart drums to propel my march. One step, then another. My stomach clenches hard. I stop, my hands wrapping over my belly.

"Naoko?" The light from the lamp swings in my direction to land on my cheeks.

I straighten and take a deep breath. "I'm coming." We are so close. I step up and onto the bridge, glancing over as I hurry past. The water churns under a thin sheet of ice, trapping the koi below. Goodbye, my old friend *Ganko*, persistent fish. This time I will not return.

"Naoko?" She whisper-shouts. She's at the gate. The lamp sits near her feet. My bag toppled over on its side. She works the key in the lock as I approach but turns, flustered.

"Sora? What is it?"

She shakes her head, spewing large clouds of vapor. "It doesn't work. It's not—"

"What?" My gaze drops to the key in her hand, then up to the gate's lock. "Here." I take the key and try. Maybe it's just cold or frozen. My heart stops. The teeth won't thread. I try again, and again. Lifting the key, I study it, then look to the lock. *Oh, no.* "This isn't the right key."

Our eyes anchor to one another in shock.

"Now what? I'm not going back. I can't." I fold. The cramping returns.

"Please, Naoko. You must stay calm. You haven't been well." Her arm rests on my shoulder.

I stay half-bent, holding myself, breathing through the strange sensation until it passes. "I am fine. Try again."

Sora tries the lock once more, then shoves at the gate. It only creaks with the sway. Looking around she finds a rock. One strike after another creates only smashed fingers. I watch, frozen in fear. My midsection squeezes in another unpleasant hug.

What happens now? What if we cannot get out? I watch Sora hit at the lock again and again and focus on the fence. Bamboo is known as both yielding and triumphant. I want it to yield, so I can be triumphant.

I want out.

I fix on the three-inch stalks strung and woven together with *shuro nawa*, black palm fiber cord. "Sora, try the twine. Strike the twine." We should have brought a knife. Why didn't I think of this? *Because she drugged me.* "Ah…" Again, I hunch over and grimace in pain. I try to stay quiet so not to distract her. Please let it work. *Please.*

Sora tries a sharp edge and tries to slice through it, but it only frays. She growls in frustration. "It's not working." Another strike, then again.

"Wait." My eyes go wide as I consider the lantern. A flash of excitement engulfs the thought. "It may not budge, but it will burn."

Her bleak expression brightens. Dropping the rock, she digs deep and produces the small book. Inside, there are only six or so matches left. She looks back and forth along the fence and steps to the ones beside the gatepost.

She runs her hands against each other while blowing warm breath on the crisscrossed twine. One strike of the match and it sparks to life. We huddle together and hold the small stick to the cord and wait. A thin transparent wisp of smoke rises above it, then the match at her fingertips snuffs out. We try again and again.

It's not working. "Wait!" I remove the lantern's glass cover and crank the wick high. Holding it at an angle, the flame licks the bound cord. There's smoke. Small spindles climb the air. The twine bubbles and retreats, exposing the cane.

"It's working!" Sora and I look at one another and grin.

I hand her the exposed lamp, and she lowers it to the next knot to patiently let it smolder and smoke. Again, bare cane is revealed. She works each crosshatch nub, then moves to the next stalk and the next.

I watch, still holding my belly, praying for this baby to hold on. Just awhile longer. A few minutes of patience will earn a lifetime of peace.

After each row is complete, Sora wrangles the shoot free. Then two…now five are down. We require a few more. She works quickly to get us out. I stay still to keep my baby in.

Sora reaches for my bag, tosses it out and motions for me to go next. I turn sideways and wiggle through, scraping my belly and backside against the slats, but I manage to get free on the other side.

Freedom fills my lungs.

Sora follows and looks back and forth in either direction. "Which way?"

The train station is to my right, and in my mind, I have retraced those steps ten thousand times, but know I can't go home. So, I look to my left and move along the endless bamboo fence, my arms wrapped across my belly. It tightens but I step through, my contorted face hidden behind my scarf. *Just a little longer.*

"Where?" Quick steps catch up to mine. "Where will we go, Naoko? And what if your baby comes?"

"It is fine. The baby will settle as soon as I can rest, and the nuns and monks walk by here every day, so their monastery cannot be far."

The endless fence of the Bamboo Maternity Home turned a corner. However, we did not. We walked straight, continuing until we discovered the small monastery community. A bamboo fence also surrounds this property, but it is only half as high. The grounds are tended, but not lavish in ornamentation. Another locked gate. Instead of out, we want in.

I'm exhausted.

Sora and I now wear whatever clothes remained in my bag and sit huddled together on the case, bundled, layered and warm. My middle still cramps, and I do my best to hide it. I fear the exertion has started an early labor, so I try to stay calm and think only agreeable thoughts.

"I am glad you're here, Sora." I snuggle on her shoulder with heavy lids, the surge of energy from before now depleted, leaving me lethargic and drained.

I drift in and out, a meditative slumber, disturbed only by the tightening of my midsection. I think of Grandmother's teacher and student story, the one with the spider, and imagine one descending from the sky to rest on my belly. It is an ugly creature and stares with several beady eyes. I want it to leave, so I blink away the vision only to have it return.

In the story, the student reports the spider to his teacher, saying he plans to place a knife in his lap, so when it next appears he can kill it. The teacher advises him to bring a piece of chalk. "When the spider appears next," he says, "mark an X on its belly, then report back."

When the spider appears again, the student does as the master suggested. Later, the teacher asks him to lift his shirt. There's an X. The story's meaning? We often wish to destroy what we're scared of, but by doing so, we destroy ourselves.

Yes, I am scared, but I have embraced my fear. Chiyo refused, just like Aiko, and so many others. How do they feel knowing what they have done? Does this not destroy their hearts?

"I'm grateful you have seen the spider on your belly, Sora."

My voice sounds distant. I am not sure the words were spoken or that I'm even awake. "Ahhhhh!" My stomach tightens, and I fold over to wait it out. It's intense. Something warm and wet pools between my thighs. "Sora... *Sora!*" Another contraction.

No. Not yet.

THIRTY-THREE

Japan, Present Day

I took slow steps toward the traditional house and the woman who gardened at its side. My heart pounded in my ears as I stepped from the road to the grass, then found the gravel path, kicking up pebbles.

She turned with wide eyes.

I stopped, just as surprised, but then regained my composure. "I'm so sorry, I didn't mean to scare you." I took a few steps and a deep breath, but the building pressure across my ribs didn't ease. "Are you a member of the Nakamura family by chance?"

She removed her visor, folded it and preened the hair that worked loose from her bun. She stared, first at my silk scarf, my blazer and then at my face. While she studied me, I gazed at her. She was elegant, with paper-creased skin and onyx hair banded gray with age. Pinned up, it exposed a delicate neck and bone structure. She was about the right age, but was it her?

I smiled and adjusted my blazer. "I'm Selby Porter," I said, using the pseudonym I wrote under. I lowered my voice as I neared, afraid I'd spook her. "I'm working with Yoshio Itō from the *Tokyo Times* and we may be doing a story on your family and the trading company in Yokohama, and even the family home." I gestured to the house.

She turned and glanced where I'd indicated.

"It's beautiful, by the way." I took several more steps until I stood in front of her. "The flowers are absolutely stunning." The herbal scent filled the air. They were the same kind of flowers displayed at the Nakamura Trading Company on the reception desk. A type of white chrysanthemum, but unlike the common variety found in the States and almost three times larger.

The woman only stared.

I tried again, my heart beating erratically. "Are you a member of the Nakamura family? The family that has had the property for generations?" I dropped my shoulders. Maybe it wasn't her. The woman my father wrote to could speak English. I dug into my bag for my father's letter, wanting to show her the address.

"Yes, this is my family home."

I glanced up slowly, surprised by her words and the delicate tone of her voice.

"I am Naoko Nakamura."

It was her.

I found her, Pops. I had really found her. "It is so lovely to meet you." The words were almost whispered. "Would you mind if I asked you a few questions? About the home?"

There was a considerable pause but then she gave a small

bow. "I was just about to have some tea. Would you care to join me?" She motioned to the pebbled path that continued around the house.

I followed through a small gate to where a low table held prepared tea on a moss-covered patio. Was this where my father had gone?

While the exterior of the house was spectacular, the gardens took my breath away. It was a landscape of perspective. The pond reflected large rocks as though they were distant mountains, and moss-covered boulders placed within the water appeared as islands. White sand created the shore and pebbled paths led in either direction to vanish within the expanse of ornamental trees and groundcover.

"Sit, please." She gestured to a floor cushion positioned on a *tatami* mat, then with careful hands poured a dark, grassy tea. "It's strong, like bitter truths." She offered me the tall, ceramic cup.

My fingers slipped into the grooves as I took a polite taste—pungent and earthy.

She smiled, creating starburst crinkles around her eyes. Such a tiny woman, and yet the way she held herself—stately, focused, composed—filled the space, and me, with unease. I didn't know how to begin and feared her reaction.

"You are writing an article on my family's home?"

"I'd like to, yes," I said, tasting the rancid lies as they rolled off my tongue. I took another sip and looked around to regain my composure. "Both the house and gardens are beautiful." The same dense, low-growing plant with large white blooms carried over from the side yard.

"Not as beautiful as your scarf," she countered, eyes fixed on the hand-painted textile in hues of red. "May I ask where you found such a treasure? The details are exquisite." She leaned in for a closer inspection.

"Oh…" I offered an abbreviated smile. "Thank you. It was a gift." I almost said from my father but caught myself, not ready to transition to my real intent. I twisted its tattered edge, then flipped it over to reveal the badly repaired seam. "It's a bit worse for wear, I'm afraid."

"Ah, *kintsugi*." She straightened. "This I understand. In Japan, repaired objects hold even more beauty as the restoration becomes part of the object's history. Like my family's summer tea bowl." She nodded to the ceramic container beside her. "See how the jagged split is filled with gold? It interrupts the painted pattern but adds to its value."

"It's beautiful." The design mimicked the flora in the garden.

She tracked my gaze. "My cherished mother's favorite flower. The bowl broke because I once served her an unfair serving of selfish soup. Many years passed before I discovered she'd repaired it." She smiled. "She had melted her best gold jewelry and ground it into a fine powdered dust. Then she mixed it with lacquer and pieced it back together. Now, in knowing of both her sacrifice and forgiveness, this tea bowl is also cherished. So, you see? Its true life began the moment I dropped it." Her brows arched. "Is it not the same for your mended scarf?"

I half shrugged. "It was just carelessness, really."

"You must have cared considerably, for not only have you repaired it, you wear it even now." She smiled. "So, Miss Selby Porter, what would you like to know about my family's home?"

Patches of guilt warmed my face and neck. "Well…" Manipulating a source to attain sensitive information played well within the boundaries of investigative journalism, but the lies I told crossed lines of decency. And with the way she studied and cataloged my every move, I feared my lies, and whatever lines they tangled, stretched transparent. I had to tell her the truth. Pops would have wanted me to.

I set my tea down. "I'm afraid when I said I was here to write an article about your home, that wasn't entirely true. While I *am* a journalist, and I do write under the name of Selby Porter, it's not my real name."

"I know who you are."

I sat back. *She knew?* My chest swelled with emotion, making another breath almost impossible.

Naoko smiled at my surprise. "You have your father's eyes. They capture the same light, like the bluest water absorbing the sun. There's no mistaking the resemblance. I knew the moment you approached."

I flushed again, causing my thin blazer to build with heat as if it were wool instead of cotton.

"And, of course, you are also wearing my scarf."

"I'm sorry?" I asked, certain I heard wrong.

"Your beautiful scarf." She motioned to the decorative silk around my neck. "It was a gift from my father, and I in turn gave it to yours." She angled in for a closer look. "I thought I would never see it again."

"This was my mother's," I said without thinking, and covered it with my hand.

She straightened with a small smile. "Forgive me. I'm of course mistaken." Her eyes glanced toward the scarf, the one I still clutched. "Your mother's scarf is beautiful. The red-and-white pattern suits you."

The memory of my father's words wiggled its way between worlds to layer with hers. *I always intended for you to have it. It's important.* I relaxed my hand, but not the realization that gripped me. Mama's beautiful scarf had originally been Naoko's. I didn't know what to say.

"Since you now know my name, and we are officially acquainted, might I finally learn yours?"

I never did say. "My name's Tori. Tori Kovač."

"Tori?" Her lips parted with the last syllable frozen between them. The hand that held her tea trembled.

I shifted forward. "Are you okay?"

"Yes. Yes." She steadied herself, looked away and blinked at nothing.

I took a long drink. I'd finally spoken the truth, but her reaction to it confused me. "Forgive me, but if you knew who I was, why did you play along?"

Her gaze sharpened and locked on mine. She arched a brow. "Is that really the question you traveled so far to ask, Tori Kovač?"

It wasn't.

I reached into my pocket and produced Pops's letter, the one addressed to her, the one returned.

Old eyes narrowed to focus, then brightened in recognition. "A letter from Hajime?" She covered her trembling lips with a frail hand, eyes fixed on the envelope, but I wasn't ready to hand it over, not yet.

Instead, I smoothed out the creases, trying to connect the lines of time, picking my words with care, so I wouldn't trip over them. "This letter left me with more questions than answers. Not just about my father, but about everything. I know from reading this that I have a sister." My heart lodged in my throat. I pushed down the emotion. "I was hoping you could tell me where she is and what happened. I'd like to know the story of you and my father, so I can understand." I clenched my jaw, nervous of her reaction.

She folded her slender hands across her lap, glanced at the letter in my hands for a long time, then met my gaze. "And I, in return, would like to learn yours."

"Mine?" I shook my head. "I'm afraid I don't have one."

"Ah, but you do. The story of what led you to travel half-way around the world to hear mine." Her eyes sparkled like black diamonds.

She wanted to hear about Pops. I understood. It made sense and was only fair. I gave a nod and answered in earnest, "I can only tell you what I know."

"Then we have an agreement." She refilled my tea, then hers, took a measured sip and regarded me from the rim. "My given name is Naoko Nakamura. My married name is Naoko Tanaka. And once, for a short time in between—" her gaze held mine "—it was Naoko Kovač."

Naoko took another sip, then released a slow, long breath. "My grandmother often said, worry gives a small thing big shadows. Yes," she said, nodding. "I believe that shadow is where this story begins."

THIRTY-FOUR

Japan, 1958

S ora shouts in a panic to wake the whole monastery. "Please, my friend is having her baby! Is there anyone who can help us?"

I sit wide-eyed and doubled over at the gate, the cramping now stronger and coming in fast pronounced surges. *This child will no longer wait!*

Sora repeats her pleas, her voice high in her throat, her words tumbling together to whoever can hear. "Please, help us! She is having her baby! Tell someone we are here!"

At once, the small buildings light up. Footsteps, bouncing lantern lights and frazzled voices charge in my direction to open the gate. Buddhist nuns emerge from one side of the compound, monks from the other. The women direct the men how to lift me, what speed to move and where to go.

"Ahhhh!" Another contraction rips through my spine like fire along a fuse. A burn that threatens to combust. I am carried through the pain. Faces and voices blur.

Inside a small building, everyone is shooed away except for Sora and two women. One, old and stoic, the other, composed and knowing. They peel my layers off and point questions at Sora.

"How old is this girl? How far along is she? Where's her family? Where's the father?"

My screams bury Sora's answers.

The nuns' robes, stained in rich saffron and turmeric, swoosh around me. Aloeswood scents the air, its sweetened beginning and bitter end mixes from repeated burnings to smell of dried seaweed.

Sora strokes my head, trying to keep me calm. The older nun with a weathered face holds prayer beads and chants. It comes from deep in her belly and vibrates through her throat in a series of elongated words and breath. It's beautiful, but I mar it with my cries.

"No voicing. Stay quiet," the one with wire glasses and steady eyes tells me.

We are not supposed to express our discomfort during the birthing process. This is what we learned in the maternity home, not that anyone listened. I thought the housemother lied to silence us, but here, they say the same.

Doubled over, I scream, anyway.

I am done being quiet.

My lower back is raw and burns with fire. I don't know or care who's helping me, I just want this baby. "Ohahh!" My head lifts, and I grab my knees. I am squeezed so tight I cannot breathe. Every muscle contracts in a violent embrace. Fighting it makes it worse.

"It is okay, Naoko. Everything is okay. Stay calm. Stay

calm." Sora recites this comfort over and over as much for her benefit as mine. Her eyes are wide in worry, maybe fear. This will be her before long.

He who begins ill begins worse. I was weak to begin with, now I am spent. Every ounce of energy was used to escape, and any I had in reserve is exhausted. The waves come one on top of the next, and again I'm up, red-faced and holding my breath to endure.

"Breathe. You must breathe, child," says the nun with glasses, waving her hand to coax. Her ruddy cheeks puff and release to demonstrate.

The other nun chants louder, her long sounds cut in half. Her robe sways in graceful trails of autumn. It is as though she floats on air.

I try to breathe…a deep inhale through my nose and a hard exhale through dry lips. Again, I breathe in and out. *Did Hatsu come here? I want Okaasan. Okaasan! And Hajime.* My thoughts are spiraling. Another tightening folds me in half. "Ahhhh!"

"Push now, child. Push."

The intonation grows louder still.

"Push!"

"No. I can't. Wait. I need to stop." My words strangle with gasps of air, meaning nothing. "Ahhh!" The pain has hit a piercing threshold, the duration of each contraction increases to make it worse. My bones want to loosen and separate from the constant force.

The main nun now stoops. I see only the top of her shaven head and the fuzz that covers it. The chanting nun stops behind her, singing words of peaceful entry.

"Yes! That is it. I can see the crown." Excited eyes see what I cannot. "One more. Ready? *Push!*"

Sora grips my arm. My hands hold my knees tight, and I rock forward in agony.

"Again. One more. Now!" It is said with authority, and I surrender to it.

My nails dig into flesh, and I squeeze my eyes, my stomach, my being. A growl releases between clamped teeth. My lips pull up to expose them.

"Ah, the head is out, okay. Okay." She pats my knee. "Now wait. Be still."

I fall back in a heap. Sora catches me in her arms. For a second, I have relief. Pain has numbed me, but I sense the new pressure between my thighs, the foreign shape that rests there. I don't dare move. My heart thuds against my chest. The nun speaks in hushed tones, but in fast speech. I hear words but cannot decipher them. Spots dance in front of my eyes.

"Now we deliver. Ready? Help her up. Help her up, child."

"No…no…" I need another minute. One more minute. I am so tired. But no one listens.

Sora reaches under my shoulders and pushes me up. My insides burn and twist. The pressure builds from within. Their spoken words are nonsensical and garbled. Blood trumpets in my ears. The grip of my knees causes the veins in my hands to bulge. Chanting swallows the room. *Do more stand outside the door?* One voice becomes many. My scream rides them all.

"Ahhhhh!" I bare teeth.

I push.

I push.

I push.

And then my whole body trembles with release. My chest caves in with a breath. Sora sets me back with care.

The song is done.

"You have a girl. You have a girl!"

A girl. I lie still, breathing, watching. *I knew it was a girl.* Voices bounce back and forth. I do not know what they are saying. "Small," I hear, then something about weight.

Sora strokes my head and smiles. The nuns busy themselves with my baby. I catch only glimpses of her. Dark hair,
she has dark hair. My ears prick, desperate to hear her cry. I
need to hear her cry.

I watch their hands for pinching fingers.

"Do not touch her face!" I shriek, eyes bulging, trying to
see. "Do not touch my baby!" *Why does she not cry?*

Please let her cry. I cry for her, panicked.

Then a sputter and gasp, followed by a solitary note of
anger that fills the air.

It is the single sweetest sound I have ever heard, a potent
declaration of arrival softened by lungs too small in size. My
breath hitches by three and releases with steady tears that
stream down my cheeks.

She cries.

She lives.

We did it.

"Please," I say, reaching out with open hands, hungry for
her skin. "Please, my baby…"

The nun with glasses swaddles her in cloth of apricot and
speaks in a soft, low tone. "Once, Buddha was asked, 'Are
you a healer?'

"'No,' Buddha replied.

"'Are you a teacher, then?'

"'No,' he replied again.

"'Then, Buddha, what are you?' asked the student, exasperated."

The nun walks close and holds out my daughter. "Buddha
replied, 'I…am awake.'"

The nun's eyes meet mine as she places my daughter in my
arms. "She is tiny, but she is also awake."

"*Oh…*" I gather her close; she weighs nothing. I am worried but enchanted…by her sound, her smell, her miniature everything. How she fits in the palm of my hand.

A daughter. Hajime, we have a daughter.

A tuft of black hair sprouts from the top of her narrow head like a carrot. I blink, concerned, and look at the nun with glasses.

She smiles. "Hair will fill in." She looks to the other nun and they chuckle. A secret shared from knowing.

I soak up every detail, needing to see every minuscule inch. She is so thin. I stroke her cheek and trace the diminutive indent in her chin, then laugh. *Just like Hajime.* I smile at Sora and the nuns and point it out. "It's like her father's. Just like his."

They gather close and we admire her.

Her puckered lips quiver. Every breath a soft gurgle.

"Her lungs aren't fully formed, but you are lucky to have a girl," the nun says. "With boys, the lungs develop last—at least she has a chance." The sister adjusts the cloth to better see her face. "A small one, but there is a chance."

The baby's hand springs free from the blanket to wave in the air. I bring it close to inspect. Five slim fingers with delicate nails wrap around mine on instinct. She is early, sick and perfect.

"Hello, my *akachan*."

Her huge, liquid eyes strain to focus.

"Look at that," says the older nun. "She knows you."

I bring my early baby close and gaze into her dewy eyes. They are like deep waters, reflective and inky, and I am lost in them. Yes, my child knows her mother. We share a private conversation then and there. It says, *I have been waiting for you* and *Here I am, here I am.*

Yes, here you are, Little Bird, here you are.

Awake.

★ ★ ★

Humming…a soft throaty hum stirs me from my sleep. I blink. Afternoon light fills the small room and falls across the chanting nun's face. She smiles without showing her teeth. Her nose wrinkles like an accordion, and deep, long lines frame contented eyes. I cannot help but smile back. In my arms, my tiny baby sleeps.

We are warm, together and safe.

She is early, and struggles for air, but she lives and my heart could not be fuller.

When they offered to take her, so I could rest, I refused. I cannot let her out of my sight. So, someone stays with me instead. This is to ensure her safety as we sleep.

Bundled, her little head peeks out, and her arms pull up tight. Since she is no longer red from crying, I can see her skin. She is a shade lighter than me but there is an odd sickly tinge. It is offset by jet-black hair, dark lashes and pink squished lips that should suckle more than air. Tears well because she is weak, but she is beautiful.

"You have been so kind," I say to the humming nun. "I'm so lucky we are here, thank you." The room is bare, holding only the side-by-side futons and a chair, but it is filled with peace. One I have not experienced in some time.

"Many have luck, but few have destiny." The chanting nun's voice is raspy but soft. "You can toss the coin, child, but fate covers both sides. This is where you are supposed to be. Luck has nothing to do with it." She smiles, gathering in her lips as if she doesn't have teeth.

Maybe she doesn't? I smile back and cast my gaze to my baby's fingers. They tremor near her open mouth as she yawns. I laugh. Her every movement is amazing.

The partitioned door slides, and the nun with glasses, Sora and another woman walk in. This new woman is not a nun.

She wears a dark winter wool kimono with snow-covered pine trees woven into the design. Her hair is pinned tight in a twist at the nape of her too-short neck. Her gaze drops to my baby.

"Oh, hello…helloo," the new woman coos with a soft melodic tone. Her crescent eyes carry warmth, even if the color is flat black.

I hold my baby tighter.

"Naoko, do you remember my name?" the head nun with wire glasses asks. "I am Sister Sakura." She points to the chanting nun who has been sitting with me. "She is Sister Momo, and this is Hisa. She'll be your baby's wet nurse."

Wet nurse?

Sister Sakura stifles a laugh, and her glasses slide farther down her nose. "You barely have meat on your bones. I doubt you will be able to bring enough milk, if any at all. So, we'll fatten you both up, eh?" She holds her hands open and wiggles her fingers for me to hand over my sleeping baby.

I look first to Hisa. Her round, full face conceals any wrinkles that would snitch her age. My gaze casts down to my baby, her sunken cheeks with creases like crumbled paper. She needs to nurse.

Reluctantly, I loosen my hold. "She will feed here, though, okay? Only here." I want her in my sight always.

Hisa bows with a soft smile, and I relax a little.

"Of course." Sister Sakura lifts my baby and hands her to Hisa, leaving my arms too empty.

"Naoko…"

My eyes are on Hisa and my baby, every muscle on alert ready to snatch her back. She's hungry but fails to latch on to the breast. My heart aches because I am unable to feed her and she struggles.

"Naoko, Sora tells us you were being kept at a maternity clinic, by a Housemother Sato?" Sister Sakura asks.

The mention of the home and the demon midwife's name grab my attention and sends chills. I shift my gaze and nod. She and Sister Momo exchange a nebulous look.

Sister Sakura pushes the wire glasses higher on her nose. "And you could not leave, you are both sure of this?"

This time, Sora and I share a look. A confused one. There is something in her tone.

I shrug. "Yes, why? Did the housemother contact you? Is she here?" My heart hammers hard.

"Sister Momo will bring you some lunch, then assist you with a dried ginger root sponge bath to aide in healing." With high brows and a soft smile, she nods.

Why doesn't she answer? "Sister, what about Housemother?"

Her eyes sideswipe to Sister Momo, then back to mine. Her lips pull tight. "Brother Yuudai, our abbot, wishes to meet with you both when you're able. You'll discuss Housemother Sato with him."

She nods again to close the subject and glances at the wet nurse, Hisa, and my baby, who has yet to feed. Her brows lower, causing her glasses to slip again on her nose.

My stomach rocks uneasy. "She's not feeding."

Sister Momo sighs. "She's early, child…sick and frail. We will keep trying. But let us prepare for you to eat, as well, yes?" Another nod in my direction, and she swishes out, followed by Sister Sakura.

I meet Sora's eyes, worried for my baby and for us. *Why does the abbot wish to talk about Housemother Sato? What if they've contacted her?*

As soon as Hisa leaves, we have much to discuss.

Like Little Bird, I am also *awake*.

THIRTY-FIVE

Japan, 1958

It's been a few days since Little Bird's arrival, and until today, I partook only in sponge baths with dried ginger root. Even now, after a full bath, its sharp smell sticks to my skin and burns my nose, just as the kerosene from the small paraffin heater Sister Sakura brought us does. At least it keeps away winter's bite and our room is cozy.

Hisa, the wet nurse, rocks my baby and sings a lullaby while I tug at my still-damp hair, working to untangle its knots and the uncertainties in my mind.

It's January.

Hajime left in September for Formosa. His service was up soon after, so he'd have traveled back to America for release. Has he returned to our little home in the village and found me missing? Did he go to Zushi to look for me there? I fear

Grandmother and Father have sent him away with lies, so I asked Sora to seek news and leave the truth of my situation with my neighbor Maiko.

My baby has lost weight she couldn't spare and struggles with every breath, but she is still alive, so we continue to try to feed and fatten. Sister Momo brings me warm meals of soup and *mochi*, rice cake, to see if I will plump, too. My head and body ache from lack of Housemother's poison tea. Does the baby's hurt from the withdrawal of poison? I glance to her in Hisa's arms. My baby is swaddled, contented, cared for and loved, but does she suffer?

"What song is that, Hisa?"

"Oh, just an old cradle tune. She likes it, though, I think. You do, yes?" She lifts my draped baby higher and makes silly smiles near her face. "Oh, yes. Yes, you do."

I laugh. "I like it, too."

Normally, after birth, a daughter stays in her mother's home for almost four weeks. Okaasan would have loved to sing lullabies. Even Grandmother would make a fuss if things were different.

If Grandmother were different, she still could.

I do not expect to remain here four full weeks, but where will I go? And feeding my baby is still in question. How will I pay Hisa? My weary heart plummets, so I sigh from the length of my soul, then blink to refocus. With the way Hisa holds Little Bird, only a tuft of blue-black hair sticks out. I set the brush on my lap and smile. "Her hair crowns her head like a strawberry cap."

Hisa tries to press the stem flat with two fingers. It stands right up. She laughs. "Have you thought of a name for this little berry?"

Normally, the entire family would gather for the *meimei*,

naming ceremony. My baby will have no ceremony, but yes, she will have a name.

"I thought of naming her after Okaasan," I say, twisting my hair into a braid. "But then she would have a traditional Japanese name, and…" I glance at Hisa and speak the obvious. "She is not a traditional Japanese baby. So, instead of a name that attempts to blend in, maybe one to stand out? But I have not decided."

Hisa just nods. What is there to say? With my baby's lighter skin and rounded eyes, my Little Bird will stand out regardless.

"Hello, Naoko, Hisa." Sister Sakura heads straight toward the baby as she walks in. Her robe of mustard spice hangs stiffly as though freshly dried from the sun and not yet loosened by her movements. The burnt ochre fades where the cloth has worn, but the rest is bright like the smile lifted on her cheeks. "And hello, little egg with eyes."

I stifle a laugh with memory. Hajime thought "egg with eyes" is an odd term for *beautiful*. I told him it is a great compliment to have a perfectly shaped oval head and big beautiful eyes. Our baby's eyes are massive on such a little face.

The sister's smile fades as she and Hisa speak in hushed tones. She has brought a syringe to siphon collected milk for the baby. They fear she is dehydrated, she is not gaining enough; her cries have weakened. Worrying builds nothing but sorrow and empties the day of strength.

Little Bird needs my strength.

With the syringe filled with milk, they prepare my baby. Shifting, I pull myself upright and move to sit beside her.

"Hold her up, we don't want her to choke." Sister Sakura places the dropper into Little Bird's mouth and squeezes. "We want just a dab on her tongue, so she can manage it."

I stroke her head, whispering words of encouragement.

"There you go." I smile when her lips close to taste. "You can do it."

"It works!" Hisa laughs. "Look at that."

Sister Sakura pushes her glasses up. "And you will be able to feed her, Naoko. Here, try." She hands me the dropper. "Careful. Only one drop. And only after it is gone do you add another."

I beam, delighted. "At this rate, she will always feed."

"Yes, this way there is hope, yes?" Sister Sakura places her hand on my arm. "Are you ready to meet with the abbot?"

My smile and stomach drop in tandem.

"Why this face?" Her brows bunch, and the wrinkle of her nose causes her glasses to slide. "He only wishes to talk with you and Sora. There is no need for concern, child."

I nod with a compulsory smile, then refocus on feeding my baby, but my mind circles scenarios. Housemother Sato lost not only my fee, but Sora's, and Hatsu's. I imagine she is out looking for us.

Unless she no longer needs to.

When Sora steps in from the doorway, she won't meet my eyes. My heart falters. *Something's wrong.*

"Hello, child." Sister Sakura looks over her spectacles at Sora, then shifts her gaze to me.

"Can Sora and I have a moment alone?" I look to Sister Sakura, then to Hisa.

Hisa stands, but I object to her leaving with my baby. "No, I will take her. It's okay. I will continue to feed her as soon as she wakes." My arms are already outstretched. Housemother may be near.

Hisa carefully hands her over, then eyes Sora with a curious expression.

Sister Sakura pats my arm. "I will let the abbot know you both are here."

I nod, then make room on the futon when they leave. "Please, Sora, sit. Tell me what you've learned."

She sits, but her lips hold a tight line.

I need to pry them open, need to know what secrets are inside. "Sora, did you find my neighbor Maiko?" My heart rises high in my throat while I wait.

"Maiko wasn't there." Sora's shoulders drop with a sigh.

"Was her daughter there watching her little brother?" Tatsu's handsome face flashes in my mind: big eyes, long lashes and covered in mud. I lean closer, causing the baby to stir. "Sora?"

"No." She shakes her head. "There wasn't anyone living there. It was empty."

"Empty? Did you go the right house?" My heart pounds an irregular beat. "Did you go to *mine*?"

Her knowing eyes level to my desperate ones.

I sit back and swallow, biting at my worried lip so hard I taste blood. Not knowing is bad, but not knowing doesn't change what is. "Sora, please, just tell me. Whatever it is, it's okay." I nod to encourage her.

She takes a deep breath. "An old woman who calls herself Grandmother Fumiko—"

"Yes!" The familiar name gives me hope. "She helped me get ready for my wedding."

"She said Maiko's family moved on to another village."

"Oh..." I nod. "Okay, yes. I guess this is common within these—" I stop on the word. *Eta* move where there is work. I just never thought of it. "Did she say where? Did she see Hajime?" My thoughts are frantic, so my words are rushed.

Sora pulls back her shoulders, looks at her hands.

"Sora?"

She looks up and shifts so she's closer. "He...well..." She wrings her hands. "Naoko, Hajime has not returned." Her chin drops. So does her gaze. "I am sorry."

"He has not returned? At all?" My heart writhes from the pressure. I don't understand. He'd have left word. I reach for her arm and shake it. "Were there any letters left at the house?"

She tilts her head. "Since your house sat vacant, another family has moved in. So, there was nothing."

Nothing.

My fingers fall away from her sleeve.

Now I cannot breathe.

As Hajime was detained, I feared we'd lose the house, but I expected word. I thought Maiko's family could take me in for a while. Grandmother Fumiko lives with another family already. I glance at my sleeping baby and try not to panic, but it bubbles up. "Now what?"

Sora takes my trembling hand in hers.

I look up. "In my mind, Sora, I saw Hajime's return at least a hundred times." My shoulders fall, my words a mere whisper. "He'd search for me, frantic to know where I'd gone. I even saw him traveling the train to Zushi. Running up the hill to my family's house and calling out for me."

"Then what happens?" Sora asks, leaning over, pressing her forehead to mine so we form a triangle over my bundled baby.

"'Naoko,' he'd say, and Obaachan would hobble to the door, wearing such a frown." I blink Sora into focus through tears.

She squeezes my hand.

"Hajime would believe nothing she'd say. He'd keep looking until he found me. Then he'd pull me into his arms, saying, 'I love you, Cricket. Where is our Little Bird?' You see, in my mind, Sora, it was always Grandmother's or Father's lying that would send Hajime away." I blink back the daydream and lift my eyes through wet lashes. "I never imagined they wouldn't need to." I shake my head with quivering lips pulled high and wide to hold it in.

Sora's hands cup my cheeks. "Maybe he *couldn't* get back, and his letters went unanswered? Maybe he learned others inhabit your house, and he thinks the return trip isn't welcomed?"

Or maybe he's left me.

Maybe I was blind, after all.

The baby stirs and with puckered lips cries in silence. I cry loud enough for us both. My shoulders shake from the earthquake of emotion. Sora strokes my hair, and I think of Obaachan. My family. Hajime.

How much I have lost.

I cry and cry, then exhausted from it all, I think of nothing. *Has this all been for nothing?*

"Sora, Naoko?" Hisa leans in. "The abbot is on his way."

Sora and I share a look of "what if…" *What if Housemother has contacted him? What if she is here? What if they expect us to leave with her?* But before it's given to voice, the abbot has arrived.

"May I enter?" His rich robe colored of boiled bark and tubers hangs heavy without ornamentation. He is slight in size but centers the community and commands the space.

If the abbot is of fertile earth, then the sisters and monks are its bounty. A succession of spice in shades of curry, cumin and turmeric follows him in.

Sister Sakura has her glasses off and makes quick introductions as she cleans them with a cloth.

I hear nothing except the beating of my heart.

Is no one else coming? Sora and I share a curious glance.

"Hello, girls and new little life," the abbot says, observing my baby as Hisa attempts to feed her with the dropper. His joyful smile pulls high and rounds out his cheeks. His eyes squint with soft crinkles in the corners. It is infectious, but I do not smile. Neither does Hisa when he asks if my baby now feeds? Instead, she shakes her head.

"She will," I say to them both. "Please, keep trying."

We form an informal circle with Sister Sakura to my left, Sister Momo, Sora and the abbot to my right. I am still on edge and ready to snatch my baby from Hisa and dart away.

"I would like you to start at the beginning. How you came to be at our door." The abbot folds his hands inside his over-size sleeves and rests his eyes on me.

They are kind, but are they understanding? "We were at the Bamboo Maternity clinic down the road." I wait and gauge reactions but get none, so continue. "My mother just recently passed, so I was home, and..."

The baby stirs, allowing me pause to consider my words. *How to explain everything?*

"I had some trouble with the pregnancy. We were afraid I could lose the baby, so my Grandmother sent for a midwife. She wanted to do further tests, so I was taken to the maternity home, but..." I tense and look down, not sure how to speak of Grandmother's intent. "How do I explain what I myself don't understand?"

"Naoko, just speak your truth." The abbot's voice is soft and reassuring. His lips turn up at the corners. "Sometimes you have to push the stick in the thicket to drive out the snake."

The words find their way to my lips, and once I start, I cannot stop them. They flow in a rapid sequence to string together the events of the last year and a half. I tell them of Hajime, our wedding, about my family. Even Satoshi and how he was my family's choice. I explain how Housemother locked the gates and then, glancing across to Sora, I tell about the babies.

All those babies.

How they cried, and how they did not. Yoko's, Jin's, Aiko's, Chiyo's…so many more.

I do not just push the stick, I jab it, to reveal Housemother Sato.

They listen without interruption and, as far as I can tell, without judgment. Hisa's eyes have moistened with tears and she dabs at them. The sisters shake their heads. Even Sora's eyes water. She was not with Jin, Hatsu and me. Maybe she didn't know the full extent of Housemother Sato's heartless cruelty?

Sora picks up where I left off to explain the state she found me in, the tea, our escape and journey here.

The abbot sighs. His smile vanished as though it were never there.

The baby fusses and I reach for her. Hisa hesitates, but I insist. I don't care if this pulls their patience. Right now I'm still unsure of everything. Everyone. Better hungry than missing. "Is she here?" I blurt, not able to hold it in any longer. "Has she come for us?"

"That woman?" Sister Sakura asks, her face folding. "No, no, child. We simply wanted to learn your story."

"And I wish to thank you both for sharing it," the abbot says, sitting taller. "And for your bravery."

Small nods of soft agreement fill the space.

"What will happen now?" Sora asks.

Sister Sakura readjusts her glasses. "We will inform local officials, so they may consider the matter, of course."

"But they will not do anything," I say in protest, looking from one face to the next. "An inquiry won't make a difference."

"That depends on who you ask," the abbot says. "Once, a man was walking along the shore when he spotted a monk reaching down to the sand, picking something up and very carefully throwing it into the ocean." The abbot frees his hands and uses them to demonstrate. "As the man got closer, he called out, 'What are you doing?' The monk paused, looked up and answered, 'I am throwing starfish back into the ocean. The sun is up, and the tide has left them here to die.'"

I rock my baby and listen.

"The man looked up and down the vast shoreline, then back to the monk. 'Do you not see the miles and miles of stranded starfish? You surely cannot make a difference.' The monk listened politely, then threw another starfish into the sea, past the breaking waves and said, 'It made a difference for that one.'" The abbot grins, his eyes shine in amusement. "See, Naoko?" The abbot lifts his chin. "Did you not help Hatsu? Did you, Sora, not help Naoko? Did your actions not make a difference for that one?" He nods to my Little Bird.

The abbot leans forward to stand. The sisters and monks rise, as well. Only Sora and Hisa stay behind. I glance again at my sleeping baby. Grandmother always said, "Even *nothing* is something."

She is something.

"Brother Yuudai?" I call out.

The abbot turns, stepping back through the door, brows arched high. "What is it, child?"

"Please, if you can make arrangements, I need to see my father."

I have not come this far for nothing.

THIRTY-SIX

Japan, 1958

Hisa suggested I nap while my baby does, but I only slept for a moment. Now I stare at the tall pine silhouettes through the *shoji* window screen and sigh. My nightmare haunts me.

It was summer, and I was running through the open fields of tall grass. With my arms outstretched, my fingertips raked the seed heads. Feathery plumes swayed before me, like a sea of cascading waves. I stopped, lifted my chin to the sun and let the heat warm my cheeks.

In the clouds, I saw Hajime's ship. The breeze kicked up, and he sailed farther and farther away. Then Brother Daigan took my baby, and when I called out to him, he disappeared, my voice lost in the wind.

All around me were cries, the *mizuko*, water children, waiting for *Jizō*, waiting for me. They wailed. Then birds. A dozen, maybe two, flew overhead in a panic. I watched their soft underbellies until they blended into the sky, and I was alone in silence. Then something stirred behind me. I turned.

The majestic tiger.

Amber eyes with pinprick pupils fixed right on me. There was a familiarity to his stare. His lips curled into a snarl, a warning growl from deep within its throat. I could feel his breath; we stood so close.

He was a monster of ginger orange. His length was of two full-grown men, and his girth, of four. Its tail, as long as me, twitched in aggravation.

My heart beat like a jackrabbit. He stepped to the left and crossed one giant paw over the other in a slow, calculated movement. I stepped to my right. Our eyes stayed locked. Another sneer bared yellowed teeth, but he did not attack.

Instead, we circled one another, around and around in the tall grass. I woke, his roar held in my ears even as I shifted over from sleep. Sweat beaded on my brow, and I wondered if he could still devour me.

I wonder that now.

The partition door slides open, and Sister Sakura leans into the doorway. "Hello, Naoko. Are you ready?"

"Do you remember the story of the two tigers?" I cannot shake my nightmare.

"Yes, of course. Hello, little-*chan*." Sister Sakura's voice rises and falls in singsong as she holds her finger under the baby's reaching hand. "It tells of the man who climbed a vine to reach a strawberry and was trapped there by two mean terrible tigers. Then mice nibbled away on either side." She makes faces to Little Bird as she talks. "Yes, they were very scary." Sister Sakura's glasses slip, but instead of pushing them up, she lifts her chin higher and continues to flirt with silly expressions. "But you're not scared, are you?"

"I am," I say, watching them. "I'm like the trapped man reaching for the strawberry." I reach for her now.

Hisa appears in the doorway. "Your father's here, Naoko, are you ready?"

The monastery grounds are expansive. It is a training center with over one hundred monks and nuns in residence. Between the lecture hall, bathing houses, living quarters, temples and classrooms, there are at least thirty structures. Meditation gardens surround them. I have only seen the front gate and my room. And now, at dusk, the sun rests on the horizon with its arms outstretched in a wide yawn of yellow and orange, so I see it only in shadows.

I follow the abbot and Sister Sakura, a half-step behind, staying close to Hisa, who carries my bundled baby. We turn into one of the many covered corridors. It's narrow with exposed beams along the high ceiling. Small lanterns attach to the supporting poles and tease with flickering light to guide our way.

The corridor opens to a wide room that acts as a reception hall to the attached temple. As we pass, I cannot help but glance inside to the monks in colored robes of rust and brown who sit in a lotus position or with foreheads to floor. The nightly devotional pulsates through the building, through the floor, and reverberates even in my weary bones.

The abbot turns to find me stopped. "Meditation serves to quiet the monkey mind. Close your eyes, Naoko. Listen."

I shut my eyes and picture Jin and Hatsu while listening to the long-drawn-out syllable sung over and over. Some hold the note, while others begin. With theirs held, the others start again. The layered chants reverberate deep from their diaphragms. The hum is many voices as one, and it speaks to me. It fills the cracks in between my racing thoughts and overtakes them, like the rise of a quick tide over a rocky shore.

"What is it you wish? What is it you need? What is it you seek?" the abbot asks.

I open my eyes. Chanting is not a prayer, it is not asking. "It is nothing."

The abbot smiles so every line in his face pulls high. "Then you are ready." He crosses the wide room and slides open the door to another.

I fix my baby's hair again, then share a look with Hisa. She will stand in the hall outside the entry with Sister Sakura when I'm invited in, then when the time is right, I will present my baby and ask for my father's acceptance.

My stomach winds tighter into a knot, the truth of my situation settling in. I am nervous and excited. It is as though fire ants crawl over my skin and bite. Despite everything, I have missed my family, but what will my father say?

My hands wring one inside the other, not feeling as confident to meet with him. I know in my heart Father would let Grandmother tend to women's things. But then is *Grandmother* the tiger from my nightmare, or are they both tigers like in the story, waiting to devour me and my little strawberry in the middle?

The door slides open.

I look at my baby's sleeping face in Hisa's arms and say a quick prayer for strength. If I keep my head and my heart focused in the right direction, my feet can follow. One step then another leads me closer and closer. Then I peek in.

Father faces the abbot, his back to me. He wears a white dress shirt and tan pants. They hang off him now. *Has he lost weight?* I step inside, stealing a glance at Hisa and my baby, then with shaking fingers I close the door behind me. When

I turn, I'm eye-to-eye with my father. I do not move. My skin bumps.

It is just as in my dream.

The abbot beckons me with a wave. The russet sleeve swallows the motion. "Come in, child."

Father's eyes are black with contrasting bands of red jasper and deep honey. I search them. Do they hold anger? Hate? Will he pounce? But I see only sadness. Guilt fills my churning belly, and I shrink so small. A child hiding behind a parent's leg, but I have no parent.

Instead, I have become one.

"Please, Naoko, come in." The abbot waves again.

Father is larger than life. His word within the family is law. Am I still family? I close the distance between us and bow low to show submission.

The abbot nods with a soft smile. His voice is melodic and calming. "Naoko, your father and I have spoken at great length about the maternity home and how you have come to be with us…"

The rest of his words fade under my racing thoughts. My eyes shift from the abbot back to my father. The gray that clings around his temples has whitened and is more prominent than I remember. Creases sit deeper between his brows and hug the corners of his mouth to camouflage any pleasing expression. He is regal and intimating.

"…and I will leave now, so you may discuss your future." The abbot bows to us both, and on the way out, touches my arm with a reassuring squeeze.

Father motions for me to sit, and I do, but not with my back to the door. I need to watch the shadows, to know my baby is just outside. The image of Brother Daigan disappearing with her keeps replaying in my mind.

I meet Father's eyes, but I cannot find any words. Breathing is hard enough, so I wait for him to begin.

"I am glad you had the abbot contact me." His voice is raspy, as though he has not used it in some time, or have I forgotten its coarse sound in my ears?

I focus on my hands, look to his face, and then to the screen over his shoulder. The shadows. My baby. My words rise in anger. "Did you know what that...*that place* was?"

"No." His eyes close for a moment. When they open they are softer. "And yes."

"Yes?" My jaw drops slack. So, he is the beast? To consider something and to believe it are not the same things. "Why? How co—"

"Wait." His hand is up. "With the bleeding, Obaachan feared, we *both* feared, for your health. We believed the baby was lost, it was too late, you see? When that happens there are certain things...procedures that must be—" His hand lifts and stirs the air, as though it could wave away the uncomfortable words he leaves hanging there.

We stay fixed. His words go around and around and stalk me.

His lips tighten, and a guttural sigh heaves from his chest. "I know this because your mother lost a baby once." He does not look at me. Instead, he looks somewhere in the past. "It was after Taro. A boy."

My shoulders drop. *She never told me.*

"They had...procedures that had to be done to clear the womb. This I remember." For the first time in my life, I witness my father in battle. A battle of his own emotion. His face tenses to mask it, but just like in the last war, there is nothing to be done except surrender. The building moisture is released only to be quickly pushed away with a clearing of his throat.

"This is why you were allowed to go there. Understand? It is a place for such things."

"I did not lose my baby."

Father's lack of response is response enough.

"So why did you continue to pay Housemother Sato?"

His thick eyebrows furrow. "What do I know of these things? I was told you needed this to be well, and Obaachan agreed, so of course I paid."

I sit taller and ask the next difficult question. "Obaachan agreed? Did *she* know?"

His eyes narrow. "Obaachan has her strong opinions of the matter, but her intent was to ensure your health. We'd just lost your mother and…" His head shakes, and he scrubs a hand over his jaw.

The shadows shift behind him, and my thoughts return to my baby. "I wish for you to meet your granddaughter." The words are said and I cannot take them back.

Father straightens but says nothing.

This is my chance, maybe my only one. I stand, bow and walk with purpose to the door. The sudden movement as it opens startles Sister Sakura and Hisa, but Little Bird is ready.

"Please." I hold out my arms.

Hisa hands her to me, and I peer down at my daughter's face, her determined sprout-like hair and blameless eyes. Then I glance up to Sister Sakura. Nothing is said, but the implications of this first meeting hang thick between us.

I am desperate for my father to see her beauty and innocence. We are expected to leave the monastery in a few days, and we have nowhere to go. We need his acceptance.

I make myself breathe deeply to steady my nerves. Turning, I walk back in, shut the door and march right in front of him. "This is your granddaughter." My voice is soft, hope hidden in its tone.

He observes the bundle in my arms.

The ground beneath my feet shifts, causing outward trem-
ors in all directions. We stand on a cultural fault line, the
fracture running miles deep, and the potential aftermath ca-
tastrophic. My intent may displace sides, but this baby connects us all like a bridge. If only my father is willing to cross.
Please let him cross.

My baby stirs and makes a gurgling noise. Her eyes are
open wide as if she knows how significant this meeting is. I
wet my fingers and push down her stubborn hair.

"She rarely cries." I study him as he takes her in. "She is
not much trouble at all." Stepping closer, I tilt her up, so he
can really see her.

Father scans her from top to bottom, but his face is un-
readable.

This is his granddaughter regardless of the baby's father.
She blows a spit bubble and wheezes.

My father has no response.

I do. My heart is sinking. I scramble for the right thing
to say, tears welling. "Her skin is only slightly lighter, and
look…" I step even closer. "Her eyes, almost black just like
mine." Her hair sticks up between my fingers. "That is only
tsumuji." A cowlick is thought as a sign for genius. "See? There
is no curl or wave. She will not stand out. And she will get
stronger. I know it."

My father lifts his chin and stares past me.

He is done looking at her.

His hands clasp behind his back, and he rocks on his heels.
My arms reposition my baby across my middle. I brace myself, to not only speak the truth, but to face it.

"Hajime was called away. You know about the threat with
Taiwan. And now his service is up." I swallow my pride and

continue. "He has not returned." My eyes fill with tears, but I will not cry in front of him.

"So, you will return to your house and wait."

"No." I focus on his chin, the rise and fall of his Adam's apple, anywhere but his eyes, his empty eyes. The lump in the back of my throat grows, so I almost fail to get out the words. "I cannot return there because…" My head lowers in humiliation. "Because without payment, the house has been rented to another family."

He puffs a breath from his nostrils, flaring them, and steps back to process this new information.

I wait. Ten seconds. Twenty? It seems a thousand until he speaks again.

"And do you expect his return?" His tone is even and soft, as though he knows the strength of his words might blow me over.

They could.

Tears overflow to wet my cheeks. My lips quiver. My teeth lock hard against each other, and I suck in a fast breath. I will myself not to cry, but it is too late. I am on the vine, between two tigers. The hungry mice gnaw away to force my movement up or down. I do not know the direction I should go. *Which tiger is worse?* I lift my eyes and speak my truth. "No. I do not expect his return."

I wait, staring at my father for some reaction. The air is too heavy. Too still. My heart pounds hard. Little Bird stirs in my arms. I pray she doesn't fuss.

His jaw is tight. "And your plans?"

He is going to make me ask.

Insist I grovel.

Demand I beg.

I glance at my baby. *I will beg for her.* I bend low. "I would like to return home, Otousan. To help with Kenji and Grand-mother. I would like to take my place as—"

"And what of her?"

My eyes lift and level with his. "She is my daughter."

"She is sick." He huffs and starts to pace.

"She will get better. We found a way for her to feed." I do not mention how little she does.

"We cannot bear the weight of such a child. The required medical expense is too much."

"I will take care of her!"

"You must also think of our family name, and if not that, think of this child. She's small, sickly, could have develop-mental problems, and what of school?" He pivots on his heels, his voice picking up speed along with his stride. "Where will she go?"

"I will teach her myself."

"She cannot expect a decent marriage or a job." He con-tinues talking as if I did not speak. "*If* she even survives, she will be a costly burden."

I step in front of him, pleading. "She will be fine. I will make sure she fattens and is healthy. I will teach her and take care of her. Please, I need her with me."

"Enough!" His hand slices the air. "You need. You will. You want. *Enough!*" Father's face sours. "What you want is what brought you here. What you want now is of no impor-tance, Naoko. This time, it is about what's *best*." Father steps toward the door but stops.

He speaks over his shoulder. "What is best for you and what is best for that child are not the same thing. *You* are welcome home. Do you understand this? You alone."

Another step, the door slides, and Father is gone.

I understand he was the tiger, after all.

THIRTY-SEVEN

Japan, Present Day

Naoko took a deep breath and dabbed moisture from her eyes. "So now you know my story, Tori Kovač, and I in turn would like to know yours."

The sound of my name snapped time like a wet towel. The sting jolted me from the vibrant colors and rich culture of 1950s Japan to the crisp, hard lines of present day. I blinked to align the young Naoko of seventeen—a girl ostracized for who she loved, cut off from everyone she knew, blamed for her mother's death and forced to make an impossible choice—to the aging Naoko of seventysomething, the one my father wrote, loved, had a daughter with.

"Thank you for sharing it," I said, aware she hadn't shared it all. Of course, I hadn't disclosed everything, either. I glanced to Pops's letter still in my hand. To learn the rest of her story, I had to share what I knew of my father's.

She gave a slow bow, eyed my near-empty cup and, lifting the pot, poured more.

My heart pounded my ribs. "I can see what you were up against. And while I'm confused by your father, I admit, I'm also confused by mine."

My eyes drifted from her back to the letter. "Did my father write before?" I needed her to say yes. I needed to know he tried. His letter to Naoko had snuck in through the past and, like Wendy in *Peter Pan*, stitched a dark unruly shadow to my feet. I couldn't shake it. Everywhere I went, it followed, whispered—*What if he abandoned them? What if he's to blame?* It challenged everything I knew and trusted about my father, and after hearing all she went through, I needed her to set that shadow free.

She took a moment, searching through the past. "In the beginning, I think Hajime wrote. At least, I like to believe he did." Her brows twitched, and her gaze returned to mine. "But I suspect if he had, Father and Grandmother would have kept his letters from me. And the few letters that came after, I never read.

"Instead, I buried them with my sorrow."

My heart jumped. I leaned forward. *"Why?* Didn't you want to know if he tried to return?" The question came out quick, forgetting myself.

"What good is knowing when it could change nothing." She looked at the envelope I held as though seeing ghosts.

I saw my own and held the letter up. "Knowing changes everything for me. All I've done since I read this is question my father's character because it doesn't make sense." My eyes searched hers. "How could my father, a man who lived for his family, leave another one behind? A young wife? A *child*?

311

How could he *do* that and then never even mention it? That's *not* my father. Something must have happened."

"Then you already know and have answered your own question."

I sat with her words, confused.

Naoko tilted her head. "Was Hajime a good father?"

"Yes. He was the best."

Her brows creased. "Then how does knowing anything else alter *that*?"

And there it was.

A truth.

A personal one. And maybe the only one that mattered. "You're right. It doesn't. The man I knew was a great father." I shrugged, frustrated at the emotion that strangled my words. "But I knew the man, Naoko. Not the boy that got him there."

"And I knew the boy, not the man he would become." She again threaded her fingers together in her lap. "So, you see? Knowing more does not change anything for me, either. It does not change how a young man from America loved me so much he practiced and learned my language and customs to meet my family for tea. It does not change how he rented a small thatched hut and planned a life with me there. It does not change how he professed his heart in a magical wedding under the trees."

"It also doesn't change that, for whatever reason, he didn't return."

"Yes, true, and yet..." Her eyes glinted. "Grandmother always said, 'Man has a thousand plans, heaven but one.' And heaven? Oh, how heaven laughed at ours, but..." Naoko tilted her head, her lips curved to a thoughtful smile. "Even heaven herself cannot change truth. Despite it all, we loved."

I gave a nod and smiled, but then it faded remembering

another truth. Their daughter. "According to this—" I held up the envelope "—my father didn't know where his daughter was or what happened." My pulse quickened. "Can you tell me? Please?"

We sat in silence then. Her, with Hajime's daughter, and me, with the woman he once loved. The question of their baby wedged between us, unmoving.

"*Okaasan?*"

My chin snapped up at the familiar word.

Naoko's glance flickered. She turned to the patio door where a woman appeared, then greeted her in Japanese. But the woman who called for Okaasan wasn't looking at Naoko, she stared at me.

I sat frozen.

Blood drained from my head. I'm sure I was as white as the ghost I yearned to see. She was older than me, but of the right age? It was hard to tell. My emotions ran feral. I searched her face for my father's, only to find she looked like Naoko, but maybe? At a certain angle? She had the same bone structure as Naoko and the same warm black eyes.

"Hello," she said, and bowed.

The same lovely manners.

I managed a slight nod but couldn't speak.

Hell, it was hard to breathe.

"Tori, this is Shiori," Naoko said. "Shiori, this is my new American friend, a journalist who is doing a story about the house for the *Tokyo Times*." It was Naoko's turn to give a sideways glance.

I held it, confused.

Did her daughter not know about Naoko's past, or maybe she didn't want to embarrass the guest who had lied?

Naoko looked back toward her daughter. "Oh, yes, the flowers." She stood and retrieved the bamboo basket she'd placed at her side. "Every week I pick the best flowers for my daughter, so she knows her importance to me." She nodded and handed it to Shiori.

"And enough for all of her friends," Shiori said in English with a soft smile. She slid the basket to the crook of her arm just as her mother had earlier, and they again conversed in Japanese.

I watched, analyzed—stared. This woman could be my sister.

With a small bow Shiori spun to leave.

I watched her walk away, the obvious questions loaded and ready on my impatient, American tongue. When she stepped from view, I set it free. "Was *that*— I mean, is *she*...? I *have* to know... Please." Tears blurred my vision.

Naoko didn't answer, and instead motioned to the cushion.

I offered a trade and held up the envelope. "She needs to read this, to know my father, her father, thought of her. That he loved her. Will you let me do this for my father?" The last part hitched in my throat.

Naoko's eyes glinted with moisture.

"Please, Naoko. If Shiori is my sister, I'd like to tell her about him. Ask her forgiveness on his behalf and..." I clutched my heart. "To forgive *me* for having the father she never had. But if she doesn't know, and you prefer it that way, I understand. But then *you* should know..." I held it out, pleaded with my eyes. "I know it doesn't change anything, but this letter *means* something."

When she didn't reach to take it, I extended my arm farther. "Please, it would mean something to me, too. Let me do this for my father." My voice cracked, losing the battle of emotion.

Naoko eyed the tattered envelope, glanced to me, then with utmost care took it from my hand. She removed Pops's letter as though the words were fragile and unfolded the single sheet to find the small piece of yarn. "He kept it." She smiled.

"The red string of fate," I whispered as the connection resonated from her story. "That's the yarn you gave him in the note."

"Yes." She nodded, eyes glistening with tears. She squinted at the letter. "And he still writes so small." She laughed, holding it for me to see. "He used to leave me notes, and I would tease, saying, 'It is too small, Hajime, too small.'" She handed it back. "Maybe you can read it for me?"

Taking Pops's letter, I glanced at his words. I cleared my throat to push down the emotional grip that constricted it, and with a breath, read it for the hundredth time, so Naoko could hear it for the first.

"My Dearest Cricket,
"I hope this letter somehow finds its way to you, and that it finds you in health and surrounded by loved ones and family. I pray that family also includes one of my own.

"Please, without any expectations, I wish only to know our daughter is well and, if it's within your heart, for our Little Bird to know she's always been in mine. Even now.

"I'm an old man, Cricket, at the end of my life when pain comes due. I need you to know, in loving you, I've never had a single regret. But in losing you? In the how and the why? So many.
"Your Hajime"

Naoko covered her mouth. This time, when I handed her the letter, she claimed it with both hands and clutched it to her chest.

I shrugged. "I know it's short…"

"What else is there to say? He loved me, he wishes it were different, he remembers our Little Bird." She nodded, took a deep breath and released it as though held for a lifetime.

We smiled at one another.

With a deep inhale through her nose, she looked to the sky. Then she squared her shoulders and, with knitted brows, her eyes found mine at last. She tilted her head, and I knew.

"Shiori isn't Little Bird, is she?"

"No. I am sorry."

"I think maybe I knew that." There was nothing left to do but ask the palpable question that bridged between us. The same one that brought me thousands of miles around the world. "If Shiori isn't my sister, Naoko, then *where* is she? I can't leave until I know. I can't."

Her shoulders released. "I think maybe *I* knew that." Carefully she folded the letter and returned it to the envelope in her lap. Then she took a sip of tea and regarded me from above the rim. "To just know such a truth is not enough. First, you must understand. And it requires bravery from two people. One to speak it. And one to listen."

At the hospital, Pops's had asked, "Are you listening?"

"I'm listening," I answered.

She nodded. "My father gave me an ultimatum. Yes, he was the tiger, after all. His words repeated in my mind. 'What is best for you and what is best for that child are not the same thing.' The conditions of living in my father's house allowed for only me. To live on my own didn't allow for me to care for my baby. So, what was I to do? I hung on the vine, holding my strawberry between two tigers, and I had to hurry, as the mice were nibbling away..."

THIRTY-EIGHT

Japan, 1958

In the monks' covered Zen garden, I sit with Little Bird and sort my father's words. *What is best for you and what is best for that child are not the same thing.*

With my toes, I push the cool sand around. The garden is meant to be viewed from the surrounding corridors, but I am on the large, flat rock, smack in the middle, messing up the perfect lines with my feet.

A storm in the monks' sandy sea of tranquility.

I stroke my daughter's fine hair with my fingertips. It is soft and dark like mine. Though her skin is much lighter, she tinges yellow from jaundice. It almost glows against the black of her lashes. She is too thin and struggles to breathe.

I struggle for perspective.

I wish I could visit Okaasan's burial site. A single erect

slab with both Father's and Mother's names engraved in the smooth front. Mother's name in black to signify she has gone, while Father's remains red to signal he waits to join her. All graves are inked this way. It is as beautiful as it is disturbing.

The cemetery is a strange miniature city of stone, a sprawling metropolis for insects, but I would draw comfort there. I would ask for guidance. Wait for a sign.

Without money how will I protect my baby? Provide for her? Feed her? Oh, I will love her, but love does not nurse a baby back to health or keep one safe and warm.

Look how love has left me.

My father made a significant donation to the monastery and, for it, expects my quick return. The abbot believes my father yields. He doesn't know it is a welcome home for only me.

"Naoko, is that you, child?" Hisa calls from the pathway.

"I am here," I say as she does the unexpected and treads through the Zen garden, adding ripples of her own.

Sister Sakura surprises me more because she walks a step behind. "The monks will have a fit in the morning." She laughs, noticing how I've disturbed their peaceful labor. She slides her glasses up as she gazes down at Little Bird bundled in my lap. "Has she eaten?"

I shake my head. I couldn't get her to take the dropper of milk.

It's as if she knows.

My voice cracks. "We have nowhere to go."

"What do you mean?" Hisa asks. "Your father was here."

"My father wants only me." I stare at my baby, sad for his stubborn stance. "He refuses her, saying she has no place in our family. He claims she is too sick regardless, that health care will be costly and pointless." My words stammer for breath. My heart aches for refuge.

Sister Sakura gives a heavy sigh. "In some ways, child, your father is right."

"What?" My head snaps up. "How is he *right*?"

Sister Sakura lowers her chin. She threads her fingers, so the robe's sleeves swallow them whole. "She is very sick and not eating." She shakes her head. "I fear it is only a matter of time."

"No..." Tears trickle down my cheeks. I don't bother to wipe them. "She *was* eating." I turn to Hisa. "Can she not just stay here with you? I will come back every day or I will stay. She will eat, I know it, and..." Emotion strangles my words, so I almost choke. "I will find a way to pay." I nod, pleading back and forth between them. "I will pay. Somehow I will."

"Naoko, it is not about a fee," Sister Sakura says, sitting beside me. She wraps me with her arm. "I am sorry, child. There is nothing to do but wait."

"What about the home?" I ask, sliding up and away. "The one in Oiso? The one for mixed-blood babies?"

Sister Sakura tilts her head. I turn to Hisa but she casts her eyes away.

"They will take her." I'm crying now, squeezing my baby close. "Can you help me take her there? *Please.*"

Hisa wipes her eyes. "There, she'd only die alone."

"No! You don't know that!" I stand, shaking my head. A warm stabbing sensation builds. It rises and flares my nostrils with each clipped breath from trying to hold everything in. I have no words.

I have only anger.

It rips through me and releases a string of accusations. "How can you say that? Why did you pretend to care before, and now won't help?" My shoulders quake as I curl into my baby. "Why will no one help us?" My cries make no sound because I can no longer breathe.

I can't breathe.

"Naoko, please." Sister Sakura and Hisa stand, trying to console me.

I'm beside myself. My lips peel back to release a cry of desperation. "No. *No...*" I spin and run from the Zen garden. I run to my room.

I run from their bitter truth.

In my room, I rock my baby. Hisa sits outside the door in case I call, but I won't. I wish to be alone.

Curling on my side, I wrap around my sweet daughter. Tears roll down my cheeks one after the other. I let them fall. My insides are raw from deciding between such miserable fates. Everywhere I turn, no matter what I do, it is as though fortune has decided.

For now, I tell my Little Bird stories. She fell asleep hours ago, but I talk, anyway. I talk until I am hoarse. I yawn but refuse the trap of sleep, for it is a thief that steals precious time away, and I have none to spare.

"Let's see, I told you the gift of insults, and the one about stealing the moon...*oh*, but not my favorite tale. This one I have not shared." I reposition myself and clear my throat to give the best delivery. "This one I used to make Grandmother tell me over and over. Her voices made me laugh.

"Four monks are sworn to silence..." I fall silent, not able to continue because I know she will never hear Grandmother's version.

Instead, I tell her of Hajime through tears, of how we met and how we loved and of his proud reaction that day on his ship when he told our young guests he would be a father. I tell her of Okaasan's valiant heart and how she brought me her wedding dress. How she stayed to see me in it, how much I need her now.

I tell Little Bird my whole heart because it breaks beyond repair.

What else? I stroke her sunken cheeks. *What more can I share?* That I want things to be different, but what I want is not what is best? "I am sorry, Little Bird," I whisper near her ear as tears run down my cheeks. "Know you were wanted and loved, and I will think of you every day of my life. Every day, I swear." She's wheezing now. It is as though she knows.

"Jin, Hatsu and I made a pact, you see," I say, leaning away to see her eyes and stroke her hair. "We promised one another we would spare our babies from Housemother Sato's bony fingers of death, that your spirits would never be left waiting." I kiss her head and wipe at my eyes.

"And I pledged if I could not keep you with me or keep you safe, to seek out Brother Daigan. To allow him to take you with honor and respect to a better home." My shoulders shake. "But I do not want to, I swear."

I curl around my baby and cry, heartbroken, gutted. So foolish to believe my capacity for pain had been reached. I am bottomless.

I look to the window. The sun stalks me. It stirs the shadows with a thick haze of sleepy light to shoo them away. My baby barely moves in her swaddling. Does she even breathe? I place my ear near her mouth and listen. It is faint. "Little Bird," I whisper, and place my finger under her tiny hand, then kiss it. "I will keep my promise. I will seek out Brother Daigan."

She blinks up with inky eyes, and I know she understands.

The vine is threadbare.

It's time.

My throat swells, and a balloon inflates my lungs and threatens to burst. It crushes outward as I try to hold everything in. My chest convulses without breath. My face hurts from the pressure. I will keep my word, for her, I will keep my word.

I glance outside. The time is now.

With my baby wrapped tight, and me, again wearing every piece of clothing I own, I sneak around Hisa and out the door. I left a note for Sora. *Thank you,* I wrote. There was no need for more. The nuns will help her deliver a strong, healthy baby, then make arrangements for her baby at the adoption home. Hisa said Little Bird would only die there alone. I will not let that happen. Brother Daigan will not let that happen.

With hurried steps, I dart away. The cool air nips at my warmed skin as I work my way toward the entrance gate. Passing through, I all but run the long stretch of road.

I do not look back. I will never return.

Destiny's coin tosses high in the air. I hope for a miracle, some twist in fate's design, but both sides read the same. *What's best for me and what's best for my child are not the same.*

So, I will find Brother Daigan, and I will pull my daughter close, just as Okaasan had done with me, and just as quick, I will hand her over and set my Little Bird free.

I.

THIRTY-NINE

Japan, Present Day

I choked back tears and looked at nothing. To give her daughter up after all that. How could Naoko stand it? I wiped the moisture from under my eyes, trying to regain my composure, but the slight wobble in my voice gave my emotion away. "I'm so sorry. I can't imagine how hard that was."

Her brows lowered over tear-filled eyes. "While I have no regrets in loving your father or our daughter, that love carried a lifetime of consequence. And after?" She looked away. "After, I couldn't bear it. It was an impossible darkness, so I tried to drown my sorrow in the river of three crossings."

I covered my mouth with my hands, scared of what she would say.

"But the pain I'd cause Kenji with another loss outweighed the rocks I'd placed in my suitcase. How could I cause him more pain? And I had made a pact with Jin and Hatsu, so I untangled the rope of clothing from around my waist and sat on the shore, measuring the sins of Housemother Sato against my own. I decided my life sentence of punishment was to ensure Housemother received hers."

It took everything not to reach over and squeeze her hand. "Did she?"

"The abbot kept his word and informed the authorities. They, in turn, came to me. Housemother was arrested, tried and found guilty." Naoko's shoulders fell. "Although she served only four years."

"Four?" I creased my brows and shook my head. "That's it?"

"Yes, but they closed the maternity home. So, you see? The abbot was correct with his starfish story. While Sora and I could not save them all, our efforts made a difference to that one, and to that one."

"And to me," I whispered, because she had given my sister up. I sat with Naoko's words, acquainting myself to their truth. My heart ached for her, for them all, but it also lifted with hope. My sister was still out there, somewhere.

As a journalist, research was my backbone. With renewed purpose, I fired off questions. "Do you know where Brother Daigan took her? What adoption agencies he worked through? Did she end up at that home? If she stayed in Japan or ended up in the States or if they registered a name?"

"A name?" Naoko's eyes widened. "To me, she is only Little Bird. With that name, I set her free. And by sharing my story, I had hoped to set you, Hajime's daughter, free, as well." Her chin dipped, her brows furrowed.

I sensed she wanted me to leave it alone, but I was so close to finding my sister. I'd come all this way. "I know I can find her, Naoko." I knew who to call and how to search. "Maybe I don't have her name, but you gave me Brother Daigan's and

the home in Oiso." My heart pounded my ribs. "Is there anything else you can share that might help me find her? Anything at all?"

"No." She shook her head. She took my hands in hers,
squeezed, then turned my hands palms up. "I've given you
our story, and the story of our Little Bird. Now what you do
with it is in *your* hands."

She let go and I held my hands suspended in front of me a
moment, then clasped them together and brought them to my
heart. She had given me her most precious gift, so I needed
to return a gift just as precious that was never really mine.

I untied my mother's scarf from around my neck. Every
thread held a memory. Sunday drives, silly sing-alongs,
blond hair tousled by the wind. But knowing the threads
ran through Naoko's memories first, I held it out. "I believe
this *is* yours. Pops said he meant to give it to me, but my mom
found it and, well, what was he gonna say?" I smiled with a
one-shoulder shrug. "He gave it to me before he died, telling me it was *important*." I held it out. "Now I understand all
the reasons why."

Naoko ran her fingers over the beautiful silk but didn't take
it. "With its return, you've helped Hajime keep his promise." Her gaze met mine. "May I now ask you to promise me
something in return?"

"Of course, anything."

"If you find my Little Bird, you will give her this scarf.
Tell her it has passed between fathers and daughters and husbands and wives and traveled the great ocean twice. That it
carries not only expectations, but all of our love." Her eyes
glistened with a tight-lipped smile.

I promised.

"Naoko?" An elderly man in tan trousers and a blue pin-
striped shirt peered out from the house.

"*Oh*, my husband," Naoko said, rocking forward to stand. "He's here to escort me home."

I tilted my head in curiosity, then rose.

He strolled through the patio door, caught sight of us and continued in our direction. The lightest of gray fuzz slicked back over the top of his head. His sharp, square jaw touted the same gray in an unshaven shadow. And like Naoko, he exuded an understated sophistication in presence and manners.

He offered a small bow.

I wasn't sure what to say since we hadn't spoken of him at all. Embarrassed, I simply returned the gesture.

"Forgive me, but your eyes." His smile lengthened, his chin dipped. "I haven't seen eyes so blue since the famous movie star Marylin Monroe honeymooned in Tokyo. And I'm afraid, like hers, they've hypnotized me."

My heart leaped to my throat. Those were the same words said to Naoko in her story. Was it him? The pressure shot the words like a cannon. "You're *Satoshi*?" Maybe we had spoken of her husband, after all. Many times. Of course it was him. The way he stood—tall and strong. The way he spoke—thoughtful and measured.

When he didn't respond, I sensed my mistake. "I'm so sorry. I just assumed because of the stories that you were the boy she spoke about." My cheeks warmed, and I knew they had flushed red.

He laughed, full and rich, then touched my shoulder. "Please, I'm honored for such an enthusiastic greeting."

"And I'm extremely embarrassed." I looked at my feet with a small, apologetic smile.

"I am the one embarrassed," Naoko said to ease the awkwardness. "For I spoke with such detail, you of course knew him at once. Please allow me to officially present my husband, Satoshi Tanaka."

"It is you." I beamed. The inner light lifted my smile. "And I'm so glad it is. I am." I nodded, looking at them together. Naoko *married* Satoshi. This was right. I couldn't stop my grin.

He bowed, still smiling. "I only hope to live up to such an introduction."

"You have. Absolutely."

"And this, Satoshi, is my new treasured friend, Miss Kovač. *Tori* Kovač."

"Tori?" His smile softened. Satoshi turned toward Naoko and a shared glance lingered between them. An entire conversation without words.

For the first time, I wished for a translator.

"Well, I won't keep you any longer." I took a step, but hesitated. "Naoko, if I find anything..." I wasn't sure how much to say in front of Satoshi. "I mean, do you want me to contact you? Would you want to know whatever I learn?"

A silence fell between us.

"I've met you, Tori Kovač, and what I want, what I hope, is for you to finally make peace with your father's past. Know that by meeting you, learning your name, you have allowed peace in mine." With that she stepped back and bowed from her waist.

I wanted to hug her. Hug them both. But I bowed in turn, then held up the scarf, to say, *I wouldn't forget, thank you*, a million unspoken things.

Satoshi and I exchanged warm smiles, then with a slight bow of the chin, I turned to go. As I approached the road, I spun back a last time.

Naoko's family house on the hill was surrounded by blooms of white. This is where my father met for tea with a king of an empire, dreamed a different life and fought against heaven's wishes.

I'd probably never be back to see Naoko or Satoshi, but I'd

never forget either one. With Naoko's scarf, I carried their story—*our* story—forward with hope and love.

My flight didn't leave until morning, but I could catch a later one if needed. I refused to leave without visiting the monastery and inquiring of Brother Daigan and the orphanage.

FORTY

Japan, Present Day

Riding the train to Hiratsuka to visit the monastery, I stood, wired with "what-ifs." *What if* the monastery had lots of information on Brother Daigan? *What if* the orphanage he worked with had records? *What if* I found my sister?

I stifled a laugh. I was getting way ahead of myself. Because *what if* the monastery had no idea who Brother Daigan was? And like my father's military records, *what if* it was another dead end?

What then?

I would visit the Girl with Red Shoes statue. Even if it meant a later flight. I owed it to Naoko, my sister, to Pops— for what he'd tried to tell me. The Girl with Red Shoes stands at each port on either side of the ocean to remind us of the thousands of innocent children lost between them.

Who were *still* lost.

What if one could be found?

There's a tether linked between families and there's a natural pull to reel them in. I could feel it. I was close. I sat down, wiping tears from my cheeks. My emotions ran rampant.

The train coasted to a stop, letting more passengers off than on, and leaving my car near empty. *Almost there.* My stomach twisted in anticipation. Hiratsuka would be next, and the monastery a quick walk away.

I planned to run.

Settling into a seat, I watched the landscape roll past. The sleepy countryside I imagined from Naoko's stories didn't match the urban sprawl of modern buildings that now covered it. On the other side, the train line hugged the sea. Even that intoned of industry.

We slowed, and I jumped up, ready to go. Stepping out onto the platform, the sea air greeted me with a salty kiss and damp embrace. I debated my direction. Naoko said it was a straight shot from the station, but the street split in two.

"Excuse me?" I asked, but the woman smiled and kept walking. I sidestepped a bike only to force a moped to swerve. I spun around, trying to get my bearings. Shops, office buildings and traffic with bicycles in between. Hiratsuka was not a sleepy rural city in the least; in fact, it bustled.

And yet my phone wasn't connecting to maps. *One bar.* I approached a shop and peered over the counter. An old man sat in front of a small TV, eating. He smiled.

"Hi. Is the monastery this way?" I asked, and pointed down the street. "Monks? Brother Daigan?"

He wrinkled his nose and lost his smile. I repeated myself, then gave up, stepping the way I'd indicated.

The more I walked, the farther apart the buildings became. They changed from cubed offices to stacked apartments to modest, stand-alone homes, many of which were abandoned. Some had partially caved-in roofs with windows and doors missing. I'd read that over eight million homes were abandoned due to Japan's aging nation and shrinking population, but to see it in person was eerie. A real-life ghost town made ominous by the fading sun. I walked faster. Afraid I'd find the monastery closed. *If* I found it.

Naoko also said the walk wasn't long, but I had walked awhile. I asked a few others but couldn't understand them. One pointed left, another right. I thanked them with a bow and kept going in the same direction.

A high fence ran along the road across the street.

My heart jumped. A *bamboo* fence.

I hadn't even considered the maternity home could still be there.

Crossing the street, I peeked between the stalks, but found only dense brush on the other side. I remembered Naoko's words, *We're trying to get to the other side. My child, you are on the other side.*

She had wanted out and here I was, some fifty years later, desperate to get in. Instead of a locked gate, an open arch covered the entrance. I ventured through, careful not to trip on the uneven pavers embedded in the walkway. The late sun mottled under the canopy of trees, casting inconsistent shadows that swallowed the street behind me. Birds trilled warnings of my uninvited arrival.

There were more woods ahead and thick forest on either side. I spun around to consider going back when someone called out in Japanese. I was trespassing. I shouldn't have been there.

The man's bald head appeared first over the raised incline, then the rest of him. A monk in white. His robe swayed to and fro as he approached, like a broom sweeping away debris.

He carried a small bag as if he'd just returned from the store. Calling out, he thwacked his walking stick on the ground.

I gave a wave and approached him. "Hello, is there a maternity home back there?"

He blinked and stared. Maybe he didn't speak English, but as a monk, he might recognize the name. "Do you know of a Brother Daigan?"

His thick brows furrowed.

"*Brother Daigan*, he helped babies?"

His chin lifted. "Ah, babies." He patted his belly and then pushed rounded cheeks high into a smile. His eyes creased like crescent moons. "*Ojizō-sama*, Brother Daigan?"

"Um, yes?"

"Okay, yes. Come." He floated ahead. When I didn't follow, he repeated himself, waving with fervor. "Babies. *Ojizō-sama*, Daigan, come."

Maybe it still was a maternity home? I hoped he didn't misunderstand and think I was pregnant.

I caught up to walk beside him. Water trickled somewhere ahead. A stream? Yes, and a small footbridge. Naoko's persistent fish! I smiled and gazed over as we crossed. Fish with fins of gold, white and black circled below in shallow eddies. Naoko and Satoshi were in this exact spot discussing the story. And he'd been right: Naoko was like the fish, she had persistence and fight. And Naoko had been right, as well. She had needed it.

Ahead, the trees parted. A building with rust-colored tiles peeked through. Or maybe the color was cast from the sun hanging low overhead. It had several newer buildings constructed around it. "Is that the maternity home?"

He shook his head, then veered away from the house to a side path, pointing ahead. The new path was smaller and somewhat overgrown. We had to walk single file. I stepped faster to keep from trailing behind. The property sloped, dipped, then climbed and climbed.

With the sun setting, I worried I made a huge mistake. That the monastery had closed for the day.

"Okay, babies." Ahead, the monk had stopped. The sun shone bright before him, rolling long shadows off his back.

A branch snagged my arm; I stopped to release my sleeve.

"Come." The monk beckoned me forward like the lucky blessings cat.

Pushing through the thicket, I took one final wide step to stand beside him, then squinted in the light and gasped. Wild red blooms decorated the unkempt grasses as far as I could see.

"See?" The monk offered the field. *"Babies."*

I covered my lips with a hand.

Naoko's words whispered from memory, *From the clearing's mouth, the earth bleeds red, and I peer into death's pregnant, bloated belly.*

It was beautiful and disturbing. The concrete sculptures with fabric bibs and caps of red stood every which way, without any set order. Some sat in neat rows, some climbed the embankment, others faced one another in silent conversation.

The monk turned to leave, but I tapped his arm. He'd misunderstood. "No, I'm wanting info on Brother Daigan. Brother Daigan who *helped* the babies."

"Yes. There."

"There?" I blinked.

He indicated to a statue. *"There."*

"That's a *Jizō* statue. I'm wanting info on Brother *Daigan*."

"Yes, *Ojizō-sama*, Daigan. There." He pointed to another one. "And there."

I pushed past the monk to encroach the clearing below, needing to understand his meaning. A *Jizō* smiled up at me, its bib of red faded pink from the sun. I spun to the monk at my heels, then pointed. "This? *This* is Brother Daigan?"

"Yes. *Ojizō-sama*, Daigan." His thick brows pushed down.

"And this one?" I asked, almost yelling while pointing to another.

"Yes." The monk again presented the field of red. The one we now stood in. "All *Ojizō-sama*, Daigan."

Prickly fingers crawled the length of my spine. Fingers that pinched little noses and covered their cries.

"*Ojizō-sama...*" I said it slower, breaking the syllables apart. "*O-jizo.*" My jaw dropped.

Jizō statues.

All.

Naoko said, "*Mizuko*, water children—the stillborn, miscarried and aborted—cannot cross over alone. *Jizō* wears the baby's clothing, a bright red bib and cap, to show their connection."

Tears welled up. Brother Daigan *wasn't* a monk who helped babies find a new home, at least not a living one. He was the spirit that helped the babies cross over. Naoko had told me as much.

My heart jumped.

Oh, my God, the pact.

"If we could not keep our babies or keep them safe, we would seek out Brother Daigan and allow him to take them with honor and respect to a better home.

"After, I couldn't bear it."

Oh, Naoko.

I spun around, breathing hard, and searched the landscape for the monk. *"Wait!"* I yelled, then chased after him. "Wait! *Please.*"

He turned. The white robe shifting a beat behind.

"Where are the other babies?" My heart bulged with chaotic beats. Fear strangled it. "Um, half, *Hafu.*" I pointed to the field. "Where are the *Hafus?*"

"Ah…" His furrowed brows lifted and then the monk took the lead.

I followed, taking deep breaths, fearful for what I might find. *Jizōs* with little stone faces watched us as we passed. One had chubby cheeks and smiled. Another scowled. Some prayed in silence.

"There." The monk pointed.

A grove of nonnative trees just like Naoko described it. Dark gray bark and leaves like spindly fingers. Some climbed the sky and towered above. Most were just over my head. *This is where the mixed-blood babies lie,* Hatsu had told Naoko.

I turned to take in the landscape, expecting small mounds of unmarked dirt. Instead, there were dozens and dozens of *Jizō* statues scattered every which way, except under one prominent tree. There, *Jizō* statues stood huddled in a perfect circle, their bonnets and bibs of red contrasted by blooms of white—I gasped.

Chrysanthemums.

Every week I pick the best flowers for my daughter, so she knows her importance to me. And I gather enough for her friends. The remembered words of Naoko and Shiori punctured my lungs.

Blood rushed my ears. Tears fell one after the other. I took a step, then another and another. Until I was face-to-face with Naoko's truth. My father's.

My own.

I dropped to my knees, folded into myself and cried.

I found her, Pops. I found my sister.

She was surrounded by friends.

One, two… I counted six. Hatsu escaped as did Sora, so one for Jin's baby—*the one with the homemade scarf?* Aiko's, maybe

Chiyo's and Yoko's—the girl Naoko never met but heard the baby's cries. I couldn't think of more.

Each had its own face—two smiled, two cried, one slept—and my sister's, with the most flowers around its base, and the only one with a wooden marker, looked right up at me.

We shared a private conversation just then. One long overdue.

It said, *I've been looking for you* and *Here I am, here I am.* I blinked back tears, fixed on the kanji-styled symbols etched in the wooden grave marker and painted red. *What did they say?*

I turned to ask the monk, but he had gone. I fumbled for my phone, snapped a picture of the writing and ran back through the nonnative trees, yelling for him to wait.

"Hello? Sir?" I wove through and around one burial plot after another. I spotted him in the distance, approaching the embankment on his way back to the trail. "Sir?"

He turned.

I ran faster, my heart pounded, and when I reached him, I couldn't catch my breath.

Phone in hand, I clicked the image and held it out. His eyes darted from the image to mine.

"What does that say?" I pointed to the image. "That." I motioned, trying to coax his words. Desperate to hear them.

He reached into the deep pocket of his robe and pulled out reading glasses. The wire frames balanced on the tip of his nose. He squinted. "Oh, *Chīsai tori.*"

My heart jumped. "I'm sorry?"

"*Chīsai tori.*" He smiled.

I didn't understand.

"Ahhh…" Using his finger and thumb, he showed a small space between them. "*Chīsai.*" Then he looked up to the sky, looked left, then right. "There, *tori.*" A brown bird flew overhead with a tan underbelly. He flapped his arms and pointed again.

"Bird? Tori is 'bird'?" Tori is "bird" in Japanese? "*Chīsai tori*, Little Bird."

I looked to the picture on my phone again.

To the grave marker.

To my sister's name.

My name.

The name we shared.

Pops didn't forget Little Bird. He named *me* after her. And maybe I never would know his full story of wants or dreams, or what had happened to keep him from them. It didn't matter because I knew Pops's heart. And just as he said in his letter to Naoko—he carried her there.

Through tears I thanked the monk and wandered back to my sister, my mind swimming.

Letters. Naoko said there were more letters and she "buried them with her sorrow." Did she mean she buried them here? Did my sister have Pops's other letters all along? If so, Little Bird knew for certain the *how* and the *why*, even if I never would. But knowing the man my father was and, through Naoko, meeting the boy that got him there, I believe with all my heart he tried to return.

There was only one thing left to do.

Keep my promise.

I unfastened my mother's silk scarf—Naoko's scarf—from around my neck and carefully wrapped it around my sister's *Jizō* statue. Surrounded by blooms of white, it not only wore a cap and bib of red, but now a scarf that had traveled the great ocean twice and passed between fathers and daughters and husbands and wives. I told my sister how we shared the same name and, in passing this scarf to her, how it carried all our love.

Her mother's, her father's and mine.

In parting ways, Naoko had said, "What I want, what I hope, is for you to finally make peace with your father's past. Know that by meeting you, learning your name, you have allowed peace in mine."

In learning my sister's name, I have, too.

Like Okaasan had done with Naoko, and Naoko with her Little Bird, after a night of long conversation, telling stories and shedding tears with my sister, of sharing everything I could about Pops, *our* father, the man I *still* adored and knew, I set the past free.

I set it free for both of us.

For all of us.

The bird no longer in my hands.

EPILOGUE

Japan, Present Day

Time, I have said before, does not discriminate. It does not care if we are happy or sad. It does not wait, slow or hurry. It is a linear creature, traveling in one direction, and it is constant.

But is it forgiving?

I often wonder this.

For years darkness had weakened my bones, so I could not walk away from the past. It haunted me, whispering *if only* and *what if*. Satoshi said it was just my sorrow working itself free, and only by allowing the process could I face my ghosts.

I'd been clipping flowers when I saw Hajime's.

I placed a stem in my basket, then shooed away an irate bee. I motioned again as it buzzed near my face. When I looked up, I caught sight of a man walking down the road toward the house. A man wearing tan pants and a white button-up shirt with the sleeves rolled up. I squinted into the afternoon glare but saw only dancing sun spots of yellow and blue.

I shielded my eyes and narrowed them to focus. There was something familiar to the man's long, stretched-out steps and natural, easy stride. I tilted my head as he neared, disoriented. He had the same dark hair, but longer. The angular jaw with indented chin just like Little Bird's. My basket of flowers dropped as did my heart, and I stared in disbelief.

"Hajime?" It was not quite a whisper.

My legs wobbled. My hands covered my mouth. There was not enough air for my lungs and my chest ached for trying.

The sun spots followed him as he moved around me, orbs with tails of light like the *hitodama* soul fires that accompany living spirits. Was Hajime visiting from a dream? Or was I dreaming of Hajime? What was real? The memory of our match meeting played out in my mind. The words I said that quieted Grandmother. *Instead of which is real, maybe it is both. True happiness existing in the in-between.* Had I somehow found my place between them, once again?

We stared at one another and shared a silent conversation.

Cricket, I love you, I tried to return.

I know, I cried. *I know.*

I reached out to touch him, but my fingertips grazed only light.

When Satoshi called from the house, I turned. He asked what was wrong, but I was unable to speak. When I looked back, the vision of Hajime had vanished.

A figment or a gift? Maybe it was both. For after, I was able to love again with an open heart. I hoped it had allowed Hajime the same.

After meeting Tori Kovač and learning her story, I knew it had.

And in sharing my story with Hajime's daughter, I realized it wasn't mine alone. It also belonged to Jin, Hatsu and Sora, to every young woman and serviceman who fell in love and faced unimaginable choices and hardships. To every baby born between them, to the hundreds of children who were adopted and to the *thousands* that didn't survive.

My story also belonged to Tori, and I hope as a writer she shares it. Because like the starfish story, it might matter to that one, and that one. Maybe Hatsu's daughter will recognize the wedding story of twinkling lights and find her way home. Maybe others will know that their parents tried. That despite the world's prejudice, they loved.

I hold Hajime's letter close to my heart, shut my eyes and picture the distant flicker of a thousand lights, knowing Grandmother's wisdom was wrong.

Sorrow and happiness do not pass. They burrow in deep and become our bones. We stand on their uneven legs, trying to keep balance when there is none.

There is only love. Only truth.

And this is mine.

★ ★ ★ ★ ★

AUTHOR'S NOTE

Although *The Woman in the White Kimono* is a work of fiction, I crafted it from real events and stories, including my own—or rather, my father's. His story of the beautiful Japanese girl he loved while enlisted in the US Navy. Her family had invited him to a traditional tea, but upon meeting him, an American sailor, he was refused. From there, research and my imagination took over.

I worked backward from what I knew—locations of ports, service dates and my father's story. Then forward with research, digging through international marriage and birth registry laws for the United States, Japan and the military. From all three, I found only bureaucratic red tape designed to thwart interracial marriage. The small percentage of servicemen permitted to marry confronted strict immigration quotas and, when they returned home, America's anti-miscegenation laws. And while Japanese brides faced serious discrimination in the US, it was nothing compared to those left behind in Japan. Exiles in their own country, these women had no means of support.

Over ten thousand babies were born to American servicemen and Japanese women before, during and after the Occupation. *Ten thousand.* Out of those, just over seven hundred children were surrendered to the Elizabeth Saunders Home—an orphanage in Oiso, Japan, created in 1948 by Miki Sawada, the Mitsubishi heiress, specifically for abandoned mixed-race children.

But how and why did this happen?

By answering those questions, I was able to create a probable narrative, but it was in finding the real-life survivors—the children of the Elizabeth Saunders Home—and in learning their stories that *The Woman in the White Kimono* took on a story of its own.

The Orphanage in Oiso

I based the orphanage for mixed-race babies in Oiso that Naoko learns about on the real-life Elizabeth Saunders Home created in 1948 by Miki Sawada, the Mitsubishi heiress. In her autobiography, Miki states that in 1947, while riding on a train, the dead body of a mixed-race baby wrapped in layers of newspaper and cloth fell from an overhead compartment onto her lap. This horrific incident inspired her to start the orphanage.

The home took on the name Elizabeth Saunders in honor of the orphanage's first donor, a Christian Englishwoman who spent forty years in Japan as a governess in the service of the Mitsui family.

Naoko, Jin, Hatsu, Sora, Chiyo, Aiko and Yoko

Naoko and the girls in the maternity home are inspired from real-life stories of the many adoptees from the Elizabeth Saunders Home I met and interviewed while attending the first US reunion held on Shelter Island in San Diego. I continue to be a part of this wonderful community through the Elizabeth Saunders Home Reunion Group on Facebook, which is run by the great-niece of Elizabeth Saunders.

The Bamboo Maternity Home

The Bamboo Maternity Home is fictional, but I based it on the Kotobuki Maternity Hospital in Shinjukuin, Japan. In 1948, Waseda police officers, working from a tip, found the remains of five babies. When the autopsies revealed they had not died of natural causes, they searched the property and discovered seventy more. However, due to the expansive grounds, the exact death toll remains unknown.

Housemother Sato

Miyuki Ishikawa, the real-life "Demon Midwife" who ran the Kotobuki Maternity Hospital in the 1940s, inspired the character of Housemother Sato. Tried in the Tokyo District Court, and based on testimonies, they charged Miyuki Ishikawa with over one hundred and sixty infants' and children's deaths. Found guilty, they sentenced her to eight years in prison.

Because of this publicized incident, on June 24, 1949, abortion for "economic reasons only" was legalized under the Eugenic Protection Law in Japan, and a national examination system for midwives was established.

In 1952, Miyuki Ishikawa appealed the eight-year sentence, citing she had inadequate economic means to support the influx of unwanted babies born in her maternity home, and won. The Tokyo High Court reduced her original sentence to just four years.

The Girl with Red Shoes

The song and the stories that inspired the statues are all true. The little girl's name was Iwasaki Kimi, and the original statue in her honor stands in Yokohama, where the orphanage once stood. On June 27, 2010, to commemorate the one hundred and fiftieth anniversary of the Port of Yokohama, Japan, delegates from Japan presented a matching "Girl with Red Shoes" statue as a gift to their sister city, the Port of San Diego. The statue stands on the shore of Shelter Island near the US naval base.

The Village in Taura where Hajime rents a house

The village in the real town of Taura is fictional, but I based the community on the real-life *Eta* hamlets that once existed in Japan. *Burakumin* were a socioeconomic minority within the larger Japanese ethnic group. They were members of outcast communities in the Japanese feudal era, composed of those working in occupations considered impure or tainted by death, such as executioners, undertakers, butchers or tanners. Historically, they suffered severe discrimination and ostracism. Although the *Burakumin* class was officially abolished in 1871, their descendants still face discrimination.

Jizō statues and *Ojizō-sama*

In traditional Japanese Buddhist teachings, *Ojizō-sama* is the monk known for helping babies cross over to the afterlife. It is said *mizuko*, water children—the stillborn, miscarried and aborted—cannot cross over alone. A *Jizō* statue wears the baby's clothing, a bright red bib and cap, to alert *Ojizō-sama* they are waiting for him to smuggle them into the afterlife in the sleeves of his robe. *Jizō* statues are common in cemeteries throughout Japan.

Pops's and Naoko's tales

The Great Divide story is based on the navy's rite of passage for young sailors in their first Pacific crossing over the Meridian and International Date Line. There is a giant anchor outside the Womble Gate entrance at the naval base in Yokosuka, an American town near the base with a statue of Lady Liberty, and yes, nearby you will find "Blue Street," so named for the blue and white stone chips embedded in the asphalt. While I created Pops's stories around those real locations, I pulled Naoko's tales from Japanese myths and folklore.

Although I set this novel aside several times, it called me back again and again. With knowledge comes responsibility, and since I knew—*ten thousand babies*—I bore a responsibility to share their story. It is my sincerest hope that *The Woman in the White Kimono* shines a bright light in multiple directions without blame or forced resolution. It is through their acknowledgment that these children live. Like Naoko's Little Bird, I place my story, *their* story—a beautiful and tragic truth—within your hands. What you do with it is up to you.

ACKNOWLEDGMENTS

I am indebted to the following colleagues for their time, assistance and support: critique partners from the beginning, JC Kang and JC Nelson. My heartfelt thanks for your sharp eye and unwavering enthusiasm for Naoko and Tori's story. You both have been instrumental in their development. Thank you to critique partner and friend Leanne Yong, for always pushing for more, and to the following for countless reads and thoughtful advice: Amy Anhalt, Stacey Zink and Kris Mehigan. I'd also like to acknowledge the wonderful writing community of Scribophile and specifically thank the following: Patti Jurinski, Julia Satu, Shannon Yukumi, Colleen Maloney and Steven Wade.

I must also thank my brilliant agent and friend, the lovely Lorella Belli of Lorella Belli Literary Agency, for her belief, encouragement and business savvy, and Jeff Kleinman at Folio Literary Management for his support and enthusiasm. And of course, my keen editor at Park Row Books, Erika Imranyi. Thank you for seeing the story's potential and pushing for me to reach it.

Resounding debts are owed to the Elizabeth Saunders Home Reunion Group. In sharing your truths and beautiful stories, they are forever a cherished part of mine. And a thank-you to the Yokosuka Naval Base, Past and Present FB group for your service and your time.

Last, my sincerest thank-you to AJ, who imagined, and Marvin, Kirklen and Garrett, who have lived with this story from the absolute beginning, and with unwavering conviction believed.